LIGHTNING
TREE

SARAH DUNSTER

Bonneville Books
An imprint of Cedar Fort, Inc.
Springville, Utah

This is a work of fiction. The characters, names, incidents, places, and dialogue are products of the author's imagination, and are not to be construed as real.

ISBN 13: 978-1-59955-959-9

Published by Bonneville Books, an imprint of
Cedar Fort, Inc., 2373 W. 700 S., Springville, UT 84663
Distributed by Cedar Fort, Inc. www.cedarfort.com

LIBRARY OF CONGRESS CATALOGING-IN-PUBLICATION DATA
Dunster, Sarah, author.
Lightning tree / Sarah Dunster.
pages cm
Summary: Fifteen-year-old Maggie survives the trek across the plains to Utah Territory only to lose her parents, her older brother, and her baby sister. She and her sister are taken in the Aldens, but the girls know something is amiss when they find their mother's china locked in Ma Alden's trunk.
ISBN 978-1-59955-959-9
1. Mormon pioneers--Fiction. 2. Mormon girls--Fiction. 3. Orphans--Fiction. 4. Frontier and pioneer life--Utah--Fiction. I. Title.

PS3604.U577L54 2012
813'.6--dc23

2011049366

Cover design by Angela D. Olsen
Cover design © 2012 by Lyle Mortimer
Edited and typeset by Melissa J. Caldwell

Printed in the United States of America

10 9 8 7 6 5 4 3 2 1

Printed on acid-free paper

To the wonderful people in my critique group in Utah, who helped me turn this story into something worth reading, and to those in my new critique group in Idaho—without you, my stories would read like molasses and I would still be making up adverbs.

To my children for helping me to keep my priorities in line, and to my husband, whose support and enthusiasm have been the engines to keep me writing.

To good friends who have read my manuscripts and given me honest feedback, and to all those who have supported and helped me in the LDS arts community and at Cedar Fort—what a blessing you have been in my life.

Thank you.

CONTENTS

Prologue 1
The Mattress 3
The Aldens 27
Dreams 43
A Charity Case 58
A Secret Uncovered 80
A Strange Sparking 91
The Porcelain 108
Changes 124
The Incident 141
At the Hosters 159
A Close Call 180
Tales of Murder 210

A Story 238
The Letter 251
Back to Aldens 277
Cradlebaugh 307
Hepsedam 324
Hellos and Good-byes 352

Discussion Questions 373
About the Author 375

PROLOGUE

THE LINE OF MEN STOOD AT ATTENTION WITH MUSKETS tucked up against their bodies. Mud and red paint dripped off their faces and onto their bare chests like dark blood.

"Ready," a resonant voice called out.

"Aim!" Suddenly all the men moved in unison. The stocks of their guns foreshortened in Maggie's vision and became small blotches against their pale shoulders.

They didn't wait for the next order. It came unexpectedly—a giant explosion that filled Maggie's skull with ricochet noises of screeching metal and a peppery smell of gunpowder.

She yelled and flew into a sitting position. She whipped her head around, confused. All of a sudden, it was dark. And instead of powdery earth and prickly weeds under her bare feet, she was sitting. On something soft and lumpy . . .

Maggie's heart slowed as she felt the straw poking into the back of her legs. She reached over and found her sister's warm head on the pillow beside her.

"Maggie," Giovanna muttered. "It was just a dream. Go to sleep."

THE MATTRESS

It could be said of Magdalena Chabert (and many in Provo *did* say it) that she was an old woman in a fifteen-year-old's body. She moved carefully and kept her limbs tucked close to her, almost as if she were nursing rheumatism. She looked at a person shrewdly and unapologetically. She didn't say much, and when she did say something, she hardly meant a word that came out of her mouth. It was all too subtle and unsettling to most people, because outright sarcasm was a thing that she saved for her friends. And exactly two people fell into that category.

On this morning, Maggie stood in the crowd that spilled over the edges of the scrupulously laid block of town square, careful to touch as few people as possible. The air was refreshing and cool, though it wouldn't be long before the sun blazed high in the sky and scorched through calicos and flannels. For now, the jagged shape of Squaw Peak loomed above the crowd, hiding the sun and providing welcome shade.

"I reckon Brother Brigham's gotten long-winded over something," Henry's twangy voice cut into Maggie's awareness.

She turned and squinted at him. "Reckon that's not unusual."

Henry chuckled and edged into her space. "Like as not, he's gone on about the proper thickness of bread crusts again. After all the hol-der-oll, I'da thought he had some big news for us."

Maggie nodded. She felt her throat thicken, her stomach clench. Where was Mariah? She would feel so much better if Mariah were standing in the crowd beside her. Didn't she know about this? She had to, being a member of the prophet's extended family. The fact that she wasn't here seemed a bad omen to Maggie.

The people around her were beginning to jostle each other a little, and the murmuring started, a low buzz that made hearing even more impossible. *They all know what it's likely about,* Maggie thought. *We're all just standing here, waiting to hear it from the preacher's mouth.*

Information was a free commodity in a pioneer town like Provo, even with all of the extra population she'd gained of late. And something as big as a letter of pardon from the president, in the face of all the fear and expectation that had built over the summer—

S'il vous plaît, Maggie's thoughts began in French as they occasionally did, especially when she was agitated.

Immediately she shook her head. "Say it in English," Ma Alden would say. Did say, all those months and even years at first. "We got nobody here who speaks your funny furrin' words, girl. You've got to start talking and thinking like you're in America."

Maggie forced herself to think the words in English: *Please, give us one more month.*

She shook her head again, flicking away the sorrow that reared and threatened to pour over in a dark tide. She rose onto her toes and craned her neck, but it was useless, as she had known it would be. She was at least a head shorter than everyone in front of her.

"You want a lift? I could get you up on my shoulders." Henry was staring at her with something like concern.

Maggie offered Henry a freezing smile—the sort that often sent people away without further comment.

He grinned back at her, unfazed and apparently reassured. "Fine, then. Can't say I didn't try to be a gentleman."

Maggie snorted appreciatively. "Very fine manners—hoisting a young lady of fifteen up t'your shoulders so a hundred people can count out the holes in her stocking."

The crowd around them was growing restless. With the buzz of muttering, Maggie couldn't even hear a dim echo of what the prophet was saying.

"Where's Mariah?" Henry asked suddenly.

Maggie shrugged, keeping her face neutral. "Likely had to stay home and mind babes. Her ma likely wanted to be here."

Suddenly the whispers increased in volume, all around them. Maggie stood straighter and craned her neck; it was like the air was charged, the feeling of thunderclouds full of rain about to burst.

"What's he sayin'?" she whispered to Henry.

"They're all headed back north, then." It was Cindy Holden's voice. She was pushing through the crowd, her gangly husband in tow. "Just as you thought, Shedrick."

Shedrick Holden stroked his pointed beard, his face

unusually solemn as he followed in his wife's wake. "Not much surprise to anybody."

"I admit I'm feeling relief," Betsy Clegg said, leaning around Henry and Maggie so she could see her friend. "It's been exciting, but it'll be good to have our east pastures back again for grazing. David's been worrying lately how to get the sheep fattened with wagons camped out on his best grass."

"It'll be sad to see some go," Cindy said, sighing.

Maggie felt something like an iron band tightening around her heart. "When?" she croaked.

"Brother Brigham said he's shipping out today. Got his wagons all loaded up already."

At this, Maggie's pulse raced.

No wonder Mariah wasn't there. It had been her worst fear.

She didn't wait to hear any more; she stepped quickly through the crowd, leaving Henry with his mother and father. When she got enough space, she began to run toward the town square, but soon had to slow again, waiting for animals and carts to pass. Center Street was already so thick with people running and walking, shouting out orders, saddling animals as they stood by the side of the road, and loading up wagons, that there was no room for a body to pass through untouched.

They're ready to shake the dust of this place clear off their feet.

This was her bitter thought as she made her way through the square. A sudden flare of pride came with it, slowing her pace. She stopped outside the door, second from the left along one of the long, narrow lean-tos where the prophet and his family had lived these last few months.

I'll head home, she thought. *Mariah don't really need me in all this mess. Likely she'd rather I leave her alone to pack.*

After a moment's struggle, she rapped once on the door. It was opened immediately by a harried-looking woman holding a broom.

"Hello, Sister Liz. Mariah around?" Maggie asked.

Elizabeth Young shook her head. "They've cleared their things out already. They were one of the first ones out—likely you'll find them east of town headed for the benches."

Maggie's heart pounded in her temples. She felt moisture start at the corner of her eyes.

Mariah didn't even plan on saying good-bye. She just up and shipped out.

She trudged down Seventh, feeling sick to her stomach.

She thought it had been something special, what she and Mariah had. Or at least, it had been infinitely special to Maggie, who had never had a bosom friend before. Not a girl friend at least.

Henry don't count. She picked up a stick and struck savagely at the tall weeds that lined the shallow water ditch.

He's a boy, she argued to herself, quashing the prick of guilt that followed her uncharitable thought. *And besides, going fishing for suckers isn't the same as talking your heart out 'til you felt full and sure that someone knew you.*

Mariah.

Maggie shook her head and began running again. No, she couldn't leave it. She just couldn't. It was too much. She would have too much to regret if she didn't try to say good-bye. There was no room for pride here, not with the searing ache in her middle, the lump in her throat. She didn't care if she made a fool of herself. Mariah's companionship, even though it had been for only a few short months, had meant the world to Maggie.

It had been odd—threatening, even—at least at first.

Maggie had thought that girlish friendships were not meant for her, or that there was something about her that just made it impossible. She thought it was because she wasn't refined enough or because of her funny foreign way of speaking.

It was really Maggie's solemn countenance and unnerving way of studying people that kept the Fourth-Ward girls at a distance. Which was why it was such a miracle that Mariah had sat next to her during Nancy Wall's quilting party that Saturday in March. And it was also a miracle that, in spite of Maggie's silence and one-word answers, the girl stayed next to her and continued to talk for three long hours instead of changing seats to sit next to Julia Huntington, for instance. Instead, Mariah weathered the long silences, waiting for Maggie's answers and talking as if the conversation was proceeding at quite the normal pace.

The third miracle happened the next day, when there was a knock on Maggie's door. There stood Mariah, with one of her mother's aprons folded over her bodice and tied around her waist. Her dimples framed her grin like parentheses, and her eyes glittered as if she knew a joke. Maggie couldn't help but let her in, couldn't help but offer her a place by the fire, couldn't help the fact that her emotional dam began to crack and the words started to pour out slowly, like molasses from a pitcher.

Mariah had never once teased Maggie about the way her skin browned in the summer. She never made a remark about Maggie's unruly, often uncombed hair. She never looked scornfully at her hem, the way it rode up on her shins instead of falling at her ankles, as a proper young lady's should. And she would ask Maggie questions about her family—about her mother, her father, and what had happened on the plain.

Maggie had never talked of her times with Mariah with

anybody. Maggie, who had only had the Clegg boys as friends, had learned what it was to be a girl that summer. She learned that there was fun to be had outside of fishing and mud fights, and that a confidante could sometimes lessen a burden carried inside. She still couldn't take pleasure in sewing, but she and Mariah had spent long hours poring over books and picking flowers and pressing them, or just taking walks along the wide, dusty streets in town. Mariah, with her sweet smile and friendly disposition, naturally attracted attention and warmth from those around her, and some of that warmth had settled on Maggie too, as they were always together. More people had gotten to know Maggie's name in the last few months than had ever known it these last four years since she settled with the Aldens in Provo.

Anyhow, there's been pecks and bushels more people at all these last months. Maggie hurried east toward the line of wagons and carts, carriages, and every moving contraption there was known to man. Tongue to tailgate, they lined the rough road that led up along the benches, past Provo and Battle Creek and Evansville, all the way to Great Salt Lake City. The line moved slowly, stirring up plumes of dust that looked almost like smoke.

As had become her habit, Maggie scanned the faces she saw carefully, even in her haste.

No Samuel.

But it wasn't a sad or frustrated thought; it was only matter-of-fact—almost absentminded. She hadn't seen her brother in four years. His face, in her mind, was blurry, and his very existence, to Maggie, seemed blurry as well. It could be he had come south. He was supposed to have been taken in by some tradesman as an apprentice up in Great Salt Lake City, when Maggie's family parted ways on the plain: Mama and Papa to heaven, Maggie and Giovanna to the Aldens', who ended up in Provo. And Samuel, somewhere in Salt Lake City. That is the way Maggie had come to think of it.

At least it's not muddy. She stopped running. She scanned the horizon and felt a start of recognition. That was surely Mariah's crazy quilt, hanging over the canvas of the third wagon in line.

She walked toward it, feeling a lump gather in her throat.

"Hello, Maggie." Lucy Young smiled down at her. "Mariah find you?"

Maggie walked slowly, keeping pace with the wagon. "No."

"She went after you. Wanted to say good-bye."

Maggie nodded. Jubilation—and relief—surged through her, so that she didn't trust herself to speak.

"Reckon she went to the Aldens'," she finally managed. She turned on her heel, poised to run back in the direction she came, and nearly ran into Mariah.

"Megs," Mariah said, grinning at her.

Maggie hugged her fiercely. It startled both Mariah and Maggie, who were unused to such a demonstration of physical affection from Maggie.

"Good-bye," Maggie choked out.

"It's all happened so fast, hasn't it?" Mariah's voice was also rough with emotion. It did Maggie's heart good and made her even sadder at the same time.

"I'll miss you." The words were so hard to say. They felt like they had been wrenched out of her, leaving gaping wounds. "Do you—are you—?"

"I'm sad to leave, Maggie," Mariah said after a moment. "Silly. I'm glad we're going home to Sugar House, but I'll miss you awfully. You've been such a friend in all this."

"You're kind to say it." Maggie wiped her nose with her sleeve and grimaced. "Don't have any clean kerchiefs."

Mariah took one from her apron pocket.

"No, I won't be able to give it back to you."

Mariah pressed it into her hand. "You can take it to remember me by, then."

Maggie wiped her nose on the edge of the soft square and tucked it into her bodice. "But you'll write too?"

"Of course. You'll write back?"

"I'll try."

Mariah's face became stern. "You'd better, Megs. What do you think Sister Clegg made you that journal for?"

"I'll practice," Maggie promised. "I'll write you, long as you promise not to show my poor letters to any soul but yourself."

Mariah nodded. Her lip trembled, and she slid her arms around Maggie again. "'Bye," she croaked, and then stepped into the wagon box. "Likely we'll see each other again sometime."

Maggie nodded, even though she knew it was just pleasantries. "See you."

She walked along with the wagons until they reached Temple Hill, and then she sat in the long grass, chewing on the sweet ends of stems and watching the people pass. She wanted to follow them further, but she knew it wouldn't be safe that far outside of town walls.

Why? she wondered, chewing on the brittle stems. *Why is it I can count on one thing: that is, if I start depending on somebody, they end up gone from my life?*

Ma, and Pa, and Samuel. And now Mariah.

It was an unfair thought, and Maggie knew it. There were plenty around who hadn't left her. Henry, Hyrum.

Ma and Pa Alden, her foster parents. Her two foster sisters, Etta Mae and Patience, and of course, there was Giovanna. Giovanna would always be with her. Giovanna had survived the prairie, just like Maggie. The thought was less comforting than usual, though.

It was Giovanna who found her there, an hour later.

"Mama says come help with chores," Giovanna said breathlessly, running up to Maggie and flopping onto the ground next to her. "What're you doing?"

Maggie stretched her arms and carefully rose. "Nothing. Mariah left, and I said good-bye to her."

"She going back to her house? I'll miss her. She told me that story about the princess who slept on all those mattresses with the pea underneath it. Do you think you could tell it, Maggie?"

"Maybe." Maggie began walking back down the road, her shoulders hunched over, her arms folded tightly to her chest. She gave a minute nod to Cindy Holden as she passed their fenced-in front yard. A half-dozen little redheaded children played around Cindy, while she knelt weeding the carrot patch.

"Hey, there. Do you have mind to tend the children on Saturday? I've got a meeting with Sister Wall."

"She had her baby, yet?" Giovanna called over the fence.

"Nope. Still a few weeks, I think. Maggie?"

"Sure," Maggie said, avoiding her gaze.

"Could you come by around ten? You'd get lunch for them."

"Fine."

Maggie and Giovanna quickened their pace as they turned into the Aldens' drive.

"Are they cross?" Maggie asked.

"No. Just wondered where you'd got to." She pulled the door open recklessly, letting it bang.

Maggie stepped over the threshold of the Aldens' two-story adobe home.

Ma Alden, Patience, and Etta all sat in chairs around the pile of mending in the middle of the main room, while Pa Alden and Father Fort sat on the hearth, as usual, fiddling with bits of repair.

In the corner by the door was Jed Forth, who grimaced at Giovanna. She stuck her tongue out at him and scurried over to Patience. Maggie skirted Jed warily on her way to the empty rocker on the other side of the room. It was obvious he was in a mood.

"Bodyguards," Uncle Forth was saying. "Always has them around now. I think ol' Brigham's relieved to have it all resolved, to be able to move everybody back up and pretend like none of this ever happened." He made a harrumphing noise, something between clearing a throat and harsh laughter.

Maggie hated that noise. She hated it, and the talk. And when Uncle Forth was around, there was plenty to be had of it.

The main room of the Aldens' home was an airy, pleasant room during the day. At nighttime, when the furniture was pushed to the walls and the straw ticks were laid out on the floor, it also served as the four girls' bedroom, and could get drafty in the cold of winter. The girls would sometimes take the blankets from their beds and huddle up together next to the fire that Pa Alden kept banked in the stove for their warmth.

Maggie moved to sit in the remaining empty chair, but Ma Alden made a shooing motion with her hand. "We're hemming linens. I don't trust your stitches. Change the ticks and air them out, if you please, Maggie."

"Upstairs too?"

Ma Alden paused and then nodded. "Yes, the bed up there needs to be turned over. You'll find the clean linens on the line outside. Got some good washing in this morning; there was nobody else up at the crick."

"They're all packing to leave," Patience added. "Did you get to say good-bye to your friend, Maggie?"

"Streets choked with contraptions and dusty—hot as hades," Uncle Forth interjected, speaking to nobody in particular. "That was some bit of planning ol' Brigham did, wasn't it?"

Pa Alden looked up from the bit he was working on. Seeing that no answer was required, he offered none.

Maggie nodded to Patience. "Caught her up by the benches."

"Canyon road's going to be nigh untrav'lable for weeks on end," Uncle Forth put in, glaring at Maggie, as if she had caused it all.

Maggie dashed up the stairs. She stood at the top, waiting for her emotions to ebb once more, and looked the bed over. She had never turned the upstairs mattress by herself before. It was horsehair, covered in canvas, so it was heavier than the others. She was generally clumsy too; she'd have to be careful to move Ma Alden's lamp, which sat on the big chest at the foot of the bed, before she tried it.

She took the lamp and put it in a corner of the room. Grunting, she tugged the heavy cedar chest out of the way. She stopped for a moment, running her fingers over the smooth lacquer of its surface. All of Ma Alden's prized possessions were in there, things from the Aldens' previous life in New York before they joined the Saints and had to leave most things behind, not once, not twice, but three times.

She could hear the words in Ma Alden's voice. Ma Alden always said it like that: "Not once, not twice . . ."

Maggie kept her mind filled with inane thoughts such as this, in order to keep the more painful ones at bay as she went about the work. She pulled the quilt off and bundled it in another corner of the room. She pulled off the linen sheets and piled them on top of the quilt. Then she bent, steeling herself to lift the floppy, heavy mattress. She stood on the bed frame, steadying it, and then leapt out of the way as it fell hard on its other side. The dust rose up, eddying in the streams of bright light that came through the little east window.

Maggie grabbed the sheet from the corner, bent to tuck it around one of the mattress corners, and then froze. She stared down at the mattress, her knees ready to lift, her arms underneath it, poised to heave it over onto its other side, and felt her mouth go dry and her heart flutter against her ribs like a bird in its cage.

What was this?

"Magdalena Chabert," she whispered, reading the writing along the seam of the mattress. It was faded—only a shadow on the yellow canvas. But the hand was neat and flowing. It was somehow familiar. And the name was her own.

What was her name doing on this mattress? Would Ma Alden have some reason for writing Maggie's name on the upstairs bed?

And then the shock came.

Mother.

Maggie was named after her mother. The name was

her mother's—did her mother write it? Had this mattress belonged to her mother?

Maggie stared at it, her back aching from her awkward position. Slowly, she tucked the sheet along the edge of the mattress, smoothing it over the surface. She walked around the bed and tucked in the other side as well.

She stared at the bed for another long moment, then bent and ripped the sheet off. She was reading from the other side, and so the words were upside down in her view this time but . . . *Magdalena Chabert.* It was unmistakable.

This had to belong to Maggie's mother.

But, Maggie argued with herself, *Ma Alden told me all Ma and Pa's stuff was gone. Sold, to pay for . . .*

Maggie stopped again and stood, the corner of the sheet in her hands.

The yellow pitcher. The old, worn Bible with its leather cover. These objects swam into Maggie's vision, murky with the wear of memory. Sold, she had thought.

But this mattress hadn't been sold. Wouldn't a mattress fetch a pretty decent price, especially out there at one of those lonely trading posts? Maybe not more than the china, but the Bible, surely . . .

There's only one real answer.

Ma Alden had lied.

Had she lied?

Maggie shook her head, and rubbed her eyes, hard, with the palms of her hands. This mattress was her mother's and obviously hadn't been sold. Ma Alden had said everything had to be sold for money to pay the cost of setting her Papa's broken leg, and still the Chaberts had left a debt behind when they died.

Maggie's mind was as mixed up as winter stew after the

shock of this morning, and now this. It was too much.

Almost savagely, she grabbed the quilt off the floor and threw it over the mattress. She shoved the chest up against the bed frame, bruising a toe in the process.

She didn't even notice. She was numb—numb from the neck down, and completely foggy from the neck up. Her body took her down the stairs in a jerky stride that nearly sent her sprawling at the bottom.

"Where are you going?" Ma Alden called out to her as she headed for the door.

"Digging segoes." The words came unprompted to her lips, and she dashed out the door.

"But—"

Maggie didn't wait to hear Etta Mae's protest. She knew it wasn't the right time of year.

She ran around the back of the house to the barn and found Jed Forth harnessing the mule to the cart. The Forths and Aldens shared a barn, a backyard, and Ma Alden. She and Dale Forth were brother and sister. Jed, Uncle Forth's son, was sixteen, old enough to do a man's work.

When she saw it was Jed, she nearly doubled back toward the Aldens, but again, her need was too great.

"You going out to the sheep?" she asked, approaching the cart.

Jed nodded.

"I've got to go get some segoes from the riverbanks."

Jed squinted at her. "They'll be stringy and bitter this time of year."

Maggie breathed out slowly. If Jed was talking, he couldn't be in too much of a mood. "There's no arguing with Ma Alden," she offered.

Jed shrugged. "Hop up, then. Go on, now, quick."

Maggie quickly grabbed the edge of the wagon and hoisted herself up. She had learned, long ago, to keep away from Jed's bad side.

The rocky road and the rickety wheels of the cart made Maggie's teeth chatter. It was a welcome distraction. She tried to forget, to fill her mind with nothing but the heat that cooked her shoulders through her bodice, and the pungent, whiney smell of cottonwoods.

He drove out of the press of moving bodies and wagons as fast as he could, making a circuitous route that avoided both Main and West Main, and the roads that lead off to the canyon way, which were now so packed that nothing could move more than a few feet at a time.

They passed the old fort field. Maggie swatted mosquitoes away from her face. She didn't really see it—the bare foundations and the little hill of earth, where the cannon first sat when the settlers came—there were other images flashing through her mind, flooding her vision. Too much to see, too much to feel. That was why Maggie had put these memories away for good in a dark corner of her mind. And here they were, all summoned at once because of a line of faded handwriting.

Jed turned the wagon north and began to head west to where the Aldens' pastures lay on the south side of the river. When they stopped by the pasture fence, Maggie dropped heavily to the ground and walked to the water. She found a broad-trunked cottonwood and sat against it, watching the waters rush over the long roots that stretched into the stream. She pulled out the little journal that Mariah had mentioned. It had been a birthday gift from Sister Clegg. It was homemade—leather tanned from one of the Clegg's calves, and pages carefully cut and saved from any papers lying about that seemed decent enough and had blank backs. She could only write on the one side because the other mostly contained newsprint. One had an address on it; the carefully smoothed-out paper had once been a thick mailing envelope. It was a tiny book with pitifully few pages—precious space, not to be wasted.

If Maggie hadn't found the mattress, she would have slowly and painstakingly written a curt line or two detailing the events of the day, without bothering to detail her own woebegone feelings of having been left behind.

But this was so much. There were no words, even if she had them all at her disposal, even if she could write as swiftly as Patience or Etta. She was so stuffed full of oddness and hurt and fear, so blocked up with it all bucking and rearing inside of her, it was like there was no room for words, even practical ones.

So she lay there in the tree roots, with the journal resting face-up on her lap, and looked up at the pieces of blue sky that shone through the leafy greenness of cottonwoods. She hoped perhaps that, if she lay still enough, it would calm, and then all could ooze out of her, watering the ground as readily as any rain shower.

Or maybe the stream could rise and rush over her, carrying it all away.

A few minutes of quiet did seem to help things settle a bit, at least. And a sort of funny thought suddenly came to Maggie, bringing with it a little bit of relief.

She sat up slowly and put pencil to the page.

"Its shir od," she wrote, "of all tyms Ive put lynins on that old matris and never I seen it before."

She paused and then scrawled another line.

"Saynts out of toun. Canin rode is chokd clear up to the mowth."

Then she shut the journal with a resounding slap of leather on parchment and tucked it back into her bodice.

Guess that's all, she thought.

But it wasn't.

Maggie could remember some of the details of what had happened to her family when they had crossed the plains four years ago. The Campbell Company, it had been.

Most of the journey had been fine. Good going and plenty of feed for the animals, and enough for all the people too, right up until the end when the winter weather and scarcity of food began to complicate matters. But the Chaberts had still gotten along fine. Mother somehow made the food stretch enough to keep everyone in good spirits and energy to do what they had to, to keep on going.

And then there had been Papa's injury.

Maggie had very clear memories of that time. Her mother—ungainly with her large belly—sat wrapped in a woolen shawl tending the campfire. Her father lay in the wagon, his leg bound up from hip to ankle.

Me and Giovanna went to the Aldens'. Mama and Papa went to heaven, and Samuel went to Great Salt Lake City, Maggie repeated it to herself, like a mantra or a memorized map of her family's geography.

What was odd were the things Maggie could *not* remember. When she thought back on those several months of travel—leaving their little mountain village, the boat, and the few months by wagon—it all seemed one jumbled mess of events, places, and people. She had known very little English at the time. It had been so much for her ten-year-old mind to take in.

Before today, she had believed Ma Alden's account in every particular. On the few occasions Maggie had found to bring up the subject, Ma Alden had always related the same tale, and Maggie had no reason to doubt the account: Samuel was given to another family. Ma Alden couldn't remember the name particularly. This rumored family had promised to give him his keep and some books and letters. They had settled in Great Salt Lake City, Ma Alden thought. The girls had come to the Aldens' with nothing but "the clothes on your backs and hungry bellies for the feeding."

This had always been a mystery to Maggie, how all the family's goods had been lost. But it was nothing significant; many families had to leave goods behind on the prairie. She did have a very clear memory of the white porcelain pitcher, gilded along its rim and handle, that her mother carefully packed and moved around throughout the trip to keep it from breaking. There were some cups too, round, with little round handles. She remembered the family Bible, which Papa read out of every evening, even on the frostiest ones. He pulled the mitten off his hand and turned the thin pages delicately with his bare fingertips.

And she remembered her father's face on the day that he died, the strange, skeleton calm of his features. She had read to him from the Bible then, skipping over or guessing at words too long for her to sound out, turning the pages as carefully as she could with her clumsy, stiff fingers.

This was too painful, though, to think on for very long.

It had been a shock, a sudden burst of memory, to see her mother's writing there on the cotton, to see her mother's name . . . her own name.

Did shocks, as a general rule, tend to come severally within a short period of time? Maggie hoped not. Or perhaps she hoped so. Was she due for another shock if she asked Ma Alden about it today? Perhaps she could mention it, offhand, sometime during the long, quiet afternoon whilst the woman sat around in the cabin with their mending? Could there be more things that Ma Alden hadn't thought to catalogue among the Chabert's remaining assets?

Are the pitcher and the Bible still around, then? she wondered to herself. Perhaps they were hidden someplace. In the chest under the upstairs bed or the chest of folded linens in the front room, or even buried, like treasure from those yarns Henry liked to yammer to her about that he read in his fifth-form primer . . .

Guilt seared through her mind at the thought. In a way, it was like accusing Ma Alden of stealing. But an equally guilty piece of her wanted this truth, wanted Ma Alden to have deceived her, for the sake of the porcelain pitcher. And for the sake of her father's Bible. What price, after all, would a family Bible bring? It was odd that she'd never thought of it before. If Ma Alden found no use for it, had she simply thrown it aside, like so much garbage? She doubted it. That would be most unlike Ma Alden, who was thrifty to the point of hoarding even the most useless of scraps—Etta Mae grumbled every time she rooted through the rag bag, which half should've gone into the hens' nesting boxes because they were not even fit for rug-making.

The sheepdog's barking brought Maggie back to the present. Jed came over the hill and pointed imperiously at the wagon. "Get up. Your Ma's going to be in a fuss if we don't get going." He looked around and then at her. "Where's the segoes?"

Maggie shrugged. "Couldn't find any worth digging. Are you all coming over tonight?" she asked.

"Dunno. Likely, I guess." Jed strolled off, holding his prodding stick across his shoulders.

Maggie settled herself into the back of the wagon. Jed clucked to the horses, not bothering to glance behind and see that she'd settled herself properly. Maggie held on tightly to the side as the contraption rattled down the winding little path that led off the bench and back down toward the valley where the little town nestled. From up here, the streets were like seams of delicate stitching; the houses lined up along Main Street, cunning little buttons.

"Looks like the ways've cleared out. Nobody wants to leave this late in the day, I guess."

Maggie nodded, though Jed wasn't looking at her.

The Seminary building and Redfield Hotel stood tall, along with the scattering of buildings along Center, or Seventh, as some still called it. Seventh Street, which had most of the businesses in town, had been teeming with trade all spring and summer. It seemed forlorn now, surrounded by empty streets. She picked out a few carts and a horse and rider here and there but that was all. Town Square was empty too. The long, narrow lean-to buildings that had housed Brother Brigham's large family were still there, but there seemed to Maggie little other evidence that the Prophet had lived in their midst for so many months. He had departed, and so they were no longer the gathering place. They were once more a mere settlement, Fort Provo, looking hopefully north toward the Great Salt Lake for information and counsel, and anything else of consequence.

Samuel is there. Suddenly, the thought seemed frighteningly tangible. If she had more than a hazy memory of his features, Samuel's face would have come to her, sharp and real.

Samuel was alive. Somewhere.

It was like this name on a mattress was some kind of

proof, real evidence that Maggie had been a part of a different family once. That Mama and Papa and Samuel weren't hazy, fairy-tale creatures to offset the harsh reality of living in Provo with the Aldens.

Samuel might be in Salt Lake, not more than a day's ride north.

She had thought about the fact that he might have come south, that they had been mere miles apart these last few months, but it had been like looking for a falling star, something one didn't expect to see.

Samuel was real, and he was alive.

It was almost unbearable, the thought that she might have missed an opportunity. He could have been in Provo, even.

But perhaps she would not know Samuel if she saw him, or he, her. It was even possible that Samuel could recognize her and still have very little desire to have much to do with her.

When they pulled into the Aldens' yard, Maggie felt as if her heart might burst clear from her rib cage. She tripped as she descended from the wagon, landing on all fours on the ground.

Jed snorted.

Maggie blinked her eyes free of moisture and rose slowly to her feet. As she walked toward the front door, she felt like someone else's feet carried her.

"Hello, Maggie." Patience smiled at her as she entered.

She didn't smile back. She turned her gaze on Ma Alden, who still sat in the corner with her mending. "Where is my brother?" It came out hoarse, almost a whisper.

Everyone in the room froze. Giovanna, who was playing on the hearth, turned to gaze at Maggie. Pa Alden looked up from his whittling, his eyes dark with some strong emotion.

As Maggie met his gaze, he looked away.

"You're brother's up in the city," Ma Alden said. "I've told you before, he's been apprenticed. What's . . .?" She shook her head. "Why you digging up dirt all of a sudden?"

"What d'you mean by that?"

"By what?" Ma Alden's lips thinned out, and her eyes got a look in them that Maggie knew meant trouble.

"You hiding something from me? About Samuel?" Maggie's voice rose. "About my family?"

Ma Alden rose from her chair. She set her mending in the seat. "Those are some uppity questions, coming from the girl whose back I clothed and whose belly I've filled these last four years." Her mouth shook.

Etta, rocking in her corner, made a tutting sound.

Patience rose and put a hand on Ma Alden's arm. "It was so long ago, Maggie. Don't worry over it. You're here now." She smiled. "You've got a family—us."

Maggie nodded, but she didn't sit. She watched all of them settle back into their places—Ma Alden in the middle, Patience and Etta next to her, Giovanna on the hearth with Pa Alden, who sat silently whittling, as if nothing were happening.

She watched her sister, the way the firelight brought out the red in her dark hair; the paleness of her face; her large, dark eyes.

Mother. She looks like mother.

Maggie touched Pa Alden's hammer where it lay on the table. She wrapped her fingers around the handle.

She walked upstairs. She stood at the foot of the bed, her shins against Ma Alden's old trunk. She saw the mattress with linens tucked around it. *Ma Alden's linens, and her quilt neatly spread over the top*, Maggie thought bitterly.

The lacquer surface of the trunk looked hard. Ugly all of a sudden. It seemed full of secrets. *If she hid things, she'd hide them here,* Maggie thought. The iron lock and bracings seemed like they held Maggie prisoner.

She lifted the hammer and paused for a moment, thinking of the family downstairs, chatting, mending, whittling.

Her hand began to tremble. Finally, she lowered the hammer, twisting her apron around it to hide it. She walked back down the stairs.

THE ALDENS

MAGGIE SET THE DISHRAG DOWN AND PEEKED OUT THE back door for the third time that morning.

He was still there—Pa Alden's figure leaned against one of the fence posts. He was so still, he could have almost been a fence post himself. *If somebody'd be so foolish as to make a fence post out of a willow bough.* After it'd been through a few months of stiff wind, it might look something like Pa Alden.

He stood, looking over the vegetable garden. He reached up, from time to time, scratching his head.

It was not at all unusual. He got stuck like that lately—still, staring, and no words for whatever it was going on inside him. Pa Alden had always been a man of few words. But now, he never talked in company at all. *Around Uncle Forth or Ma Alden, he doesn't hardly even say the things that ought to be said by a human.* Not a word even when Ma Alden asked him if he wanted breakfast; she asked half-desperate, inane questions as if she were worried he would lose the ability to speak from lack of practice. As if she were worried she'd forget the sound of his voice.

Maggie reflected as she wiped grease off the cast-iron pan.

Last summer, that's when it had started. That last Indian mission—he had come back haggard. Jumpy. He stooped, as if carrying a burden or ashamed to show his face.

Something, Maggie thought. *Something happened that week.*

But he had been back up in Provo before all the shooting happened, she was fairly certain of that. Before the Indians started the killing. Women. Men. Children . . .

Maggie rubbed her eyes with the back of a hand, as if trying to erase the image there, in her mind. The image from her dreams.

She had no notion of what exactly had happened down in Cedar. There were rumors, to be sure, but the sort of rumors that little girls only caught a word or two of, before grown-up people hushed up in their presence. Thanks to Uncle Forth, though, just enough words had been spoken around Maggie to start those nightmares. Men painted up with mud, with something red. Men with guns, trained on her, and then the giant, horrifying explosion. Or sometimes it was Maggie who held a gun, to the face of someone she loved—to Giovanna. To the watery-faded image of her mother. To Mariah . . .

She had told only Mariah of her dreams, though she couldn't hide them from Giovanna, who slept next to her at night. Maggie was ashamed that her mind could come up with something so awful.

Maggie shuddered and wiped her hands on the dish towel. There was still the big stew pot to do, but she needed to collect eggs sometime this morning. *Might as well be now,* she thought.

She wandered out into the yard with a basket in her hand. She came to a stop next to Pa Alden.

"Counting the leaves on the cabbages?" she asked.

Pa Alden started. "Split some fence rails?"

That's it. Four words. No "Maggie-girl, you feel like splitting fence rails with me this morning? I've been telling your ma, you're near as good as a boy with that axe."

No "I'd sure love your company in some splitting, little bella."

"I have to do dishes and get ready for Twelveses' barn raising tonight," Maggie replied. "You fixing to do some splitting?"

Pa Alden passed the back of his hand over his brow and shrugged. "Reckon. Weeding. Your Ma Alden." He shrugged again.

Maggie nodded as if she knew what he was trying to say, as if it was normal conversation. "Seems to me it needs weeding." She climbed through the little door in the henhouse and collected two dozen warm eggs. She washed her hands with water from the well. She returned to the house and her place at the wash-barrel. Patience nudged her way in next to her and took the stew pot from her hands.

"We'd best hurry these dishes along. Ma wants to start baking."

Maggie nodded and began on the cups from the table. "How many are we baking for?" she asked.

Patience added water to the pot. "Twelveses, of course, and the Bells and Baums, Turners, Holdens, and I think the Cleggs are planning to come. And Bishop and Sister Wall, of course."

"Lots of baking, then."

"A fair amount. Sister Nancy Wall asked that there be

enough to leave some with the Twelveses after, and to make up hampers, of course. She's not had her baby yet."

"I'd planned on bringing in some fish. We could have it for dinner tomorrow."

Patience gave Maggie a look. "The Clegg boys will be busy this afternoon too, I'm sure."

Maggie reached over and gave the bottom of the pot a vicious scrub, dislodging the last of the blackened stew. "There," she said. "You got to set in with your shoulders to get the worst of it off."

Patience raised an eyebrow. "Thanks." She daintily wiped away the grime and lifted the pot onto the stovetop to dry.

"Does Ma Alden need me especially? She knows I'm no hand at cakes."

"I suppose you could ask. Giovanna's off playing at the Forths'; she could likely stand to help a little in the kitchen."

Maggie stifled the sudden dart of worry, reminding herself that Jed was helping with the Turners' wheat harvest. She hurried her hands, glancing at the door. In spite of what Patience said, it was likely Henry would be by soon. Henry liked to get his fishing in before the full, blistering heat of noontime hit. And he had been very keen on fishing lately.

"Where's my blue thimble?" Etta Mae's fretful voice came from the rocking chair, which was turned toward the fire. "Second time I've found my bags disarranged inside a week. Do we have mice, I wonder?"

"Likely little hands seeking sweets or treasures," Patience replied. "We've had the Holden boys over recently. Cindy Holden came to trade some scraps."

"Little cubs haven't learnt to keep their hands to themselves," Etta agreed.

Maggie didn't say anything, but the guilt seared through

her. Maggie knew who had rummaged through Etta's things, and it wasn't the Holden boys.

It had become a routine, ever since the day she'd discovered her mother's name on the mattress. She checked it, every day when she found herself alone in the cabin, to see if it had been some strange dream or fancy on her part. But it was always there, indelibly blued into the seam. The thought of the porcelain, and the family Bible—what a bolt of lightning it was—the thought that they might be around somewhere. The possibility, remote as it was, had driven her to search every corner of the cabin. Every box or bag. She'd even taken to knocking on floorboards to see if there were some secret space somewhere. She'd pulled out the box of winter underwear and gone through it. She'd even looked in and under the henhouse. The well taunted her—surely Ma Alden would never throw a Bible down a well? She was too religious for that.

Maggie had even stood over Ma Alden's cedar chest. She stood at the foot of the upstairs bed, staring at it. Last time she'd slipped one of Pa Alden's hammers into her apron and spent something like fifteen minutes alternately deciding and then backing away, shaking her head.

"Have you looked amongst Ma Alden's things?" Maggie asked. She set her clean pot aside. "She may have borrowed it—I, I thought I saw her the other day using it. Well, there the dishes are done. I think I hear the Clegg's cart along the street." She stumbled over the consonants a bit and stepped outside before Patience could plague her further about taking Henry away from his chores.

She ran around the side of the house toward the vegetable garden, feeling her heart beat in her temples. Henry wasn't there, of course. He would come by way of the street and pull up against the hitching post. Pa Alden was at the far end of the garden. His long, lean body was bent over, moving rhythmically along one of the rows.

It was a strange sight, Pa Alden weeding the kitchen garden—women's work. Last year at this time, he would be trading work, likely picking peaches or apples in a neighbor's orchard, and expecting a return favor for this fall's corn and potato crops. At the very least, he should be up with Jed tending the sheep and fences.

We're two peas in a pod now. Doing things we wouldn't do. Acting like we're touched in the head.

"Hey-O!"

Maggie shrieked and jumped a good few feet. A warm hand grabbed her elbow, steadying her and turning her around.

"Sorry," Henry said, grinning down at her.

"No, you ain't."

"Aren't," Henry corrected. "What kind of girl are you? Don't even know your ain'ts from your aren'ts. Bet you don't know your aren'ts from your uncles, neither."

Maggie gave him a look. "Reckon it took you the whole way from your house to here to think of that."

"Nope. Old joke of my Pa's; he's said it ever since I was little."

"It's either, not neither."

"Part of the joke," Henry replied agreeably. "Get it? Correct someone, and make a mistake doing it. Makes it funny instead of irksome."

Maggie shook her head. "Let's go catch us a few irksome trout. Wait while I go get my pole. Hyrum coming today?"

"I brought it. You left it at my place last time, remember? No. He's busy in pa's shop."

It was odd, climbing into the driving seat beside Henry.

Just the two of us now.

They turned their cart out on West Main Street, moving up the west side of town square. The sheds were starting to come down now; lumber was far too dear and hard to come by to lie around useless for long. There were a few wagons out today headed north, but the steady stream had gone down to a trickle as this third week came to a close.

"Pa's helping to take it down today," Henry said, clucking to the mule and nodding in the direction of the line of sheds. "They're thinking on using some of the Bells for fencing 'round the east fields down by the canyon toll road."

"People causing trouble again, then?"

"Nope, not much since Fanchers," Henry said. "Just good practice, though. And now we've got a crop of soldiers milling 'round places, people're a little uneasy and more of a mind to pen things up a bit."

"Henry," Maggie started, and then stopped, rubbing the hilt of her fishing pole thoughtfully.

Henry was not stupid, and he knew Maggie well enough to know she was upset over something. He clucked to the mule again. "Your Pa Alden's a good man," he said.

"I know. I ain't fussed about that no more. I reckon whatever happened down in Cedar, likely Pa's just upset over it. He's got a soft spot for those Paiutes. Can't believe they'd do something like that. And Uncle Forth and all his chatter about how it weren't just Indian ruckus, it was the bishops as ordered the—"

"People talk. It's those as listen, and worse, those who move the stories along, who are the fools."

"I know," Maggie repeated, clearing her throat carefully.

"You haven't had any more dreams, have you?"

Maggie stared at Henry. "Mariah told you about my dream?"

Henry shrugged. "It came up."

"How, I'd like to know. How would my dreams come up in a conversation between you two?"

"You're both of our's friend. You come up a lot." Henry shrugged. "Mariah was worried. Said you were worried over it, that your Uncle Forth's been talking a pack of lies and you've been taking it keenly."

"Yes, well . . ." Maggie put her pole across her knees. "He talks about a lot of things."

"What're you upset over then?"

Maggie was silent for a long moment. "Henry, do you reckon there's a way to tell if someone *is* lying to you?"

Henry chuckled. "I'd never lie to you, Maggie. I'd hate to be at the receiving end of whatever you'd give me when you found me out."

"I know you don't lie, Henry. That's not why I asked. But do you reckon there's a way to know, for sure, for real, if someone tells you the truth or not. I mean, is it easy for a person to pretend something—I mean, have you ever had anyone lie to you for a long time and you didn't know they was lying?"

The smile melted off Henry's face. "Who's been lying to you?"

Maggie shook her head. "Nobody. That I know of for sure. Just wondered."

"Well, I suppose you could pray about it."

Maggie sighed. "I suppose I could."

They were riding close to the old fort now. The furrows in the earth left from the foundations of cabins that no longer stood, and the mud wall that enclosed it to the town walls, emphasized the melancholy Maggie was feeling.

"At any rate, it's done and over, and all is well. You shouldn't worry on something you can't do much about."

"You're just chock-full of advice today," Maggie snapped. She jumped down from the cart, which slowed as they approached the riverbank where it curved along the northwestern corner of town.

It was a beautiful day, still with the heat of summer, to make the shady riverbank a nice resting spot. Gentle breezes brushed through the cottonwoods. Maggie sat on the flat, warm surface of a boulder that overhung the bank and cast out. Henry walked a little further upstream, where the river widened a bit into a long, calm stretch of pool. He was particular about the sort of fish he caught; Maggie was happy with whatever suckers or catfish she managed to snag. She was no discriminator of fishes. She quickly caught mottled catfish, all on the small side. She threw the smallest back.

Water. What was it about the sound that calmed one so? She could fall asleep, leaning here on this warm stone and the water to lull her, with no trouble at all. Perhaps she could set her pole aside and dangle small, bare toes into the cool surface of the water, and a nice, silver-finned bass would wake her with a nibble.

It was Henry who woke her an hour later. "Time to get to town, if we want to make the Twelveses' to-do."

Maggie stumbled to her feet and pulled her string of fish from the water. "What'd you get?"

"A couple trout. I'll give one to you; ma's getting right sick of 'em. Traded that half dozen I collected Saturday last. To Brother Stewart, for some salt pork. Trading my fish for salt pork; that's what it's come to at my house."

Maggie chuckled, and her stomach rumbled. Salt pork

was not the most attractive thought, if you were thinking on the sorts of meats you've had in your life. But this time of year, just before harvest and hunting time . . . even salt pork began to run a little scarce. Turnips just didn't fill up a person too well as a substitute.

It was odd, Maggie suddenly realized as they turned back onto Seventh. Just her and Henry. It had always been a threesome before. Hyrum used to come with Maggie and Henry. And just about the time Hyrum outgrew his tendency to go fishing every chance he got (preferring the company of girls in town and the dramatic association his brothers were a part of), there was Mariah to make up the threesome. *Though it must be admitted, Mariah wasn't never much of a fisher.*

Maggie suddenly felt shy. It was possible Henry felt something of it too, because they were silent all the way to the Twelveses', and he didn't have any smart remarks for Maggie before she leapt off the wagon bench and ran toward the crowd that had accumulated in the field where the Twelveses' joined timbers were stretched along the ground, ready for raising.

While Henry led the mule over to be hitched with the other animals lined beside the Twelveses' old barn—a one-story building with a sod roof that was falling in—Maggie quickly took in her appearance. Not too bad, as she hadn't gone wading, she decided. She ran her fingers through her hair and wound and knotted it at her neck as best she could, and tied a loop of grass around, with her usual futile hope that it might stay most of the evening. She smoothed her skirt down, adjusting her bodice under her apron in the hope that it might hit her a little lower on her shins.

The chatter and laughter carried over across the acres of grain that lay in front of where the new barn would be.

Maggie trotted through, keeping to the already-broken path that the others had taken through the field, and stood for a moment as the tall, triangular frame came into view. Men laughed and talked as they climbed and hammered, straddling trusses and working together to get the beams across the framing. Women scurried around off to the side, laying out long lines of quilts and blankets, setting the dishes there and stopping to scold small children from being too close to where the work was being conducted. Somebody had brought a harmonica, and already there was a lively tune playing, inducing foot tapping and humming from the busy gathering.

Ma Alden found Maggie devouring fried chicken and biscuits, sitting on one of the corners of the Cleggs' old rose-of-Sharon quilt. "We're over by the oak tree, there on the other side," Ma Alden said. "Patience could use your help with the girls."

Maggie started. She couldn't look Ma Alden in the face. Hadn't been able to at all, lately. The black thoughts that welled up inside of her—they had to be visible. Ma Alden would take one look at her and know.

Maggie nodded at Sister Clegg, who smiled back.

"Come talk to me sometime before you go," Sister Clegg said.

"You take too much advantage of Betsy and her family," Ma Alden chided Maggie as they sat. "Taking her gifts. And you spend too much time with those boys. Likely people will start to talk, don't you take more care." She slapped her palm emphatically on the quilt's surface. "Set for a bit, then we'll need you to help in the clearing up."

Maggie nodded again, keeping her eyes on her food and trying to keep a dam on her resentful feelings. If Ma Alden was so worried over proprieties, why did she care so little that Maggie's hems came nearly to her knees as she sat there on the blanket?

As if to punish Maggie for her ungratefulness, Liz Ellen Hoster walked by just then. Her skirts dusted her knees as she walked. Several crudely sewn patches covered the back of her skirt. She walked past the Aldens and Forths and plopped herself down on a ragged quilt spread out over the grass, without taking care to keep her skirts decent. Two boys sat on the quilt with her. Both had her matted sandy-blond hair and freckled complexion.

"Heifer!" Jed called out, grinning

Patience gave him a reproving glance. "Have some charity."

"Charity's the job of the womenfolk," Jed answered back and took a large bite out of the apple he held. "Honest, I could have used a worse name. Heifer's the nicest thing she could be said to smell like."

"Jedediah Eldridge Forth," Patience spat out. "Your pa'll hide you when he hears what poison you been spouting about your neighbor."

Jed shrugged. "Don't think that's too likely."

Patience sighed and picked at her chicken leg.

Liz Ellen and her brothers were called Heifer, instead of Hoster, by some of the more mean-spirited people in town. Jim, the older of the boys, worked for Brother Higbee as a hand. In return, they were given a tiny, sod-roofed log cabin that lay in ruin close to the Higbees' property. Liz Ellen, who was maybe a year younger than Maggie, kept house and took care of the younger brother. They owned only one thing of value, and that was a rust-colored heifer. They had no barn for her, and so the three children just slept with the beast on a pile of straw, next to the cabin's tiny hearth, right in the middle of the floor. The heifer gave them milk to drink and to sell, and provided them with warmth. It was almost like the heifer was the real mother in the family, and that's how the nickname came about.

There, but for the grace of God, and the Aldens, Maggie reminded herself dutifully as she watched Liz carefully ladle potatoes onto her brothers' plates.

As if sensing the intensity of her gaze, Liz glanced up from her plate and grimaced at Maggie in a most disgusting manner, then tucked into her food with ferocity.

Well, may be that they ask for it, Maggie thought with some annoyance. Being a charity case is one thing, being strange and unsociable is quite another.

The sun beat down on the Aldens and the Forths, causing them to squint and hurry with their eating. Etta was fluttery and nervous and even more fretful than usual. Finally she got up and went to talk with Julia Harrison and Mary Wall, who stood in front of the half-framed barn. *Chattering like banty hens.*

"Etta's got a right bee in her bonnet," Jed remarked, sucking the last bits of meat off a chicken leg.

"Elias said he'd come for the raising," Patience explained, apparently forgetting her pique.

"Thought he was up in the canyon with Brother Jones," Maggie remarked.

Patience glanced at Maggie and smiled. "Got back from his Injun meeting this morning. And I saw Hyrum Clegg when I was in line, Maggie," she added.

Maggie felt her cheeks redden. For some reason, Patience and Etta were sure she was in love with Hyrum Clegg. She had no idea how that notion had entered their minds. "That's nice. Think he'll ask her?"

It took a moment for Patience to process the quick change of subject, back to Etta and Elias. "Don't know." Patience shrugged. "Let me fix your hair," she added.

"You know it won't make no difference," Maggie snapped. "I don't care, anyhow."

"Sure about that?" Patience grinned.

Maggie made a noise somewhere between an impatient growl and a sigh. She stowed her plate on top of the pile of empty dishes, then hopped to her feet. "Let's go see about packing up the rest of the food. Sister Clegg asked me to help fill hampers."

"We'll all go." Ma Alden set her plate aside. "Gigi, don't you go off and get into any trouble now."

Giovanna nodded. "Lizzy wanted to show me a bird's nest over by the crick."

"Fine. But don't get wet."

"All right."

Maggie waited until Patience and Ma Alden were off a ways and then turned to her sister. "Stay out of the crick," she said quietly, scowling at her.

Giovanna scowled back.

The two of them made a funny picture, standing in the middle of the field. They stood out. It had something to do with their unruly dark hair and strong profiles, but it was also the way they stood and their identical expressions: fierce, black eyebrows, and calculating, dark eyes.

"All right," Giovanna finally conceded. "But I don't see it does anyone a harm if Lizzy and me gets our ankles wet."

"Lizzy and I. You don't know where the currents are. Lizzy don't know this stretch of stream well enough; they just bought this piece last year."

"All right. You don't got to light my tail on fire."

Maggie swatted her sister and turned to run after Patience. Instead she ran face-first into a red flannel shirt and a hard chest.

"Hey there," a familiar voice said.

Hyrum Clegg, of course—who else would it be she would run full tilt into with her hair resembling that bird's nest her sister was so keen to find?

"Hello," Maggie mumbled, working to untangle her skirts. She hoped beyond hope Patience wasn't watching her right now. She didn't really feel like being teased tonight.

Hyrum grabbed her elbows and steadied her. "Sorry. I came right up behind you. Thought you knew I was here."

"Uh, that's just fine. You're—it's no trouble. Sorry."

"You coming to the hotel tonight? We've got up a real good few pantomimes this time."

"Wish I could."

He nodded and turned to walk away.

"I've got to help make hampers," she mumbled at his back.

"Oh," he said, turning suddenly. "I forgot I came over here to ask. You seen Julia Morrison anywhere? We've got some lines to go over. I've been looking for her all afternoon."

"Seems to me I saw her over by the barn," Maggie replied.

"I'll go look there, then."

Maybe she doesn't want to be found. Not by you, anyway.

She shook her head and moved toward the cluster of women who were gathered over the spread of food, carefully wrapping and portioning out the leftovers to give to people like Liz Ellen Heifer. *Hoster*, Maggie corrected herself.

I'm lucky.

She repeated it out loud, like a prayer of penance.

I'm lucky to have the Aldens, lucky to have skirts to my shins and not my knees. Lucky I don't live with a big, smelly cow and no way of knowing next time I'll have a good piece of meat to chew on. Forget about the mattress, Maggie, and stop being such an ungrateful chit.

She went about the mindless task of filling hampers, of folding up blankets, of nodding to people who she saw . . . she tried to concentrate on what was in front of her eyes, what her hands were doing. *That's the good thing about life in the wilderness . . . if you wanted to, you can find enough work to clear your head of almost anything unwelcome or troubling. You could find labor that'll clear your soul of almost anything at all. For a few moments, at least.*

DREAMS

THEY WERE SITTING AROUND THE HEARTH IN THE FORTHS' one-room homestead cabin by the river. Maggie knew, because she could smell the choking smoke from the hearth fire. The chimney on that old homestead had never worked well. Uncle Forth had built it too narrow at the top.

There was also a strange, sweet smell Maggie couldn't identify. She felt the warm bricks of the hearth under her legs and suddenly felt Giovanna sitting next to her. All in the family watched Ma Alden stroke a little baby girl with a head full of dark ringlets. Patience was smiling, Etta cooing at the baby and trying to get a smile. The baby had wide, dark eyes. Her face seemed familiar somehow.

Maggie just had time to get the thought in, "Who is that baby? She don't belong in this picture," when, slowly and deliberately, Ma Alden took a pillow from the bed and placed it over the baby's face.

Maggie sat, horrified, unable to move—frozen somehow. Sick.

The baby thrashed frantically, pummeling Ma Alden with its tiny legs; Ma Alden held it away from her and waited until it stilled, then stopped. Then she placed the baby back in the crib and went to sit calmly in her rocking chair.

Maggie trembled. A scream rose up in her throat. She struggled, struggled, struggled to unfreeze herself, to loosen whatever it was that bound her still; she had to get up, and to run, quickly. She would yank the baby away from Ma Alden's grasp—

That was when she woke, feeling for a frightening few moments like she couldn't take a deep enough breath to calm the beating of her heart.

What? Maggie trembled. *What was that?*

The dream. It wasn't the guns dream, it wasn't anything anybody had talked about, anything she'd thought of or seen at all, or—

Maggie tried to collect her mind and scrape together the few scriptures she knew by heart. That nearly always sent her to sleep, repeating the rhythmic words of psalms.

They were all gone from her mind. The sweet-sick feeling of fear and an empty stomach kept her awake, kept her mind racing away like a runaway colt.

She gave up when she saw the sky began to lighten. She stood, careful not to jiggle the mattress and wake Giovanna. She looked down at her sister, who lay in the path of the tiny window by their heads. The soft light colored her peaceful round face and brought out red lights in the mess of curls that tangled across her neck.

She glanced around the room, at the stove and fireplace, at the quiet bedstead by the other wall where Patience and Etta slept. Maggie and Giovanna's pallet was usually stacked on top of the bedstead during the day, only to be spread on the floor at night. Father and Ma Alden slept upstairs, of course. On the canvas mattress. Nobody was stirring yet.

She slid her feet into her moccasins, laced them up her

calves, and then pulled Ma Alden's thick, woolen outside shawl over her shoulders and wrapped it around her frame. It covered her past the knee, concealing her nightgown. She closed the back door quietly behind her and breathed in deeply, enjoying the cool, vanilla-spice scent of the weedy field that divided the Alden's house from the Forths'.

Maggie's heart hurt in a queer way. It was like it had caught on her rib cage and something was tearing away with each breath she took.

She walked over to the stone lip of the well and sat there, trying not to think of her dream. Her thoughts skipped over and settled on Hyrum and Julia. Maggie didn't care, as much as Patience and Etta would like to think so, about the idea of Hyrum and Julia sparking; it was more the thought of Hyrum moving on and growing up that bothered her.

What sort of woman would Maggie be? Right now, it seemed to her as if she wouldn't grow beyond a girl. Womanhood was an impossibility. It was something for girls who had already started to wear their skirts down to their boot-tops and had people helping them do their hair up. And she was not refined as Patience and Etta were; she knew no music, not even singing. Her voice was rusty like a crow's when she tried scales. She knew no fine needlework, though she could darn and hem and sew a fine, clever patch with the best of them. Most other girls her age had started on a trousseau of linens and things.

What was being a woman on the prairie worth, anyhow? Maggie wondered what good a lace tablecloth would do if one didn't even have a real roof over her head. Elias, for instance, was building a homestead cabin, whenever he got a break from fieldwork and trips with Brother Jones to talk to the Timpanodes or Paiutes. The roof was sod and branches, and the floor was dirt. Maggie had to think that those dainty doilies and fine embroidered pillowcases would stay packed away for a good long while, even if Etta and Elias married before the year was out, as many around speculated they would.

Maggie reckoned that the things that would prove useful to a pioneer wife were also the things that most girls were supposed to pretend they knew little about. Birthing and how to tend sicknesses in animals and people. Likely, a husband out here would appreciate a woman with strong arms and shoulders who could hoe a row quick as he could more than he'd appreciate a finely painted screen for the scraped-log walls of his first home.

The rooster crowed. Maggie sprung up from the well and headed for the henhouse to collect eggs, thinking to herself that she reckoned Hyrum would, at least. Julia was no kind of girl for Hyrum to court. *It ain't female cattiness,* Maggie thought, *as some'd likely say if I spoke aloud such a thing.*

Just pure, clean truth. Maggie nodded to herself as she collected eggs.

Julia ought to marry something like George Smith Jr., whose father likely'd already set up a living and had a fine house ready for all kinds of cultured arts.

The morning wore on, tiresome, full of disturbed thoughts on Maggie's part. "You need anything at Stewarts?" Maggie asked, after she had finished the breakfast dishes.

Ma Alden frowned at her. "You have something taking you there?"

"I think I might get a letter from Mariah."

"Likely not. Settling in takes some time, and the post's been delayed from Great Salt Lake with all the travel."

Maggie nodded and moved to sit down with the mending basket.

"Still, if you're raring to go, I do have a need for molasses. Think you can get someone to haul a barrel back here?"

Maggie jumped up again and took the coins from Ma Alden. "Guess I'll find someone. Thanks."

She skipped out the front door, ran down the path to the gate, swung it open, and jumped over the muddy ditch where the water ran beside West Main Street. She met Mother Turner there and offered to help her carry her large basket, overburdened with eggs as usual.

"They haven't slowed down laying," Maggie remarked, grunting as she hefted one of the handles.

"No. I don't know whether to be grateful or not. We're bringing in a pretty penny lately on egg money, but I have to haul them myself and collect them twice a day, before the hens start pecking at 'em. Boys are over helping with the Walls' wheat harvest sunup to sundown, and Father Turner's busy keeping our lot free of pests and the corn watered."

They stumbled down the street and turned the corner at the bustling main street. Someone held the door for them as they entered Stewarts.

"More of them today then?" Brother Stewart nodded at Sister Turner and cleared a space on the counter. Maggie helped heft the basket up and sighed. She wandered around, running her fingers over tightly woven linens and soft woolens that lay folded on the shelf along the back wall.

More than likely Sister Clegg's work was in there somewhere. She was the best weaver around. All these goods were made, for the most part, right there in town—there were no trains or big rivers to bring fancy premade things to Provo.

There were a few things that came, on occasion, though, through trade with the settlers that came through the towns on their way west. Right now, several open barrels with crackers and spices, and one of salt, stood by the counter. They cost more than most could pay, and so they sold slowly. No skin off of Brother Stewart's nose, though . . . spices lasted forever.

Maggie longed to tuck a finger in when nobody was looking and then lick it off, but this was something a little girl would do. As well, she avoided staring at the few large, glass jars that held colored candy sticks and balls of various sizes—homemade, most of them, in trade for other goods. But still, candy was hard to come by.

Finally she turned back to the counter. "Ma Alden wants a barrel of dark molasses. And we were hoping you could help us find it a way home too."

Brother Stewart nodded. "You live just off West Main, half a block up, I think?"

"Right." Maggie dug into her apron pocket and set the coins on the counter.

"Molasses's gone up," Brother Stewart eyed the coins. "I can give you half a barrel and some change."

Maggie nodded. "Fine, then."

Brother Stewart opened the door in the wall behind the counter, leaned in, and yelled up the stairs. "Junior! We need the cart."

Andrew trundled down the stairs. He nodded politely at Maggie and then turned breathlessly to his father. "Brother Bell is saying they's sending judges to judge us, Pa."

Brother Stewart frowned at his son. "You ought not be up there listening to things you can't figure, instead of down here helping me at the counter."

"They said Sinclair up in the city's been given task to turn over the courts and take Brigham to arrest. And another feller's coming soon too, from the gov'ment to judge all the bishops."

Brother Stewart simply shook his head. "Get the mule harnessed up and take this barrel and Miss Alden here up West Main to deliver, if you please, son. Have a seat." He nodded at Maggie.

Maggie sat at one of the stools that lined the counter. "Chabert," she said.

Brother Stewart squinted at her. "Miss Chabert," he corrected.

"Sorry." She tried to bite her lip, to stay out of the conversation—but it was too much for her. She didn't need more to worry over; she really wouldn't be able to stand keeping much more in.

"Brother Stewart," she asked.

"Hmm?" He looked up from the notebook he was scribbling in.

"They couldn't really, could they? Send people to take over courts like that?" It came out in one breathless stream, the words almost too fast to understand.

Stewart shrugged. "Likely not. Everybody's trying to find something else to get het up about, now the war's over. Bad for business, having more than half the town leave at once."

"Brother Bell's not like that, though. He's not one to shoot off his mouth."

"Little gal like you ought not worry over such matters, surely."

Maggie felt her face turn red.

He winked at her and drew up one long, green-and-brown-striped stick from the jar, then another. "Give one to your sister," he said. "Came tripping in here yesterday with one of her little friends, begging a sweet. Can't say no to a face like that."

Maggie felt her cheekbones grow hotter at the thought of Giovanna's impertinence. "Sorry," she murmured.

"It's nothing. Nice to see something cheerful around here. So much doom and gloom being preached, and now it's like everyone's sad none of it came to pass. It's a good reminder to the rest of us, to see the joy of children. You've a year or so of childhood left in you, Maggie. Soon you'll be turning fourteen and putting your hair up," he shook his head.

"Likely you're right, sir." Maggie nodded to him, not bothering to correct him that she was already fifteen, and slid off the stool. "I'll go and see if the cart's ready."

"Good morning."

"Good morning. Thanks for the sweets."

She walked around back to the little lean-to where the delivery cart and mule were kept, just as the boy had finished tightening all the buckles and straps of the harness. She hopped in back, leaning against the little half-barrel.

She hoped Ma Alden wouldn't be displeased at her. Likely she'd say Maggie ought to have talked him down.

A sudden yodel sounded nearby, and Henry's long, slender figure leapt up beside her. "You going home?"

"Yep." Maggie avoided his gaze, tucking the candy into her pocket.

"You don't have to share," he teased. "I just need to walk out that way and figured your Ma would have a bite ready for lunch."

Maggie struggled for a moment—*Henry and me, alone? Again?* But she couldn't stem the tide of relief that washed over her. Ma Alden would be much easier to face today if

Henry were there to take her mind off things.

"She'd welcome you for lunch," she said, in a more kindly tone. "They're for Giovanna," she added, patting her pocket.

"You don't want to split one of them with me?"

Maggie chuckled, took one of the sticks out, and bit it in two, handing the larger piece to Henry. She sucked away at the sweet, smooth candy, feeling the bliss of it wash away her previous chagrin.

They waved at Brother Greene, and Maggie slapped her forehead with her hand. "I forgot to ask if I had a letter from Mariah," she said at Henry's raised eyebrow.

"Likely not. Have you sent her one?"

"Two," Maggie replied, biting her lip.

"Likely she's glad to get them. From what I've heard, all is not peaches and roses up there."

Maggie turned to Henry. "Did you hear something about bringing in judges from the government to take all the bishops to court?"

Henry stared at her, consternation on his face. "Where'd you hear talk like that?"

"I was just at Stewarts," Maggie shrugged.

Henry shrugged, too. "Well, I ain't heard much either. Just about that one up in the city, who's making ruckus. Sinclair. But there's been rumors that they're bringing in another one to come down here in the south parts. Rumors've been going on a while, though."

Maggie felt her stomach clench. "I thought with the move back north, that letter and all, that they were leaving us alone."

"They are; they will," Henry said, swatting her shoulder. "Don't go all silly over it. People're just trying to find something new to be worried at. Worry's like a tonic to some folks. Keeps them getting out of bed in the morning."

Maggie sighed.

"What's worrying at you today? Not the judges. It's something else, I can tell. Gigi go off with Lizzy Twelves into the wilderness again and get back after suppertime?"

"No, but I hear she's been begging sweets off people and going about Main Street causing her own brand o' ruckus."

"She's only a little girl. Like Ma says, you've got to let children be children. You worry over her too much."

"That's not what I'm worried over, pert-head," Maggie retorted.

"Well, then, what?"

Maggie shrugged. "Do you remember your dreams very often?"

"This again?" Henry sighed. "Maggie, dreams are dreams. They're just mixed up mumbo jumbo—mind clearing itself, you know."

"I don't know what could have got into my mind to give me a dream like I had last night."

Henry frowned at her. "You really are in a state over this. Well, tell it to me, then. That's the best way to get rid of it."

"I'm not sure I should."

"You shouldn't be upset over a dream. You can't decide what to dream, you know. And sometimes, dreams are messages."

Maggie stared at him.

"And sometimes not. Go on, tell it."

And so Maggie rehearsed the entirety of what she had dreamed, lowering her voice, finding it hard to get the words out, when she got to the part where Ma Alden smothered the baby.

Henry frowned at her and then looked thoughtfully at

his boots. "Land sakes," he mumbled. "That's a dream, all right."

The cart stopped, and Andrew was turned around in the driver's seat, eyeing them expectantly. Henry and Maggie leapt down, and Henry helped her lug in the little barrel.

"Molasses went up," Maggie explained at Ma Alden's look. She was grateful for Henry's presence then, as it stayed Ma Alden from voicing her complaint, which was clear in her face. "Henhouse needs mucking out today," she said instead.

Maggie nodded. "Is dinner close?"

"Done. Leftovers in the pot, and there are some corn biscuits in the cupboard."

Maggie set out two plates and served Henry and herself. They ate quietly, quickly, stuffing their mouths full and barely chewing before swallowing. Henry didn't ask for seconds as he usually did, and when they went out the door, he followed her around back, and took up a shovel.

"You don't have to help me."

"Dirty outside work oughtn't to be done in skirts," he said.

"My skirts aren't fine enough to worry about." Maggie chuckled.

"That color looks pretty enough on you."

Maggie flushed and then shook her head. These Clegg boys were sure raised right—chivalry in every situation. Even down to complimenting a muddy-legged wren of a girl. "Thanks," she managed, and set to digging out the straw and mess, tossing it onto the rapidly growing pile in the wheelbarrow. Henry worked beside her, doing about two shovelfuls to her one. They soon cleared the floor and then went to the shed to get large armfuls of clean, sweet-smelling straw.

"I think it was just a dream," Henry said out of nowhere, startling Maggie so that she tripped over the doorway. "Nothing more."

She steadied herself on the little, hinged half-door. "What makes you say so?"

Henry tossed his armful of straw to the floor and dusted off his hands. "Everyone's been running their mouths off about the business in Cedar. That's likely what brought on that dreams about the men shooting you've been having lately. We've all heard bits and pieces. Just enough to scare us clean to our socks, not enough to benefit from good, solid truth about the matter. Your mind was just clearing itself of chaff, is all."

"And the baby?" Maggie wrinkled her forehead. "I've never seen nor heard about nobody smothering a baby before."

Henry considered her. "I don't know," he said finally. "Is there some worry you've had lately might explain it?"

Maggie shifted her gaze to her feet.

The mattress. It swam into her vision, the writing clear and sharp against it. It was etched in her mind, now; she didn't need to rip the bedding off and look. It was truth, now.

She opened her mouth, but just couldn't find her voice to say it. "Guess you're right," she mumbled instead. "Likely just all this worry. All the ruckus with everybody taking off back for the city." She turned her back on Henry and loaded herself up with more straw, so he couldn't see her face.

"You ever hear any tidings of your brother, Maggie?"

"What, Samuel?" Maggie shook her head. "Not hide nor hair. All right, though, don't really expect to. Likely he'd've sought us out by now if he could, or really wanted to."

"Likely he wants to, Maggie. Reckon he doesn't know where to look."

Maggie nodded and kept shoveling, her mind not really on Samuel. Samuel was a topic that waxed and waned; overshadowed easily by her more recent concerns.

When the task was done, Maggie stood and brushed off her skirt. She turned back toward Henry, who still leaned on his shovel, studying her as if she were some kind of exotic game animal and he was trying to learn her habits.

Don't shoot me down, Henry, she thought. *I'd make poor eating.* The thought made her chuckle.

Henry's eyebrows shot up. "What's so funny?"

Maggie shook her head.

"If it makes you feel better, Maggie, I've had a few dreams I'd rather run around town wearing a barrel hammered full o' nails before I'd tell. Reckon everybody does."

"Oh." Maggie was curious, but something in Henry's face forestalled her questions.

"Do you think your Ma would mind if you went fishing?"

Maggie took a moment to get her head around the abrupt change of subject and then nodded. "I'll ask."

"I'll come with you."

He knows Ma Alden. Knows she's more likely to say yes if he's there.

Just as they walked in the back door, Giovanna barreled through the front door. Her boots were filthy, and the front of her apron covered in dirt.

"Where've you been?" Maggie hissed.

She gave Maggie a wide-eyed glance, and then turned to Ma Alden. "Do you reckon I can go over to Twelveses' for supper?" she asked, nearly jumping with excitement, scattering clods of dirt across the floor.

Ma Alden pondered for a moment as she filled a pot with kitchen scraps. "Fine," she said. "Just take these out to the hog first."

"All right," Giovanna gulped, grabbing the pot and scurrying out the door to the corner of the Forths' yard where the hogs were penned.

"She'll change her dress before she goes," Henry said suddenly.

Ma Alden frowned at him, surprised.

"She'll change," Maggie answered, feeling the hot anger of defense. "We wouldn't send her off to dinner in the state she is."

Henry wrinkled his brow at her tone and then nodded. He looked for a moment at Maggie's apron, which was worse, after mucking out the henhouse, than Giovanna's had been. Maggie followed his gaze as it traveled to Patience, seated primly on a stool, hemming a linen handkerchief, and Etta, who sat in the rocker, knitting at something in a soft blue wool.

They look so refined. Their pale-colored skirts coming to the tops of their boots, their hair sleek and slicked back.

"You two fixing on going fishing? Are you sure Betsy doesn't expect you at home?" Ma Alden asked.

Henry glanced at Maggie, his face unreadable. "You're likely right." He nodded at Ma Alden and ducked under to doorway.

Maggie stood, watching him walk down the path toward the road. Confusion, anger, and embarrassment rendered her completely immobile, like she had suddenly turned to stone.

Apparently she had done the impossible—offended Henry Clegg.

But, she mentally argued, *it was his own fault, mouthing off about Gigi. Who was he to do so? He had deserved her sharp reply, and Ma Alden's. Didn't he? She and Maggie couldn't help it if . . .*

She had an odd, choked sort of feeling as she sat on the floor against the wall, and dipped her hand into the mending basket, taking out the darning needle, fingering a pair of Pa Alden's worn wool socks.

Much later that night, after restlessly tossing until she fell asleep, she woke again suddenly, nearly choking on her own tears.

It had been worse this time. She had seen the baby's face; purple, swollen, mouth parted in distress. The eyes were wide open—Giovanna's eyes.

Her mother's eyes.

At least it had awakened her before any other horrifying images came into being. There were no painted men, no rifle butts.

Still, Maggie felt driven to crawl out of bed, to assume her shawl and boots. She slipped outside, stared for a moment at the dazzle of the summer night sky.

The porcelain. The Bible.

It was an insidious whisper in her mind.

The moon was bright enough to see by. She searched around the well stones and privy, and even slid her body under the henhouse, though it was so dark that she would never have been able to find anything, even if there were something to find.

A CHARITY CASE

THE DANCE FINISHED. MAGGIE CURTSEYED AWKWARDLY AT Samuel Clegg's bow and then quickly made for the food tables. Ma Alden had been giving her an eye every time she passed by; she and the other ladies were busy removing plates of meats and savory things to make room for pie.

Maggie approached the food tables. "Yes, ma'am?" she asked Ma Alden.

"Take this hamper to the Hoster girl and her brothers. And tell them not to forget to return the basket this time." Ma Alden handed a covered basket to Maggie. It smelled of bread and pickled ham.

Maggie's stomach turned a little; she'd had too much of the pickled ham already. "I don't know where they're at."

"You've got legs. Go take a walk around and find them. Last I saw, Liz Ellen was sitting at the children's dance over to Town Square, and her two brothers dancing. Likely they're over there still."

Maggie walked away from the bowery, in the direction

of the center of the grassy square, feeling her feet drag. She did not feel like being the bringer of charity to Liz Ellen Heifer.

She turned, hearing a quick footfall at her side.

It was Sister Clegg. She also carried a hamper. "Happy Twenty-Fourth," she said. "Haven't had a chance to chat with you."

"Happy Twenty-Fourth," Maggie replied.

"I'm looking for the Twelveses." Sister Clegg patted her hamper.

"Hosters."

"I think they're over in the square. Henry's playing the comb over there. Maggie, I've been meaning to talk to you. I want to make over a few of my old frocks, and Lavinia's. We're both grown too wide, and it's a waste to use the fabric on quilt squares, as I've thought I might do. Do you think you and your sister could find use for them?"

"Ma Alden wouldn't let me accept," Maggie said, without even bothering to think on the issue. She knew what Ma Alden's reaction would be, if Maggie were to take Sister Clegg up on such an offer.

"Won't be charity," Betsy Clegg said, shifting the basket to her other arm. "I'll need some work out of you for them. There's some nice cotton and cambric in those dresses—brought them across from Illinois. So they're worth a little."

"But I—"

"Honest, Maggie," Sister Clegg said, putting a hand on her shoulder, "I could use another woman about the house, with all the men I clean up after. And with all the whispering over Etta and her beau, I figure your Ma wouldn't mind not having to do the work of making new things for you this year."

Maggie stopped short then and stared at Sister Clegg. "Why me? Julia Harrison's got much finer stitches. And she'd likely put a new frock like that to good use. From what I hear, she's got a bit of time on her hands too."

Sister Clegg's lips quirked and her eyes wrinkled at the edges. "I'm not asking Julia Harrison. I'm asking you."

"I'm a bit 'shamed to say, I don't know much more'n basting and darning. And I don't darn too well, neither."

"I'll teach you finer work. Make you more useful," Sister Clegg replied, patting Maggie's shoulder. "And Giovanna too," she added, as if she could see the worried thought flit through Maggie's mind. "If we can get her to sit still for long enough. I don't mind giving you the dresses. Honestly, I'd rather put them to use than let them get wrinkled and yellow in storage."

"I'll have to ask Ma Alden. She might not like the idea too well."

"Let me talk to her. I know, since you go off with Henry for so much fishing, that you've got a bit of time to spare for it. Well, see you soon, then, Maggie. I think I see Sister Twelves over by the run with her little ones."

It took a moment for Maggie to process what Sister Clegg had said. When she did, Maggie felt suddenly as if she had been kicked in the stomach.

She wants me to stop spending so much time with Henry. She's worried about us being alone, without Hyrum or Mariah.

All the things she and Henry had been doing lately flashed through her mind. She winced, picturing her muddy skirts, hoisted high on her hips as she waded the river with a fishing pole tucked under her arm. Alone, just the two of them. She could see how it might worry a mother. Her own, Ma Alden, had only done her usual, a sneer or a disapproving glance to express her opinion of Maggie's activities. How was Maggie to know how to behave?

As she watched Sister Clegg walk away, she felt as if the ground under her suddenly grew unsteady.

How much longer could a friendship such as hers and Henry's survive? They were both rapidly growing out of the innocence of boy- and girlhood.

Maggie sped up her pace, so she was nearly running toward the center of town square, to a bare spot of ground where a group of children were screaming and pulling each other about by the arms to the beat of a little band made up of drummer, wood-whistler, and comb-player.

When she reached the edge of the group, she stopped again, feeling like her moccasins were rooted to the ground.

She spotted the oldest girl right away. But she didn't want to give Liz Ellen Heifer a charity hamper. Who was Maggie to give charity, anyway? Apparently, according to Sister Clegg, Maggie was the charity case.

Finally she shuffled forward, approaching the dirty-blonde, tangled head that was Liz Ellen, who sat on the grass cross-legged, watching her brothers dance.

Maggie leaned over and plopped the hamper into Liz's lap. "Ma Alden sent me with this," she muttered and moved quickly away before Liz could give her another of those demonic grimaces she was so good at.

"Hey!" Liz Ellen called out.

Reluctantly, Maggie turned. "Yeah? It's just bread. And things. Ma Alden said—"

"Maggie. That's your name, right?"

Land's sake, she does smell like cow. She took an unwilling step closer. "Yeah. Magdalena."

"Magdalena," Liz Ellen repeated. She stood and walked

toward Maggie. She seemed oddly hesitant. She opened her mouth, then shut it, and considered Maggie for a long moment.

Maggie had never noticed before, how Liz Ellen's arms and face were spotted all over with freckles, and her eyes an unusual brownish-green color.

"Well?" Maggie snapped. "You don't have to give me a kiss for it. Bread's likely stale anyhow. Ma Alden says to return the basket at the bishop's storehouse."

Liz Ellen shrugged. "I'll try to remember this time. How's things for you at the Aldens'?"

Maggie took a moment to register the abrupt subject change, and then she felt fury overtake her. So did Liz Ellen, of all people, consider her a charity case? Sister Clegg was one thing. Liz Ellen—Maggie did not need the pity of a ragged, rude, clearly backward sort of person such as Liz Ellen Heifer.

"Fine," Maggie snapped. "Though what business is it of yours, I can't think on."

Liz looked seriously at her. "Well, I've noticed you and Giovanna about town lately. Your sister played with my little brothers the other day. And it seems," she said, shrugging. "I dunno." She made a line in the dirt with her big toe. "Just thought I should ask after the two of you sometime. I know how things can be."

Maggie made a mental note to give Giovanna the scolding of her life. "Oh?" She managed to keep her tone even.

"And if things ever get . . . bad or . . . I don't know. If you ever find yourself in need of a place," Liz shrugged. "Sometimes it's better to be on your own. Know what I mean?"

Maggie shook her head. "Aldens are good to us," she said. "Don't know what you've been hearing or seeing, but you're mistaken."

Liz nodded. "See yer 'round, then." She turned abruptly and ran back to sit down at the edge of the circle of children, who had linked arms and were playing crack the whip to the tune of "Turkey in the Straw."

Someone ought to take sand and soda to the whole lot of those Hoster brats. Nothing else would take off all the dirt. And then they'd need a good, long dunk in the river—supposing it wouldn't kill off all the fish.

This was Maggie's defensive, spiteful thought as she broke into near a run, back toward the tables under the bowery.

She felt miserable all around.

The light began to fade. Lanterns glowed in the soft light. She slowed her pace to a walk, thinking that the lanterns looked like giant lightning bugs, hovering in the bowery. It made her think of fairy tales.

It also brought a sudden memory that was so clear, it stopped Maggie in her tracks. Of those warm, peaceful nights on the prairie at the beginning of the crossing. They weren't quiet, those evenings. They were filled with all the musical noises of the wilderness: strange chirpings, night birds, and the occasional ominous rattle that sent men searching around the camp in ever-widening circles. The soft, flickering lights were a mystery to the Chaberts, until Samuel caught one in his hands. Maggie remembered, suddenly, her keen disappointment, seeing the strange little bug, cupped in his palms. She had thought they were guardian angels or something else equally miraculous.

Maggie nearly jumped out of her skin as something tugged, hard, on her skirt.

"Ma says we're to go home." Giovanna's face was sticky with some red substance— jam, most likely.

Maggie licked a finger and moved to swipe at her sister's cheek, but Maggie dodged out of her reach. "Ick," she said.

"Go find a rain barrel," Maggie snapped, feeling exasperation well up inside of her. Giovanna was far too old to be running around, face mussed and hair like a black tornado. "And a comb," she added.

Giovanna scowled. "Ma'll be in a state if you don't come right now. She's been looking for you. Elias Smith's asked to talk to Father tonight."

Maggie stopped still. She thought of Pa Alden, who was likely sitting by the fireplace at home, whittling. Ma Alden had begged him to come to the celebrations, but he hadn't even bothered to voice an answer. And when the time came to walk the few blocks over to Town Square, he wasn't to be found. Maggie hadn't seen him all day.

"Well, why doesn't he just go over and ask him? Why've we got to all leave?"

"I dunno. They're starting for home, though, and Ma's already cross with you."

Maggie followed in her sister's wake, winding around bodies and skirts until they found the rest of the Aldens and Elias Smith, waiting on the other side of the trickling run that ran alongside Town Square. As soon as Ma Alden spotted them, she gestured impatiently. She handed Maggie a basket that contained some leftover baked goods.

"Thought they were putting all the leftovers in hampers to give away," Maggie remarked.

"There was a lot left over. We contributed several things; it was only right we bring some back too."

Maggie nodded.

"To hear you talk, a person'd think you were above taking charity."

Maggie was puzzled for a moment at the annoyance in Ma Alden's tone. And then she remembered Sister Clegg's proposal. Had she already spoken to Ma Alden about it then?

"There's never been the need for charity. You've always provided plenty," Maggie said quickly, feeling her heart pick up speed.

"I've given you clothes to warm your back," Ma Alden continued, as if Maggie hadn't interrupted her. She touched Maggie's shoulder. "That frock is fine—sturdy calico. Last a few more seasons."

Maggie nodded, trying not to look down at her exposed shins.

"You're just a girl, anyway. You act like a girl, ignoring your needlework, going about tasks like splitting wood. If I made you long skirts, you'd just rip them and muddy them in the river fishing. Betsy said today she's going to be giving you dresses. What you'd be needing with more frills . . ." Ma Alden shrugged. "It's not as if you're going to get any beaux calling anytime soon. I'd have given you petticoats and long skirts if I thought you'd needed them. Seems to me you ought to be used to your lot by now. Why you'd go and complain to Sister Clegg, after four years living this way," she shook her head.

Maggie felt her face burn, for the second time that night. "I didn't run and complain to Sister Clegg," she said.

"Or to Henry? Don't tell me you don't paint your life a picture of misery for him, whining over things that you ought not worry about anyhow. What are you going to turn out to be anyway, Maggie, the rate you're going? Laundress? Help? You've no prospects, that's for sure, and I don't see why Sister Clegg would waste time on you when nothing I've done has gotten through your stubborn, thick way of thinking."

As usual, when Ma Alden let loose, Maggie had no words—nothing. As usual, it took several minutes for the tide of angry words to sink in, and as usual, the moment had passed by the time she got her head around what she would say in return.

My mother was a refined woman.

My father was a good man. Both of them could read and write, and taught me, and you've not even bothered to put Giovanna in school at all.

Where is my father's Bible?

Where is my mother's china?

She wanted to shout the words, but emotion—and her sudden, loosened grip on her English—made it impossible. As usual, she said it all in her head in rapid French, imagining that the silent words were stones, pelting Ma Alden's narrow, stern features and slim, straight torso. Infecting her with venom. Killing her with bruises. "Giovanna migh' do well." Maggie slurred over the consonants, sounding more French than she usually did.

"Mayhap. Her English is a mite better than yours. If she learnt some refined ways. But here on this savage prairie, she'll always be one of the Chabert girls. Eye-talian, foreign, a charity case, not fit to grace a husband's table."

"If you'd teach her manners, she'd learn."

"Don't you back talk," Ma Alden hissed. "I do what I can for you. But there's only so much I can do with what I'm given. I was given you two girls—ungrateful, wild, grabbing up everything around them, going off with boys and getting their clothes muddy and torn. But a mother has to put up with what she's given."

Maggie stared at Ma Alden. "You," she said, deliberately biting off the consonants, "are not our mother."

In front of her, Etta stopped, turned, and gave Maggie a look that could peel bark off a cottonwood tree. "Shut, you ungrateful chit," she hissed. "We don't want any scenes tonight." She glanced up the street toward Elias's retreating form. He hadn't noticed the rest of them stop; he seemed to be in a rather preoccupied state of mind.

Ma Alden took Maggie's chin and jerked it upward. Maggie stared up into Ma Alden's stern grey eyes.

"You can go to Betsy's to help her," Ma Alden said, after a long moment. "But don't let me hear of you sitting around scribbling in that diary of yours instead of helping her at her mending, or loping off to the crick and leaving tasks undone, as you're wont to do around my house. Betsy is not as tolerant of sloth as I am. Believe me, you'll earn those dresses."

At the mention of Sister Clegg, and of fishing with Henry, all of Maggie's courage suddenly fled. She felt the humiliation of that earlier conversation, and the implications of it, come oozing back. "I know, ma'am." She swallowed hard.

"She's going to have you at fine needlework."

"I know."

"You've been balky enough about it. I've never pressed you to learn fine sewing. She'll be a hard taskmistress. It won't be all rush-and-hurry-through so you can go after your boy fishing."

Maggie felt as if her face couldn't get any redder. She felt like her skull might explode.

Patience came up behind them and placed a soft hand on her mother's shoulder. "Elias's probably at the house, now," she said. "Ought we to give them a few minutes?"

Ma Alden started. Her grip slackened, releasing Maggie's chin. "No need." She quickened her pace. "It's not as if none of us know what'll be said. I'll need to be there to make sure—"

"Pa Alden will be fine. He's expecting it," Patience said, hurrying after her mother. "It might be best if we just—"

"We never know what father might be about these days. Or what odd things might come out of his mouth," Etta put in, breathlessly. "Here we're at the gate, anyhow. Hello, the house!"

Ma Alden and Etta tripped into the doorway at the same time and nearly fell to the floor of the candlelit room in an undignified pile of petticoats and cotton skirts. Etta flushed. She untangled herself and moved aside to let her mother go ahead.

Pa Alden and Elias Smith were seated next to the fire. Elias's face was pink, and his quiet words came to a halt as the women filed in. Ma Alden and Etta began to chatter loudly about the party and bustle around putting things away. Pink-cheeked, Patience picked up the sewing basket and dragged the rocking chair to the corner of the room opposite where the men sat. Maggie and Giovanna followed her.

Maggie was surprised to see Giovanna take a crumpled scrap of linen, decorated in vivid red and orange yarn, from the bottom of the basket. It had been months since she had worked on the sampler Ma Alden had given her last Christmas. Had she heard what Ma Alden said to Maggie and somehow understood something?

Maggie's sharp, dark eyes stayed on her sister for a few minutes, taking note of the clumsiness of the finger movements, the way she scratched her knee, wiped her nose on her sleeve . . .

Maggie sighed. She was fair used to the idea that she might not end up with a husband or children or a warm hearth of her own to sit on. But what would become of Giovanna? Her heart ached with the question.

Elias rose from his position, and everyone froze for a moment. Giovanna pricked her finger, yelped, and began sucking it. Patience gazed at the lace she was knitting as if she were studying some perturbing verse of scripture.

"Etta?" Elias jerked his head toward the door.

Etta Mae couldn't keep the grin from spreading over her face as she followed him outside.

Pa Alden stood and dusted his knees. "Jed and your brother're to Turners again for wheat tomorrow," he said. "I've traded for the Turners to come help us at potatoes come October."

"Right." Ma Alden's voice cracked.

"Going to check the drainage round the carrots and cabbages." Pa Alden slipped out the back door.

Ma Alden sighed. Patience moved out of the rocker, allowing her to sit, and took Pa Alden's place on the hearth.

"We should have stayed east." Ma Alden sighed again. "Pa Alden was so much more cheerful as a gentleman farmer."

A gentleman farmer, Maggie thought. *What's that, exactly? A farmer who wore kid gloves while he scythed the corn?*

"I'm for bed," Ma Alden said finally. "Pa Alden will come when he will."

They all rose, retreating into the cold little nook off the main room to change into their nightgowns. Etta and Patience brushed their hair; Maggie took the comb after Patience was done. She held it for a moment, looking at her reflection in the small hand-mirror that lay on the bed, and began to attack the ends of her thick, unruly curls.

"Put that light out," Ma Alden said irritably.

"Yes, ma'am." She blew out the candle and combed as best as she could by feel, hurrying through the routine. She had wanted to do Giovanna's that night, but it would have to wait until morning.

Ma Alden was likely right. Why did Maggie make this kind of effort at all? Nobody would see her as anything more than what she was—Magdalena Chabert, poor Italian immigrant. She and Henry and Hyrum would part ways as they grew up. They were already parting ways—Hyrum now treated her with the formality and stiffness that a polite, grown-up man might bestow upon a childhood playmate.

Maggie would make out all right when real life happened to her and she ended up mixing medicines or folding linens for someone. Becoming a laundress or a midwife's helper, maybe. But it hurt. It hurt, because of Giovanna. Giovanna deserved better. She could do better. She had lighter skin and their mother's wide, dark eyes and sweet smile. She had the flat vowels and consonants of someone who you would never guess had come from anywhere else.

Giovanna can do better.

Maggie went to the Cleggs' house after her chores were done the next day. This ended up being in early afternoon, after lunchtime, because suddenly the henhouse needed mucking again, and the kitchen garden weeding, and there was some wood Ma Alden was very keen to have split. But when Maggie finished up all these, she was allowed to wash up and run a comb through her hair. Ma Alden even loaned out a clean, starched apron. Maggie felt so light and clean, it was hard to keep from skipping out of the door, down the road toward the Cleggs'.

The hard work had exorcized some of the bad feelings

from the previous evening. The things that Sister Clegg had seemed to imply, as well as the things that Ma Alden said outright, still hurt. But it was more like the pain of pinpricks, whereas last night Maggie had felt as if she had been wounded to the quick.

And so she gulped down her nervousness. She marched up the adobe-brick steps and gave a sure, steady knock on the Cleggs' smooth box elder door.

When Hannah Clegg poked her face out, Maggie's heart began to beat faster, but she forced a polite smile to her face. "I'm here for Ma Clegg," she said.

"The Alden girl's here," Hannah called over her shoulder. She grinned at Maggie and tied her bonnet strings. "I'll be off, then. Betsy says you'll be her helper around the house."

"I'll do my best, ma'am," Maggie replied.

"Well, I really appreciate it. I've got a lot on my plate right now. Ward service meeting, and I'm meeting with Sister Wall this afternoon about an important issue." She nodded and paused, as if waiting for Maggie to ask what the important issue was.

"Well, I'm here," Maggie replied lamely. "Should I go on in?"

"Oh, sure." Hannah nodded and moved aside, holding the door open. "See you later, Betsy! Could you wake Jerry in a little while?"

"It's fine, Hannah," Sister Clegg said.

Maggie walked inside as Hannah bustled out. The hardwood floor shone with wax, and the pleasant smell of drying flax and wood smoke helped Maggie relax a little more.

"Well," she said. She swung her arms and then twined her fingers together behind her back.

"Hello, there."

Again, the broad grin. The gentle, clear eyes and the friendly tone. It took Maggie completely off her tack of self-pity and defensiveness. She swallowed, feeling her heart beat in her throat. "Hello," she managed.

Sister Clegg took her shoulder and pulled her inside. She twitched at one of the long apron strings that wrapped twice around Maggie's middle before tying in back.

"Far too big for you. I'm guessing you'd fit better into one of Lavinia's old ones. I packed them away, but if memory serves they're near the top of the cedar chest . . ."

She walked into one of the two other adjoining rooms, leaving Maggie to stand alone in the middle of the main area of the house. As always, it was clean and comfortable; the kitchen stove gleamed with wear and polish.

They'd brought it with them across the plains, Maggie remembered suddenly. Henry told her one day how they tied it onto the back of their wagon. And Sister Clegg hadn't had much use for it until she had a home of her own; those first few years living in the fort had been difficult for even so genial and stouthearted a woman as she.

Sister Clegg liked to tell the story of when they came into the little, weedy valley bordering the glittering blue lake, how she had looked around and expressed her deep discouragement, and her son Benjamin, though young, reminded her that things looked darkest before the dawn of the day. Sister Clegg often remarked upon that lesson—grilled it into her sons, from the way Henry spoke about it.

Looking at the weathered stove made Maggie ache inside. It was a piece of history—something completely unarguable, something from the Cleggs' past that they kept and treasured even though there was no doubt at all Sister Clegg could afford better now. It was a reminder of where they had come from.

If she had her family's Bible, she would be able to run her fingers over it. She'd have something written in her mother's hand. It would be real—all that had come before the life she was living now.

Sister Clegg emerged from the room, smoothing a small, white apron over her front. "Smells a little of must; sorry about that. I'll air it out good for next time. Where's that sister of yours? Here, let me have that."

Maggie obediently untied the apron Ma Alden had lent her. Sister Clegg folded it neatly and set it on the long, low couch that sat underneath the window. Maggie pulled the apron over her shoulders and found the ties met exactly at her back.

"Thought so." Sister Clegg nodded. "Lavinia wore that when she was about twelve. We're not built small in our family." She chuckled.

"Gigi didn't want to come," Maggie answered her earlier question.

"Ah."

"Ma Alden said she didn't see a need to needle her about it; she was just as well out of your hair, playing with Lizzy or one of her other friends. She don't know any fine stitches, either."

Sister Clegg frowned. "Right," she said. "Well then, speaking of needling, I've got a few things set aside for you to start on. Have you ever done any fine basting or hemming?"

"I'm no hand at it. Ma Alden's tried, but she never lets me near her finer things."

"We'll learn on these, then." Sister Clegg pulled a stack of fine, fluttering linen squares from the large ragbag that sat next to the couch. "You use a tiny stitch. The thread makes a difference—it's thinner than the normal sort you use for bed linens and such. Be careful tugging at it. The idea is to leave yourself room and pull it just tight enough but not too tight—like so."

She demonstrated, leaning over Maggie's lap and deftly winding the needle along the edge of the square. "See here, I've got a few on here . . . now I'll pull through and loosen the thread a bit, making sure the stitches are all even and as small as I like. You see?"

Maggie nodded doubtfully, peering at the delicate line of stitches that trailed behind Sister Clegg's needle.

She took it in her hand and tried to duplicate the movements Sister Clegg had made.

"No, you must start from the other side," she corrected. "See here . . . yes. That's the way. No . . . don't you worry about it," she added, seeing Maggie's despairing expression as she examined her own warbling, wandering line of stitching. "Time and patience. There's a whole stack here to practice on. You'll do the last near perfectly, you'll see. I'm making a late dinner for David; he'll be coming in. Don't mind us. Just keep trying at it."

Maggie's neck grew stiff and her thumbs sore and red from needle pricks over the next half hour. She almost wished for Ma Alden to come by and snatch the work from her hands, as would have happened at home, and hand it to Etta or Patience.

A few minutes in, Brother Clegg came in by the back door. He sat down at the table and ate quietly for a while. Maggie looked at him now and then. He seemed tired.

"Anything new about town?" Sister Clegg asked mildly.

"Nothing much. Everyone's buzzing about Cradlebaugh as usual. Talk now is he's come down here to settle the Cedar murders."

Maggie's almost set her sewing aside, and then realized it would draw attention to her and perhaps lead Sister Clegg to tell him to hush his talk. She bent over her work and kept quiet.

"I thought they said they couldn't identify all the Indians that did it," Sister Clegg said.

"Wasn't just Indians, Betsy."

The even thumping sound of Sister Clegg's kneading halted suddenly. "What?"

"Talk is some of the folk down there dressed up as Indians. Putting on paint and dirt and so forth, so to blame it on them, and others got the Piedes riled up to cover things further."

"Who's spreading such blasphemous rumors?"

Father Clegg raised his eyebrows and shrugged. "Erastus's said a few things. He's looked into it some and says it's not all straight up, the way . . . the way some've told it. He say's that the Indians he's talked to say they joined in after the initial siege started, and witnessed the shooting of—"

At this, Sister Clegg made a hushing sound. Father Clegg glanced over his shoulder in Maggie's direction, and Maggie hastily bowed her head again—she hadn't been able to keep from looking up in surprise.

Her gun dream. She called it that, now . . . and the other one was the baby dream. She hadn't had the gun dream in a while. But if she could have chosen, she would have kept it over the baby dream.

She had taken Henry's advice and passed both off in her head as fiction, just her mind clearing itself of all the chaff. They were still disturbing and awful, and frightening, but it had been a comfort to tell herself that they were nothing more than jumbled-up nonsense. But here Father Clegg was describing a scene right out of her dreams. Men painting their faces. Men with guns.

And yet, dreams. Could they be anything, really? Only prophets dreamed about past and future happenings. She surely didn't want some of these things she'd dreamed lately to be any sort of vision.

Maggie sighed and fixed her tongue against her teeth, struggling to concentrate on her stitching, to get rid of the image that readily came to mind at this line of thought: the tiny baby's struggling limbs, and Ma Alden's grim, casual satisfaction as they stilled.

After Brother Clegg finished his lunch and hastened back out the door, Sister Clegg breezed around the room, stirring this and kneading that, washing up dishes. At one point, a wail sounded from one of the other rooms and a few moments later, a rumple-headed little boy emerged, rubbing his fists into his eyes.

"You can set that aside for a moment. Take Jerry? My hands are covered in flour."

Maggie set the stack of handkerchiefs down, clasping and unclasping her fingers to stretch and steady them. She noticed her arms were shaking as she held them out to the little boy. He walked toward her hesitantly, climbed carefully into her lap, and put a thumb to his mouth.

"There you are," Sister Clegg spoke in a soothing tone and held out a warm, buckskin bottle. He took it readily, throwing his head back and closing his eyes as he sucked rhythmically at the nipple.

As Maggie felt the small body settle against hers, she felt the horror surge through her again. She searched her mind for something—something that she could say, that rid her mind of the awful image that hovered there. "When's

Hannah going to be back? I mean . . ." Maggie stumbled over the title. "The other Sister Clegg?"

Sister Clegg smiled. "Still with Sister Wall, most likely. Like I said, she doesn't take much pleasure in inside work."

Maggie stared down at the round eyes, now open as the little boy sucked.

"I don't mind," Sister Clegg added. The bench creaked as she sat down at her loom. "I've gotten good at raising little boys."

Maggie watched, almost hypnotized, as the large, muscled hands drew the shuttle through the taut threads at a speed too fast to easily follow with her eyes. The crank of the pedals, the warp and weft—they set a rhythm to the room that Maggie found herself rocking to, found herself starting to doze, with Jerry's hot, heavy head on her shoulder . . .

The men smeared the dye across their cheekbones. They circled the dye barrel, the tips of their fingers dipping in, coming out dripping scarlet, then flowing over the haggard planes of their faces, leaving a gleaming welt of red behind. They knelt and rubbed great handfuls of sandy mud on their faces and into their hair, which made it stand on end, then started with the paint again—brown on red, on brown, on red, until the faces became lumps with muddy, unrecognizable features, with scarlet rivers running over them. It seemed almost to be a ceremony: the dipping, kneeling, and mussing, in such a rhythmic flow of movements, and in such soberness and silence.

"Nobody'd know you from an Injun even if they was nose-to-nose with you, Fred, after you get your getup on, so stop your twitching," one voice finally broke the uneasy solemnity.

"You think so?" The voice was Pa Alden's.

Maggie felt the world turn around, slowly, slowly, until she was looking directly into his pale, careworn face, oddly free of mud and paint—the washed out gray-blue of his eyes, the lines of anxiety framing his mouth.

"You think I could pass as a Piede on account of some mud and paint, Brother?" His mouth moved slowly, deliberately—it was how he spoke when you knew he was greatly bothered.

"Reckon Erastus himself wouldn't know you from a redskin," the other voice answered. Then came a chuckle and a slap on Pa Alden's shoulder; Maggie saw the shoulder and arm, and the flat palm come down, and she saw Pa Alden wince. "In or out, Fred? Now's the time to decide."

A sound—loud, like a gunshot—sliced through Maggie's dream, jarring and waking her. She felt her heart racing, the cold sweat on her neck.

"Don't bang the door so."

Maggie jumped again, startled at the sound of Sister Clegg's voice. She looked up at her, then across at the person she addressed.

Henry leaned casually against the doorframe. His boots were crusted on the bottom with mud, his trousers soaked clear to the knees. He'd removed his hat, leaving mud streaks across his forehead from the dirt on his hands.

"And don't come in on my clean floor till you've knocked the dirt off. What have you been doing? Catching catfish with your bare hands?"

"Hello, Maggie," Henry said, walking obediently to the hearth and tugging at his boots.

Maggie shifted the baby to her other shoulder. The one he had been lying on was now numb, and would no doubt be stiff with knots when the feeling got back into it.

"I'll take him." Sister Clegg finished her row, set her shuttle aside, and rose, gathering Jerry into her arms. "It's time he woke up and had a little porridge anyhow. You can get going on those handkerchiefs again. I told Cindy you'd mind her babes this afternoon for a while. Hope you don't mind."

"No," Maggie replied automatically, though it was the last thing in the world that she felt like doing at that moment. She pictured all the Holden children, with their red-and-tow-colored hair and freckled, mischievous faces, and suppressed a sigh.

Cindy Holden needed the spelling. That was for sure. She was a woman who intimidated Maggie, which was not easy to do. But her bright smiles and nimble words always somehow made Maggie feel at a disadvantage. Luckily, she generally had enough words for both of them.

"That'll be fine." Maggie stuck her tongue between her teeth, willing her mind and fingers to concentrate.

A SECRET UNCOVERED

"WHAT ARE YOU MUTTERING ABOUT?" ETTA SNAPPED. "Hurry up and finish that; I need help into my stays. I've finished the corset, and I want to try it to make sure it fits right." Her bothered expression slowly melted into a blissful grin as she held the garment in front of her, turning it to examine her handiwork.

Maggie flushed a little; she hadn't noticed that she was muttering under her breath. *Talking to myself. Getting more tetched in the head each day, Maggie-girl. Careful, or you'll end up like* . . . Well. Pa Alden wasn't a lost soul, by any means. At least, Maggie hoped he wasn't.

She finished scrubbing out the pan and went to stand behind Etta and pull on the cinches. It was a delicate process; Etta had fussed and worked her fingers to the bone (as she often said) over this piece of frippery. She had stitched and embroidered and added lace trim, making all the stitches as tiny and neat as any Maggie had ever seen. Truly, Etta had outdone herself in this piece of her trousseau. Ma Alden had given Etta an old corset from her own girlhood to take pieces from, and so Etta had the whalebone and metal eyelets and all that made it possible to cinch a waist as tight as could be.

Maggie pulled as hard as she could, thinking uncomfortably of all those seams, but it seemed to work just fine. Etta leant against the bedpost for a moment after all was done, and gasped. "It's fine. I've just got to get my breath," she said at Maggie's skeptical look.

"Why are you wearing it today? I thought it was for your wedding. You won't be able to husk corn in that."

"Trying on my wedding dress," Etta managed. "Darn corn harvest. If we hadn't traded with beans to come help with potatoes in November . . ."

"Then we'da had to do it all ourselves," Maggie finished, reasonably. "And you'd be planning on spending your honeymoon with clods of dirt under your fingernails."

Etta winced. Maggie hadn't put any more pressure on the laces; she knew that Etta was remembering it, the painful sensation of fingernails slowly separating from the fingers. It happened every potato harvest. It was something that one could prevent a bit by using work gloves, but inevitably, by the end of the season, everybody had a bad case of it.

"Why'd you two fix on end of October, anyhow? We'll all be bone tired after corn harvest and slaughtering, and two weeks of potato picking after."

"Oh, Maggie." Etta shook her head, and her eyes glazed over a little. "It would've been after Christmas otherwise."

"Seems a much more likely time to have a wedding."

"It's in three months."

"So?"

Etta shook her head, smiling in the way that always frustrated Maggie, as though she wasn't going to bother explaining something to somebody without the intelligence or refinement to understand something.

Maggie gave an extra tug for good measure.

"Ouch!" Etta stood up straight, groaning, and gave Maggie a baleful glance. "Ma's coming over in a few minutes from Sister Wall's; she was doing the finishing on the hems. If it fits, then we'll put it all away for the wedding, when corn harvest is done. Thank heaven—it's all got done in the nick of time. I didn't think it was possible."

"I'm to go over to Cleggs'," Maggie replied. "I won't be here to husk for the first loads of corn."

"I imagine that's fine," Etta said mildly, turning and doing her best to admire her figure, though she couldn't bend at all to see much of it. "How do I look?"

"Fine, I guess."

Etta gave Maggie a sharp glance. "Green eyes don't look well on you."

"I'm not jealous."

"Yes, you are. Every girl is. When I was your age, I was jealous of every fine-figured lady in a pretty frock that walked by. Don't worry. You'll get your chance someday. Growing up isn't all it's made out to be, anyway."

Maggie frowned and shrugged. "Don't reckon I will," she said. "Hey, Etta," she added, suddenly remembering the source of worry that had nagged at her all morning. "If Giovanna ends up in the cornfields, could you see about her?"

"Hm?"

Maggie bit her lip. Would she be causing trouble? "See about Giovanna, that the boys don't get her riled up?" She felt like she was choking around Jed's name.

Etta turned, frowning, just as Ma Alden came in, carefully keeping the bundle of lace and white material from touching the floor. Relief came over Maggie at the interruption; that was not a discussion she wanted to have right then.

Etta wrinkled her nose. "Stinks to high heaven in here," she said.

"Walls' gotten going on their corn. Husking all the time. We'll air the dress out before the wedding," Ma Alden reassured her.

Unlike Etta, Maggie loved the sweet, dusty scent of corn husks. It was so comforting. This would be the one smell riding over everything else for the next several weeks. It warmed her heart and made her fingers ache in anticipation—husking was woman's work, but it was no small job.

Patience came in after. "Sister Wall said make sure we do up all the buttons and have her walk around the room in it."

A sudden dart of real worry hit Maggie. "Where's Giovanna?"

Patience shrugged. "Went off to the Twelveses' to play, I expect."

Maggie started out the door, but Ma Alden laid a hand on her elbow. "Let her play," Ma Alden snapped.

Maggie nodded and walked out the door and down the path. The fresh air did her good. *The air inside is a bit close. It's been getting closer and closer, the closer we get to Etta's wedding.*

She chuckled. Henry would like that one.

"Hello," Sister Clegg called as Maggie opened the door. "Quilt squares. On the floor by the rocker. They need to be sewn together, just like I showed you the other day. Do you figure you can do it on your own?"

"I can try," Maggie replied and sat obediently in the rocking chair. She picked up the pile of soft-colored squares of material and placed it on her lap. "Any particular order to the colors?"

"I'll leave it up to you. It doesn't signify much, I'd guess the Hoster children won't notice colors so much as how much batting's in the middle."

Hoster. Why did it seem that ragamuffin bunch was being constantly thrust in Maggie's direction lately?

A few moments later, Sister Clegg came into the room wiping her hands. She sat at the loom and began organizing her threads.

"What are you making today?" Maggie asked.

"I'm going to do some boiled wool for Father Clegg's winter coat."

"Ah." Maggie squinted at her seams. She had stitched half a dozen together for the first row. They seemed fairly even so far; it helped that the quilt pieces were so exactly square.

"So," Sister Clegg grunted as she leaned forward to untangle a couple of threads, "Henry says you have some concerns about the Cedar murders."

Maggie froze. She felt her face burn.

It was completely unexpected . . . the broaching of the subject at all, the fact that Henry had been talking with Sister Clegg about her. About *Maggie*. Why?

And the word *murder* coming from the prim and motherly lips of the woman who sat next to her.

"I—I know I ought not talk about such things," Maggie began.

"Nonsense. Your Uncle Forth talks anyone's ear off about it who'll listen. It's no surprise at all to me you'd be fretting over it. And a body can't help what dreams she has. Fair natural to talk to friends about such troubling things."

"I know I . . . ought not listen, though. And dreams are just . . . mixed garbage coming out when the mind's not busy. Henry said." Maggie felt her face grow hot, mentioning his name to Sister Clegg.

"Well," Sister Clegg replied, "it's disgraceful for a man to be bringing up such things in the presence of young ladies and in front of children. Your Uncle Forth ought to be horsewhipped, and that's a fact."

Maggie nodded and went silent. Sister Clegg was also silent for several moments. The creak of the loom seemed to talk for both of them. The thoughts raced through Maggie's head: protestations, questions, worry over what Sister Clegg thought of her.

"Your Pa Alden was down there when it happened," Sister Clegg finally broke the silence. "Am I right?"

"Yes," Maggie croaked. She cleared her throat. "Well, no, not exactly. He was there just before, came up before . . ." The unspoken words hung between them.

Before the shooting.

"He's been odd," Maggie finally continued. "And such things are whispered on about—have been, ever since. I don't want you to think I'm . . . that I'm interested in those sorts of things, that I listen to the stories when I can help it."

"It's plain your mind is a fair muddle of worries right now," Sister Clegg agreed. "Do you get enough rest at night? Have the Aldens been working you too hard?"

Maggie started at this question and then shook her head. "The Aldens are always fair and kind to me and Giovanna. I don't know why my mind's a muddle. It seems it all started when I saw . . ."

She paused again, then, unsure she wanted to tell Sister Clegg all that had occupied her mind those first weeks after the "Move Back North." All her suspicions, her sneaky searches. It didn't reflect too well on her, and she already worried over Sister Clegg's opinion of her.

"Saw?" Sister Clegg prompted, staring at her with a furrowed brow and real concern in her gray eyes.

Maggie sighed. "I found my mother's name on one of the mattresses the Aldens use. The bed in the front room."

"Oh." Sister Clegg frowned, clearly puzzled.

"Well, you see," Maggie hastened to explain, "Ma Alden told me, when I asked a few years ago, that there was nothing left from my family. From Italy, from Papa and Mama and the plains. She said not a scrap remained to their name; all were sold to pay for the doctoring of Papa's leg . . ." Suddenly she found herself stuttering, and her mouth felt as if it twitched downward of its own accord. And then the onslaught came—tears, pouring down Maggie's face.

How odd, she thought as she felt herself sobbing, felt Sister Clegg come to her and put soft arms around her. *Why am I doing this?*

Her mind was completely removed from this strange shuddering her body was making, almost as if she were watching from a distance as this overwrought young girl sobbed her heart out.

"There," Sister Clegg said after a while.

The voice grounded Maggie; she shuddered and wiped her face with the proffered handkerchief, feeling intense shame steal over her suddenly. "I'm sorry," she groaned, disentangling herself from Sister Clegg's embrace. "I don't know what all that was."

"The dams burst," Sister Clegg said. "And no surprise."

Maggie shrugged and blew her nose. "Well, anyway, I'd better get going on these quilt squares."

"I remember when you came to the valley. You and your

sisters." Sister Clegg's voice had a note of stubbornness in it; she wasn't letting the subject drop.

Maggie forced herself to look up at Sister Clegg, who was regarding her with a mixture of solemnity and concern.

"You came in from the prairie with the Aldens and settled in the Forths' old stead by the river. I brought over some bread. Do you remember?"

Maggie nodded. "You gave dolls to us. Giovanna still sleeps with hers."

"Those little corn husk dolls? Land sakes. I've got an old rag doll of Lavinia's I ought to give your sister. No use sitting here getting moldy in my trunk. Anyhow, I remember how struck I was, seeing you and your sisters. You looked solemn and full of care. It was like looking at a grown-up face on a girl's body . . . you were tired out, used up by that prairie. And Giovanna was like a little bird, tiny and all big dark eyes. And the baby had those same dark eyes and a tiny, pinched face. Like a baby robin asking for food."

Maggie stared at Sister Clegg, feeling shock course through her system.

"It did my heart good, Maggie," Sister Clegg continued, putting a warm hand on her knee. "Seeing you grow younger every day. Getting enough food, and your sister filled out and grew rosy and just as a girl should be."

"Baby?" Maggie whispered.

Sister Clegg frowned at her again. "Your baby sister, who came over in the wagon."

Maggie's fists were clenched so hard, her nails dug into her palm. "I have a baby sister?"

Sister Clegg stared at her, an odd, almost frightened sort of expression on her face. "Your baby sister? You don't—Naomi, I think her name was. Your Ma Alden called her Jane."

"Noémie." The name immediately came to Maggie's lips, with the softer French vowels and consonants. And suddenly she remembered, just a flash of an image—wide, dark eyes, and a pale face framed by dark curls. And then she remembered. Her mother's ungainly figure, in the wagon. Her mother's—

Her baby sister.

"What happened to her?" Maggie could barely get the words out; it felt as if all the air was being squeezed out of her lungs.

Sister Clegg removed her hand, and her expression became more troubled. "You truly don't remember?"

Maggie shook her head.

"Well, mayhap that's a good thing."

"What happened?" The words burst from Maggie, far louder than she had intended.

Sister Clegg put a hand to her face. "It was very sad," she said after a long moment. "I—I didn't know you . . . I wish I'd not said anything. The mind plays funny tricks on us sometimes, Maggie-girl. Likely you didn't want to remember. You were fair wild with grief, that day they found her, wouldn't let her little body go. And afterward you were always running off to sit on the little grave they dug for her up above the homestead."

"What happened?"

"They found her one morning. Like I said. In the crib. Still, and pale and cold—it happens sometimes, to babies. Nobody knows why, Maggie." She shrugged. "Nobody knows why."

They were both silent again, Sister Clegg's fingertips pressing into Maggie's thigh like a hot brand.

"I think I—I want to go home now," Maggie managed.

"I'll send some baking home with you," Sister Clegg said. Her voice was husky, like something had caught in it.

Maggie carefully set the quilt blocks on the floor. She didn't wait for Sister Clegg's offering. She didn't even feel her feet on the floor as she walked out, leaving the door standing open behind her. It was like some outside force led her. Her feet, one in front of the other, moving up Main Street past the city run, up past the old fort, carrying her body with them.

The sun blistered the top of her head, because her bonnet hung limply down her back, and the heat sunk into her dark hair, the curls hot against her cheeks. The sweat ran down between her shoulder blades. She walked and walked, and when she finally reached the old adobe homestead, she continued walking on up the hill until she found the little piece of wood. There was a name on it, burned into the wood with rough-formed letters.

"Baby Jane," Maggie read aloud.

She knelt, shivering, and folded her arms against her chest.

Baby Noémie.

A million images seemed to flood her mind: rosy baby cheeks, solemn dark eyes. The adoring smiles and coos of a younger Patience and Etta, and Ma Alden's softened gaze as she held a little, dark-haired bundle in her arms.

Her own mother, thin-faced and pale, clutching a tiny, red-faced babe with trembling arms. The moment that the life went out of that face, when the breathing stopped rattling and the face seemed to blur and set—the features like yellowish, pale wax. When Maggie knew, knew beyond doubt, that Mother was gone for good.

And that terrible morning. The cradle.

She couldn't see it. It was like her mind was closed to it—the sight of her baby sister's death.

She lay down in the grass on her side, her body circling the little marker. The sun beat down on her, the birds chattered deafeningly. She felt the heat lull her into a strange kind of stupor, and then finally her breathing calmed and slowed.

It was the sun's setting that startled Maggie awake—a sullen, red ray hitting her directly across the eyelids, painting her sleeping vision pink. She opened her eyes and blinked, then slowly rose.

She had no way of explaining herself, she realized. She would walk back, and Ma Alden would be completely outraged at her. The way she was untidy with dirt-stains on her apron and twigs and grass in her hair, at her strange half-sunburn. The fact she'd been out so long.

Maggie figured, though, that she wasn't the one who owed somebody an explanation. This was her grim thought as she slogged her way home, her wet moccasin shoes collecting dust and leaving damp prints in the road.

A STRANGE SPARKING

MAGGIE KNEW THE ROUTINE BY NOW, AFTER FOUR SEAsons of it. Stoop, gather as many as possible, toss them in the wagon, bend and gather some more. Giovanna ran along in front, picking up the corn even as it fell from the scythes to the ground, dodging and giggling as Jed purposefully tossed one in her direction.

This is one time when I'm not sorry for her boundless wind and gallop. Maggie smiled to herself. Her smile quickly faded, though, as it tended to do lately. Dreams. They tortured her. Not every night, but not knowing almost made it worse: would she dream tonight?

And the other question was, did she want it to happen, or not? The dream of the baby. The dream of the guns, not so much. Maggie could live without that one. But if, for a small, brief moment, she saw the face of her baby sister, even with all the horror that would come right after—

Just then, Jed managed to peg Giovanna in between the shoulder blades with the sharp tip of an ear.

Giovanna tripped in surprise and fell flat on her face. Maggie stumbled over a hoe, which Jed had let fall to the ground, in her rush to help.

Giovanna's eyes were wide with surprise and hurt, but she didn't cry. "It's fine, Megs," was her irritated dismissal as Maggie brushed at the dirt smears on her face and elbows.

For the rest of the row, Maggie tossed ears recklessly at Jed's head. She waited until he wasn't watching, of course. She wasn't stupid.

She hit him a few times. It made her feel better when he turned around, red with annoyance, and couldn't see who was to blame.

Sweat. The scent mingled with the sweet scent of plump, yellow kernels, millions upon millions, which lay tucked inside the fat gold spades they threw into the wagon. They'd already loaded up the Aldens' and the Forths', and now they were using the Bells', who carted back and forth to an ever-growing pile by the homestead, waiting husking and shucking. A great deal of it would be left in the ears, but to make cornmeal one had to shuck, twist off and dry the kernels, then cart them all over to the gristmill.

Eating through the winter is a tiresome business, Maggie thought as the last hours of the afternoon wore away. Maggie was so exhausted she was starting to fumble. She'd grab for an ear and miss; she'd toss it and it would fall short of the wagon by a good three feet. In front of her, Giovanna continued as cheery as ever, skipping along and tossing ears into the wagon like she was playing a game.

"Right, then, Maggie-girl, into the wagon." Pa Alden's voice, so close behind her, startled Maggie so badly she jumped.

"We headed back for the day?" she asked, feeling

a prick of pleasure in her chest. It was the most he had said to her—six words—in a long time. He'd used the nickname—Maggie-girl.

She felt his firm hands lift her by the forearms up onto the pile, and then Giovanna, giggling, landed beside her. Etta's and Patience's ascents were more graceful, with Pa Alden and Jed holding to their hands and giving them a boost up.

Maggie watched Pa Alden for a while. He seemed more cheerful than usual. He even said good-bye to the Bells as they parted ways on the main road, nodding and affably touching the brim of his hat. *Has something happened, maybe something Brother Bell said to him in the fields today, to make him this way?* Maggie wondered.

Maggie slid back down into the wagon and lay there in the corn, feeling the itchy, crackling husks against her back, and breathed in deeply. Giovanna sighed in a satisfied way.

"One day done," Etta grunted.

"We'll likely husk some tonight," Maggie reminded her.

"Don't remind me. What a fair state my hands will be in the day I get married."

"Lily-pale skin and soft hands on the prairie signify vanity and foolishness," Patience put in.

Etta turned and frowned at Patience.

"Sister Wall says it," Patience replied, shrugging. "Tells all her boys. 'Look for a girl with healthy color and calluses, and you'll find yourself a useful partner.'"

"Good thing Elias isn't in Sister Wall's Sunday school class," Maggie put in, then rolled quickly to avoid the ear of corn aimed in her direction.

"Being able to keep up appearances in the midst of dirt and degrading work is the sign of a true lady," Etta said, theatrically dusting her hands.

"Who said that?" Giovanna asked.

"Me."

"No real lady's got an aim that true." Maggie tossed the ear she'd avoided at Etta and missed completely.

"Stop throwing the corn overboard," came Ma Alden's furious voice from the front. "Behave yourselves, ladies. We're about to ride through town."

"Ladies," Maggie said under her breath. "Sure."

Patience gave Maggie a reproachful look and then struggled from her prone position. She held on to the side of the wagon for balance as she tried to make her back ramrod straight, curling her legs and ankles underneath her for support. Etta followed her example, but Maggie and Giovanna lay in the corn and gazed up at the sky, which was clear and full of stars.

Sleep came easily all that week. Hands grew chapped, and scratches from the dry stalks tended to show up wherever skin was bare: on the neck, on the wrists, and the back of hands. On the forearms too, because the women retreated inside to do the husking and left the men to fend for themselves on the field. The pile next to the Bells' homestead grew to enormous proportions. Eliza, Emily, and Mary sat constantly in the house, husking, and were nowhere near keeping up. Lizzy, the little four-year-old girl, and the two-year-old boy, William, played with the husks, tying them around their heads and playing Indian, princess, and many other games. The two babies sat or lay on the floor while their mothers worked.

The noon meal was always a welcome respite, and Ma Alden glowed with praise for her baked goods and her pears, which she continued to bring every day. Mother Forth was busy and silent as usual, and Uncle Forth not as vocal as he usually was, and Pa Alden said a few more words than usual. Maggie was grateful. She was sure it had something to do with Brother Bell, who was one of the chiefest of patriarchs around and known for his loyalty to Brigham Young. He was also very involved in dealings with the Indians. Maggie wondered, more each day, what it was Brother Bell and Pa Alden had to talk about so earnestly. Or, at least at mealtimes, Brother Bell talked quietly under cover of the loud chatter of the women and children, while Pa Alden listened, nodded, and grinned on occasion. Uncle Forth would saunter over to whichever corner they were sitting in and try to overhear, and Brother Bell would immediately smile and start talking to him. *To his frustration*, Maggie imagined, watching the pained, forced-pleasant expressions on Uncle Forth's work-red face when Brother Bell addressed him. She noticed the awkwardness of his posture as he tried to sneak up on them.

The first of the husking bees was approaching. That evening, in fact. Maggie had determined not to go. It was the first free night she would have in a long while, since Etta and Patience had been invited and were planning to attend, and Mother and Pa Alden had decided on an evening at the Forths' and some husking of their own, and Giovanna wanted to go with them to play with the little boys.

Just as Maggie settled onto her straw tick with her journal, there was a banging at the door. Maggie sighed, padded over to the door in her stocking feet, and opened it to find Henry standing there.

She stared at him. He looked odd, somehow. Smelled odd too.

As if suddenly remembering, Henry snatched the hat off his head. He nodded at her.

"Hi, Maggie." He spoke strangely, clipping off his

consonants. His tone was strange too, as if he were forcing his voice lower in his throat.

"Hello?" Maggie's voice made it into a question.

Henry nodded at her—nervously, as though he couldn't help his head bobbing on his neck. "I was wondering."

"Wondering?" Maggie frowned. He must be playing some trick on her. When she said the right word, he'd have some punch line to make her look foolish and laugh. She sighed. "All right, Henry. What were you wondering?"

"Wondering if you'd been invited," Henry said.

"If I've been invited? To what?"

"Well, I mean, *I'm* inviting you to come up to Walls' for the corn-husking. If you'd like. Or," he shrugged, "like as not, we could go fishing or something."

Maggie nearly laughed out loud. He looked so uncomfortable, and his hair was slicked so tightly to his head it almost seemed painted on. When he removed his hat, there was a mussed spot in back, where a quarter-size tuft stood straight up on his crown. "Don't look like you're dressed for fishing," Maggie managed finally, keeping her laughter inside.

Something in her expression conveyed her amusement. "Well, no," Henry retorted, blushing and jamming his hat back on his head. "So if you're not of a mind to go to the Walls' husking bee, I'll just go on ahead myself then."

Maggie sighed and glanced behind her at the empty main room. It would have been so lovely, having some solitude. She still hadn't written anything about what'd happened the week before—when she suddenly remembered Baby Noémie and visited her grave and the thoughts that had come back into her head all about the Aldens and what they may be hiding . . . it was like to make a girl burst, carrying all that inside. She was in fair need of writing or at least, thinking with her book open, which was more what she could do. A few, scrawled words; it would be enough.

But it seemed Henry was in fair need of her company to the husking. Likely trying to impress some girl, Maggie decided. Well, she was a friend. She could play along. Henry wouldn't want to show up alone, looking foolish in front of whomever it was he'd gone all gentlemanly and slicked his hair back for.

"Wait," Maggie said. "I'll change into a nicer frock. I've been on the fields all day in this one."

Henry shrugged. "Looks just fine."

"To you, maybe. But trust me; we'll get sniggered at if I don't change."

Henry's eyes opened wide as he considered this. "Right," he said. "All right. Just don't be too long."

"Right," Maggie replied. "I won't." She slammed the door and hurried through changing into the faded yellow housedress that Patience had taken in for her a month or so ago. It wasn't too bad; the flowers still stood out, white and fresh and pretty on the mellow background color, and the stitching was impeccable. And most important, it had the longest skirt of all the dresses Maggie owned, falling nearly to her ankles, covering her boot-tops. She'd asked Patience to save as much of the material of the skirt as possible, but she'd still had to cut a good twelve inches of hem off, in the end. Well, she'd be at least halfway decent in it.

After she finished lacing up, she had another thought.

She went to stand in front of the mirror on the wall in Mother and Pa Alden's bedroom, dipped the hairbrush in some water from the rain-barrel, and ran it carefully through her hair, smoothing it as best she could. Feeling guilty, she rummaged through Patience's things until she found a bit of white lace that matched the white flowers on her dress, and tied her hair up awkwardly in back.

When she ventured out, Henry didn't say much. He nodded at her and took her arm. It was odd. Formal, and stiff. They'd always pushed and shoved one another down any street they walked, or skipped, or ran races. They'd never walked like this, like a couple trying to act like they might be courting.

It made for strained conversation. Henry commented that the roads were quite dusty. Maggie agreed and added at least there wasn't any mud. Henry agreed and then there was a long stretch of silence.

"This is stupid," Maggie finally burst out, wrenching her arm away from Henry. "Let's just walk like normal folks, and when we get there we can do . . . this thing," she gestured with her elbow, "If you want. When we walk in."

Henry squinted at her. "All right," he said, in a tone that made it clear he thought she was entirely crazy. He took a step away from her and they paced, side by side.

"So, Hyrum still drilling with the Legion?" Maggie asked. She attempted a skip. It felt good, so she skipped again.

"Yes," Henry said. "He drills most every day. Rumors've come back from the city that there might be need for the militias, and more people to join up."

Maggie stopped skipping. "What rumors?"

Henry shrugged. "Just the usual stuff. Judges brought in by the government to turn over the city courts."

"Oh, the judge thing."

"Yeah, that."

"I've only heard a little about it. Just heard that the judges might be coming down to look into the Cedar Murders."

"I heard that too. And the Parrishes, down south in Peteneet."

"Haven't heard about that. What happened to the Parrishes?"

"Well, way I heard it told, Parrish was found in a ditch—confound it, Maggie!" Henry burst out, interrupting himself. "This ain't the sort of thing I ought to be talking to you about tonight. Why can't you just behave like a girl ought?"

Maggie felt as if she'd been kicked. She swallowed. "I-I'm sorry?" she ventured, finally. "I—I know it ain't proper. I'm just . . . with Pa Alden, I can't help but be . . . you know. Curious."

"No." Henry nodded at her and scratched his head. "No, don't figure on it," he said. He straightened up. "I'm sorry I spoke so crass," he added in the strange, clipped formal tone from before. "Takes a while for a fellow to un-learn some words."

Maggie stared at him. "What sort of game you playing at, Henry?"

Henry gave her a look that was half confusion, half frustration, and slid back into his customary stoop, shoving his hands in his pockets. "Nothin', I guess."

Maggie was relieved when they reached the Walls' home. A general shout for them to enter came at Henry's knock, and they found a large group already gathered there, husking.

Maggie managed to squeeze between two of the Wall girls. Henry went to sit with his brother Samuel. They all sat, nearly two dozen of them, around a large pile of ears just like the ones Maggie had been tossing into the wagons the whole week long.

"You've got a late start," Mary Wall said. "Here, you can have some of mine."

Maggie smiled and shrugged. Mary had the biggest pile already. Her large, capable hands moved faster than a person could watch.

Each person in the circle grabbed and husked as fast as he or she could go, throwing the husks aside and collecting the ears in barrels and tubs, set aside to be shelled. Sister Wall liked to save the nicest husks for all manner of things. She made little dolls, like the one Sister Clegg first brought Maggie and Giovanna when they came to the valley. Sometimes she dyed the husks and made them into wreaths that were lovely to behold.

Everyone was in high spirits. Maggie reflected as she worked, listening to the hilarity and noisiness and the quips that flew around the circle. In spite of what all people said about hard work being a way to get off too much energy, she figured hard work did nothing but stir it up. Especially when there was the prospect for games and jokes. She watched as Henry and Sam Clegg kept funning and setting everyone to laughing. Maggie couldn't help herself, she laughed so hard that, by the time the evening was getting on, her stomach hurt like it had been kicked.

And then Hyrum and Julia entered. Maggie felt funny, watching them come in the door. It was obvious the two came together; Hyrum had Julia's elbow in the same manner that Henry had tried to take Maggie's.

They sat next to each other, so close their arms were touching, though they seemed to say little enough to each other. Julia looked really beautiful, Maggie forced herself to admit. She wore a russet-red housedress and a ribbon of the same color, carefully tying her long, brown hair up in a neat bun. Maggie touched hers and winced at the mass of fluff she found there.

Hyrum turned often to participate in his brothers' banter, and Julia flew grimly through the pile, husking.

Now, that is odd.

Odd enough, that Maggie couldn't help but be curious. Usually Julia was the type that ignored tasks at hand in favor of smiling and talking to whatever boy is striking her fancy lately. Maybe she meant to impress Hyrum with her focus on the task at hand?

Maggie found herself glancing up from her pile every moment or so to see what Julia and Hyrum were doing. It was ridiculous of her, she knew. It painted her as green-eyed and jealous, and yet what sort of claim had she on Hyrum? None. She didn't think of him that way. She didn't think of any boy that way. Still, she couldn't help herself. Her eyes were drawn to Hyrum's lithe form, his shiny dark hair spilling over his forehead as he peeled back ears.

And then Maggie watched as Julia pulled back a husk, revealing a glint of soft red. Maggie's heart sank . . . Julia had found a red ear of corn. So that was what her intent had been, pouring through those ears like her life depended on it. She wanted the first red ear.

But what good, Maggie wondered, *will it do Julia?* There was the rule at these events that if a boy happened to find the first red ear of the evening, he had to kiss the girl sitting next to him. But a girl who found a red ear was expected to chuckle over it, perhaps make a joke, and toss it into the pile. No girl would be forward enough to demand a kiss. *Of course, Julia's quite an interesting sort of girl. Who knows what she's capable of?*

As Maggie watched, Julia looked around the room carefully. Maggie looked down for a moment as she saw Julia's gaze move in her direction. When she glanced up again, she saw that Julia was smoothing the husk back over the ear. And then, with a deft, subtle movement, she tossed it into Hyrum's pile.

Chit.

It was an uncharitable word to come to mind, but she had no other way of expressing the indignation that swelled within her at the contrivance. What was Hyrum about? Girls like Julia played games. Was the girl Henry was trying to impress—was she like Julia?

Most girls are like Julia, Maggie admitted to herself. But Hyrum and Henry both deserved to be with friends who were honest, forthright. Girls who had more up their sleeves than silly tricks.

Maggie's attention was irrevocably riveted now. There was no going back to her own husking race. Her hands slowed, as she couldn't tear her gaze away from Hyrum. She winced when she saw his hands come perilously closer to the ensnaring ear. She said a prayer that someone else would find one. Soon . . . anyone. She would even be willing to be the one kissed, if it came to that. Of course, she was sitting next to two girls, and so there was no real danger there

A few moments later, Maggie's heart skipped a beat as she watched Hyrum's face go red. Julia was pretending not to see; she had turned to fuss around with her apron strings.

Maggie barely restrained her shout of laughter as she watched Hyrum smooth the ear over, just exactly as Julia had done, and toss it quickly in his husk pile.

It was all Maggie could do to keep the laughter in for the next little while; she watched as Julia's face fell further and further as time went on and Hyrum made no mention of any red ears.

The boy with the second red ear ended up being

Archie Billingsley, who shrugged and turned a little pink. "Foolishness," he said and threw the ear in the pile of husked corn.

Maggie watched Henry as he joined in the chanting and the goading. Samuel Clegg began swatting Archie on the back. "Kiss! Kiss! Kiss!"

Finally Archie shook his head, shrugged, then turned and gave his sister Martha a kiss on the cheek.

It's lucky for him she's sitting there. Eliza Wall, who's sitting on his other side, looks a bit miffed, Maggie thought.

The laughter came and went in waves. Shedrick Holden slipped in at some point, and his jokes never failed to set a room to rocking. His sparkling black eyes, and the quirk to his mouth only apparent by the way his cheeks curved out above his devilish pointed beard, made the things he said seem more wickedly funny. There was a lot of sparking going on of course, with boys rushing to help a girl carry a load of husks out to the husk pile. Toward the end of the party, Hyrum stood up with Julia and walked out with her, both their arms overloaded with yellow silk and crackling husks, and Maggie's heart contracted. Would he take the opportunity to give her a kiss or some other such nonsense? She tried not to allow her eyes to follow them out.

"You really like him, don't you?" The abrupt words, directly beside her, made Maggie jump and whip her head around to behold Henry, sitting beside her.

Maggie felt her face go red. Henry too? She had enough of teasing about Hyrum from Etta and Patience. "When did you come over here?" she snapped.

"Been sitting here a good while," was his mild response, but something in his face told Maggie he wasn't feeling mild, at all.

"I'm sorry," Maggie said. "I'm not in the best of moods. And it's nothing to do with liking anybody," she added, seeing the belligerent gleam in his eyes as he opened his mouth. "How're you getting on husking? I've no chance of winning at this point."

"Sam's going to win. That was decided almost from the beginning. Got some bee in his bonnet—I think he's trying to get Mary Wall's attention."

"Ah."

"Maybe I ought to take a page from his book. Nothing else seems to be working."

Maggie frowned. "Likely you're doing just fine. That arm thing seemed to work on Julia. You should try it on whatever," she viciously tossed a handful of husks into her pile, "girl you're worrying yourself over, all slicked hair and fine manners." She flicked a belligerent glance of her own at him.

"Codswallop," Henry snapped.

Maggie's head snapped up. She had never heard that sort of anger in his voice before. He wasn't looking at her; he had his gaze trained on the floor, arms folded over his chest.

"We should just shove it and go home," he said. "I'm tired. And I'll be working the fields tomorrow."

"I suppose," Maggie ventured after a moment.

"Well, let's go then." Henry stood.

Maggie brushed corn silk and husks off her lap and stood as well, taking the hand Henry offered. When she stood, he kept her hand—kept it and held it firmly when she tried to slide it out of his after she had her feet under her.

Maggie felt strange. It was strange. If Henry was trying to impress some girl, wouldn't she think he was already, well, already sparking Maggie? If she saw them walking with their hands . . . holding hands, like this.

The cool air was nice after the stuffy warmth of the Walls' main room. *Laughter somehow heats up a person,* Maggie thought as she breathed in the cool night air. *And stars, they cool a person back down.*

"Stars are real pretty."

Maggie nodded, keeping her gaze trained on the sky, trying to pretend she didn't notice, didn't notice at all the warmth, the hard calluses, and lean, strong fingers around her palm. "These summer nights the sky is clear. No chimney-smoke to muddy things up."

Henry stopped suddenly, tugging on Maggie's elbow. "Maggie, I reckon I've got something to say to you," he said.

Maggie stopped and frowned, feeling annoyance and something else—something rather like hurt, or fear, rise up inside of her. "Reckon I do too."

Henry released her hand and sighed. He turned to face her. "Fire away, then," he said. "What I have to say can wait. It's been waiting a while, anyway."

"Well, Henry, I s'pose I just want to say I don't see why you need to be different all of a sudden. I understand you might fancy a girl or two, but that doesn't have to come in on us. I mean, we don't have to change anything; we can go on being friends, right? You don't have to go off like Hyrum did, Henry. I need—I mean, I like . . . having you 'round. Makes things a bit easier for me. At the Aldens, and just . . . all the time, better. You don't have to go off and leave too, Henry."

Henry's face was shadowed so that Maggie couldn't see his face, but she heard the perturbation in his voice. "Different? How? And why would I go off and leave you?"

"Well, the way you're slicking your hair down. The straw hat. Keeping to proper topics. Doesn't suit you, Henry.

Hyrum started all that last summer and now he's—now we never see him. You wouldn't really want that to happen to us, would you?"

"I guess . . ." Henry said. He scratched his chin. "I guess the real question is, would you want it to, Maggie?"

Maggie shrugged. "Well, of course not. I'd miss you, of course. I mean, wouldn't you miss me?" Her voice was impatient, sharp, because inside there was a gaping fear of what the answer might be.

Henry chuckled. It was a strange sort of chuckle, with a sort of exasperated puff of air that started it off. "I reckon I would," he said. "I'd miss you a lot, Maggie. And I s'pose that might be enough, for now. C'mon, then, let's get you home."

He turned, oddly abrupt, and began walking. Maggie followed. She nearly had to skip to keep up.

She felt a certain hollowness in the region of her stomach. *For now,* he'd said. Because, of course, some day he would have to move on. Maggie wouldn't be enough. He'd be a man, someday, and he'd want someone to fall in love with, someone to hold hands with and give a kiss to . . . Maggie's heart beat strangely, and her throat felt full and tight.

At the gate, Henry gave her a little nod, lifted his hat, and turned back, leaving Maggie to stand there for several moments, watching the shadow of his retreating form until it disappeared from view.

The world is going crazy, Maggie thought as she let herself in.

The lights were out. Etta and Patience were breathing deeply, slowly on their straw tick in the south corner. Giovanna, on their pallet, tossed a restless arm over her head and rolled onto her stomach, muttering.

Maggie removed her clothes, put on her nightgown, and slid under the linens next to Giovanna. She laid her head on the stiff pallet and shivered, willing thoughts away, willing sleep to come, but sleep didn't come for a long while. And when it did, it was full of strange figures, strange forms, and strange words. Like a mix of all the nightmares she'd had lately, only with no understandable sequence, no real way of following. Just frightening flashes: faces, gestures, and strange places—crude stone buildings, steep, green hillsides. The scent of water heavy in the air, and evergreen trees—different from anything she'd smelled here in the valley. The scent was familiar and heartbreaking. She had no idea why.

THE PORCELAIN

ON THE LAST DAY OF THE BELLS' CORN HARVEST, MAGGIE took a short walk along the river. She left during dinnertime, with the full intention of just walking—just seeing, once. She wouldn't have the opportunity again, not safely. She was here on the river and so if something happened (like a run-in with Indians), she could call out or run or something.

Soon it will be winter. This is my last chance for a while.

The river's trickling sound tickled her and made her feel thirsty. She skipped for part of the way and then slowed and walked as the roof the Forths' old homestead came into view, just over the top of a small hill. A small hill with a flat little piece of wood stuck in the ground.

She veered around it, unable to quite face it, and walked into the homestead.

She walked around the inside, took a couple of laps of the one room. It smelled like dust, like old cinders.

It happened when she came to a stop, the second time around, in front of the fireplace.

A feeling.

A memory. A memory?

The picture of Etta swam into her mind. Etta, at fourteen, was a slender girl—prim, neat, her hair screwed back from her face. Her delicate little toes peeped out from under a starched skirt.

Even though she was going barefoot at the time, she was always a lady first. Still the same fussy, bossy girl.

A picture of Etta setting the table came to Maggie. The table, it stood . . .

Right here. Maggie walked over to the little east window. *So the morning sun could come through and shine on our breakfasts.* Etta would stand there, laying a pink-and-white porcelain cup at every plate. In the middle stood a teapot—no, a pitcher. A pitcher, with yellow flowers. And two of the cups were not pink, they had yellow flowers—

Maggie shook her head. It was her own wish, come to haunt her, invading her memories. That pitcher had never been on the Aldens' table. The last she had seen, it was nestled carefully in the straw, wrapped in a ragged piece of linen, lying close by her mother in the wagon.

Maggie sat with her back against the wall, feeling the sun on her head. The vision swam back into her mind—setting the table. Etta dropped one of the cups, and it clattered to the floor, chipping its rim as it hit the table's leg. The handle came off and rolled in the fireplace. Ma Alden had given her a talking to, then. She'd run a finger along a crack and clucked, after chewing Etta out, fretting that there was "nothing to mend it."

Etta, clearly aghast, shook her head. "We can set it aside, Ma. Put it in your chest and then when there's something to mend, it we can—"

"No. Not like it was anything valuable. Came with the girls. I just fancied them. Pity, now we're short a setting. Just toss it in the chest. Put the rest of them in there too."

Maggie shook her head again. Was she having dreams by day now? Was she so fussed that her mind was spilling over into her waking thoughts?

She dropped to her knees. Wincing as she felt the ash collect under her short fingernails, and, chuckling at herself, she dug around in the dusty, crumbling ashes that remained in the crude brick fireplace.

Maggie shook her head and snorted. She was surely going crazy. A teacup handle, hidden in the ashes. What was the chance it would still be there, even *if* it had really happened? If she was making up daydreams—inventing. *If* the china had made it to the Aldens'. *If* Etta really did set out two of the yellow cups and the pitcher that day. *If* one of the yellow cups really had—she stopped still and felt her heart take off, like a bird fluttering against the bars of a cage. Slowly, she drew her index finger out of the ash.

Curled there, around the tip, was a little white piece of porcelain. A handle.

A teacup handle.

She sat there, staring at it as it lay, gleaming white against her sooty gray fingertip.

After several minutes kneeling there in shock, she rose and tucked it carefully into her apron pocket. Her heart seemed to pound in her head now. She felt pains in her stomach as if she'd eaten bad meat.

She turned, slowly, and looked at the room.

Where had the cradle been?

She couldn't remember. She tried hard, squinting so tightly she saw stars. Then she opened her eyes, scrutinized every corner, every worn, smooth floorboard.

No, it wasn't going to come.

She walked out the door and around to the back of the homestead.

She sat down next to the marker. She touched its weathered surface.

After a few moments, she forced herself to stand again and walk. The Bells would be back in the fields soon. And tomorrow was Etta's wedding.

On the ride back down to town, Maggie watched Ma Alden's profile. What if she pulled the teacup handle suddenly from her apron and presented it to her? What if she asked—what if she said, *I know. I know about the china.*

I know about Noémie.

"Do I have a smudge of something on my face?" Ma Alden snapped, waking Maggie from her ruminations.

"No, ma'am." Maggie slid back down to sit against the wagon's headboard.

The morning of the wedding was cold. For the first time since the previous winter's end, it was cold enough to require woolen shawls to be worn out to the chicken coop for egg collecting. Giovanna and Maggie flew through the outside chores as fast as they could and ran into the house shivering.

"You'd think you gals'd be used to it. Happens every year," Ma Alden chuckled, watching them. "Guess it's your 'talian blood."

"French," Maggie said quietly.

Ma Alden raised her eyebrows.

"Me and Giovanna are *French*," Maggie repeated, feeling the blood start to churn through her veins as her limbs warmed up. "We lived in Italy but spoke mainly French. And we lived up the mountains, where the ice froze over the rain barrel 'bout mid August. So this cold's nothing."

Ma Alden opened her mouth as if to retort, then closed it. She squinted at Maggie for a long moment, and then turned abruptly back to the baking she had been fussing over.

The burning in Maggie's chest was from more than the cold. It was odd, this sudden impulse to say something, when she never had before. It felt good, saying it. She wanted to say more.

The porcelain. The Bible.

Noémie.

Maggie fingered the little lump of the smooth porcelain handle—she'd wrapped it and tucked it into her waistband—and opened her mouth.

"Maggie, could you come here a minute?" Patience's clear voice pierced Maggie's thoughts.

She jumped up from the side of the fireplace to help with some last minute fussing over Etta's gown, holding knots and draping and smoothing material.

For the rest of the day until evening, it was little tasks like these that kept her busy, so that she forgot to think too hard about anything.

In fact, the whole family was busy enough that they forgot to eat. Perhaps Ma Alden didn't forget, but she seemed to find an endless stream of tasks for herself and everybody else—dashing between the house and Town Square with parcels and chairs and tables and quilts and doilies and all manner of things she seemed to constantly be remembering she had forgotten.

And then the time came for Etta to get over to the Walls' for some quiet time before the evening ceremony. Bishop Wall wanted to "talk to the young couple" for a while before he married them civilly, before all the guests and bustle showed up. Etta fussed, staring at her face in Patience's little oval mirror. "My hair's not quite—"

"It's fine," Ma Alden snapped.

Maggie pursed her lips at Patience, hiding a smile. It was saying something, when even Ma Alden had no more appetite for fussing.

Etta slid on her overcoat, grumbling about the weather and how, with the way Patience was bundling it up, she would disarrange the folds of the wedding dress.

Ma Alden fairly had to bustle her out the door. Patience and Giovanna followed in their wake. Pa Alden was somewhere.

Likely staring at a thistle patch.

She sat in the rocker. It had been a while since she'd had a task-free moment. She watched the patterns of the burning coals and thought of that daydream she had experienced in the Forths' homestead.

Fourteen-year-old Etta seemed to materialize in front of her.

Etta bent and placed the round, gleaming pitcher into the chest and then carefully cradled the cups around it, tucking in some linen to separate and protect them. She stood and turned the key in the lock.

Maggie blinked free of her daze. *Ma Alden's chest,* she thought.

The chest, upstairs at the foot of the bed. The chest that she'd stood over so many times, hefting Pa Alden's hammer. Thinking she'd never have the nerve to do it. Unsure she wanted the nerve, either.

It's odd.

Her feet seemed to move again of their own accord, taking her up the stairs two at a time.

It was odd, how all along she should have looked in the place she was most afraid to breach. She'd tried to find the key, of course, but Ma Alden kept it somewhere she hadn't been able to find, not in all her searching of the house over the late summer. If she had, she would have already looked.

She was going to have to break the lock this time; she knew it as she lifted Pa Alden's hammer from the nail by the hearth. The daydream had made the decision for her. This was a decision that couldn't be unmade.

Trembling, she knelt down at the foot of the bed and heaved the chest out from under it. She pulled the hammer from her pocket.

She winced with her first swing, and the blow glanced away, marking the soft cherry-wood with a pale, sickle-moon shaped dent.

She stared at the gleaming, polished surface of the chest, feeling a mix of guilt and fear. And then a strange kind of fury overtook her. She stood up, swung the hammer back over her shoulder, and slammed it down on the lock with all her might. Once, twice, three times, until the latch wrenched away from the wood, and then four, five, six times for no reason at all against the fluting on the edge, breaking off a section.

She stopped then, her chest heaving, and forced up the lid.

It was all neatly, beautifully packed. It was the picture of gentility, with the soft colors of fine, old fabric inside the dark wood of the chest. It was like looking into another world, something from the Aldens' past that didn't belong here on the rough, dirty prairie.

On top, a beautiful satin infant's dress lay spread out, as if it was on display. It was yellowed from lying in storage. Carefully, Maggie picked this up and laid it on the bed.

She picked up some intricately stitched lace pillow shams, also yellowish, and a little brittle from starch and storage. Next, she found Ma Alden's wedding dress—soft, gleaming yellow muslin on a pattern of blue, and removed it with hands that trembled a little. Ma Alden had brought this out when Etta was engaged, Maggie remembered. And Etta had been quite upset that she was unable to do up the buttons. Ma Alden had said there wasn't enough fabric to let it out for Etta's fuller figure. This was what had lead to Ma Alden giving Etta the corset instead—

There.

If Maggie had said it aloud, it would have come out in a shriek—half exultation, half horrified surprise.

There, underneath the dress, were the pitcher and cups. She knelt and stared, unable to believe her eyes, unable to really internalize the manifestation of something she had still been half-certain was only her imagination—something from a dream, from another life.

After a few moments, she picked up the pitcher and cups and set them carefully on the bed next to the other things. She repacked the wedding dress, the shams, and the baby's dress. She shut the chest once more as best she could. She tried to hammer the latch so that it was somewhat flat once more, but she knew it was no use; there was the gouged-off area of trim. And that mark on top where she'd hit the surface of the chest with her first shaky try.

It was a matter of time, Etta knew. And Ma Alden couldn't be stupid enough not to know which of those living in her house would want to remove the china, over all other things. There'd be no escape from this.

It's only a matter of time.

There's no going back now.

As she shoved the chest back against the bed, turning it to hide the damage, Maggie felt shame. And anger, and bewilderment.

Tears spilled over her face, rolled down her nose, and her whole body shook with silent sobs as she ripped back the bedding once more, looking for that name . . . the thing that had started all of this, that had upset the life with the Aldens she and Giovanna had settled into over these last four years.

Of course it was there, still, undeniable. The faded name was along the seam. It chided her, made her remember things . . . things she'd thought were better to be forgotten. Where was the Bible, then? She hid the Bible someplace.

This worry was nothing, though . . . not anymore, in the face of one gaping, raw question: Noémie.

The Aldens never mentioned Noémie. It was like to them, she didn't exist. For a while, she hadn't existed for Maggie as well. Maggie had really forgotten about her. How could she? How could Maggie simply forget? Why couldn't she remember?

The dreams.

Real?

If they were real, then that meant that something unspeakable had happened. Something so horrible, Maggie couldn't even voice it, couldn't even think the word.

Ma Alden had . . .

She . . .

Even as she thought it, the images from her dream filled

her mind: Ma Alden holding the pillow over the tiny, struggling form until it stilled.

Footsteps downstairs gave her such a start that she nearly felt her heart would burst open inside of her. She jumped up, pulled off her apron, and tucked the porcelain in, then bundled it under her arms, up against her skirt. She ran down the stairs, turning sideways as Patience and Ma Alden came up past her.

"Doing laundry?" Ma Alden asked, seeing the bundle in Maggie's arms.

Maggie nodded. She didn't trust herself to speak.

"There's more whites that need to be done. But not tonight. We'll do them in the morning."

"I don't have another clean apron," Maggie managed. "I—I forgot to put my one from yesterday in—"

"Take one of Patience's," Ma Alden snapped, and then continued up the stairs.

Maggie ran down the stairs, ran out of the house, and paused and leaned against the henhouse, feeling sick.

She had absolutely no place to hide anything. It was the same problem that she had rejoiced in earlier, when she was looking. Not many hiding places meant only a few places to search. And, in the end, she knew it was going to come down to Ma Alden's chest.

A new dart of fear shot through her. Was Ma Alden going up for something from the chest? It was Etta's wedding day; perhaps she meant to give Etta the shams or something else from the chest.

With that thought, she picked up her skirt, apron and china bundled in it, and ran, pell-mell, down west Main Street. She ran as fast as she could around the corner, ran to the only place her feet seemed to know to take her.

She knocked on the door and waited, her head throbbing, her breath rasping, and her throat so dry, she felt as if a gulp of icy water wouldn't even be able to force it open again.

Sister Clegg opened the door. The welcoming grin quickly melted from her face, leaving a puzzled, concerned expression.

"Come in and sit down," she said.

Maggie stood there for a moment and then moved across the threshold. She walked, dazedly, to a chair. She sat, and the china clinked as it shifted in her skirt. She pulled it open, revealing the delicate white pitcher and cups, with their pattern of yellow flowers.

"My family's," she said shortly at Sister Clegg's questioning gaze.

She lifted the pitcher. It felt so light. So very fragile. One at a time she lifted the teacups. One was missing its small, round handle.

Maggie took the handle from her apron pocket—the little piece of china that she had found in the ashes—and matched it to the cup. It lined up perfectly.

"Found it in the homestead," she said. "In the fireplace."

"And—where did you find these?" Sister Clegg asked. She touched the teapot, fingering the china detail on the handle.

Maggie's shame choked her.

She began to cry silently again, her shoulders shaking, tears making hot tracks down her face. Sister Clegg came up behind her, patting her and making comforting noises.

Somehow she said it. Said what she had done. Sister Clegg was perturbed. Maggie could see the concern in her eyes, but she said nothing.

"I'm in big trouble," Maggie added, after she managed to get it all out. "Big trouble. When Ma Alden's seen what I done to that chest of hers—" She shook her head. There was no way of knowing how such an act would be dealt with. Maggie had never done anything even approaching this level of naughtiness since coming to the Alden household.

"I don't know what to do with this," she continued, shaking her skirt gently so the porcelain dishes clinked against each other. "I believed her. I never thought she'd— she'd go and lie about something—something so small as this."

"Doesn't seem to be such a small thing to you," Sister Clegg answered. "You're saying these dishes came with your parents from Italy?" She reached for the pitcher, picking it up this time. She examined it carefully. "Beautiful."

Maggie nodded, wiping her eyes on her sleeve.

She felt self-conscious, suddenly. What sort of a crazy person did she seem to Sister Clegg? Rushing in here with no provocation or reason, with a skirtful of china. Breaking open, defacing Ma Alden's most valued possession. Did Sister Clegg think she'd stolen from the Aldens?

Sister Clegg was still examining the pitcher. At Maggie's glance, she placed it back in her lap. "Well, what are you going to do with them?"

"I don't know. Maybe go put them in the old homestead? Or someplace." Maggie shook her head. "I don't know."

"You can leave them here if you wish."

Maggie looked up at her, surprised. "You—you believe me, then."

Sister Clegg seemed to know the thought going through Maggie's mind. "I know you're no thief, Maggie-girl," she replied. "And I have a little space in one of my chests if you'd like to keep them there."

Maggie didn't know what to do with this. No scolding? Sister Clegg wasn't even going to tell Ma Alden? She was even willing to go so far—she trusted Maggie so much—that she'd help *hide* the things? Why?

"Thank you," she whispered. "Can I tell you something, Sister Clegg?"

"Sure, of course."

"I—I've been having dreams. Not the ones about the guns. Different ones about . . . about Ma Alden." Quietly, she told Sister Clegg about her dream of Ma Alden and the baby.

Sister Clegg's face sharpened with concern, her eyebrows drawn together in the middle. "Dreams are just dreams, Maggie. And I did tell you, remember? It came to you as quite a surprise, when—"

"No. I was having them before. Before I knew about . . . *remembered*, Noémie. It was after you told me about her, after that, I knew who she was."

The silence spread out between them, thick and troubled as a cumulous cloud.

"When I found my ma's name on the old mattress on the bed upstairs that one day," Maggie added a few moments later. "It started after that."

"Well, Maggie." Sister Clegg shook her head, as if helpless. Maggie had never seen her be helpless before; it scared her a little. "What are you saying? That you think your Ma Alden . . ." Like Maggie, she couldn't finish it, couldn't voice the words.

"Do you reckon God gives visions to fifteen-year-old girls?"

Sister Clegg chuckled, a little wildly. "Well," she said. "Well, we know He gives them to fourteen-year-old boys.

Knuckleheaded as we both know boys can be." She sighed and sat at her loom.

Maggie rocked, keeping her hands on the cool, curved surfaces of the china in her lap. It felt alive, somehow. Like she was touching flesh.

"Henry's gone and joined the drillers over in Kolob," Sister Clegg said suddenly.

Maggie started and looked at her. "The Legion, you mean? I thought he was too young."

"His pa," Sister Clegg shook her head, "went and gave his permission. Against my wishes, of course."

"Well, that's . . ." Maggie searched for a word to describe the sudden coldness, the dart of fear that had seared through her. Henry? Like Sister Clegg said, he was little more than a boy.

She thought of him as she'd last seen him: jumpy, awkward, with his attempt at hair-slicking all up in a rooster tail on back of his head, and something seemed to squeeze her insides. "Why're so many joining all of a sudden? You reckon it's true they're expecting something soon?"

"I don't reckon. I just keep my mouth shut and my hands kneading and weaving. . . all I can do is fill bellies and cover backs."

Maggie stared at Sister Clegg, surprised at the bitterness in her tone.

"I think we should have something to eat," Sister Clegg said, rising abruptly from her chair. "And maybe some cool water to drink."

"Sounds just fine," Maggie said faintly.

Sister Clegg's oatmeal biscuits did seem to restore something in her, though. And the cool water was nice on her dry, hoarse throat.

"Dreams," Sister Clegg said, shaking her head. "Maggie, I think dreams sometimes are there because our mind is so chock-full of things, it can't help but spill over when we're not awake and can't fuss."

"That's sort of like what Henry said one time."

"But sometimes," Sister Clegg went on, "dreams are a message, I think. From God. I've had them." She gazed at Maggie. "I don't know about your dreams, Maggie. But perhaps you've found some truth in them. Don't take that to mean it's all truth—the mind is a funny thing. Really you ought to pray about it, I'm thinking. Or leave it be. Sometimes our mind hides things from us for a reason. Sometimes, if we go digging at things, we don't like what we find."

Maggie nodded and smiled, not really listening so much as enjoying the calm, mellow tones of the older woman's voice. It was wonderful talking like this to Sister Clegg, not being scoffed at nor bossed, but just like they were trying to figure things out together. "Maybe I should pray about my dreams," she said, tracing her fingers absently along the cup's edge, staring at the pattern of flowers on the china in her lap.

"You might want to pray that Ma Alden will be merciful when she sees what you've done to her chest too," Sister Clegg added wryly. "And don't you have a wedding to get over and help with?"

Maggie's heart sped up. She took a long gulp of cool water. "Yes," she said, rocking a little faster. "But Ma Alden—"

"You'll have to face her sometime. You're a tough little thing. It might seem like the world is ending, Maggie, but you'll manage. And I can have Moses or David look at that chest and see what can be done to make it new, if your Ma likes. You can work for me to pay it back."

Gratitude welled up in Maggie again. She nodded and drained the rest of the water from the glass.

"We're bringing some chairs and baking tonight. Tell your Ma Alden I'll be free after suppertime to come and help her arrange things." Carefully, she lifted the pitcher and cups from Maggie's lap. "I'll put these up high where nobody can get into them."

CHANGES

MAGGIE WALKED BACK TO THE ALDENS'. WHEN SHE WALKED inside the door, she winced, as if waiting for some kind of explosion.

"Hurry and put on a clean apron," Ma Alden snapped at her. "We've got to take the baking over. Thank you for washing the dishes."

This unexpected thanks stunned Maggie and sent a fresh wave of guilt through her. She watched Ma Alden for a moment as she bent over, gathering platters where they sat, stacked and ready, on the table.

"I'll go up and get the spread," Patience said. Maggie's heart began to thump, hard. Did she mean to go get something from Ma Alden's chest? She wasn't ready to talk about it, what had happened this afternoon, nor the explanation about what she had done. She wasn't ready to demand answers to the questions she had.

She took a large basket and began tossing bread and buns into it.

They rushed out of the house together, loaded down with their burdens.

Maggie felt another dart of fear as Patience ran up behind them with neatly folded bundle in her arms. "Got it," she said breathlessly. Maggie waited for her to mention the chest, but nothing came.

It must not have been in the chest. Maggie felt like her muscles might melt in her relief.

"Hurry up, girl," Ma Alden called over her shoulder.

When they got to Town Square, Maggie looked around in amazement. The bowery was completely transformed. Neat rows of mismatched chairs were decorated with leftover late summer flowers. There was a wide aisle through the middle that lead to a cleared space in front of the chairs, where a high little table served as a podium. It had a large wildflower arrangement on the ground in front of it in Ma Alden's glass vase. Behind the podium were long tables with delicate lace tablecloths; like the chairs, they were obviously temporary donations from several women in the ward and neighborhood. Already, the tables were crammed full of baking and various delicacies, and on one table were large platters of meats: cured pork and beef, fowl and fish, sausages, and all manner of savory things.

Maggie shivered. She wasn't hungry.

She walked around the tables as if examining the food and finery, really seeing none of it. She then turned and began to walk down the wide aisle, which had been laid down with straw.

"You could help me with the posies," a voice said close behind her. Maggie turned and was startled to see the grim, freckled countenance of Liz Ellen Hoster. She held, in her skirt, a large bundle of woody-stemmed flowers: black-eyed

Susans, purple yarrow, and bunches of that starry-flowered grass that grew all over the prairie.

"Sure," Maggie replied.

"Just take a grass and twine it 'round the bunch, then you can lay it on the ground next t'row. I've done all these, and I reckon I ought to go home and check on things." With that, she dumped the entire bundle of flowers into Maggie's waiting apron and ran off.

Maggie gritted her teeth, then shrugged, and began to make painstaking little bundles, trying to get an even number of flowers in each one. "Silliness," she said under her breath.

It wasn't like Etta would remember something as miniscule as whether there were wildflowers at the end of every row.

Well, really, knowing Etta, it's quite possible. And it was likely that she'd stop her walk up the aisle and demand that the situation be remedied, right in the middle of the ceremony.

Maggie chuckled. It came out more like a sigh.

She'd nearly gotten to the end of the rows. She was feverishly sorting yarrow for the last four bouquets, when another voice, close behind, startled her out of her countenance.

"Hey, there. Want some help?"

Maggie jumped, sighed, and turned. "Henry."

"Hello." He grinned and shifted his hands in his pockets. "Been a while."

Maggie stared up at him. He was badly sunburned. His skin was a mix of brown and red, complete with peeling pink spots on his prominent nose. His eyes were almost ghostly, light as they were, staring out of that weathered face, and his hair was bleached to nearly straw-colored.

"If you think it'd be as exciting as running around in

the mountains likely has been," she said, unable to keep the retort out of her voice.

"Nope." Henry knelt to take one of the bunches of flowers. "Right fun, drilling. I know why so many've been joining up now. I should've done it sooner."

"Your ma's nearly in tears over you."

"The day my ma spills a single tear that you can prove, I'll promise to muck out the henhouse every day as long as I live."

"You ought to be careful the words that come out of your mouth."

"I am," Henry said, grinning at her. "I mean every one of them." He looked at her keenly for a moment, and Maggie felt the heat go to her face. They were both thinking of that evening, the last time they had met, when he'd been acting queer and Maggie had begged him to keep being friends with her.

She couldn't look at him; it was too humiliating. She turned back to her flower arrangement. "Fine," she said. "Well, just put them at the end of the rows, then. I'm going to make these into table decorations." She piled the leftover flowers into her apron and stood.

"You look mighty pretty in that color, Maggie. Save one of those Susans for me." His voice had a strange quality to it. Was he teasing her somehow?

Maggie felt herself flush again. She turned away from him and marched up the aisle, making sure to keep her back straight and her head up, so he wouldn't see how his words affected her. If she ignored him enough, he was sure to stop. She hoped he would, at least. She couldn't stand to lose another friend right now.

Her fingers trembling, she arranged the flowers along

the edge of the central table, the one holding the glorious, two-tiered wedding cake that Sister Wall had made, complete with candied cherries and strawberry slices. *Mariah*, she thought suddenly. *I wish I could talk to Mariah, right now. She'd love all this—the flowers and decorations.*

"Hello, Maggie. You looking for a task?"

Maggie turned around. "Hi, Sister Holden. Not right at the moment, thanks."

Sister Holden nodded, frowning a little. Her hair, slicked back neatly, gleamed orange in the sun. It contrasted shockingly with her bright blue eyes. Maggie couldn't help staring at it.

"You all right?" Sister Holden asked, moving a little closer, bending down.

"No, I mean, yes." Maggie shook her head. "Yes, I'm fine."

"Well, all right," Sister Holden said.

Sister Holden always intimidated Maggie a little. She was too perceptive for Maggie's liking, and her tongue was too fast to keep up with when she got going on a subject that fascinated her.

"Thanks," Maggie nodded.

"Well, you ever need someone," Sister Holden said, shrugging, "to talk to, Maggie, heaven knows I could stand a little womanly company anytime I can get it."

Maggie pursed her lips. "Thanks," she said. What about her made it so obvious she was unsettled inside? Or what about her situation made all the matrons in Provo think that Magdalena Chabert needed to be taken in hand? She shook her head. *Small towns.*

"I'm going to go get dressed," Patience said, walking by the table. "Do you want to come home with me?"

Maggie shrugged, feeling relief well up inside of her at the intrusion.

Sister Holden nodded at her and walked back over to where the fiddler's platform was being constructed.

"Reckon this'll do." Maggie looked down at her light calico frock. "Don't have nothing much better, anyhow."

Patience's eyes sparkled. "I don't know," she said. "Let's go home and see what there is. Where's Gigi?"

"Giovanna's likely off with Lizzy Twelves."

"Well, let's go by the Twelveses' and round her up, then."

They started off, Patience slipping her arm companionably through Maggie's. She seemed in a rather good mood, better even than usual. Patience was usually quite content and even-tempered, but today she seemed almost to skip with happiness, and her cheeks were rosy with excitement.

"You going to dance tonight?" Maggie asked her.

"Of course. You are too, aren't you?"

Maggie shrugged again. "I s'pose I'll have to. Wouldn't be seemly, to skip out on Etta's wedding. And if someone asks me, wouldn't be polite to say no."

"Hyrum Clegg'll likely be there."

"And Julia Harrison too," Maggie retorted. She had a sudden thought—did Patience fancy someone? If she did, she hid it well. She glanced over at her foster-sister; at her delicate profile, with the nose slightly turned-up, and the light brown hair pulled neatly from her face.

They cut through the Twelveses' wheat fields, now a carpet of golden stubble. They found Giovanna and Lizzy up in the barn playing with some kittens. They persuaded Giovanna to come down and made a fast track down Seventh Street. Patience was walking faster and faster; she was almost running now, and Giovanna giggled, skipping as she kept up. Some of Patience's excitement seemed to be rubbing off on her.

Maggie, however, felt a great deal of her nervousness return as they entered the cabin.

I ought to just fess up. Waiting to be found out's like being the chicken with its head on the stump, always twitching and wondering when the ax's going to fall.

Patience walked into the main room and stood by the little bed that she and Etta shared. She turned to Maggie with a big smile.

Maggie frowned at her. "What's got into you? It's just a dance, not like we haven't been to a hundred already. You got some fellow on a string all a sudden?"

Patience scoffed. "Me? No. Look!" She gestured toward the bed.

Maggie saw then. Spread out on top of the quilt were two dresses. White dresses, trimmed with lace. "That's nice," Maggie said. "You'll look pretty in it."

"They're not for me," Patience said. "Silly. They're far too small, look."

Maggie shook her head, about to speak, and then realization struck her.

"Did Ma Alden—?"

"No," Patience said. "These are the dresses Sister Clegg did over for you. She took them in and re-trimmed them. Brought them by just now. I happened to be here looking for more baskets. She said they used to be one of hers and Lavinia's. Said she did a few alterations. Made it sound like naught, but look at them." Patience shook her head. "I doubt she just took them in. More like cut pieces out of the skirt, sleeves, and bodice and made up two whole new dresses. That ribbon looks new too. You'll have to thank her, Maggie."

Maggie touched the sleeve of the larger one, feeling equal parts wonder and embarrassment. After this morning. This, from Sister Clegg. "For me and . . . Giovanna?"

Patience nodded.

Giovanna howled and grabbed for the smaller one, which had a yellow-ribbon sash.

"Wash your hands first," Patience said sternly, whisking the garment away from her. "And for that matter, get your neck, face, and arms. And your legs and feet. Maybe we should just dunk you in the rain-barrel." She tossed the dress on the bed and hustled Giovanna toward the back door.

Maggie lifted hers carefully by the shoulders and held it up against her. It looked like it would fit well, and the skirt came all the way down to her ankles. Room to grow still. Instead of a yellow ribbon like Giovanna's, her sash was a dark blue that shimmered when the light hit it.

Wonder where she got such fine ribbon. Not at Stewarts, that's fair certain. No, it had to have been taken from something else. Something the Cleggs brought with them all the way from back East, or something that Brother Clegg brought back from one of his missions, maybe.

She put on the dress and stood in front of the mirror, brushing her hair, dipping the brush in a glass of water, and trying to tame her curls.

Patience and Giovanna came back in, breathless. Giovanna was giggling. Her hair was sopping wet but looked clean. Patience flicked a comb through it and then braided it tightly. Maggie turned and watched as Patience slid Giovanna's head through the neck of the dress and felt her heart contract. The shining dark hair, the clean, pale face, and shining dark eyes against the white of the dress—Giovanna was beautiful. Nobody who looked at her tonight could say she wasn't looked after, that she wasn't a proper little lady.

"Here, let me help," Patience said briskly. She took the brush from Maggie's hand and dunked it into the water, gave her hair a few strokes, then dunked it again.

"You just have to get it real wet," she said. "Do you want to wear it up?"

Maggie felt herself blush. "I guess." She winced as Patience pulled hard on it and began twisting it so tightly the skin on her neck and scalp burned and tingled.

"Don't have any pins, so you'll just have to make do with something. Here." She got the bit of lace that Maggie had used to tie her hair back the night of the husking bee.

As they finished up, Ma Alden rushed in. "Anyone see the little embroidered purse of Etta's? It's got Elias's ring."

Patience shook her head. "Do you need any help getting ready?"

"No, I reckon we're all about as fine as we'll be, considering all this dust." Ma Alden shook her head and ran up the stairs.

Maggie watched her go up, feeling her heart thrum in her chest.

"Wait!" Patience said suddenly. "Wait, Ma. I think I might have seen it." She ran to the corner and began digging through the mending. "Here it is," she called. "Must have fallen in with the mending or got mixed up with it or something."

Ma Alden came downstairs, snatched the purse, and ran out of the house. Maggie felt limp and dizzy with relief. She collapsed onto the bed and sat there, watching as Patience finished up with Giovanna.

"All right. Well, it's about time to be getting over there," Patience said, examining her own reflection. *She looks prettier than usual,* Maggie thought. She wore a yellow cotton dress, and her hair gleamed like honey. She'd taken time to tuck a black-eyed Susan into her bun, and excitement made her eyes gleam.

"How does Etta look in her dress?" Maggie asked as they began to make their way back toward Town Square.

"Very nice. The cut turned out beautifully. Very becoming to her figure. You'll see. Oh, I feel like I could just dance right now."

"You'll likely get to later."

"You too. You look beautiful, Maggie."

Maggie felt queer, stiff almost. The white dress, the hair—she felt like she was a different person. One who sat down like a lady and arranged her skirt, who wouldn't just spout off sarcastically. She felt guilty too. *I don't deserve all this,* she thought. *Not after what I did this morning.*

They went and sat in the front row on the bride's side, beside Pa Alden, Uncle Forth, and Jed. Maggie noticed her flowers were wilting a little and hoped Etta wouldn't notice.

More and more people came to sit. Elias's mother and father were there in the front row on the other side of the aisle, and two of his older brothers with their wives, having come in from Peteneet that morning. Past the first few rows, people from the neighborhood and the ward just piled into the seats without consideration for bride or groom; they knew both equally well.

Maggie noticed the Cleggs filing into seats a few rows behind her. They filled two whole rows. She counted them, out of curiosity. There was Sister Clegg, who sat on one end with Father Clegg. Next to them was Moses with his three wives, Rebecca, Ann, and Jane; Benjamin with his two, Mary Ellen and Eliza, and Baby Benjamin. In the row behind them sat William, who wasn't married yet, next to his younger brother Joseph, who had his wife, Phoebe, and their little son, Joseph Jr. And then of course there were Harvey and his wife Margaret, then Samuel, Hyrum, Henry, Alfred, Orson, and baby Jerry, who sat on the end of the second row of Cleggs with his mother, who was Father Clegg's other wife, Hannah. The only one missing was Lavinia, who lived with her husband in the city. Twenty-three people. How would it be to have so much family 'round to no end all the time?

Maggie grinned, watching Hannah struggle with Jerry, who clearly wanted to be in the front row so that he could play with his nephews. She quickly turned back around when she thought she saw Henry looking her direction.

The ceremony was simple. Bishop Wall presided and gave the vows. Etta's voice trembled as she repeated back the words Bishop Wall gave her. After all was done, he pronounced them man and wife, put a hand on each of their shoulders, and grinned.

Etta blushed as Elias leaned in and kissed her, but she seemed to kiss him back happily enough, Maggie noticed.

The band started tuning up then, at the other end of the square. Benjamin Blanchard, William Smith, and Levi Curtis up from Springville were all three fiddling. Two more men were sitting on the platform with them. One was deftly running his fingers along a washboard. Another held a harmonica to his mouth and was blowing at the holes, trying out his notes.

"Bound to be a rollicking time," a voice said, startling Maggie. She whirled around. Her heart sank a little, oddly, when she saw it was only Pa Alden. He leaned against one of the chairs in the back row.

"You fixing to dance?" Her voice reflected her surprise.

"It's my daughter's wedding." Pa Alden shrugged. "Been a while. Hope my steps haven't gotten too rusty."

"Doubt that." Maggie felt her heart lift. She loved to dance with Pa Alden. He was nimble and quick and graceful, and he prided himself on the trick steps he could put into a dance pattern. It was easy to follow him too; his arms seemed to send you messages of what he was about to do and made a girl feel as if she were the finest dancer around. Before the Cedar troubles made him odd and scarce at such events, he had always danced once with each of his daughters, Maggie and Gigi included, though of course with Gigi it was mostly just him whirling her about while she giggled.

Maggie gave him a quick grin. "Best go see if Ma Alden needs help," she said and headed for the refreshment tables again. Pa Alden followed her. It was his old, nonchalant stroll from before. She glanced back at him, wondering what it was that had him so much easier tonight than usual.

What was in the air? Everyone seemed to be in the best mood possible, frisky and silly, giddy like school children. Except, of course, for Ma Alden. She stood over the tables, her face lined and grim. It seemed to Maggie that everything a body could do had already been done, but there Ma Alden was, fussing. Moving things an inch to the left or right, fluffing up the bouquets, sliding the tablecloths a little, smoothing out imaginary wrinkles.

"Come on, Ella-girl," Pa Alden said, strolling forward and grabbing her hand away from the platters. "Band's tuning up. Got to warm up my steps."

Ma Alden frowned. "Can't, Dale, I've got to—*Fred?*" She looked up at him, and the worry seemed to slide from her face. Her lips quirked. "You're dancing?"

Pa Alden raised his eyebrows. "Of course I'm dancing at

my own daughter's wedding. All these questions. I'm starting to get an idea nobody fancies my dancing. Maybe I should just go sit and watch—"

"No, no." Ma Alden quickly stepped around the table and took his hand.

Maggie watched them stroll away with a curious warmth in the middle of her chest. She felt her feet move to the tune of the reel that the band was experimenting with—stopping, tuning, and then starting up again. She felt heady and a little dizzy. The air was ripe with dry grasses, spicy with wildflowers, and the sickly sweet, tangy undertone of the river cottonwoods.

She looked up, saw Henry ambling in her general direction, and turned hastily back to the tables, taking Ma Alden's place worrying over platters that didn't need moving and cloths that didn't need straightening. Her heart pounded in her ears as she waited for a tap on her shoulder.

After a few minutes and no interruptions, her heart slowed. The intoxicating feelings seemed to drain out of her, leaving her with a sudden knowledge of how exhausted she was after the day's events. She dragged her feet over to an empty chair and collapsed into it, tapping her fingers to the rhythm of the music.

There was a fair crowd now, gathered between the rows of chairs and the platform where the fiddlers played. Maggie could easily pick out Etta, with her billowing pale skirts. *Elias is a good whirler,* Maggie thought, *though not quite to Pa Alden's skill.* She saw Betsy dancing with Brother Clegg, and a few of the Clegg boys with various of their wives. She didn't see Hyrum or Henry but was startled for a moment when she caught a glimpse of Alfred dancing with Gigi, a solemn expression on his face as he carefully turned her through the steps. Gigi seemed to be enjoying it; she giggled with every turn. Maggie cursed herself for forgetting to see to her sister's hair again; her braids had unraveled and her hair swung down her back, a riot of tangled curls.

She shook her head and sighed.

"Don't look so down in the mouth about it." A voice startled her for the third time that evening. "Like as not, someone'll ask you soon enough."

Maggie looked up into the sharp, strong features of Samuel Clegg.

"Evening," she said, falteringly.

"Sure is." He nodded, glancing over his shoulder to look at the dancers. "Evening, all right. Well, let's go then."

Maggie stared at him, flabbergasted. She gave him her hand, and he pulled her up out of her seat.

"Can't stand to see a nice girl look so downhearted at such a rollicking event as this. Three fiddlers!" Samuel whistled and whirled her around unexpectedly as they walked to join the group. "Your ma's outdone herself."

Maggie laughed and began to be caught up too in the whorl of colorful skirts and stamping feet. Dust rose up off the ground, making her cough a little, but coughs readily became more laughter at the improbable steps Samuel lead her through. He turned her far too many times on the way back from the front of the line, and they missed their beat.

"How do you like my dancing?" he asked her solemnly when they had taken their place at the rear.

"I've been spoiled," Maggie replied, jerking her head in the direction of Pa Alden, who was still dancing with Ma Alden, two couples in front of them.

"Ah," Samuel nodded. "Poor fellows who try to impress

you with their steps after that. Henry's got his work cut out for him."

Maggie felt her face grow hot. "How is your dramatic society coming?" she asked primly.

"Fine. We're doing a play gotten up by Sister Cindy Holden; it's off some of Byron's poems. She's written a little story around them."

"Sounds fine."

"You should come see it. Hyrum and I both have a speaking part."

"Does Julia too?"

"Sure. She reads the best of all the girls. Given Hyrum some lessons to help him along. He's come a long way with his reading." He glanced down at her and then twirled her again.

"That's nice," Maggie said, her breath catching in her throat. "For them, I mean." She looked down in confusion; she didn't know what she meant. This whole conversation was getting strange.

"Maggie," Samuel ventured a moment later. "You know Henry fancies you, right?"

It took a moment for the words, and the sudden change of subject, to sink in. When it did, she shook her head violently. "He likes to joke," she said. "He's plagued me since I . . . ever since Giovanna and I came out here with the Aldens."

"And why do you think a fellow plagues a girl? Just, time comes in a fellow's life when plaguing should turn to sparking."

Maggie looked up at Samuel and saw that he was serious. Her heart seemed heavy, suddenly, her feet leaden. "I—I don't know," she said.

"Don't know what? Seems to me nothing could be so

simple as that. Sparking's a normal part of life. Moving on from childhood to manhood, you naturally start thinking of it. Don't tell me you haven't yet, Maggie."

Maggie thought her face must be red as boiled lobster. "*You* don't have a girl," she said. Her voice had perhaps a little more venom than was necessary.

"Isn't because I haven't had my share of sparking. Listen, you don't have to get all serious about it. Sparking isn't marriage. I mean, it can lead to that. But Henry just likes you. If you just," he shrugged, "showed him somehow you like him, too, it seems to me he'd appreciate it. I've been watching him eat his heart out these few months, and it'd do my heart good to see things resolved."

Maggie stopped dancing. "You're not joking."

"Nope." Samuel folded his arms and looked down at her, an almost stern expression on his face. "Listen, I like you, Maggie. But when it comes down to it, my loyalty's got to be to my little brother. He'd hate me if he knew I was talking to you like this, but I figured," he finished, shrugging.

Maggie stared at Samuel. She shook her head. "I—I don't—" she said. "I'm sorry," she croaked, finally. "I think I'd better go find . . . someone." She turned then and walked away as rapidly as she could without running, praying Samuel wouldn't follow her. The thoughts pounded in her head, a whorl of confusion. Sparking! Is that what they had been doing all these years? The fishing, the walks together, the sharing of chores—

She shook her head again. It just wasn't possible. Samuel was wrong. He had to be. She and Henry were fast friends, sure. But he didn't think of her that way. Didn't even find her that pretty, in point of fact; all those times he'd teased her about her brown skin and hair. The way he used to take a curl in his fingers and then release it, letting it spring back. Teasing her.

Maggie's face flushed again. It was almost as if she could feel them now, his fingers close to her neck, touching her hair.

But, Maggie argued to herself, there were all those mud-and-water fights, when he'd wrestle her under the current, making sure every inch of her streamed water. That one time he raked his hands through a stretch of wet mud and swatted her back, leaving prints . . .

Maggie shook her head violently and began to trot.

Darn that Samuel, she thought, relishing the wicked word, the vent it gave to her feelings. *He's planted all these thoughts, and now they taint everything.* She couldn't think straight.

She stopped at the refreshments stand to grab a little pumpkin cake and one of Sister Clegg's famous molasses cookies. She glanced around; everyone was preoccupied with the business of socializing and having fun.

Everything was done, really.

She wasn't needed here.

She walked slowly down Seventh, stopping at the corner of West Main to glance back. The sweet sound of a trio of fiddles nearly drew her back to the dance, but she couldn't face the idea of having to face Henry. Face her feelings, so confused and muddled. He'd ask her to dance, perhaps. What should she say to him? She just couldn't think too hard. Too many things seemed to be shifting and changing under her now. With all that had happened lately . . .

She couldn't think about it. She couldn't.

THE INCIDENT

MAGGIE FINALLY GOT A LETTER FROM MARIAH. THOUGH she read it through several times, it was not the comfort Maggie had expected it to be.

Dear Maggie (it read):

I really 'preciate your letters and am sorry couldn't write before this. Town is not a very calm place right now. Ma and I are glad we live off in Sugar House and not in the blocks round the temple. Don't know if you heard, but when they uncovered it all, they found cracks in the stone. So they have to start again.

We all sort of feel like that right now. We're starting again. Our fields of potatoes are all stunted, most of the leaves dead because they didn't get watered. No grain field really made it. We've got apples and peaches by the bushel, but they're smaller than usual and not as sweet.

As to what's happening in town, well, everything. And nothing. Most around us still haven't moved back into their houses yet. We're one of the first, and Father doesn't come visit much as he's so busy over at Lion and Beehive houses tending to his first duties. As mother's more able to shift for herself, and not one of the younger wives, and has me to help her, we've been left to it for now. And Brother Brigham looks harried enough. Older, with more lines in his face. I didn't speak to him when I saw him in town the one time we've gone—he seemed in a hurry and he had Brother Rockwell with him, which he does all the time these days.

All is well here, Maggie. I'll write you a proper letter once things get settled.

Love,

Mariah

All that weekend, Etta had been back and forth from the Aldens' to her new little cabin, carrying things and asking for Ma Alden's help with particulars of getting settled. The Forths seemed to think that, with Etta's leaving, there was now room for all of them to take up residence. They were over for every meal and often late into the night.

Ma Alden loved it; she stayed up with her brother and chatted until the coals grew dim.

Maggie hated it. She hated having Uncle Forth and sometimes Jed, sitting on the hearth as she made a dash from the little nook where she and Patience dressed to the bed. And she hated having Jed, especially, around all the time. She felt like she had to keep her eyes peeled constantly, making sure Giovanna wasn't teasing him somehow or around him when he was in a mood.

Uncle Forth's conversation ranged, as it always did, from Brother Brigham and his increasing feeblemindedness to Johnston and the new governor. Lately he'd added another subject to his usual conversation: California.

"Miles of rolling pastureland, Ella. And gold dusting the riverbeds. Sutter himself offered me a job at the mill, when we were down south with the battalion. Just before he struck it rich."

"Don't I know it, Dale," Ma Alden declared, keeping her eyes on her knitting. "But Fred doesn't reckon on moving. Says he wants to stay with the Saints."

Good thing, Maggie thought fervently. She sat on the little stool in the corner furthest from where Uncle Forth sat, picking out some stitches that Giovanna had tried to darn earlier in the day.

What a spot to be in, that would be—if the Aldens up and decided to follow Uncle Forth's nose to California.

"Fred might come 'round when the judge comes down here, to take up the matter of the Cedar happenings," Uncle Forth declared.

They talk like he isn't even here. Like he's a lump, without the means to respond, or make conversation.

As if Maggie's thoughts had somehow enervated him, Pa Alden looked up suddenly from his whittling. "The judges mean to speak to the men involved in the Cedar affair?"

The occupants of the room—Jed, Ma Alden, Patience, Etta, and Giovanna, and Maggie herself—all turned to look at Pa Alden.

"Which men?" Uncle Forth asked. The corners of his mouth quirked, betraying him in spite of his attempt at a thoughtful frown. "Wasn't it just the Injuns?"

"What's been passed around about the judges, Dale?" There was an uncharacteristic sharpness to Pa Alden's voice. "Where did you hear they're going to look into the Cedar incident?"

"Dunno," Uncle Forth replied. "Why, do *you* know something, Fred? If you do, you ought to spill it out right here. No more of this shut-mouth, tight-lip thing you've got going on. Justice needs serving."

Pa Alden shrugged, and then, all the tension and sternness slipping out of him, he picked up his knife. "Justice. Interesting word you've chosen there, Dale," he murmured.

Uncle Forth licked his lips and scooted closer to his brother-in-law. "You were down there," he said. There was a strange pleading note in his voice. "C'mon, Fred. People say you were down there for it. Were—*was* some of the bishops involved? Or maybe . . . maybe even someone, higher up. Someone from 'round here? I've heard things, Fred. If you know something—"

Pa Alden stood and brushed the wood shavings off of his trousers. He walked out the back door without bothering to retrieve his hat from the nail that hung above it. The door slammed behind him.

All in the room stared at it in bemused silence.

Maggie was afraid of sleep that night. She stayed awake for a long time, staring at the nails in the ceiling, the chink of moonlight coming from the window until the world melted away, then reformed, prickly and uneven, under her feet.

Maggie reached into a barrel. She dug into the soft, spongy ground and found a handful of mud. She smeared her face. The red paint mingled with the oozing, cloddy mud. Chunks of it rolled down past her collar and settled in her bodice.

She marched along the line of straggling settlers. Under her boots, there was mud and rocks, pieces of wood from some wagon or piece of equipment that had broken or been torn apart.

"Ready!"

Suddenly Maggie was surrounded with people. She took her musket in her hands.

"Aim!"

She held her gun to the head of a boy not much taller than she. She waited . . . waited for that last call.

Get this over with, *she plead silently.*

The boy turned suddenly, and it was Henry. His face had that strange braced, tight look it had when he dropped her off that day after the Walls' corn husking. That horrible day. Yes, Maggie saw that his hair was slicked back, saw the tuft standing up there, in the middle of his head. It will be good spot to shoot for, *she thought.*

No.

No! She screamed it, and then suddenly, pitch black, all around her, and she was sitting on something soft, something that shifted under her, with the crackling sound of straw.

Giovanna was patting her. "Quiet, Megs," she whispered. "You'll wake everyone."

Maggie lay back on the pillow. She fell back asleep quickly, but when she woke, her head felt heavy as a boulder on her neck.

She didn't speak a word to anyone during the morning chores.

After breakfast, she went to gather the eggs. She sat there, crouched inside the henhouse, with her little journal out on her knees. Her pencil trembled, but there was nothing to write. *I ought,* Maggie thought, *to be writing Mariah another letter.*

She tried but could think of nothing pleasant. Her dream kept resurfacing in her thoughts—Henry's face. Pride and disappointment. That's what had been on his face.

What was Maggie to do about Henry?

She touched her chest, as if that might take some of the

ache away. A friend, he was. Yes, she loved him, as a friend. He was her best friend. She could not imagine life without him, without any of the Cleggs. But the thought of "sparking"—it was ridiculous to her.

Who was *she*, to think of sparking? Maggie, tangle-haired, muddy faced, unrefined.

Maggie, who had taken a hammer to her foster mother's most prized possession. What an act unworthy of Henry that had been! Henry would never, ever do something like that.

Sister Clegg would be horrified, if she knew what Samuel said to me. Horrified that he thinks Henry fancies me.

But . . . that day. The Walls' husking. Did Henry do all that for *her*? The slicked-back hair and the odd, formal conversation?

For *Maggie*?

She was going to lose him.

Like she had lost most everyone in her life that made her feel safe.

Maggie shuddered, but no tears came. She just shook as if she were cold, even though it was a mild autumn mid-morning.

Uncle Forth and Ma Alden's voices swam into her awareness. *They're coming toward the henhouse*, Maggie thought. She folded her arms tight round her knees and sat quietly in the straw, hoping to go unnoticed. She knew she'd get a scolding about shirking her work if she were discovered.

She heard the sift of dirt under their feet as they approached, and the increasing loudness of their voice. *Brother and sister, two peas in a pod.* She shifted positions, straining to keep her movements quiet as possible as their voices grew loud enough to make their words understandable.

"'Twas them bishops," Uncle Forth said in a low tone as

he leaned against the thin-walled structure.

"Wouldn't surprise me much," Ma Alden replied.

Maggie heard the whisk of the pan and the thud of the scraps hitting the side of the henhouse. The chickens immediately began clucking madly and rushed out in a tide of speckled brown-and-white, stepping and clawing around and over Maggie. One lit from the roost, landing briefly on top of Maggie's head on its way out the door. She rubbed her scalp where the claws had sunk in.

"There's near proof now," Uncle Forth added. "Not that anybody who lives in these parts needs much more to know what happened. It's that blood-murder folly. Brigham preached it, and like to've told the bishops to take matters in their own hands. 'Kill, for their own good. Spill the blood on the ground to save their souls.'"

Maggie shivered. She felt slimy, listening to this. She hated Uncle Forth, hated him with a passion, when he shot his mouth off about Brother Brigham. She was so tired of it that she was almost tempted to make a great deal of noise and stop the conversation, but thinking of her compromising position, she held her peace. *Likely wouldn't stop the conversation, anyway.*

"Not like any kind of Christianity I've ever known about," Ma Alden remarked. "That's what I thought, first I heard it. Straight from the prophet's mouth. Sunday school meeting two summers ago. That was my first thought—'This isn't like any kind of Christianity I've known about, or want to take part in.' Fred, fool he is, told me not to get all bothered about it. And now look what it's done to him. To us."

"Brigham knows he can't stand up to them government men. Those judges—they're going to uncover a whole lot of ills."

"They're going to have a time of it rounding up the Injuns, if you really think the judges are coming in here to clear up all that happened down in Cedar, Dale."

"I keep saying, Ella, 'tweren't Injuns. Erastus knows. Consarn it, Ella! Most everyone down there knows. And I've no doubt in my mind Brigham himself knows, likely the one behind it. A few're even saying he gave the order for the shooting. Fred has to know too, Ella. Likely there's some worried he'll shoot his mouth off about it. Lucky for him he's played his cards so close to the sleeve."

Maggie clasped her hands over her mouth at the wild statement of her uncle's, about the prophet.

Il ne fait pas, she thought. Brother Brigham would never do something like that. If something happened, something bad—no, the prophet would never be involved in something like that. She half expected a lightning bolt to come down right then and fry Uncle Forth to a crisp.

She clenched her teeth, lowered her hands, and twisted them together, afraid she'd given herself away with her quick intake of breath.

Ma Alden's voice shook. "You think Fred's in trouble?"

"I don't know. Maybe if he came clean—talked to someone—"

"And get blood-murdered himself," Ma Alden interrupted. "Dale, you can't say a word to *anyone* on this. I've been fixing—I've been thinking about what you've said about Sutter and California. If it got to where these judges started digging up dirt, you've seen how Fred acts whenever the killings are mentioned. He goes odd; he leaves. I know my husband, Dale. He wasn't down there when it happened, by all accounts, but he's guilty as sin over something, and his poor weak heart can't take it."

"He should come clean, Ella."

"No." The word came out with the force of a whip crack. "No. If it comes to it, we'll leave."

"Just pick up and go? Remember there's more'n eight hundred men at Camp Floyd who—"

"Who'll be after bigger game than my poor Fred. He's always bowed before those with any sort o' grit or authority, Dale. We picked up and left New York, then Ohio, then Missouri, then Illinois, and now we're out here in this godforsaken place scratching for corn and taters like," she gave a wild laugh, "like these chickens. Mindless. As much of a mind to wait for the slaughter than to do anything. No, I'm sure if he's in trouble, it's on account of someone higher up giving the orders. And he mentioned some names—or at least, just *about* said some names, just the other night. He was right on the edge of it, Dale, that's more what I'm worried over." She lowered her voice to a whisper. "Not the judges, but . . . the *people,* the ones who did it. He keeps going around nearly leaking names like that and he's sure to end up in a ditch with his throat cut, just like Parrish. We'll leave, Dale. I've been thinking it over."

In a ditch with his throat cut, just like Parrish. The words chilled Maggie to the bone. *So that was what had happened, then. No wonder Henry didn't want to be talking on about it, especially while he . . . while they . . .*

"I suppose you're right, in that," Dale said after a moment. "I can see why you'd feel that way, Ella. But what about holding those accountable—"

"I don't give a fig about accountable. I want Fred, and I want my daughters safe. That's all I care about. Etta's married, and she's settling here, with Elias. Maybe in harm's way. And if we don't go soon, Patience will be stuck here too." There was a sound remarkably like a sob.

"I could look into my acquaintances in Sacramento for you."

"That might be good." Ma Alden sniffed. "I don't feel like saying anything more on the subject."

"Fine, Ella. Fine."

Their voices faded as they made their way back to the house, and Maggie was left a mass of indignation, confusion, and worry.

No wonder Henry and Sister Clegg said I ought not worry over it. If this's the way people've been shooting off their mouths all over the valley. Blood-murder, indeed. As if Brother Brigham would preach a mad sort of thing like that.

But then, there was something—something in the way Ma Alden talked of it, some strange quaver to her voice, when she said that part about going and hearing Brother Brigham preach it.

The real question, Maggie thought as she dusted herself off, *is where.*

Where did all this leave Maggie and Giovanna? Was Ma Alden rattling on as usual or was she really thinking on going to California? Would Giovanna and Maggie be going too, then, or staying in Provo?

What about Samuel? He'd be lost to them forever. The Chabert family, hundreds of miles apart, lost to each other.

"Two dozen today," Maggie said as she came in the back door. She forced a cheery note into her voice and placed the basket on the table.

"That's less than yesterday," Patience remarked. "Did you look under the henhouse?"

"I forgot—"

An angry wail interrupted her.

It sounded strange, lower-pitched, almost animal. Patience and Maggie frowned at each other. "D'you think the cats—" Patience started.

There was a louder cry, this time with a note of fright in it.

Giovanna.

Maggie dashed outside, followed closely by Patience.

Leaning up against a scrub oak tree in the front yard, Jed held Giovanna against his chest, his left arm keeping her arms pinned to her body. With his right hand, he held a pocket-knife up against her ear.

Something was bleeding already. Blood trickled down Giovanna's neck, and she was sobbing. "Let go," she screamed. "Jedediah Eldridge Forth, you let go of me!"

"Jedediah Eldridge Forth," Patience shouted, almost at the same time as Giovanna.

Maggie stood, as if frozen in place. Patience's voice seemed fuzzy and indistinct, like Maggie was hearing it through water.

And then the world sped up again, skipping a beat, it seemed, because suddenly she was across the yard. Her arms were windmilling, her legs crazy like the wooden jumping-jack toy Pa Alden had carved for Giovanna's last Christmas present, and she pummeled the flannel on Jed's chest, kicked at the leather boots, reached for his hair, his ears, and his eyes with curled fingers.

As Maggie's nails made contact with warm flesh, pictures of Jed's small tortures of her during the time she had been with the Aldens played in her mind. The little cuts with the pocketknife. The mean pinches and the horrible words hissed under his breath that Maggie hadn't understood at first. The time she went over to the Forths' to borrow sugar, and he was the only one there, and he had chased her, screaming, around the cabin, and Maggie had come back to Aldens' to get the scolding of her life for tripping on her overlong apron and ripping it.

Maggie felt the crown of her head come in contact with Jed's breastbone. He yelled something; Maggie didn't hear what it was. She nimbly slithered out of every grasp and dug in with sharp elbows.

"Get off me. Cats and their claws! Geddoff, chit! Get off!" Jed's bawdy, baritone voice cracked as he fumbled, one-handed, for her wrists.

"Maggie, stop! Jed, drop that knife, and let Giovanna go!"

Maggie didn't stop, not even when he released Giovanna and stood. Her feet rose up off the ground. Jed began to swing his body around, trying to loosen her grip. Maggie scratched at his face, feeling flesh collect under her nails before she was flung to the ground.

The landing was painful. Her hip and shoulder blade took most of the brunt.

Maggie felt Jed's long fingers wrap around her arm. She closed her eyes, sure that what came next would not be pleasant.

"Jed," Patience screamed.

Jed glanced at Patience, grinning.

In that instant, Maggie quickly kneed him in the groin, hard as she could. It was a lucky stroke; it was exactly the right angle and placement. Jed fell to his knees.

And then a large hand lifted Maggie up by her collar.

"Uncle Forth." Patience's voice was suddenly softer, scared. "Jed was trying—he was cutting—"

Uncle Forth shook Maggie, still holding her collar. "Don't you ever attack my boy!" His gravely voice resonated in Maggie's bones.

Maggie couldn't breathe. The neckline of her cotton dress cut into her throat, cutting off all ability of speech or airflow. Someone shrieked. Maggie felt something tugging hard at her dress—Patience's hands, she realized fuzzily.

Uncle Forth turned Maggie so that she could see into his watery, greenish-brown irises. He held her there for another slow, agonizing ten seconds. "Don't you ever lay a hand on my boy, again, you dirt-faced Italian chit," he said and lowered her to the ground.

Maggie fell to her knees. She swallowed hard. She gulped air in, feeling her heart race as if it were about to beat itself to death against her rib cage. Patience helped her up, tugging Maggie's dress back into place and smoothing her skirt. "You all right?"

"Don't you forget it," Uncle Forth muttered, without looking at Maggie. "C'mon, son." He jerked his head in Jed's direction, and they loped out of the yard. Jed glanced back at Maggie, an insolent grin on his face. *We're not done,* it said.

"Ma's not home yet," Patience said. "I'll put something on your throat, and she'll look at it when she comes home. C'mon, Maggie."

"You okay, Megs?" Giovanna asked anxiously.

Maggie still couldn't bring herself to talk. Shock was part of it, but she felt like her throat might as well have been cut, with the soreness of the welt and the sharp pains in her windpipe.

She followed Patience dumbly, walking toward the house. *Ma Alden'll take his side*, she thought. *She won't get tender over me all of a sudden. She'll find a way to blame me. And Giovanna won't be safe.* That last look of Jed's had said everything.

Giovanna walked beside her. She trembled, and her large, dark eyes were fixed on Maggie's face.

"I'm sorry, Maggie," she whispered when they got to the door. "I didn't mean to get you—to have that happen. I'm sorry." Tears spilled down her face. "Thanks, for . . ." she shrugged.

Something wrenched its way free, then, in Maggie's heart, and it was like a flood of adrenaline was suddenly set loose in her system.

Maggie stopped in the path just below the step up into the house. "We're not coming in."

Patience turned. "I'll do the rest of the outside chores. You need to stay and tell Ma what happened, before—" She bit her lip.

Before Uncle Forth gets to her, Maggie mentally finished Patience's sentence for her. "She won't do anything." Maggie shook her head, and then cleared her throat. "She doesn't give a fig about me or Giovanna, you know that."

There was a second—two, three—of shock. It had been said aloud, said for all the world to hear, perhaps. At any rate, Maggie knew it couldn't be unsaid. And she wasn't sorry.

Patience shook her head. "You're wrong," she said finally. "She loves Giovanna. And—and you, too. She cares about all us girls. All her daughters."

"We ain't."

Patience frowned. "Aren't what?"

"Her daughters."

"She cares about you."

"No," Maggie shrugged. "She doesn't care much for me. And Giovanna won't be safe here, not the way she lets her run off wherever she wants to go."

"Twaddle," Patience snapped. "You and Giovanna are Mama's daughters! *My sisters.* You're upset, saying things you'll regret later. Come on in. She'll be here soon. I'll back you up."

"Patience." Maggie shook her head. "Look at you—dressed the way a girl ought to be."

Patience's brow furrowed. "What . . . why . . ."

"And now, look at me. And Giovanna."

Patience's eyes flicked away from Maggie's gaze. "You're a—it's just the way, in a large family, Megs, out here on the prairie. We use things up till they're worn out. You know that. You're third down, so the things, when they get to you, they aren't . . ."

Maggie laughed, wildly, and held her skirts out. "I'm not decent for polite company, Patience. Wherever I go, I ain't decent. Nor is Giovanna. The only decent things I got, Sister Clegg gave me. We're charity cases."

"Maggie."

"And I reckon even if I'm to do others' laundry for them and clean and such for a living, and that's my lot like Ma Alden says, then I can do it where I know Giovanna and me will be safe. I thought Giovanna, at least, was family to you Aldens, and I put up with my lot for her sake. But I know now I was wrong."

"Maggie," Patience repeated, exasperation in her tone.

"My ma and pa didn't die," Maggie raised her voice over Patience's protests, "to see their daughters treated like . . . like dirt-faced Italians. Like dirt-faced *French*, Patience. Giovanna 'n' me, we're *French*, and our Mama kept us clean, and decent. She taught us letters and figures, the Bible. They read to us every night. All of us, me and Samuel and Giovanna." She pulled Giovanna's hair off her neck, exposing the trickle of blood on her pale skin. "She didn't figure on us being shoved aside, so much furrin' trash, nor to be cut on." She paused for a moment to clear her throat, to get the choky, near-tears feeling out of it. It was like the next words rose up, came of their own accord.

"Ma didn't die on the prairie for this. Nor for her daughters to be let to go out all over creation with no learning and no manners. And for her little baby to be dead, with no more consideration than a person would take killing a rat."

Patience gasped. Her face slowly flooded with color. "You—you *know*, then?"

Maggie felt her heart begin to race. That look on Patience's face—terror. Patience knew something. Maybe she saw it? Maybe she saw it happen, saw Ma Alden take the pillow and—

"Tell me, Patience," Maggie pleaded, her breath coming in ragged gasps. "It's been in my dreams since the day of the move back north: my baby sister, blue, with all the life smothered out of her. What have you to say about that?" Maggie tasted salt.

Patience put a hand to her face, so that it covered her mouth and nose. "I . . . don't reckon . . . I don't know what to say, Maggie."

Maggie stared at Patience.

C'est vrai, she thought. *It's real, then. I'm not just making things up.*

"I don't reckon I need to hear much more," Maggie managed.

Murderer.

She had been living under the same roof with her sister's murderer. All these four years.

Maggie suddenly realized that Giovanna was tugging at her sleeve. "Let's go away, Maggie," she was whispering. "Let's just go away now, please? You're going to be in for it,

Maggie. Let's go before Ma comes home. Or Jed comes back. Please. "

Maggie's fingers closed around Giovanna's hand. She turned away from Patience, away from the Aldens. It was like the world made a hundred-and-eighty degree turn of its own accord. The pale pink façade of the Aldens' adobe home slid out of her vision.

She felt herself walking away.

It was an odd feeling. Was this really happening? Was she really doing this? In all her worst moments, the thought of actually leaving the Aldens had never really surfaced in her mind. She hadn't allowed it to. It had been a buried, dark thing, waiting there to be uncovered.

She paused when they reached the gate.

Giovanna opened it. "Let's go over to the Twelveses'," she said, tugging Maggie through it, "and play awhile?"

Maggie shook her head. "Not Twelveses," she said. She had to think straight, somehow.

"Where we going, then? Cleggs?" Giovanna asked when they came to the intersection of West Main and Third.

Maggie shuddered, thinking about the mixed up business with Henry and Hyrum, and Sam at the wedding, and the china, sitting in Sister Clegg's top cupboard. "No."

"Where, then?"

It was the sight of Town Square, of the chairs still laid out with the dusty, dried bundles tied to them, which brought the idea finally into Maggie's head. With it came equal measures of relief and distaste. "Well, I s'pose I know where we can spend the night at least."

"Where?"

"Don't worry on it. *Trust* me. It'll be fine. We're not going back to the Aldens' tonight, Giovanna. Nor tomorrow."

"We're in big trouble, Maggie." Giovanna's voice had a flat, final note in it that was somehow frightening.

"No, we ain't," Maggie blustered. "We'll go somewhere just fine. There'll be a dry hearth to sleep on, warm quilts, and maybe even a bite to eat. And a couple of your friends too, from what I've heard lately."

No need to mention the smelly housemate that comes with it all. Maggie frowned down at her apron, which was filthy from the henhouse. And after all, maybe the smell of cow would take away the stink of the chickens.

AT THE HOSTERS

MAGGIE WOKE THE NEXT MORNING IN A VAGUE SORT OF panic. She felt carefully around until she found one of Giovanna's warm wrists. She sighed, and sat up—

And almost bumped her head on the roof.

She gasped as she realized that what she thought was a bundle in the quilt next to her was really the prone form of Liz Ellen Hoster.

She began to shiver, partly because of the cold, and partly because events from the previous day came rushing back to meet her.

Jed. Uncle Forth. Leaving.

She looked down at the glowing embers of the fire.

Thankfully, the Hosters did not really sleep curled up around their cow—cow and calf, actually—as rumor had it. There was a loft, and they slept in that, though it was a tiny space. Crammed up against the side, there was barely room to lie down in the piled straw, with ragged quilts as a covering. Where Maggie was, sitting up straight was impossible.

The roof peaked about three feet in the middle above the platform where all the Hosters slept.

Comfortable enough though. Surprising, considering it's just planks nailed together and no tick to speak of.

And it felt safe, sleeping six feet off the ground. Liz Ellen had pulled up the wooden ladder and laid it at their feet, after grilling her brothers and Giovanna sternly about visiting the Higbees' outhouse, which lay between the little cabin and the Higbees' brick home.

Maggie glanced at the ladder and scratched her head. There was no way to get it down without waking everybody.

Silently, she wrapped a quilt around her shoulders and moved to the edge of the platform. She turned, grabbed the edge, and lowered herself. With her arms outstretched, her toe-tips barely touched the floor. She looked down carefully to see where she was stepping; she was on the inside of where the cabin had been penned off for the large, rust-colored heifer and her yearling calf. The cow lifted its head and observed Maggie with large, lash-framed eyes.

A fresh cow pie to decorate my feet, that's what I need right now. She picked her way past the large, warm body and opened the little door that let out into the backyard. It was a chilly morning. She wished she had taken the time to put on her shoes.

She walked to the outhouse, hopping from foot to foot as they burned with the frost on the ground. As she sat, covering her nose with a fold of her skirt and looking at the back of the weathered door, she thought about what she was going to do.

It was a serious question.

I can't go back to the Aldens'. Nor can Giovanna. She spoke the words aloud, to reassure herself.

Back at the front door, Maggie paused. A sudden sense of helplessness and confusion washed over her. What was she to do?

She walked in and saw the wooden bucket, piled with the few chipped, dirty dishes that the Hoster children owned.

Well, that was a start.

A half hour later, the children were stirring up above her, scattering straw to the floor. One of the boys whined something, and Liz Ellen snapped at him. Giovanna came down the ladder in the quick, jerky way she had when she was groggy. She stumbled and missed the last three rungs.

"It's fine," she said, frowning, as Maggie rushed over. "I fell on my behind."

"Giovanna," Maggie gasped.

"Well, that's what Liz Ellen calls it. Said I would fall on it if I didn't wait a minute or two to wake up before I went down. She was right." Giovanna stood and patted herself ruefully.

"Don't care what Liz Ellen calls it," Maggie whispered. "*You're* not to mention things like that. And no spitting, and no wallowing in any mud puddles today, neither. A lady don't do such things."

"I ain't a lady," Giovanna retorted. "I'm a kid. Can I go play with Lizzy Twelves?"

Maggie felt the frustration bubble inside of her. "No. We're going out together. Sister Clegg . . ." Her voice died out as she considered the situation.

Sister Clegg would likely sniff out exactly what was going on inside three minutes. She was like that. And more than likely she'd have Maggie and Giovanna packed off back to the Aldens' in spite of any protest Maggie made.

Or she might not. A picture of the yellow china came

into her mind, stored neatly in Sister Clegg's chest.

Finally Maggie shook her head. She'd watered the Cleggs' floorboards enough lately. Not to mention Henry and Samuel. She wasn't up to seeing either of them.

"We'll go by the Holdens'," Maggie said. "See if Cindy needs her babes minded, or any other job done. And if they don't, then we can go by Turners'—"

"Get some o' them eggs," Liz Ellen interjected, running down the ladder rungs without using her hands at all. "You reckon Sister Holden would send you home with some dinner?"

Maggie frowned. "Well, sometimes she does."

"See if you can let her know you'd like it."

Maggie's frown deepened. "I don't like plaguing people for favors and charity."

Liz Ellen grimaced. "Don't guess you've got the sauce to be so choosy. Not when you're living here. There's our dinner for today." She nodded at a few potatoes and onions, which were scattered along the wall behind the water barrel. "Davy and Scotch'll be taking the heifer and her babe out for grazing. I'm to split wood for the Higbees."

Maggie stared at her. "You split wood?"

Liz Ellen bared her forearm and made a muscle. "Rent earned in wood splitted and spades of dirt."

"Fine." Maggie swallowed. "Got anything for breakfast, then? I could make up some porridge."

"If you think you could get some." Liz Ellen nodded. "Them potatoes're breakfast too."

"And supper?" Giovanna piped up, grinning like it was all a joke.

Liz Ellen grinned back. "Supper too."

"Really?" Maggie felt her heart grow suddenly heavy.

Liz Ellen shrugged. "We find enough most times. Don't worry."

Don't worry, Maggie repeated to herself.

That was likely.

She knelt down and fingered one of the potatoes. "Reckon I can make hash."

"Make some for yourself and Gigi. We're not much used to eating breakfast. Be much obliged if you have dinner waiting, though."

"Giovanna," Maggie corrected. "We'll see what . . . we can do." She stared at the potatoes for a long minute. The onions had that shrivelly look they got when they were past their prime.

She shuddered. "C'mon, Giovanna. Let's go off to the Holdens', then. Oh," she remembered, turning around abruptly. "Liz Ellen."

"Yeah."

"Don't tell nobody me and Giovanna are here, all right?"

Liz Ellen stopped lacing her boots and raised an eyebrow.

"What?" Maggie snapped. "I got my reasons."

"Just, that's going to be a mighty hard secret to keep, with you coming and going and the way people run their mouths off about anything new around here."

"Doesn't have to be secret. Just don't run *your* mouth off about it is what I'm asking."

Liz Ellen gave Maggie a foul look. "Next time I'm sipping tea and 'broidering with Sister Wall, I'll try to recollect to keep my lips zipped."

Maggie frowned back. "Fine," she said.

Giovanna giggled and followed Maggie out the door.

That girl will burn every bridge with that mouth of hers. Maggie shook her head and stalked through the field toward the road.

Giovanna skipped, and beat her to the road.

She thinks it's a fun adventure. I just hope I can keep it that way. The thought of dinner loomed over her like a rain cloud.

Cindy Holden seemed taken aback to open the door and find Maggie and Giovanna there. Two copper-haired children leaned around her skirts. Their faces lit up when the saw Maggie.

"Hi," the little boy ventured. "I made a new boat. You want to see it?"

"Hi. Sorry." Maggie looked at Cindy. Her mouth suddenly felt dry. "Just wanted to come by and see if you might need some tending for your babes."

Cindy pursed her lips. "Not today," she said.

"All right." Maggie turned around in the doorway. She felt her face reddening.

Sister Holden put a warm hand on her shoulder. "Don't go, though. I could use your help if you've got some time to burn. My henhouse could use some cleaning. It's a disaster, haven't been able to get to it for a month. And I've got a garden needs weeding too. With all these little ones, I don't get out of the house to do much outside work, and Shedrick's busy with the surveying and other town business. I could give you dinner."

Maggie turned back around slowly. "Do you reckon," she said, clearing her throat, "you could make it lunch we could bring with us?"

Cindy frowned. "Sure," she said. "Well, all right. Shovel's in the shed out back. Giovanna, I think you'd better do the weeding. Are you all right mucking the henhouse yourself, Maggie?"

"I've done it a time or two before." It came out terser than Maggie had intended. "Thank you, ma'am," she added.

"Let me give you something to go over your dress."

"Guess it don't matter," Maggie said dully. She didn't wait for a reply; she just walked around back toward the shed.

This is what I've come to. Just as Ma Alden foresaw, I've ended in doing others' work, at their charity. I reckon it's meant to be.

She grabbed the shovel and opened the henhouse door, and then grimaced at the smell.

At least it hadn't rained recently. But Cindy Holden hadn't been lying when she said it was a disaster.

Maggie got into the rhythm of the task: heave, and dump. Heave, and dump. Around her, chickens clucked and crooned, pecking at the floor, their feet black with mud. One flapped its wings wildly as it took off from its perch up near the ceiling, nearly colliding with Maggie's chest.

She got to the middle of the room when rain started pattering on the roof. She wiped a drip of sweat off her temple and continued, taking buckets of dirty straw and mud and chicken droppings out to the garbage heap until the floor was cleared.

She walked up to the back door and knocked.

Cindy opened it and stuck her head out. "Lands, its coming down, isn't it? Come on inside and warm up."

"Let me put the straw down first. Is Giovanna in there?"

"She's playing with the boys. Weeded out about a quarter of the garden. I'm going to give them some dinner, soon."

"Still don't mind if we take ours with us?"

Cindy gave Maggie a considering look. "Why? You all right?"

"Fine, ma'am."

"Sure." Sister Holden's intense gaze raked Maggie, who tried not to squirm. "Well, go ahead and finish then—straw's in the lean-to. Then come in, and I'll send you home with a basket."

"Thank you."

The job was soon completed, but Maggie was soaked through by the time she finished. She managed to keep most of the straw dry by moving fast across the yard with the barrow, but her quick feet made the mud spatter on her skirt.

"Here you are, then," Cindy said, handing Giovanna a basket with a napkin on top. It smelled strongly of chicken; Maggie's stomach rumbled. "If you need anything, be sure to let me know, Maggie."

"Fine." Maggie walked after her sister. She kept her head down as they walked along the streets, hoping nobody would say anything to her. She walked so fast, she almost kept up with Giovanna's skipping.

"Hey-O!"

The familiar call came just before Maggie and Giovanna turned into the field to walk to the little Hoster cabin.

Maggie sighed when she saw Henry's unmistakable lean figure loping toward them. He looked ridiculous. He was even more skinny and long in a giant overcoat and mud-encrusted boots. His sopping felt hat, with the brim drooping down to his neck in back and stuck to his cheeks in front, made him seem to Maggie like an overgrown mushroom.

Maggie's heart was thrumming in her temples. Sam's face swam into her mind, though she tried to keep the words out of her head.

Henry fancies you, you know.

And Ma Alden's voice saying, *What are you going to turn out to be anyway, Maggie, the rate you're going? Laundress? Help? You've no prospects.*

She could pretend she didn't hear him, couldn't she?

Would it make matters worse if she just walked on by?

Giovanna decided the matter by whipping around and calling out. "Henry! How are you? We're staying over at—"

Maggie put a hand on her shoulder and hushed her. "Hi," she said. "Just bringing a hamper over to Hosters'."

It wasn't quite a lie.

Henry strode up to her, hands in his pockets. "Hello."

"Hi," Maggie managed again. He smelled like the rain, and like new-split wood. Maggie ran her thumb over the brim of the basket she held, staring at the cloth that covered the lumps of chicken wings and thighs. "How's the fishing lately?"

Henry touched her shoulder lightly. His fingers seemed as warm as coals through the soaked cotton of her shirt. "You don't have a wrap on. You're soaked through—both of you." He put an arm around Giovanna and squeezed her up against his side, making her giggle. "Should I walk along with you? I'll be your coat."

Maggie folded her arms over her chest and managed a small smile. "Forgot them at the Aldens'. Rain came down pretty fast."

"Started a while ago." He chuckled and looked down at her dress, which had giant mud splashes all the way up to the waistband. "And what you been doing? Wrestling chickens?"

"Sort of. You—you're not in all that fine a state yourself."

"Well, I've been splitting wood." He shrugged. "Wind took a tree down over by Twelveses' new barn. Reckon I can go get some of it. I know, I'll bring some to the Hosters. Come with me. I'll go get the cart and load some up, and you two can ride. We'll drop our loads together."

"No, thanks," Maggie said hastily, before Giovanna could speak. "We're—we've got to get a move on."

"All right," Henry replied. He fidgeted with his hat, taking it off, putting it on, and twisting the brim. He shoved his fists back into his trouser pockets. "Well, won't keep you, then."

"All right." Maggie's gaze was trained, once more, on her basket. "See you later."

She waited for Henry to turn the corner before she stepped into the Higbees' field. The high, wet grasses didn't do any more damage to her skirts, wet through as they were. When she got to the door, the Hoster boys had already flung it open, jumping up and down and exclaiming over the food.

Maggie hurried in and set the basket on the floor in front of the hearth. She grabbed a chicken leg and a biscuit before she unlaced her boots and set them by the fire to dry. It was a good thing, too; there was nothing left to grab within a minute. Giovanna chortled, stuffing her mouth with chicken and biscuits along with the two boys. Liz Ellen wolfed hers down with a small degree more delicacy than the others.

Maggie sat, picking at her food, in front of the fire. She had no other skirt to change into. She suddenly realized what this would mean. She would either have to keep wearing it, continually getting it more filthy, or she would have to haul in some water and wash it and wait for it to dry, wearing nothing all the while, or she'd have to go for a swim.

Suddenly she regretted her joke, made so long ago, about the Hosters killing the fish in the Provo River.

"I'm still hungry," Giovanna complained.

"I'll make some potatoes," Maggie said.

"Sounds fine." Liz Ellen licked her fingers. She stood and pulled off her sodden wool shawl. She hung it on a nail by the door, where it dripped, making a puddle on the floor. "I'm thinking I'm done splitting for the day. Wanted to get some for us too, but it's too wet out there. I was getting chilled. We'll just have to stir up the coals real good and bring down the blankets from the loft."

Maggie thought of Henry's offer of wood but didn't say anything.

The potatoes took a while to boil over the low heat coming from the embers, and Maggie had to hold the pot close to the heat. Her arms ached and her skin, so close to the heat, felt like it might blister.

"I can rig something," Liz Ellen said. "Not used to this refined cookin'. We usually just toss the taters in the fire and dig'em out when they're done." She rushed out the back door, coming back moments later with two cross-sections of box-elder stump. She set these in the fire. The moisture of them caused the coals to hiss. Liz Ellen set the pot on these.

"They won't burn as fast," she said. "Reckon the potatoes will be done by the time they do."

"Aren't you worried about blackening the pot?"

"Ain't hoity-toity enough to care," Liz Ellen snapped.

Maggie frowned, a sharp remark on her tongue, but the look in Liz Ellen's eyes quelled her.

A knock sounded on the door.

Maggie froze, thinking of Ma Alden and Uncle Forth. "Giovanna," she whispered. "Get up in the loft."

Giovanna frowned. "No," she said.

"Giovanna," Maggie hissed, "you do as I say or you'll—I'll . . ."

What? It was on Giovanna's face—the curious tilt of her eyebrows, the amused purse of her mouth. *You'll what, Maggie? You're not my ma. You wouldn't lick me, either.*

Liz Ellen too got a wary look on her face. "Yeah?" she called out, opening the door a crack.

"Henry Clegg here. You folks have a need for firewood?"

Maggie's heart began pounding so fast, she felt it might explode. "C'mon, Giovanna," she hissed at her sister. She jerked her head in the direction of the loft.

Giovanna looked at Maggie like she was crazy. "It's just *Henry*, Megs."

The door opened wide, revealing Henry's comically drenched figure. "It's out in the cart," he said, stepping inside. "I've covered it with the canvas, but if we leave it out there much longer—oh." He looked at Maggie, and confusion flickered across his face.

"Hi, Henry!" Giovanna called out cheerfully. "Wish we'd'a saved you some chicken. None left."

"Hello, Giovanna," Henry said. "That's all right. I'm still full from dinner." He turned to Maggie. "You—you're . . ." His gaze rested on Maggie's bare feet and then on her boots, steaming by the fire.

"Hello," was all Maggie could manage.

Henry stood there for a full minute, looking thunderstruck. Slowly, he took his hat off. "You don't have any grub left, then?" he asked.

"Maggie's boiling some potatoes," Giovanna offered. "Won't be much, though. You said you was full."

Henry nodded, his glance flicking to the pot. He turned then, toward the fire, and stretched. "Tiring, splitting wood," he said. "I'm wet through. I could use a set in front of the fire, assuming you don't mind, Liz Ellen." He looked up at the loft. "That where you all plan to sleep tonight?" He looked sidelong at Maggie.

Maggie shrugged. "Hosters sleep up there. Cozy, ain't it? Well, thanks for coming. I'm sure the splitting will be much appreciated. I'm sure your ma'll be wanting you for supper, soon—no need to stay and eat so poor a meal as boiled potatoes when you've got Ma Clegg's kind of dinner waiting you."

"Don't mind," Henry said bluntly, throwing himself onto the hard-packed floor in front of the fire. "Boiled potatoes sound right tasty. Supper's a long way off."

Maggie stared at him. So, he knew, then. Knew they were staying at the Hosters'. So why was he sticking around? Did he *want* to see her, humiliated? Was this some kind of revenge for something? The way she'd talked to him after the Walls' husking bee, maybe? Had Sam told him what she said at the wedding dance?

"Maybe you should go on home," Maggie said.

"Don't reckon I will," Henry replied, holding her gaze.

"Well, I for one don't mind sharing a few moldy potatoes," Liz Ellen spoke up. "But there really ain't much to go 'round. Do you think your ma'd be willing to—"

"Shut," Maggie snapped.

"No, that's a right fine idea." Henry said. "I'll go get some grub and bring it back. And then we can tell campfire stories," he added, ruffling Giovanna's matted head. "I heard a real frightening one the other day. Give you bad dreams for a week."

The two Hoster boys looked up from their whittling with interest.

"Ooooh," Giovanna grinned.

"Be back in two shakes."

"What's wrong with you?" Maggie cried after the door shut behind him. "Don't you got any pride? I can't believe you'd just ask for food like that."

"Ain't got a chip on my shoulder the size of a boulder," Liz Ellen retorted. "And I don't know about you, but that was mighty lean pickings, what Ma Holden sent home with you."

"She ain't your ma!" Maggie yelled. "And it wasn't like she knew she was feeding the five of us, was it?"

"Well, why didn't you tell her then?" Liz Ellen yelled back.

"Because—*oh*!" Maggie shook her head, grinding her teeth together so that her jaw hurt. "You don't know what decent folks is like." She turned away from Liz Ellen and began removing the boiled potato pieces from the pot, carefully, with two long sticks.

"Just dump the whole mess out the back door and pick 'em up," Liz Ellen snapped.

Maggie didn't trust herself to speak. She continued picking out the potatoes one by one.

Suddenly a pair of hands grabbed the handles, and the pot was whisked off the fire. Maggie stood, open-mouthed, and watched Liz Ellen fling open the back door and toss out the potatoes and water, letting the pot clatter to the ground as well.

"I don't reckon," Liz Ellen said slowly, "that I need lip from you, Maggie, about what decent folk ought to be. Maybe you don't know what it's like to go two days without food, but you start to feel less picky about begging when you see it happen to your little brothers. I reckon since I've given you a place to sleep and food to eat, you don't owe me any lip at all."

Maggie felt frustration, anger, and then despair overtake her, in quick succession. "I'm sorry," she said.

"Well." Liz Ellen nodded and went outside and began picking up the potatoes.

Maggie followed her and began picking them up too.

They thudded into the metal pot. "I was going to save the potato water. It makes good bread," she ventured finally.

"Right," Liz Ellen nodded again. "If we had any wheat to make it with."

"Oh," Maggie replied.

"S'pose you could spend a day at the mill and get some."

Maggie swallowed and pushed the picture of herself, begging at the mill, from her mind. "I suppose I could. Do your hands hurt?"

Liz Ellen shrugged. "They got a little burned. Nothing that won't heal in a day or two."

Henry came back with the promised food. Maggie held back, accepting only a small biscuit, which she nibbled, watching Henry. The fire lit up his face in an odd way, making sharp lines of his cheekbones, making his long, light-colored hair seem on fire. His expressions were fascinating as he created the characters in his stories. He stood and gestured enthusiastically when it came to a dramatic point.

"I'm going to head home," he said abruptly when he had finished a third story. "Maggie, walk with me?"

Maggie shrugged, feeling her heart speed up. Would he read her the riot act? Tell her he was going to tell his ma on her, tell the Aldens where they were? "All right. Reckon you're scared to walk home in the dark after all that," she said, trying to play it off lightly.

"Giovanna, you coming with us? I'll walk you home to the Aldens'."

Maggie sighed. *He isn't going to let up on me until I say it right out, is he?* She avoided his gaze. "She'll be fine here for now."

Henry nodded. "You're staying here tonight, then."

Maggie didn't say anything in response. She pulled on

her boots, feeling her face burn, feeling that pricking in the corners of her eyes. *I'm not going to cry*, she told herself fiercely. *Not in front of Henry.*

They went out the door and walked through the tall, wet weeds. They sprung back and lashed at Maggie, spraying her with icy droplets.

They were silent all the way out to the street. Maggie studied her feet as she walked. Her arms were folded over her chest. She was trying not to shiver.

A length of wool dropped over her shoulders. It had a musty smell because of the wet, but it also smelled like fresh-cut wood.

"Thanks," Maggie rasped, tugging Henry's cloak closer to her.

"Welcome, anytime."

"I know, Henry. Thanks. You must be cold, though."

"I'll be fine."

They walked for a block or so. Maggie couldn't bring herself to look at Henry, though he walked close beside her, close enough, almost, that she could feel the warmth emanating from his body.

"Are you in trouble, Maggie?" Henry's tone was light, but the questioned curled like smoke, thick and pungent between them.

Maggie kept her pace steady. "Don't reckon," she managed finally.

"See here, Megs," Henry said. He grabbed her shoulder, turning her to face him. "Maggie, stop just a minute, will you? Look at me."

"Why?" Maggie forced herself to look up at him. She folded her arms even more tightly around herself. "I don't know what to say to you, Henry. I'm not sure what I'm doing nor what I should be doing, nor that I should be keeping any sort o' company with you t'all."

Henry's face seemed, to Maggie, to collapse. His eyes grew heavy with something, and his mouth fell in tired, sad lines. "Now, why not, Mag?"

Maggie couldn't stand to keep looking at him, looking like that. She looked back down at her shoes. "I ain't decent, Henry. Never was, but now I'm really not. I'm—I'm sleeping with cows, now. And your ma has been so kind to me, so generous. I don't think I could pay her back by . . . bringing you to not-decent company."

The silence spread out between them again. It seemed to pulse. Maggie thought she could hear her own heart beating in her ears.

"Well," Henry finally said. His voice was raw with something—anger? Hurt? "That's a load of quack, Maggie. What are you yammering on about now? Decent company? Who've you been talking to you, telling you that you ain't decent for a little mud and fishing now and again?"

"Well, fishing and mud, I'm decent for. But if you've—at Etta's wedding, Samuel was dancing with me, and . . ." Maggie couldn't bring herself to say it.

"Even the Brethren come up in favor of dancing, Megs. You looked right pretty, by the way. I'm sorry I missed the chance to dance with you."

Maggie felt her face flush, as she looked again at his face. "No, I know dancing's fine. You know I'm not—I'm not like that, prissy and worried about things like dancing. What I'm *trying* say is I'm not somebody you ought to court, Henry. Don't think your ma would—"

"Mag," Henry growled. "Nobody's asking. If Samuel said something on the subject to you, he was out of line, and

I'll tan his hide. So just stop. All right? We can go on being friends and friends alone, that's fine. I can see," he gestured back in the direction they had come, "you got a lot on your plate right now. Reckon your mind's as mixed up and scattered as a lost herd, so don't worry over it."

"Right. I won't, then. Thanks." But somehow Maggie didn't feel all that thankful or relieved. *What's wrong with me?* She wanted to shout the question out to the universe.

"And you need to trust I won't, either, for a while at least." He shrugged. "Just let me be your friend, all right?"

Suddenly, there was a giant ache in Maggie's chest. She looked up, stared up into Henry's lean face, with its funny crags and shadows. He wasn't looking at her. He was staring into nothing, his eyes fixed on something in the distance, looking over her shoulder. Still, his eyes were blinding, clear pools of gray reflecting moonlight.

"All right," she whispered.

"All right." Henry's gaze shifted to her, and he grinned. Then his grin fell away again. He began walking. "Ma's waiting on me, I think."

She scrambled to keep up with him.

"So what's going on, then, Maggie? I'll keep it in confidence."

Maggie nodded and swallowed. "I—we left the Aldens'."

"All right." Henry nodded too. "Don't reckon I should ask why; that's your business."

Maggie shrugged.

"Any chance, though, I could persuade you to move on over to my ma's place, 'stead o' sleeping in a crowded loft? And don't say anything about decent company. My ma's always going on about you. She likes you, Mag."

Maggie shook her head, and the confusion overtook her

mind to the point where the world felt like it might spin out of place. Why would Sister Clegg like *her*? After what she had done, after the times she'd broken down in front of her, blubbering like a baby, acting like a crazy person, and cluttering about with stolen china in her apron.

Who was Maggie, that anybody would like her, especially right now? Ma Alden's words, Henry's, Samuel's, and Uncle Forth's (*you dirt-faced Italian chit*) raced through Maggie's mind.

Maggie stopped in the middle of the road and turned away from Henry, trying to keep a hold on her emotions. She felt tears on her face.

He took her shoulder again and gently tugged her around to face him.

It was unreal, as he looked at her. Like they were two dream characters. She began to shiver, her teeth chattering in her head of their own accord.

"Oh, consarn it!" His breath steamed in the icy air, and there was moisture in his eyes too; Maggie could see it. "Don't cry, Maggie, please. You'll be fine. I'm not saying you can't shift it. Just know if you need, there's a place for you and Giovanna at the Cleggs'. Consarn it," he said again, his voice cracking. "Don't cry. I didn't mean nothing by it, whatever happened is your own business, Megs, and I suppose I can wait until you're ready to tell me about it. I know you got your pride. I promise I won't tread on it again. All right?"

He tugged on one of the long jacket sleeves, bringing her closer to him, and then he caught the other one, and drew her to his chest. His long arms crossed over her back and his fingers dug into each of her shoulders. Maggie couldn't quite believe it, the warmth of his chest against her face, the hardness of his lean, muscled arms at her back.

He held her for a moment, rocking her a little, and then pulled her away from his chest. He held her at arm's length, giving her shoulders a little shake. "Maggie?"

Maggie's lips trembled. She gave a tiny nod.

Henry sighed, and the corners of his lips curled up a little, a half-smile. "Come over to my ma's tomorrow at least. She missed you today."

Maggie nodded again. She felt her body turn away; she couldn't look at his face—the way he felt, against her, so warm; those hard arms around her, like he might squeeze the life out of her, or like he was holding something precious—and not do something completely humiliating, completely embarrassing. What were these strange thoughts in her head, these strange impulses?

"I'll see you, then."

"See you, Henry."

I'm broken, Maggie thought as she walked away, and her legs seemed to take off running of their own accord. She ran faster and faster and didn't stop until she reached the little cabin. She stood there for a moment, her blood pumping.

She opened the door and stepped inside and realized that she was still wearing Henry's jacket like an ungainly, sodden cape.

Liz Ellen poked her head over the edge of the loft.

Maggie looked up at her.

The two girls gazed silently at each other for a moment, and then Liz Ellen withdrew her head. Maggie heard the sound of her hushing her brothers and rustling hay.

"Are you coming to bed, Maggie?" Giovanna called.

"In a minute." Maggie stretched out in front of the fire, pulling Henry's coat over her. Her mind and heart raced.

Eventually her breathing slowed and the room grew hazy. She didn't even notice when Giovanna crept down and tucked one of the ratty old quilts around her.

A CLOSE CALL

Maggie woke when it was still dark. She felt strange, and her back ached. She sat up and suddenly remembered. It was Henry's coat that brought it back—completely dry now, but still smelling of fresh-cut wood.

Maggie's stomach crawled as a picture flashed into her mind—herself, up against Henry's chest, and his arms around her. It tied her insides in knots, and breakfast didn't seem very important.

I promised to help Sister Clegg, she remembered. *Should I go?*

She wanted to go. She had a strange feeling inside, an excitement, something that made her want to cry and laugh at herself at the same time. She was wrong—so, so wrong—to be feeling this way. Sister Clegg had done so much for her. And she had to think of that, think of what other people might think about what had happened between Henry and Maggie last night.

Or it could be I'm being a ninny. He just saw I was cold.

And was sorry for me. And I'm making a lot more of things than I need to.

Or could be all this is just my mind mixed up from all that's happened lately. Could be I just felt safe, when I haven't felt safe lately, and so I just feel safe with Henry, and . . .

Maggie shook her head. It was too much to think about. She wanted to be able to step out of herself and relax for a few minutes, to leave her body, so full of racing thoughts and pumping blood and knotted stomach and a back and neck tense from the previous two days' worry.

She had to think about what was important. And that was what she was going to do. She had Giovanna to think of.

Was she going to do something to let the Aldens know where she was? If she did, would they come back for her, force her to live with them? Could they do that? Would someone back her? Sister Clegg, or Sister Holden, maybe?

Not likely. They were too genteel to interfere like that. They would let Maggie and the Aldens fight their own battle. Would Henry back Maggie and Giovanna? Maggie's heart raced at the thought of having Henry as a defender, but then she remembered he wasn't much of a defense when it came to Uncle Forth and Jed.

And any moment, Maggie would see one of them. This town was too small for it to not happen before long. And then what would she do, or say? What was her plan?

Maggie groaned and lay back down, pulling the coat up over her head. She hadn't gotten enough sleep. Her mind needed more rest before it was going to run smoothly, give her thoughts and feelings she could actually work with.

She gave up after about fifteen minutes. There was no going back to sleep right now. She stood and filled the pot with water, then stirred the coals and added some kindling, just for something to do. She had nothing to cook.

The straw in the loft stirred, and Liz Ellen's long legs appeared over the side. Nimbly and silently, she dropped to the floor and padded across to the fire. She shivered, patting her arms. "Thanks for getting the fire on. Soon we'll have to keep it going all night. That or curl up around Ma." She nodded in the direction of the cow and gave Maggie a sideways, mischievous look.

"Oh, you don't really sleep next to her," Maggie protested.

Liz Ellen pursed her lips. "Well, now, haven' tried it yet. Doesn't mean we won't need to sometime."

"How do you stand it, Liz?" Maggie burst out suddenly.

Liz Ellen frowned, gesturing with her head in the direction of the loft.

"Sorry," Maggie continued in a quieter tone. "I mean, don't you care what nobody thinks of you?"

Liz Ellen grimaced. It was the best one Maggie had ever seen, with fearsome wrinkles all up her nose like a dog has when it bears its teeth. "I don't care about nobody except Scotch and Dave," Liz said. "Hey, are you going over to Cleggs' today?"

Maggie sighed.

"Reckon you could get a better dinner out of Betsy. She's generous in her portions. Just . . . if you were up to deciding."

"I'll go over to the Cleggs'." Maggie felt her spine tingle with nervousness, and also something else—the same perplexing feeling that she'd had since the night before and had her insides all in knots. "She's been having me work for dresses. Says she needs womanly help 'round the house. Now I've learnt to sew a straight seam at least, I s'pose I can do something for Ma Clegg. Not feel so much like I'm begging."

Liz Ellen punched Maggie's shoulder so hard that Maggie stifled a shout.

"What was that for?" Maggie hissed.

Liz Ellen shrugged. "Boulder." She touched Maggie's shoulder, lightly this time.

"I'll head out, then," Maggie announced after she had pulled on her boots. "Could you send Giovanna along when she wakes?"

"Fine," Liz Ellen said.

"Could you—" Maggie hesitated. "Could you walk her over, please? Just to the Cleggs' door. Is it on your way?"

"Not really," Liz replied. "But don't worry on it, I'll get Giovanna over there safe and sound so's you can watch her like a dog at a ground squirrel's hole."

Maggie bit her lip to keep from retorting. "Thanks." She pulled on Henry's cloak and walked out the door, keeping the woolen hem of it above the knee-length grasses. Her skirt was half-soaked by the time she reached the road. She stopped there for a moment, hesitating.

No, she had to go ahead with this chore. She had to—her guilt would not let her sleep, and she needed sleep.

She began walking in the direction of the Aldens' place.

When she got to the long, white fence, she was relieved to see Pa Alden out there, standing in the fields. She wouldn't have to go looking for him, or for Patience, as she had thought she would, and so she wouldn't have to risk coming up against Ma Alden or Uncle Forth.

She stepped over the fence, carefully disentangling her skirts from the staggered little posts, and began walking toward him.

His long, lean figure turned toward her, and then, to Maggie's utter astonishment, broke into a trot. "Where've you been, Maggie-girl?" he asked when they were within talking distance. "Your ma's been worried sick over you and Giovanna. Why'd you run off like that?" He grasped her arms, pulled her in close, and gave her a fierce hug.

Feeling the rough wool of his coat up against her cheek, Maggie felt overwhelmed, and utterly perplexed. She had no idea . . .

No idea.

She felt a lump come to her throat as she looked up at him. "Sorry."

"Patience told me you had a bit of tussle with Jed," Pa Alden offered, pulling her away from him and examining her face. "Did Dale scare you, Mag? I could have a word with him."

Maggie felt all her anger and horror return as the picture of what happened swam back into her mind. She clenched her fists, tight, inside the long coat sleeves that covered them and stifled a sudden urge to laugh hysterically at the thought of Pa Alden having a "word" with Uncle Forth. "No, thanks. Thing is, I think we're going to stay where we're at. For a while, at least."

Pa Alden's face became a little bit grim. It surprised Maggie; she had never seen any strong emotion cross his features lately.

"Stay—where?" he asked. "Why, Maggie?"

"I—I don't feel safe."

"Not safe?" He shook his head. "You've always been safe here."

"I think Giovanna and I need some time away from some people 'round here."

Pa Alden frowned and studied his hands. "I'll tan that little son-of-a-gun, sure thing, I will."

"Um," she said, floored by his language, by his words. What was this? "Well, Pa. I just came by so's you and Patience and—and Ma could know Giovanna and I are somewhere safe, and you don't have to worry on us."

"Where are you staying, Maggie?" Pa Alden asked again.

"I don't reckon I'll say just yet."

Pa Alden raised his eyebrows. "All right, then, I promise I won't come breaking down your door and drag you back. I know what it is not to feel safe, and you can come on back when you're ready. But I'd like to look in a time or two? Make sure my girls are taken care of."

It was more than Pa Alden had said to Maggie in a long time. Hearing the concern in his voice almost broke her down. She could come back, and Giovanna, and they'd have Pa Alden, at least, to help them, to keep them safe . . .

Maggie shook her head at the thought. Pa Alden would never stand up to his wife. Least of all, Uncle Forth. And looking at his emaciated arms and hollow face, she was fairly certain it would be impossible for Pa Alden to tan anybody's hide. Least of all Jed's.

But his being closed-mouthed about something, that she could trust.

"We're staying with the Hoster kids, over in the Higbees' old log cabin," she said. "'Cross the field from their brick house. If you can . . . ," she hesitated.

"Yes?"

Maggie scraped a line in the mud with her toe. "Please keep it from Ma long as you can. And Jed and Uncle Forth too. I know she's like to find out no matter what, with the way people talk 'round here, but I'd like to have a good head on my shoulders before I talk to her about it."

"Fine, Maggie."

Maggie gave him a kind of pursed half-smile and nodded. “Thanks, Pa.”

“See you sometime soon, then. All right if I tell Patience at least?

Maggie winced and nodded.

When she got back to the road, she quickened her pace almost to a run and didn’t stop until she came up to the Cleggs’ wide steps.

It was odd—surreal, almost—to be let in at the first knock by Sister Clegg, to receive her broad grin and sit down in the same chair that she had for the last few weeks, nearly every day. It was almost like stepping back into the real world, where Uncle Forth and the Hosters had all been a strange dream.

The only jarring note was when Sister Clegg’s glance passed over Henry’s coat, which Maggie still wore.

She didn’t say a word, however. She took it from Maggie’s shoulders and laid it by the fire to dry. “Want some breakfast? I’ve just got porridge on.”

Maggie nodded. The gnaw in her stomach wouldn’t let her do anything else.

She was finishing the last spoonful when a loud rap sounded on the door. Sister Clegg went to open it and found Liz Ellen and Giovanna. Giovanna tripped into the room and immediately claimed a spot on the hearth.

“Come on in.” Sister Clegg nodded at Liz Ellen.

“Naw.” Liz eyed Maggie’s porridge bowl with regret. “Got some splitting to do, and then I have to muck out the Higbees’ barn.”

“Can’t your brothers do that kind of thing?”

“Naw. They’re just eight and five, not big enough yet. But they’re a good help with carrying the wheelbarrows, and Scotch tends Ma and her babe.”

"The cow," Maggie said quietly at Sister Clegg's perplexed look. "And her calf."

"Ah." Sister Clegg nodded. "Well, Maggie, if you're staying with the Hoster kids for a while . . ." She let her voice trail off like it was a question.

Maggie managed a small nod. She stirred her spoon in the empty bowl.

I'm in for it now, she thought. *A whole passel of questions that I can't come near to answering.*

"Well then, I'll send Maggie and Giovanna home with enough supper to feed you all, and I hope you'll come by here for a bit of dinner, Liz Ellen."

"Supper might be just fine," Liz said. "Generally have some dinner with Higbees, though. But if Ma Higbee can't spare a bite, my brothers and I'll take you up on it. Thanks." She nodded and ran back down the steps.

Giovanna sat across from Maggie at the table and ate her porridge with enough gusto and obvious enjoyment to make Maggie feel supremely guilty.

"I've got some things for you to work on today, Giovanna," Sister Clegg announced when both bowls were clean.

Giovanna sat on a little stool by the stove, and Maggie took her normal place in the rocker next to the loom. She rocked and darned, rocked and hemmed, rocked and knit a little, and pieced together some quilt squares. The rocking was soothing to Maggie's frazzled nerves, and the sewing was soothing in a way too. It was a task to concentrate all of her mind on, so that she didn't have to think much of other things. Her hemlines and stitches had grown straighter lately, though she still got the yarn tangled up in the knitting needles at least once every two rows.

Maggie looked across the room at the coat lying on the hearth and tried not to think of Henry.

Would he be in sometime soon? She thought maybe he would come home for lunch.

That line of thinking began to twist her stomach back into knots again, so she kept her mind away from it as best she could. Still the thought hovered, teasing her and keeping her hyper-aware of her surroundings; every tap on the floor, every creak of a settling board and Maggie's eyes turned toward the door.

When Henry did finally saunter in, Maggie felt like something in her might burst. He didn't look very nice; his hair was plastered to his head, and he wore an old buckskin coat that Maggie remembered from the previous year.

Henry shot little wink in her direction. "Caught some fine trout," he said. "Rain brings 'em out. Reckon you're sick of them yet, Ma?"

"Better than salt pork," Sister Clegg replied. "Come over here, son. You need to warm up by the fire before you wash up for dinner."

One by one, all the Clegg men tramped in, leaving their boots at the door, and lining the walls of the main room. Moses came in with his father, chatting about a carpentry project. Samuel came in, did a theatrical double take, and grinned at Maggie, then pinched Giovanna's cheek before he filled a plate with food and lounged on the floor, his back to the wall.

Hannah whisked through the door and into another room, and then came out carrying a tousled, protesting Jerry. "C'mon, let's get us some food," she crooned to him and sat him on her lap to feed him.

Hyrum walked in. He gave Maggie a smile and said hello to Giovanna as he came in.

Maggie watched Henry ladle potatoes into his plate.

"Haven't touched your food," Giovanna said. "Aren't you hungry, Maggie?"

Maggie flushed, feeling caught in the act, and began taking little bites. Her mouth felt dry, and the food going down was like sawdust. She tried not to squirm, but she felt supremely uncomfortable with all the Cleggs surrounding her. She wondered what they must be thinking. Did any of them think, as Samuel did, that Henry liked her? What did they think of her, if he did?

She turned and watched Sister Clegg, who was laughing at something her husband had said.

It was too worrisome. She wished she could see into people's heads, draw out their thoughts, examine and untangle them like skeins of thread.

The chatter and the merriment made Maggie relax after a little while. She even managed to chuckle at a story Samuel was telling about something that had happened up in Kolob, which was the name people gave the hidden quarters for the city legion, up in the canyon. But she didn't try to get in on any conversation.

She glanced at Henry again and found him watching her. She looked away quickly, feeling her face turn red.

Henry stayed inside for a little while after everyone else finished. He sat in front of the fire, fussing with something—it looked like a broken bridle—and chatted with Maggie, Giovanna, and his mother. After about an hour, he left.

"Going back to the orchards to pull off the leftover fruit and prune the branches," he said as he left. As if someone in the room needed an explanation.

It seemed oppressively silent for the rest of the afternoon. To Maggie, the weight of things unspoken—the million things she wanted to explain, the things she was sure Sister Clegg was curious about, things *Maggie* was curious about, worries that she was stuffing to the back of her mind—bore down on her, making her head ache and her spine prickle.

When it came time to leave, Sister Clegg handed both Maggie and Giovanna a basket with rolls, chicken, and boiled eggs.

"Thank you," Maggie said timidly. "I'll be back tomorrow morning, then?"

Sister Clegg nodded. "Appreciate the help. I've got a lot to get done before colder weather sets in." She took Henry's coat from the hearth and laid it on Maggie's shoulders matter-of-factly.

"Oh, you don't—I've got a shawl . . . at . . . at home," Maggie protested, her face red.

Sister Clegg waved her protests away. "It's been by the fire all day. It's dry now, and all warmed up for you—bet it will stay warm all the way home if you leave right now. And I suppose you don't want to go after your shawl right now."

Maggie smiled painfully. "Thanks."

"Don't mention it."

"Doesn't Henry need—"

"Henry's got plenty of things to bundle up in. I'll see about an old wrap for Giovanna tomorrow."

"I really ought to go get hers from the Aldens'."

Sister Clegg shrugged. "No real need for that, though. We've got plenty and to spare. I like the blessings giving brings. I think that wool will stay warmed up most of the way home if you set off quickly."

Home, Maggie thought as she and Giovanna stepped down the steps. *We both said it and meant different things. Which is true, right now?*

When they reached the street, Maggie held open the coat, and Giovanna climbed under it. They moved as quickly as they could, trying to keep from stepping on each others' feet, as the rain poured down on them, all the way to the Hosters'.

The week passed in just this way—the day spent at the Cleggs with Giovanna, the evenings up in the loft with the Hoster children. Maggie found time in the morning to clean a little. In the evenings, she began to sit down with some of the Hosters' ratty old garments. Sister Clegg had sent her home one morning with an extra needle and some thread and yarn castoffs, and Scotch Hoster whittled a little darning hook at Maggie's directions. Her mending wasn't the nicest, but Liz Ellen seemed to appreciate Maggie's patch-up jobs. She said, at least, that she didn't mind lumpy stockings. And so, Maggie felt like she might be starting to pull a little of her own weight at the Hosters'.

On Saturday, Maggie went out into the yard and thought about a garden. She wondered how much of the area around the cabin the Hosters could claim, and if there might even be room for a little hutch for hens. She knew the Turners were certainly in the market to trade or sell a setting hen or two.

She was going about counting paces from the cabin to the road when Patience hailed her.

It was like Patience's familiar tones pierced through an alternate reality that Maggie had been cultivating for herself these past weeks. Her voice pierced and completely shattered it. Maggie froze where she was, her heart beating wildly. Images flooded her mind that she had been able to hold off—Uncle Forth's face as he held her there, suspended. The baby in her dream.

Maggie had a sick feeling in her stomach as she watched

Patience fight her way through the tall grasses and emerge in the bald space near the cabin where Maggie had been pacing.

Patience looked Maggie over from head to toe. "You're not soaked to the bone, somehow. Look at my skirts." She held them out away from her, and Maggie could see that they were sopping from the tall grasses.

"There's a path on the other side," Maggie offered. "Hosters generally go out the back way, and come out on D Street. Just on t'other side of the schoolhouse."

Patience's face lit up. "Gigi going to school then? That's a great idea. I've mentioned to Mother—" She seemed to start and then pursed her lips, examining her feet. "How are you?" she tried again, looking at Maggie. "Brought over some onions and celery." She held out a covered basket.

Maggie looked at the basket. "Does she—?"

Patience shook her head. "I just got them from the cellar. Pa said you don't want anyone—don't want Ma—to know where you're at. So I've fended off her questions and fretting. But, Maggie, I think she's really frightened. She was fair mad with fretting the night you left, wondering where you'd got to, and when Pa told her he'd seen you and you were all right, she seemed easier but I *know*, Maggie. I know she's worried over you two. She loves you and wants your safety, no matter how little you think of her."

Maggie shook her head.

Patience stood there, watching Maggie, who was still struggling with her thoughts.

"If you want, you can come in," Maggie finally said. "Giovanna'll be glad to see you."

Maggie proved to be right, though to a degree she hadn't expected. When Patience entered the little cabin, Giovanna's eyes grew wide. Her face slowly crumpled. She walked over and buried her face in Patience's blouse.

Maggie felt her throat thicken, watching her sister.

After a moment or two, Giovanna recovered her usual cheerfulness. She dragged Patience about by the hand, showing her the loft, Ma and her babe, the stove, and the pile of firewood in the little lean-to. "We're keeping house," she said. "I go to Ma Clegg's and learn mending with Maggie now, and I've darned two stockings. See?" She presented Patience with the lumpy results of the darning work that she had spent so long on the night before.

Patience had the grace to admire it. "So," she said. "You getting enough to eat?" She glanced at Maggie, including her in the question.

"We're doing all right," was Maggie's gruff reply. She was sitting next to the stove, up to her elbows in the barrel of water, rinsing out a few pieces of tattered underclothing.

"You're not using soap," Patience observed.

Liz Ellen happened to come in at just that moment. "Don't got any," she answered rudely, giving Patience one of her more accomplished grimaces. It was obvious she'd been doing some dirty job; her skirt was smeared with mud. Her hair was a rat's nest too. She hadn't taken the time to finger-comb it that morning.

Maggie felt her face grow warm.

Patience took Liz's appearance in stride. "You can make soap easy enough using ashes and the drippings from pork fat," she said. "I can show you sometime."

"We don't generally get much meat uncooked," Liz replied, dropping her load of firewood with a resounding clatter. She walked back outside and shut the door, this time with less enthusiasm.

"Ah." Patience nodded at the door, as if Liz Ellen could still hear her. She was quiet for a few minutes, watching Maggie work. "Pa's coming by sometime today." Her tone was casual, as if it were just a minor observation.

"All right," Maggie replied.

"He wants to know before he comes, do you need any help with anything? Supplies, at all?"

Maggie shrugged. "We're doing all right."

"He wanted me to let you know Etta could use your help today."

At this, Maggie stopped scrubbing and met Patience's eyes. "What?"

"Her roof fell in. Sod. The rains made it too heavy—Elias didn't put enough under it to support the weight."

Liz Ellen came in again. A flurry of white came in with her. "Freezing fast," she chattered. "First snow's come, finally. Mag, how long you think my underthings'll take? Can't go out in this without them."

Maggie nodded to the fireplace, where she had draped Liz Ellen's holey long underwear. "Reckon it'll steam dry pretty soon."

"Great," Liz said, shivering.

"What help does Etta need?" Giovanna piped up, setting down her mess of darning and untangling her fingers.

"Move all of her stuff out. Buckets of water to wash the mud out, that kind of thing," Patience replied. "All the Aldens and Forths are over there—"

"No."

"I'm going, Megs." Giovanna's brows drew together. "I want to go see what Etta's house looks like. I've never seen a fallen-in roof before."

"No," Maggie repeated.

The door opened again, and this time it was Pa Alden's lean figure, accompanied by a whirl of wind and snow.

"Shut that door," Liz Ellen snapped, pulling her quilt tighter around her shoulders.

Pa Alden did so and smiled down at Maggie, Patience, and Giovanna. "Looks like you girls are playing at keeping house," he said. "Do you suppose," he turned to Maggie, "you and Giovanna could give us a hand over at Etta's new place? Dale and Ella've got most of the furniture and bedding out, and they're over at the house cleaning and setting Etta and Elias up at the Forths' for the night."

Maggie gritted her teeth and looked down at her hands, which, somehow, had kept busy stitching in spite of the distractions. "We'll stay here and get ready for tonight," she said. "Almost out of firewood, and we don't have anything to put on for supper either."

"I've brought over those onions and celery," Patience reminded her. "With some potatoes you'd be set. And Pa brought a load of firewood. Or at least he said he was going to."

"In the lean-to," Pa Alden replied. "Come help out your family, Maggie-girl. I promise," he added, in a quieter tone, "Ella and Dale're not going back to Etta's tonight. You won't see 'em. And I'll come with you."

"Well, I reckon I don't mind," Liz Ellen said. "You being so neighborly's saved me some frozen hands, going out chopping in this. Didn't plan it so well." She frowned. "We've got to get some wood piled up in that lean-to. Usually I would, but I've been," she shot Maggie a glance, "distracted a bit, these days."

Maggie sighed. "All right," she said. "Bundle up, Giovanna."

Giovanna draped a quilt around her shoulders.

"No," Patience exclaimed. "We'll go and get her wrap. Right now."

"Not right now," Maggie snapped, surprising herself. "I mean, I'm sorry. Could you bring it by sometime? But don't—Ma Alden'll know."

They trudged along D Street, down south past Seventh, Sixth, all the way to First and the edge of town.

Etta's house was a little cabin of rough-cut logs, stacked and chinked with mud. The roof had been made of branches overlaid with sod, but right now there was a gaping hole where the chimney had fallen in.

Maggie stood in the doorway, watching, as Pa Alden instructed Giovanna and the two Hoster boys to pick up all of the stray branches and leaves, twigs, and bits of straw that had fallen over the floor.

"When the big pieces and mud are out, and we have a few dry days, Ella and Etta are going to come by with a broom," he said. "Maggie, Patience, and Liz Ellen, if you could get water from the well out around back there, and be a bucket brigade to wash all this dirt out of the fireplace and off the floor, out the door, that would be most helpful. I'm going to shovel most of it, but shoveling's not going to get the floor all clean."

Maggie stared at him. Never had Pa Alden been so focused on something, or talked so much. Not that she could remember, at least. Maybe he had, before last summer and all of the Cedar happenings.

That seemed so long ago now.

The girls set to work, pouring icy water over the wooden plank floor. The chill in the air, in combination with the dampness and moisture of the inside of Etta's cabin soon had Giovanna shivering inside her doubled-up quilt. Maggie tried to hurry with the buckets to and from the well so as to speed the task and end all of their suffering.

"That looks fine," Pa Alden said after an hour or so. "We can wait for a warmer day to do the finishing touches. Just didn't want Etta's floor to rot out." He squeezed Giovanna's shoulders. "Take her home and get her warm."

Maggie nodded.

"We're in the potato fields these days, Maggie, if you happen to want to come by. I'll give you some to take back with you."

Maggie shook her head.

Just as quickly, Liz Ellen nodded. "If you need an extra hand, I'm not a bad picker," she piped up.

Pa Alden nodded after a moment. "Come by this afternoon," he said. "Jed'll give you a ride up; he's got some business to take care of in town."

Maggie shivered and felt the bile rise in her throat at the mention of Jed's name. She gave Liz Ellen a sideways glance and frowned at her foster father.

He didn't get the benefit of her expression as he had bent over to into the fireplace again. "I think we've got it all."

"I'll walk you home," Patience said to Maggie. "Giovanna looks like she could be carried. She's shivering to beat the band over here. And—don't argue with me, Maggie—I'm getting your wraps and bringing them over tomorrow. And your . . . your dresses and stockings and underthings too."

Maggie looked at her sister, feeling guilt sear through her. Giovanna's shoulders shook and her lips had a bluish tinge to them. "Thank you," she said absently, calculating in her mind how long it would take to get the fire in the cabin going. Giovanna could wrap up in two more quilts and bury herself in the straw up in the loft.

She should have said no to Pa Alden. Or, at least, sent Giovanna on to the Cleggs' or someplace warm, while she and patience and Liz Ellen and the boys went on.

Maggie shook her head, looking at the Hoster boys. Tattered pants, lumpy stockings, and boots with soles flapping, ragged coats—how could they be the picture of rosy warmth and good health? Maybe their bodies were more used to the cold, somehow.

They set out back down the road. Patience picked up Giovanna halfway down the block, cradling her like a baby, stumbling a little with the weight of her.

The snow came down so thickly now, in wet clumps that grew thick on the sides of the road. Patience was having a hard time of it, with Giovanna in her arms. She tripped a few times. Maggie trotted after her, wishing she could do something more to either hurry the process or help carry her sister.

"There's a puddle a few yards ahead," she said.

"What?" Patience cried.

Maggie could hardly hear her, in spite of the fact that she raised her voice. The sky was deep gray, with continual falls of white making everything near invisible. Every sound was muffled by it. *And the scarf that is wrapped around Patience's head likely muffles everything even more*, Maggie thought. She ran, feeling the snow cling to her boots, making them sodden lumps that weighed her down like lead anvils. "There's a puddle," she shouted when she was just behind Patience.

It was too late. Patience, weighed down and blinded because of her burden, and as eager to get home as Maggie, waded into it.

She exclaimed and stumbled again. Maggie moved

frantically, trying to get her snow-plug feet to go faster, but it was too late. Patience went down, losing her grip on the bundle of quilts and skirts that was Giovanna.

Oh, no. Oh, no . . .

Something hissed by as Maggie ran to get her sister out of the puddle. It felt, to her, like something had been thrown at them, but she didn't have time to stop.

She was pulling a limp Giovanna from the puddle, trying to heft her, trying to gather up out-flung limbs and bundle them once more into the sodden quilt. Maggie ripped Henry's coat from her shoulders and tried to get it around Giovanna.

Suddenly Patience exclaimed again, loudly. She had pulled herself to a standing position, but for no reason at all it seemed, she fell again into the puddle. It was odd, like something had—

There was an excited whoop from somewhere behind them on the road, and a voice exclaimed, "Gotcha, you little varmint!"

Maggie managed to stand, shaking as she hefted her sister, dangling limbs and all.

Jed.

It was her first thought, and a deep, heavy dread filled her, weighing her down even more. She wouldn't be able to get away.

"Who is that?" Patience exclaimed. "Jed, is that you?" Apparently Patience had the same thought as Maggie.

"Get this rope off of me! What are you playing at? Ma Alden'll tan your hide! Go get help!"

"First time that's ever happened. Usually takes me a few tries. Nasty old mule." the voice continued. It was closer and louder. *And not Jed's*, Maggie realized as she struggled to turn, with Giovanna trailing from her arms.

"Not Jed," Maggie flung over her shoulder in Patience's direction.

"Who's playing rope tricks?" Patience called out again. "You deserve a good hiding, to play such a trick on a couple of girls, bringing me down in this snow, whoever you are."

The man's figure—it was a man, Maggie realized, seeing the bulk of the outline of shoulder, the height of the dim silhouette he made in the dimness of the snowstorm—came into full view and stopped short. Maggie looked up at him. The broad, sharp-featured face showed surprise, and after a moment of processing, intense mortification.

"Will McClelland!" Maggie blurted and then reddened at her own familiarity. She had never been introduced, just knew who he was because he was one of the boys in town girls tended to prattle on about. And his father owned the pasture south of the Aldens.

Will McClelland squinted at her through the snow. "You're one of the little Alden girls. Mary? Martha? Can't recall your name, I'm sorry. You all right?"

"Maggie. Could you—could you please help me?" The last word came out a sob.

He moved hastily, taking Maggie's load from her.

Patience finally righted herself, stepping out of a tangle of rope.

"Patience?" It came out almost as a yelp, and he nearly dropped Giovanna in his surprise.

Patience squinted at him. "This your idea of a good joke?" she said. She shook out her skirts. "I could have twisted something—even broken an ankle. I can't feel my feet, Will McClelland, and that girl is like to freeze to death, we don't get her in front of a fire as soon as possible. Get moving, or I'll say a few words you've never heard from the mouth of a girl."

"I didn't *see* you, Patience; I thought . . . consarned snow—"

"Aim was pretty good for aiming at nothing. Let's get going. Now, consarn it!" Her voice cracked sharply in the muffled air.

"Do you know where there's a fire already built up?" Maggie asked, wiping her nose. "Please."

"Take her to the Aldens'," Patience said grimly.

"No!" Maggie shouted.

Will looked from Patience to Maggie, and back to Patience. "Harrisons are just down that way. I—did I hurt you?"

Patience didn't bother to answer his question. "How far away? Can't make out where we are exactly."

"Just a hundred feet or so."

Maggie shivered and felt her stomach sink.

Julia Harrison.

Now that she was looking for it, she could see the faint shape of the building through the snow and haze. She looked over her shoulder at Will and Patience, standing and gazing at each other, and began walking, pointedly.

With Will carrying Giovanna, they went much faster, and it was only a minute until they were on the Harrison's doorstep, though it seemed like an eternity to Maggie.

Giovanna had been so quiet, her eyes shut. She had still been shivering. That meant she was still all right. Didn't it?

They knocked on the door.

Sister Harrison answered. Her dark hair was up in back, with little curls framing her face like she was going to a party, but she had flour on her apron.

"Oh, mercy," she exclaimed when she saw them. "Get your boots off and come in. Let me take her." She held out her arms for Giovanna.

Maggie scraped her boots on the step and pulled them off as fast as she could, twisting one of her ankles a bit. She stepped inside, and her wet stocking foot slid on the floor.

"Is she all right?" Maggie asked hoarsely. She righted herself and hurried to the hearth, where Sister Harrison had unwrapped Giovanna.

"Don't put her so close," Will warned. "If she's got any frostbite . . . best to have someone wrap up in a blanket with her for a while."

"Take you outer things off," Sister Harrison told Maggie. "Don't mind modesty right now," she added, seeing Maggie's hesitation and glance at Will. "Your sister's life depends on it. Turn away," she added sharply. "Or better yet, go get their ma."

"Pa," Maggie snapped, and immediately began undoing her buttons as Sister Harrison did the same for her sister. "Not Ma."

Will's face reddened, and he turned around. "I'll go—where d'you think your pa might be? I'm sorry, Patience—I didn't mean—"

"I know," Patience snapped. "Sorry," she added, softening her tone. "I—you can explain some other time, all right, Will?"

Maggie bundled up with her sister in the blanket. Giovanna's skin was clammy and cold, and her shivering made Maggie feel colder. Maggie put her arms around Giovanna, squeezing her as tightly as she could.

"Don't have to hold her so hard," Sister Harrison said. "Lay out on the floor there, by the fire. Shut the door!" she added, as it opened and two more people walked in.

Maggie felt her heart beat and felt her sister's. She counted heartbeats and breaths.

"What's going on?" It was Julia's voice.

"Patience?" That was Hyrum.

Hyrum. Not Henry, thank goodness. To see her here in this state, in her underthings wrapped up in a blanket with her sister, mud and wet from the storm—well, it didn't matter. Giovanna mattered more than all of that. Didn't she?

"Had an accident," Patience said shortly. "Giovanna—we're just trying to warm her up. You two got somewhere else you could go for a while?"

"Let me help." Julia's voice had a note of concern in it. "Do you need more wood on the fire, Mother?"

"We're fine. She'll be fine in a few moments. Go stir my potatoes, will you?"

"What happened?" It was Hyrum's voice again.

Maggie felt like Giovanna was shivering a little less. Her breathing was easier too. Maggie dug through the bedding and found one of her hands. She checked the little fingernails—they were a more healthy color.

"Can we put her by the fire now?" Maggie's voice was hoarse. "I think she'll be all right."

"I'm all right," Giovanna repeated, her teeth chattering a little. She clung to Maggie until Sister Harrison brought over another wool blanket, wrapping Giovanna in it before she set her by the fire.

Maggie folded her own blanket tightly around herself, stood, and went to sit in the rocking chair. She glanced at Hyrum, feeling her embarrassment warm her nearly as much as the heat from the fire.

Patience saw it. "You'd better go," she said to Hyrum.

"We'll be fine. Thank you. If you want to do something, then go and get your ma."

"No," Maggie snapped.

"Maggie," Patience said. "You keep that mouth of yours shut tight."

Maggie stared at Patience. She had never heard Patience speak like that before.

"You need help," Patience continued after a moment, in a more moderate tone. "I don't think pride has any place here. Look at Giovanna. Look at her! You can't take care of her yourself, Maggie. And while I understand you're frightened after what happened the other day, I can't countenance . . . I can't stand to see the two of you like this." Her voice broke, then.

Sister Harrison's face was the picture of puzzlement. She went and put an arm around Patience. "You all right, honey?"

Maggie sat and rocked, feeling the fire warm her toes. She waited, feeling her heart beat wildly in her chest.

It was the question again, rearing its ugly head. What was to become of them? What was wrong with Maggie that she couldn't take care of her own sister?

It could've happened to anybody, she argued internally. Who could've foreseen that the snow would get so bad? And Pa Alden was the one who asked for help. If Giovanna had been at the Hosters' or Cleggs' by the fire this whole time, it wouldn't even have been an issue.

She felt her anger and resentment rise, and Patience was an easy target, standing there in the room with her, weeping as if it were *her* sister who had been half frozen.

"Get out," Maggie said quietly.

Both Patience and Sister Harrison turned to Maggie.

"Patience," Maggie clarified. "You don't need to be here. Thank you, Sister Harrison. As soon as she's warmed through, I'll take her home."

"With what coat?" Patience cried.

"Mine. I—I mean, it's Henry's, but he's loaned it for a while. I have wool stockings on; I'll be warm enough for a few blocks. I have no doubt Liz Ellen's got the fire going by now."

"No," Patience said, folding her arms. "It's crazy for you to do such a thing in this weather, when I could take two minutes and get both your wraps."

"I don't trust you won't bring Ma Alden with you."

Patience groaned. "And what would be such a bad thing if I did? Maggie, you're not Giovanna's mother. You're not going to be able—"

"I'll do better than she has," Maggie spat out. "You might be able to ignore every bad thing that goes on 'round you, Patience, but I can't when it happens to me. When it's happening to Giovanna."

"What bad things?" Patience threw her hands up. "So Jed teased her. He teased me often enough when I was a little girl—"

"By holding a knife to you?"

Patience shook her head impatiently. "That's not the point, Megs. It wasn't Ma who did that to you. It was Jed."

"She's not sending Giovanna to school. She's been telling me, saying how Giovanna and I need to prepare to work when we grow older, and has never bothered to teach me stitchery and other refined things—"

"You've always refused to learn!"

"Well, didn't you protest, when you first started? All right, could be *you* did not, Patience, but I'll wager Etta did. Or any other girl with a bit of spirit. And as I said to you that day, Patience, look at me. Look at Giovanna. She's not dressing us proper, not bothering to make us presentable, fit company for genteel society. She's turning us into—into exactly what Dale Forth said. Dirt-faced Italian chits. Washerwomen."

"But we've been busy lately," Patience argued, "and she hasn't had the attention to spend on . . . on turning you into a young lady, not right now. We've had all that with the people from Salt Lake down here, and Etta—"

"I'm fifteen, Patience. I'll be sixteen in less than half a year. You're only a little more'n a year older than me, and you've had skirts down to your boots and your hair up for three years." Patience's face flooded with color. "What a silly, *vain* reason to leave the family who's given you everything—taken you off the prairie, loved you as their own. What an ungrateful attitude—"

Maggie lost all semblance of control then. She stood, shaking with her rage and frustration. "She killed our little sister!" she yelled at the top of her lungs.

Sister Harrison, who had been trying to pretend like she was ignoring the exchange, gasped.

Patience was startled as well, so much so, that she stopped talking. She put her hands to her mouth and grew pale.

"Patience." Suddenly, the need was so great—such a yawning, desperate thing. "Patience, please tell me what happened to Noémie—to baby Jane."

Patience shook her head. She swallowed, and when she spoke, her voice was husky. "I've got to go. I'll go get Sister Clegg, then, Maggie. I won't insist on bringing Mother, but you've got to have someone—she'll have something . . ." She turned toward the door.

"Patience!" Maggie repeated, but Patience ran out, back into the storm, and Maggie was left holding the door, contemplating the wall of white that hid any figure from view as soon as they got more than five feet away.

Maggie walked back in and saw that Giovanna was staring at her. Her dark eyes were wide, her forehead wrinkled—her face was the picture of consternation.

"You're all right then?" Maggie asked. She cleared her throat, which was hoarse from the yelling she'd done. "I'm sorry," she said awkwardly. She felt the shame and embarrassment descend on her. She couldn't quite meet Sister Harrison's eye.

"Right," Sister Harrison said, likewise avoiding looking at Maggie. "I think she'll be fit now. You should wait, though, if—if Sister Clegg's coming, it would be wise. And I don't really have a wrap or coat to spare."

Maggie sat on the hearth and waited. It was almost like waiting for a spanking, as she'd done one or two times when she was little. When she would do something especially wrong, her mother would tell her to wait on the little brick hearth for her father to come home—

Father.

His face swam into Maggie's mind: the way he threw his head up when he laughed, his dark beard and sideburns framing his smile, with the two crooked teeth in front that slanted together. They gave him a slight lisp that only added to his refinement when he spoke in the soft language that she had first learned.

"Le petit en a besoin de quelques fessées, et puis des baisers?"

Mother shrugged, a little exasperated, and looked at father with her expressive dark eyes.

Mother could say a million things with her eyes.

The door banged open, and there stood Sister Clegg, holding a bundle in her arms. Maggie's vision came back into focus.

"Why don't you two girls spend the night at our place," Sister Clegg said.

Maggie looked over at Giovanna, who was looking at nothing, just staring across the room at nothing. Maybe in a reverie like the one Maggie had just emerged from.

Suddenly Maggie felt a stronger wave of guilt descend on her. It made it hard for her to breathe, thinking about what had just happened, what she had said to Patience. What Giovanna had heard. What did Giovanna think, right now, right this very minute? Did she hate Maggie and want to go back to the Aldens'? Did she understand what Maggie had said?

Sister Clegg was bundling Giovanna into a coat a few sizes too big for her, and wrapping her around in blankets. "I'll make up a bed by the fire," she said.

Maggie nodded and rose to leave. She didn't have it in her to argue.

"Henry's up at Kolob with his father and older brothers," Sister Clegg remarked as they walked into the Clegg's warm front room, with a fire blazing in the fireplace.

A little bit of warm relief found its way into Maggie's shivering body. It took a moment for her to process Sister Clegg's words. "Are they going to be all right up there in all this?" she asked, feeling a dart of worry.

Sister Clegg shrugged as she laid out a few quilts and pillows on the floor in front of the fire. "They somehow manage to come back whole most times."

Maggie's chest tightened up again. *Henry's up in the canyon.* Would he be warm enough? Men were so careless about these things, toughing it out. On the prairie, dozens had died of exposure after pushing it too hard, eating too little. *Tough it out*, Maggie thought. *That's Henry for you. And I'm wearing his warmest coat.* It was almost like she couldn't breathe.

She thought of her mother and father. They used to comfort her at night, when she woke up from a bad dream, feeling like this, like her chest had iron bands around it. Her mother would kneel with her on the cold, board floor.

"Do you think we could say a prayer?" Maggie asked. Her heart beat wildly, and she looked anxiously at Sister Clegg.

Sister Clegg paused. "I think that would be just fine," she said.

Maggie knelt on the floor next to her. Silently, Giovanna came to join them, her hands still clutching the wrap at her throat.

TALES OF MURDER

TIME PASSED QUICKLY FOR MAGGIE. HER DAYS BECAME full of small tasks for the Cleggs and Hosters, and sometimes for the Holdens as well. She thought, after Patience had planted the idea in her head, of sending Giovanna to school.

It wasn't far. The schoolhouse was just across from the Higbees' lot. In the end, Maggie couldn't do it. She didn't feel safe, leaving Giovanna by herself, even in a classroom full of children and a teacher to watch after her. Who knew if Ma Alden might guess, or hear where Giovanna went every day, and she came and took her?

Ma Alden had become something monstrous in Maggie's mind at this point. Her memories were all clouded with the thing that had become almost certain in Maggie's mind—her little sister's murder. Every gesture, every word that she would remember was slanted, with extra venom and ill intent. Even the memory of her appearance became distorted. Maggie saw Ma Alden in her mind as taller, with more sharp angles, and fiercer, meaner features.

Patience didn't visit for a few weeks after the incident at the Harrisons', but Pa Alden came by nearly every other evening just for a minute. He generally brought wood, or a few potatoes and onions, and held Giovanna on his knee for a few minutes in front of the fire. He still didn't say much, but his face had the cheer and patience in it that Maggie remembered, and he took time to tell a funny little story to Giovanna now and then. Old stories that Maggie remembered hazily, with many of the details wrong. It was as if she had heard them before, but hadn't known enough English words to get the entire gist when he'd told them to her.

When Patience did finally come again, it was awkward. Maggie had not lost her burning desire to ask Patience what she knew about Ma Alden and the baby. She wanted to hear Patience say it, to hear the words out loud. Maggie thought how restful it would be just to know what was real.

But she didn't know just how to bring it up, and that first visit became a long, silent observation between the two of them. Patience sat on the hearth, clutching the basket of bread she had brought, watching Giovanna and glancing at Maggie every now and then, and Maggie was quiet as well, doing some kind of mending or cooking or cleaning.

"You're getting much better," Patience finally ventured.

Maggie glanced down at the pile of fabric in her lap. It was one of the Hosters'; she had it pulled apart and was re-stitching onto the batting and backing. She cleared her throat. "How did the potato harvest go?"

"Fine." Patience fiddled with the fringe on her shawl. "Not the best crop this year, so we won't be selling as many."

"That's too bad." Maggie paused, opened her mouth, and then closed it. She had run out of conversation.

"Will's coming by a little later. Wanted to make sure the both of you were all right."

Maggie nodded, feeling her face flood with color again at the memory of that evening. She had been so anxious for Giovanna. She hadn't thought then about the embarrassment that might follow later. He left before she began taking off her things, didn't he? He must have. Still, it was mortifying, the thought of him there that night to see Maggie and Giovanna in that muddy, half-frozen state.

Will came just before Patience left, rapping on the doorframe with his broad knuckles. "Hello the house?" he called, his voice cheerful.

"Come in," Patience returned, with an odd sort of tremble in her voice.

Maggie frowned at her and studied Will as he sauntered in. *He is a big fellow*, she thought. *Large hands, large feet, and a frame that barely cleared the doorway.* Pa Alden was likely taller, but he didn't seem it. He was too lean.

"You and your sister doing all right, then?" he asked, taking his hat in his hands.

"Fine." Maggie lowered her gaze back to her lap, biting off a piece of thread in her sewing.

"Well, it's fine enough out for a walk, Patience. You s'pose you might want to take a stroll over along old Fort Field?"

"Can't be too long," Patience said. She cleared her throat and rose from her chair. She nodded at Maggie in an odd way. "See you," she said.

The two of them left without another word. On their way out, Maggie saw Will slide his hand into Patience's.

It made Maggie think of Henry. Not that she wasn't thinking of him already; she felt like she had to nudge every single waking thought away from him and into more productive avenues in order to accomplish anything at all.

He didn't come by much. And oddly, he was never home when Maggie went over.

Sister Clegg said he was keeping busy with the Legion and doing things in town with his brothers and father. *I'm glad,* Maggie told herself. *I'm glad to not have Henry on my conscience right now to add to all the other things I'm chewing over these days.*

But there was something odd about the way she felt whenever his name was mentioned.

One time, she saw him at Stewarts. She walked in, asking for some thread for Sister Clegg and saw his tall, lean form leaning against the counter. He was grinning, chatting in a low voice to Andrew.

Maggie felt like her heart might clear from her chest. She waited, clutching her basket.

Henry turned and saw her, and such a grin came over his face that Maggie felt like all the snow must melt off her.

"How d'you do?" she asked, holding out a hand that trembled just slightly.

"Fine," he replied, taking it and giving it a gentle shake. "You and Giovanna keeping warm these cold nights?"

Maggie nodded.

"Still over at Hosters'?"

Maggie glanced at Brother Stewart. Henry followed her glance. "Sorry. Didn't know it was still a secret. Most people know, you know. I reckon your ma knows by know too."

Maggie nodded then, feeling somehow wretched. "Likely," she said. "We're doing fine. Just—fine."

Henry had simply nodded, put his hat on, and walked out. Maggie tried to keep herself from staring after him as he went.

So wore away the last weeks of November and the beginning of December. In the third week of that month, Maggie received her second letter from Mariah.

December 5, 1858

Dear Magdalena,

To answer your question, yes, we have heard much of judges, and had some troubles. Judge Sinclair took Brother Brigham to court this week. Just to try to shame him, I think. After Pres. Bucanin's letter he doesn't have anything to hold him on, I don't think. Ma went, and said it was the strangest hearing she had ever attended. It was a laffable affair according to everyone who went there were jeers in the courtroom from the jury even. But still Brother Brigham's taking caution, he does go round with a couple of men all the time. Things are looking up though. For all his trying, Judge does not seem to be finding much to bring him in on, nor anybody else, and even if he did, well, he would need to find a jury to convict anyhow. I reckon we will do fine, Maggie, no matter how many judges come in. Until whole companies come here to take up residence there is not much anybody can do now the government is given the pardon and Johnston's troops pushed off to camp around the other side of the lake. Whoever is talking to you is like to be just trying to stir up trouble. Don't trouble yourself about it, is my advice.

Harvest was poor this year. But we're doing fine anyhow. Ma is real thrifty and thinks up all sorts of ways to make a few beans and a bit of pork and broth go farther. When it was warmer, we gathered and dried lots of the greens and the roots from the creeksides. They are tough but boiled they taste just the same, and we still find there is grain to be had for the right sort of trade. Ma says it will be a pinching winter, but we will come through all right.

I think it's real fine that you are learning sewing and going to Sister Holden's to babysit. Maggie, I think you are a real smart girl, and you should also know you are fine looking and ought not give ear to those who say you aren't worth much to give learning to. Sister Clegg takes you in hand often enough and I reckon you should think on why. I know why, I knew you only those few months and still think on you quite often and send my heart's warm wishes your way whenever I do.

Does Henry still come round a lot? Say hello for me.

Please write back soon.

With Love,

Mariah

Maggie sat for a few minutes, getting her head around the letter. She had written to Mariah, asking about the judges, only two months ago. It all seemed so small and silly now, her worries over what she had heard.

But it left her feeling disturbed. The mention of Brother Brigham's bodyguards put Uncle Forth in mind, and the shocking words he had said when Maggie had been keeping quiet inside the henhouse.

Blood-murder. The words swam in Maggie's mind. They seemed obscene, dangerous, to her. When she thought on it, images from her dreams came to her, unbidden. Blood, and mud, dripping down men's faces.

It couldn't be true, Maggie argued internally. *Dale Forth just likes to go on.*

But then Ma Alden had said that thing about going to a meeting and hearing it preached, and there had been such a note of fear in her voice. Ma Alden didn't show that kind of weakness as a matter of course. She had really been disturbed by something— something real, not made up by her brother.

Maggie tried to shake off her worries as she went about her day, cooking and cleaning for the Hosters before she went over to the Holdens' for the afternoon to watch the children.

But the worry refused to be exorcised by work, or anything else. It still plagued her while she walked down Seventh, headed for the Holdens'.

"Maggie, can I go with Scotch and Davy to chop wood?" Giovanna called out, skipping after her.

Maggie sighed. "No, Giovanna. You can't. You need to stay with me and tend. Where've you been this morning?"

"Helping Scotch and Davy tend to Ma and her babe. But I *want* to learn splitting, Megs. It's a right useful skill."

"Well, *I* don't want you going hog-wild all over creation with the Hoster boys," Maggie snapped. "You're a *girl*. You need to learn to act like one."

"Ma Alden never made me act like a girl," Giovanna muttered.

The anger flared up inside Maggie so that she didn't trust herself to speak. She grabbed Giovanna's upper arm with slightly more force than necessary and brought her through the Holden's gate.

"I don't have to obey you."

Maggie looked down at her sister. The expression on Giovanna's face was ferocious—all black eyebrows and scowling mouth. It surprised and completely deflated her. "Gigi," Maggie shook her head. "Please don't do this right now."

"You don't call me that," Giovanna yelled. "You call me Giovanna! Patience and Ma Alden and Etta call me Gigi."

"Why're you acting like this?"

Giovanna just scowled even more fiercely and jerked her arm out of Maggie's grasp. She opened the Holdens' door without knocking and stormed in, slamming it behind her.

Maggie was embarrassed beyond belief as she entered after. "Sorry," she said.

Sister Holden turned her rocker around to face Maggie. "Hello there. You up to some baby rocking?" She held out her arms, and Maggie took the squirming little boy. "Giovanna upset about something?" Sister Holden added as she rose and stretched her arms. "That child was up all hours of the night. Don't know how I'm going to get through the day!"

"Don't know," Maggie replied. "And I'm sorry."

"You seem like you might be troubled about something too."

Maggie stared at her, over the bright-orange crown of the baby girl's head.

She wasn't sure what to say. "Yeah . . . reckon all of us are troubled over something, nowadays."

"Well, what's troubling you?" Sister Holden smiled and crouched down beside Maggie where she rocked, stroking the baby's little cheeks. "She'll go to sleep fast, I think."

"Nothing."

"Oh, come on, Maggie," Sister Holden said. "I can see you've got something—a lot of things—going on in that head of yours. Sister Clegg tells me you've moved in with the Hosters."

I don't want to talk about that, not with you. Not with anybody. Maggie's heart sped up, and she scanned her mind to come up with something, anything. "It's nothing, really," she said, finally. "Just some stupid dreams I have sometimes. Bet Sister Clegg's mentioned them to you, as well."

Sister Holden shook her head, still smiling fondly into the baby's eyes. "No. Tell me about them."

"Just dreams. You know how they can be."

"I've had some strange dreams before." Sister Holden rose and stretched again. Maggie heard her back crack. "Especially when I have to keep waking up at night. Being a mother, Maggie, means giving away your heart in worry, one piece at a time. One piece for every child. What's gotten you so worried then?"

Maggie thought hard. Should she? Why would she? But she could ask; the opportunity had presented itself. Sister Holden went to every church meeting; she had to have been there at the one Ma Alden was talking about. "Some things I heard said a while back," she answered finally. "Shouldn't pay any note to them. I shouldn'ta been listening, anyway. Got stuck in the henhouse, and they were talking right outside it."

"Who's they?"

"Ma Alden and Uncle Forth."

"Ah," Sister Holden said. "Then I'll guess it was something about that business down in Cedar. And your Pa."

Maggie's eyes widened. "How d'you know?"

"Your uncle's asked Shedrick some questions."

"Does—does Brother Holden know something about it, then?" Maggie tried to keep the eagerness out of her voice.

"Not much. Just that, officially, the Indians did everything but there's whispering around that some of the settlers got involved."

Maggie nodded. "That's—well. That's generally what Uncle Forth rattles on about. 'Cept he's sure that bishops were involved."

"Bishops?" There was a note of sharp disbelief in Sister

Holden's voice. "What's given him *that* idea? Why would any of the . . . ?" She shook her head.

Maggie shrugged. She felt a little cowed by the expression on Sister Holden's face—anger, and surprise. But she had to ask her question. She had to know, had to ask, somehow. When would someone else bring it up? To her, never.

"Well," she went on carefully, "He also goes on about Brother Brigham, and something they—Ma Alden and Uncle Forth—said he preached." She paused, willing herself to form the words. "Something called blood-murder." She felt, after saying those words, like she ought to wash her mouth out, like God and all his angels were listening. Would she be struck down in a moment?

Sister Holden's brow wrinkled. "I don't recall anything like that. Likely your uncle's—" She seemed to struggle with her words for a moment. "Your uncle's good imagination." She grinned at Maggie with something of a conspiratorial look.

Non, Maggie thought. *No, not good enough.* "They were going on," she continued relentlessly, "saying things about people thrown in ditches and murder such. Ma Alden seemed frightened that Pa Alden might be blood-murdered if he talked about what happened down in Cedar. She said—she said Brother Brigham preached it at a meeting she went to once, and it scared her."

Sister Holden's face was troubled now. She gazed at Maggie, and her eyes grew wide. "Blood-*murder*? Are you sure that's what your ma said?"

Maggie frowned. "Yeah, I'm pretty sure. Why?"

"Well," Sister Holden said, sitting on the ground heavily beside Maggie's rocker. "I think I know what she was talking about, maybe. It wasn't murder, though. Brother Brigham never preached murder."

Maggie stared at her. "Well . . . why . . . what was it then?" She was afraid, suddenly. Was the world shifting under her? Was she about to learn more than she wanted to?

"I'll tell you what I can, which isn't much. I think your uncle was talking about something that the prophet preached down here and around a few years ago. It was—I don't know how to explain this, Maggie. Have you gone to a lot of Sunday meetings?"

Maggie shook her head. "One or two."

"Well, now, you ought to start going. You're on your own and can decide to go or not. You don't have any strings or obligations like I have yet, either. I would love to be able to go to meeting regularly." Sister Holden sighed and glanced in the direction of the kitchen, where Giovanna and most of her older children were playing a game on the floor.

"What're you playing at?" Maggie called across the room.

Giovanna gave her a black look. "Tiddlywinks."

"I got four already!" Tim bragged.

"Anyhow," Sister Holden continued, "I asked because I wondered how to explain to you that sometimes sermons are preached about things that we are supposed to do every day. Do you know what I mean?"

"Not really." Maggie felt like she was shivering. Was she shivering?

"Well, things about how to live our lives. Some are commandments, like we shouldn't steal or lie. Some are more suggestions as to how to live a healthier life."

"Like the thickness of bread crusts," Maggie muttered.

Sister Holden chuckled. "Right. And sometimes things are taught that are deeper in nature. More—not for this life."

Maggie shook her head. "It's all right, Sister Holden, you don't have to—"

"No, it's all right, Maggie. Really. I mean," she said, nodding to herself, "things that we think about but don't really do. Things we ponder and consider on, that might be for the next life, or might help us in this one, but we're not actually asked to do."

"All right."

"I think your uncle and your mother meant blood *atonement*, which is something Brother Brigham's preached a time or two. That's actually a good example of what I mean, about things preached—theoretical. You ever heard that word before? Blood atonement is something not many understand, or understood at the time he preached it. I still don't understand it completely. But I think I'm not meant to, then. Milk before meat, as the scripture says."

Maggie felt fear and confusion stir inside of her. "So, what's blood atonement, then? Is it—did he say something about . . . about killing?"

Sister Holden was silent for a long moment. "No, he never preached that you should kill a person. Murder's a sin, no matter which way you look at it."

"Unless God tells you to." Maggie felt sick inside. "Nephi."

This effectively silenced Sister Holden for a moment. She folded her arms over her chest. "Well, that's a really tough thing, Maggie. You're right that we do have some examples of God commanding . . . that sort of thing, in scripture, at least. But it's different."

"How?"

"I'll have to think on that one a bit. But, Maggie, I was there and heard the prophet preach the doctrine of blood atonement, and I can tell you he never said people needed to kill one another. I never felt that was the intent of the message, though I can see how someone might twist it that way, if they had an agenda. And it has some to do with some very special things that we really can't say too much about here. I can't ask you to understand it, Maggie. It's not something to be discussed lightly. Certainly not something for weak-minded fools to use to justify their own selfish actions."

Maggie nodded. She couldn't hold the other woman's gaze. She nodded again and shifted the baby to the other shoulder.

"Brother Brigham had nothing to do with those murders, Maggie. Nor any member of the Church in good standing with the Lord. That you can count on. And if there are men out there who would do harm to your father, it's not because of the prophet. You have to understand that this is something that has happened throughout history. People will take what a prophet says, and distort and twist it to justify their own selfish actions."

Maggie nodded a third time.

"I have a question for you, Maggie. Could you imagine your father being involved in something like that? In purposefully killing people? Women and children, even?"

At Sister Holden's words, an image Maggie's real father—Guiseppe Chabert—flashed into her mind. Dark beard, gleaming dark eyes. She shook her head to clear it. "Pa Alden wouldn't ever hurt somebody. I can't even picture he'd do it if he had to, to save himself." *Or anybody else*, she added internally. She felt choked with bitterness.

"Well then, I think you can trust that truth above all others. And so you can put what your uncle said out of your mind. And let me say, Maggie, I know that the prophet would never be involved in something like that either, no matter what people say on the matter. That is a truth I hold in my heart, and it can't be shaken. Truth will come out one day, Maggie, and in the meantime, I think faith is all we have to go on. It's what God expects of us."

"But," Maggie started, and then stopped. She looked down at the redheaded girl in her arms. She had fallen asleep.

"Yes?"

"If somebody did . . . *murder* someone—not Pa Alden, somebody else—and Pa Alden knows something of it, could they—wouldn't somebody might want to . . . to hurt him?"

Sister Holden rose again. "I wish I could put your mind to rest, Maggie. But like I said, I don't know anything more than anybody else around here about what really happened down in Cedar. I've heard lots of rumors, to be sure, and there are plenty of people like your uncle who are happy to say whatever they don't know on the subject. But there is one thing you can do, Maggie, if you're worried for your father's safety."

Maggie bit her lip, holding back a groan. "Pray."

"It's not a little thing, Maggie. I look at you and see a girl who gets her prayers answered every day." Maggie raised her eyes to the ceiling and shook her head.

"No, you do. Have you gone without a meal yet this winter?"

Maggie felt a bit of shame run through her. "No."

"Well, maybe that's not what you pray for, but it's what others pray for you. You can think on that." She nodded and rose. "I'm going to start on the dishes. Do you mind rocking her for a while? She'll just wake up if I try to put her down."

"I don't mind," Maggie replied.

She rocked. She heard the loud chatter of Giovanna and the Holden kids, and wanted to yell at them to be quiet; there was too much in her head as it was.

What if Brother Brigham was wrong, as Uncle Forth seemed to think? What if he had said something, meant something dark and sinister—but, no. Maggie couldn't imagine it either. Brother Brigham? All the times she had seen him preach, all the small interactions that she had with the bishops in their area: Bishop Wall, with his slow grin and the way he stepped back when his wife took over; and Bishop Johnson from down in Springville, and his wide, pleasant face and clear eyes.

No, it couldn't be. It just didn't fit.

Talking with Sister Holden had been a bad idea. It hadn't comforted Maggie at all.

That night, Maggie dreamed again, but her dream changed.

The men—painting and dirtying their faces. One of them moved forward, closer and closer. The watery gray eyes of Uncle Forth.

Suddenly, he turned so Maggie saw his back, and he held a gun to his shoulder. Maggie wanted to see who he was shooting at. The world turned obligingly.

Pa Alden stood there, lean and pathetic looking, with his hands hanging at his sides. Uncle Forth fired the gun. Pa Alden stood still, an amazed look on his face for a few seconds. A bright stain spread over his breast, and he fell, stiffly, to the ground.

A flash of light. Ma Alden stood over the crib, holding down her pillow. Her face had an exultation on it now, like she was enjoying it.

After the baby's limbs stopped thrashing, she turned to Giovanna, her pillow held out. Giovanna lay down on the bed, as if she was waiting her turn.

Maggie woke up suddenly to find Giovanna shaking her awake.

"Stop it," she said. "You're waking everybody up. And

Ma Alden's not going to kill me. So just shut up your dumb mouth and go to sleep. You're crazy, and you have crazy dreams." There was a sob in Giovanna's voice.

Maggie cleared her throat. "Giovanna," she whispered. "You're going to wake everyone up. Sorry, I was—"

Giovanna flung herself into the straw, tucked as far as she could into the tiny corner where the roof met the wall. As far away from Maggie as she could get.

Pa Alden visited a few days later, but he brought Patience with him. Maggie had wanted to talk to him. To warn him about Uncle Forth. She couldn't discount her dreams anymore, not after what had happened. Not after what she had learned about baby Noémie.

But she didn't get a chance to get him away from either Patience or Giovanna, and later Will came over as well. Maggie watched Patience and Will as they sat and laughed together.

She still hasn't told me how Will came to throw that rope around her and bring her down in the snow, Maggie remembered suddenly.

But there was no real chance to talk to Patience, either, for the rest of the night. She was completely focused on Will, on every word that seemed to come from his mouth.

The weeks wore on. It grew colder and colder, until it was unpleasant to make even the short journey from the Hosters' to Cleggs' or from the Cleggs' to the Holdens'. Maggie still couldn't imagine how Liz Ellen and her two little brothers handled the cold. They were out in it practically all day. Darns and mends notwithstanding, they wore very threadbare clothing.

The dreams came every night now. Giovanna didn't shake her awake again, but she took to sleeping on the other side of the loft, next to Liz Ellen. And her sudden strange behavior toward Maggie did not go away, either. She spoke barely a word to Maggie, and when she had to say something, she didn't look Maggie in the face.

Maggie felt consumed with worry. It wasn't just Giovanna's behavior, though that hurt and bewildered almost beyond reason.

It wasn't just the dreams, either.

She felt like she was waiting for something horrible to happen. It was like the *something* hung over her, and she stood in the shadow, waiting for it to fall.

She became tense whenever she was about town. She was always on the lookout for Ma Alden's tall figure, always keeping her ears pricked for the sharp tones. A time or two she startled badly, thinking she'd heard Ma Alden call her name: *Come here, Maggie.* Maggie—it sounded like so many other English words.

Magdalena.

Christmas was approaching. The third week of December started out as it usually did. All in the little, mud-walled town of Provo had gotten into the business of hard celebrating. Sleighing and caroling parties kept people up late at nights, and there was dancing and popcorn-popping and ward functions to go to almost every evening.

Maggie kept away from most of them. She preferred to sit at home, rocking and mending. It was too much of a strain to be out in so much noise. To be out, where she would likely run into all sorts of people she didn't really have anything to say to.

The Hosters, of course, attended them all and brought home as much food and treats as their pockets and aprons and shirtfronts could hold. Giovanna had taken to slipping away with them. The first time, watching Giovanna bundle up with the Hosters on her way out the door, Maggie opened her mouth to protest. And then she took a look at Giovanna's face and shut her mouth.

Maggie sat alone in the little cabin, rocking, darning, and ruminating on these things when the door swung open.

She jumped and then put a hand on her chest when she saw it was only Will and Patience.

"Didn't mean to give you a scare," Patience said, grinning. "I thought you might like to pop some corn or make some taffy. I didn't see you at the Walls' party last weekend. Talked to Liz Ellen the other day when I happened to pass her in the street. She says you're holed up here at nights like a scared groundhog."

Maggie frowned. "Scared o' what? Just have things to do."

"Let me take that. You're making a fair mess of it." Patience reached for the sock, and Maggie flicked it out of her reach.

"I'm learning."

"Oh, well." Patience squinted at her and gestured toward Will, who sat down on the hearth.

"Want some popcorn?" he said, rattling the pan he held.

The sound of the kernels was deafening, somehow, in the empty little room. "You two're in a mood," she remarked. "Fine, I don't reckon I'll say no."

Will stirred the dying coals. Patience came over and held the pan, shaking it over the heat.

Just about at the same time the popping sounds began, the door opened again.

Maggie looked up. The dry little smile melted off her face.

She thought for a moment that she must be hallucinating, because there stood Ma Alden—as nightmarish a figure as she ever did see with gray eyes blazing, hair awry. Angry as she'd ever seen her.

Patience did a double take. "Ma?"

Ma Alden crossed the room, bent, and seized Maggie. "How could you?"

Maggie felt Ma Alden's fingers trembling on her shoulders, trembling, as if she wanted to grip her harder, to dig in and bruise her. Her terror left her feeling like she had no breath to speak, like her mind was a solid block. *Was* this one of her dreams? Was Ma Alden about to take a pillow from behind her back and . . . ?

"Ma!" Patience cried. "What are you doing here? Stop it!"

Will stood, looking uncertainly at Ma Alden, and then at Patience. "Should I go get your pa?"

It was Will's boyish voice that grounded Maggie and slammed her into reality. She began to squirm, grabbing at Ma Alden's wrists.

"You ungrateful, unfeeling chit." Ma Alden's voice trembled with rage. It pierced through Maggie, almost a physical pain. "After what I've done for you, and for Giovanna, and what I've said, and *not* said."

"Ma!" Patience tugged at her mother's shoulder. "What're you doing here? Go home! You agreed to leave it alone, to let me and Pa keep an eye on Maggie and Giovanna."

"The chest," Ma Alden hissed, ignoring Patience. Her cold, gray eyes bored into Maggie's.

Maggie's heart plummeted. The chest.

She had almost forgotten.

"Stop, Mother!" Patience exclaimed again, grabbing Ma Alden's arms. "What has she done? What has happened?"

Maggie swallowed. "I broke into Ma Alden's chest," she said. "'Twas a while ago. Before I—we left."

It felt flat, funny coming out; the words had been waiting there. It was almost like she'd practiced them, that she had been expecting this moment for so long. "She had something of mine. I opened the chest and found it . . . and I took it."

"You stole."

Maggie's shoulders tingled. She shook them and tried to scoot her chair back, away from Ma Alden. "No. I was not the one who stole."

"You broke and rustled through my precious things. My things . . ." Ma Alden let go of Maggie and gestured wildly with her hands, nearly striking Patience, who had come to stand behind her.

"The cups and pitcher are not yours," Maggie said. She stood and took a few rapid steps backward, coming up against the brick hearth. Will sat there still, his face a picture of horror and confusion.

"They came across with my family. I remember them."

At this, Ma Alden's face paled. She sputtered for a moment. "You're . . . the . . . you've never said that you wanted them. You could have asked—"

"I did. When we first came over, you said there was nothing left. You said they'd been sold. Everything'd been sold to pay for Papa's leg."

Ma Alden's face was rapidly losing the grimly furious expression in the face of sheer outrage and what looked like—confusion?

Why was this confusing to her? She knew what she was doing, lying to Maggie. Keeping this from Maggie.

Noémie. The thought filled her with boldness and righteous anger. "They were my things. Mine. So I took them.

If *you'd* not lied to me about them, then maybe your chest wouldn't be broken."

"You had no *right,* Maggie." It was Patience this time, gasping, shocked. "*You* ruined Ma's chest?" She shrugged as Ma Alden whirled furiously to face her. "Sorry, Ma. I suppose I should've told you. I saw it the day of Etta's wedding, when I was looking for linens. Saw the lock was broken, and the wood on the front damaged. I knew how upset you'd be over it, and so I didn't want to tell you about it and ruin—ruin things for Etta. I thought it was—well, I thought Maybe Jed had got to it."

They exchanged a long look and then turned to Maggie, both with stern, angry expressions. Both with arms folded over their bodices. Will's face, beside her, was a study of shock and horror, as he looked at Maggie.

"*You* haven't a right!" Maggie shouted, then. "None of you. Neither of you."

Patience shook a finger at her. "Why, Maggie, you ought—"

"No! Shut up! You haven't any right—to—tell me what to do, to pretend you're my mother." Maggie walked toward them, pointing an angry finger. "When you lie. Patience, *you* lied, too. All this time." It was a scream now, a throat-shattering scream that scared her to hear, and continued and didn't stop. The words seemed to spill out of her mouth like pus from a septic wound. "Ma Alden killed the baby, and *you* pretend nothing happened."

The slap came, swift and fast, from Patience's cool hand. It shattered the red rage that had taken over Maggie's mind, her words leaving her depleted and raw.

"Sit down," Patience said clearly, quietly. Her face was pale, drawn.

Fear. That fear again. Of what? Maggie said it already. *Say it, Patience, just say it. The word is murder.*

"Sit, Maggie. Calm down, and say your piece. Mother," Patience added in a trembling voice, as Ma Alden started forward and opened her mouth. "Let's hear Maggie out. She's a good girl. She's never done something like this before. She's clearly been upset and worried over—over something, these past several weeks. Let her speak."

Maggie's eyes were streaming. Hot liquid ran down her face. She sat, feeling as if something solid blocked her throat.

"Tell us, Maggie," Patience said and knelt by Maggie's knee, trying to look into her eyes. "What are you so worked up about? What happened with the chest? I'm sorry I—please, just tell me and we can get this out in the open."

Maggie drew several deep, ragged breaths, feeling a mixture of mortification and fear, and a moderate return of the anger. She glanced at Will. "Does he have to be here?"

"I'll go," he said abruptly, nodding at Patience. "See you later, over at the Bells' house?"

Patience nodded. She waited until the door closed behind him before she turned back to Maggie expectantly. Her expression was calm but veiled.

Maggie stared at her for a long moment. *She's hiding something.* "It started the day of the move back north. I saw my mother's name on the mattress. And a while later I found the china. A chip—a handle, in the old homestead. And I started having . . . having dreams. About Ma Alden and—" Maggie nodded.

"Mother and *what?"*

"And the baby. A baby with dark hair. Dreams that she took a pillow and . . ." She demonstrated with her hands.

Patience sat back, her hands over her mouth.

"And then," Maggie continued, keeping her gaze fixed on Patience's horrified eyes, "Sister Clegg told me. About—about Noémie. Baby Jane. I—I don't know how it happened, but my mind sort of erased it. I didn't remember until I had the dream, until she told me. And I knew what the dreams meant."

"You think I killed baby Jane," Ma Alden spoke up then.

The room seemed to grow suddenly hotter, stiller. Silence. Maggie felt a vein throbbing in her forehead.

"You think *I* would—" Ma Alden laughed. It was a horrible thing to hear, a mix of sarcasm and hysteria. "Girl, if you knew the truth, you'd be on your knees, begging my forgiveness."

Maggie whirled around and stared at her, open-mouthed. "Forgiveness for *what?* For being upset you strangled—you murdered Noémie?"

"You're asking questions you don't want the answers to, girl."

"Mother," Patience said. There was something in the tone again, that same thing as at the Harrisons'.

Patience knows something. She knows. "Tell me," she said flatly. "I've a right to know."

"She died in her sleep. As I said to you once before. Now leave it, Maggie."

"We found her in your bed," Ma Alden said, with the air of somebody delivering a fatal blow. "In *your* bed, that morning. Dead."

Maggie shook her head "My bed? What're you saying? You killed my baby sister and put her in my bed?"

Ma Alden laughed again. Maggie wanted to cover her ears against the noise. "Tell her, Patience. She'll believe you. And right now she thinks *I* killed the baby. There's no help for it. Damage's been done, way I see it."

At this, Patience's calm countenance broke. She rested her forehead in her palm. "I can't," she whispered.

A sudden uneasiness came over Maggie, as she watched Patience struggle, struggle with something—something wrong. *Something's wrong.*

Patience nodded then, and raised her eyes. "I—I don't want to hurt you, Maggie."

Maggie flicked a glance at Ma Alden. The grim satisfaction on the older woman's face. *Something's wrong.*

"We kept what happened from you because we didn't want you to know." Patience's voice was kind—and excruciating. Her face held a sorrow and concern that chilled Maggie to the bone. "You really feel you need to know, then, Maggie?"

It was like someone had nodded for Maggie, jerked her head up and down. She felt frozen in place, stiff.

Something—about to fall.

Je ne desiree pas savoir. Patience, you are frightening me.

"You killed her!"

It was Ma Alden who said it, who couldn't contain the words any longer.

Maggie frowned at her, shaking her head a little. "It's—no."

"There. Now you know." Ma Alden was breathing heavily, clutching the shawl to her chest so hard, her knuckles shone white.

Maggie stared at Ma Alden. "It's a lie."

She said it, but there was no conviction in it. She knew, as soon as the words were spoken—no, she knew it before that. She saw it in her mind, an image.

No. She pushed it away.

"First I lost Lucy," Ma Alden was going on, muttering as if to herself. She clutched her shawl tight, as if there were a blizzard in the room. "I had to bury her in a snow bank. She was dying, and I saw the baby, those dark eyes, laying in the wagon. And I took her to my breast, full of milk all ready for a baby, and I brought her home."

She sighed and sat down on the floor. "Jane. A gift from God on the trail, to make up for my suffering. And we took the two older girls too, of course. And then, six months later, she lay between the two of them, the two big girls, dead and blue, her face tangled in the linens—you took her from me." Ma Alden's voice rose now, hateful and bitter, and she pointed a shaking finger. "You, Maggie. You! I told you and *told* you, but you didn't know no English, and you didn't much care what anyone else thought or said. Always been headstrong, always wanted things your own way, always thought you could take better care of the baby—"

"Stop." Patience's voice was quiet, but there was a force behind it that somehow stopped it—stopped the horrible words.

Maggie, trembling from head to foot, turned to stare at Patience.

The answer was in her face—Patience's soft eyes, full of a wrenching sort of sadness, a regret that chilled Maggie to the bone. "It was an accident, Maggie."

Maggie stumbled, clattering over the popcorn pan, scattering white puffs everywhere.

"It was . . . an accident, you didn't mean to. You—" Patience shook her head, and then tears started sliding down her nose. Her shoulders began to shake as she cried, silently, gazing at Maggie.

Maggie tried to regain her balance. She sat down,

missing the hearth, and landed hard on the floor. "It's a lie," she got out.

"It was—'twas my fault too." Ma Alden's tone was entirely different from before—husky, ragged.

Patience turned to stare at Ma Alden. "No," she said.

Maggie seized upon it, like a drowning person making a grab for anything, anything that will keep them above water. "What did you do to her?" her voice was hoarse.

Ma Alden was to blame, she had to be. Ma Alden did it, killed her sister.

"Figured," Ma Alden continued after a moment, muttering almost to herself again. "I figured Magdalena'd gone through enough and didn't know any better, and felt the need for comfort with all three sisters. Tried to keep a closer watch on Jane's cradle to make sure she didn't take her in the tick with all those blankets and Gigi, who's always tossing in her sleep like she's having a fever fit. Maggie slept like the dead in those days right after the crossing. We had to use cold water or lift 'er out of bed and shake 'er to wake her up betimes. But one morning I woke up to find the cradle empty, and Maggie and Gigi in the bed, and I asked Patience to get the baby and Patience found her under—under—"

Maggie felt as if all feeling had left her. She couldn't look at Ma Alden, couldn't look at Patience. Her mind seemed to have become coldly logical; she thought through all that they were saying, and had said, and felt only iciness inside.

She could believe—could almost force herself to believe—that Ma Alden might lie about something like this. It was a stretch, but she could make her mind fit that possibility. But Patience? Who was always charitable, usually calm and reasonable, and who had sometimes taken her side? Patience would not lie. She wouldn't lie about this.

I killed her.

Baby Jane, baby Noémie. The flower-face, the sweet smile, and plump cheeks. So full of joy and life. The dark eyes that were so like her mother's.

Maggie's mother. The way she looked before she died, holding Noémie tight to her, keeping her wrapped close in the ragged flannel blanket where she lay in the wagon bed. And Maggie, who—

The image slid into her mind, in spite of her struggle to resist it. It was the image from her dream.

The baby, with plump limbs frantically wiggling, little fingers grabbing. Stilling, and then turning cold. Turning blue.

Maggie folded her arms tight around her chest and began to rock on the ground.

Patience knelt then too and put a hand on her shoulder. "Maggie."

Maggie brushed her hand aside. She stood and made for the door.

She ran without looking, without even realizing that she had caught her stocking on the cabin's doorframe and rent it all the way up her thigh. She ran through the Higbees' field, ran down Seventh, not caring about whom she nearly ran over, or the way people stared after her. She got all the way to the edge of town and stopped running. She stood, looking out at the wide, waving fields. She turned, then, and began to walk. Her body knew where she was going, even though her mind was nothing; it was just an empty space full of some horrible feeling.

Time seemed to stop and race furiously on at the same time. She walked, and walked, and walked, without seeing anything around her.

Finally, she found herself there. *Here, it's always here*, she thought. She took a step inside and collapsed onto the floor, breathing in dust and soot.

This is purgatory. This place. I'm dead. Or dying, right now.

Heavenly Father, please let me die.

She lay there for a long time, feeling a pulse beat steadily in her temple, up against the hard coldness of the floor.

She began to shiver. The involuntary movement took her out of her trance. Slowly she moved, one limb at a time. She rose to her feet, feeling dizzy.

It drew her like a magnet. She walked outside and around the cabin and knelt down by the little marker, and feeling flooded through her in a hot tide. She felt as if she were burning or being pressed hard on all sides with an excruciating, terrible force meant to crush her.

Her temple throbbed still. She felt like her heart must be beating, dying, in the small patch of ground underneath her.

When she stood again, she couldn't feel her feet past the ankle or her fingers. She walked back into the little homestead. She lay down and wished that she could stop breathing.

A STORY

MAGGIE WOKE ON THE COLD, HARD FLOOR. THERE WAS that cruel restful moment as she wondered what she was doing on a floor, and then it all rushed back. Agony.

She stood, shaking.

Why am I still alive? was her only coherent thought, as she walked slowly back to Hosters. Maybe she would freeze on the way home, if she lingered a little.

Maggie was so tired, so cold, that she could barely put one foot in front of the other. After what seemed like a year of walking, the Higbees' snow-piled field came into view. She waded through. She got to the little cabin's back door and opened it. She stood there, swaying for a moment. She tripped over the step and fell, headlong, on the floor.

She couldn't get up.

Liz Ellen, who was busy at the stove with something, saw her and shouted. Everything went black.

Maggie woke up again. Again, there was that moment of confusion, and again, the sudden rush of pain.

"Maggie?" It was Giovanna's voice, but it had a worried tone to it that was so uncharacteristic, that Maggie could hardly believe it really was Giovanna.

Maggie turned her head and saw her sister's dark eyes and furrowed brow. "Maggie, do you need help?"

"Go back to the Aldens," Maggie mumbled, and turned on her side, so that her back was to her sister.

"Megs." Giovanna touched Maggie's shoulder.

Maggie shrugged it off. "Go home," she snapped. "Stop crying. I can't do nothing for you, Giovanna. Leave me alone."

The only bearable thing was sleep. Maggie slept, and slept, and slept. When she would wake, she covered her face with the quilt and tried not to move much, to make it easy for her body and mind to go back to sleep again. Sometimes she lay like that for hours, just listening to her own shallow breathing. A few times, Liz Ellen tried to get her out of bed. Maggie just batted her away silently or gave her a look that could rival one of Liz Ellen's own.

The day faded into evening and back to day. Maggie woke up sometimes when it was dark, and sometimes when it was light. She felt weak and knew she must be hungry and thirsty, but for some reason it wasn't enough to get her out of bed. She began to sleep longer, with just short periods of waking. Life became a half-dream for Maggie; she dreamed about Ma Alden and Patience, Liz Ellen, Henry and Hyrum, and Sister Harrison and Sister Clegg. She dreamed of Samuel. She didn't know what was real and what was a dream. It all began to run together.

And then, suddenly, she was jostled awake when a pair of arms picked her up.

She cried out; it felt wrenching, cruel. She opened her eyes, half-expecting to see Ma Alden there, bent on torturing her some more.

Instead, it was Henry's face. Henry? That couldn't be real.

Maggie blinked, shut them tight, and opened them again.

Still Henry. And now she was being bundled—roughly, it felt like—into a blanket.

"No," she said, only nothing came out of her mouth. Her voice was rusted away from lack of water.

"Quiet," Henry said grimly. "You're coming to my ma's whether you like it or not."

"Where you going with her?" Scotch asked, wrinkling his nose as Henry walked past him carrying Maggie.

"Never you mind," Henry snapped. "Just tell your sister I've taken her. Where's Giovanna?"

"Back at the Aldens'," was the mild reply.

Something like shock ran through Maggie's system. She thought of Uncle Forth, and of Jed. Giovanna, back at the Aldens'?

Maggie groaned and shut her eyes tight. She had done it. She had told Giovanna to go back there.

But what did Maggie have to offer that was better? She was a murderer. At least Uncle Forth and Jed didn't kill people. Giovanna was better off with the Aldens.

But her uneasiness had been roused, and her mind couldn't quite settle back into the stupor that she had maintained over the past few days.

As Henry carried her outside, Maggie began to struggle a little bit.

"Stay still."

Maggie frowned at him. There was something in his voice—was he angry at her?

He lowered her into a wagon. He ran back inside and came out carrying another quilt, which he bundled around her. "Hang on," he said. "It's going to be a little bumpy."

Maggie managed to get herself into a sitting position, clinging to the side of the wagon, by the time they pulled up around back of the Clegg's house.

"Don't bring me in there," Maggie said when Henry came around again. "Please."

"Maggie, you need help. I don't care what you say or do. You can take a bite out of me if you like. But you're staying here for a while."

Maggie began to shiver violently. The humiliation of it all was too much. She felt tears begin to pour down her face. "I didn't ask for help," she croaked.

"Well, you're getting it. I don't mean to let you wallow, Maggie. Patience told me what happened. She's been by a time or two, but Liz Ellen wouldn't let her up to see you, and she got worried. I figured Liz Ellen might let me up into her precious hayloft. She's learned to trust me better."

"Patience told you? Does—does everyone know now?"

"Maggie, you can't stew over this. It wasn't your fault!"

"It was my fault," Maggie said dully. "Didn't Patience tell you?"

"I know there's no reasoning with you right now, Maggie, so keep quiet."

Maggie flinched at his tone.

"Ma's expecting you," he continued as he shoved open the door with a shoulder. "She's been just as worried as I have. One thing you need to learn, Mag. When people love you, you're accountable to them. Time to throw away that pride of yours, because what happens to you isn't just your affair. It's not . . ."

And there, Henry's voice broke. He kept his face turned away from her as he set her gently on the rocking chair in front of the fire. He turned on his heel and left, then, shutting the door behind him with a bit more force than was necessary.

Sister Clegg came in.

Maggie blinked at her. The room seemed dotted with drifting speckles of light; they collected at the edges of her sight, threatening to blind her.

"Can you walk to the bedroom?"

"I killed my sister," Maggie rasped again. It wasn't what she had meant to say—it just came out.

Sister Clegg went to the kitchen and came back with a cup of water. She held it to Maggie's lips. "Let's not have any of that talk right now. You need some nourishing, and you need to clean up a bit. I've got the washtub in my room full of hot water and some soap. Think you can manage?"

Maggie's used her arms to lift herself a little out of the rocking chair. Sister Clegg slid an arm under her, just as Henry had, and lifted her.

"You must be made of nothing," she remarked. She unbuttoned Maggie's dress, and peeled her out of her underthings. She tossed these in a pile on the floor and lowered Maggie into the tub. "I'm afraid to leave you," she said. "I'll just sit here on the bed and let you soak a bit."

Maggie had no pride left. She didn't say a word, but she took the washcloth and dabbed at her underarms and at her face and neck.

The room spun around her, and her heart felt like it was beating very slowly, thrumming against her ribs.

She pressed the washcloth to her face, and suddenly had the urge to vomit. There was nothing in her stomach, and so it was just dry heaves, over the edge of the tub. Tears came with them. *Maybe*, she thought, dizzily, *maybe I'm only crying?*

Sister Clegg took the washcloth from Maggie's hand, lathered it up, and ran it quickly over her limbs, shoulders, over the small curves of her chest and hips. Maggie barely had time to be mortified before Sister Clegg wrapped a blanket around her shoulders and pulled her out. She laid her on the bed, as if Maggie were a little child, and then covered her with several quilts. She laid a hot brick at Maggie's feet.

"I'll be back with some broth. Try to stay awake, Maggie. I don't want to have to wake you. Like as not, the broth'll knock you right out, after not eating for three whole days."

Maggie felt like her shame was choking her. She laid her head on the mattress and wished something would happen—the ceiling would fall in on her.

Sister Clegg came back in a few minutes later. She sat on the side of the bed, close to Maggie's head and gestured for her to sit up.

Her face brooked no argument. Maggie slid up into a sitting position.

"I can do it," she protested when the spoon touched her lips.

"Let me help you," Sister Clegg said.

"You already do. Too much."

Sister Clegg spooned some broth into Maggie's mouth and sat back, regarding her with a bit of sternness. "No, Maggie. I don't. What I do is only a small fraction of what I wish you'd let me do for you and for your sister. You're like a daughter to me, and have been ever since you and Henry and Hyrum used to scamper around those muddy riverbanks together."

At the mention of Henry, Maggie turned her head aside.

"Maggie?"

"It's not right," Maggie replied after a long moment. "I plague you by giving Henry a bad name. People talk about us."

"People 'round here don't have much to talk about, and so they make things up. I know how people are. I've never given a straw for anyone's opinion that I didn't respect. And, Maggie, nobody says anything like that about you and Henry, anyhow. People know you're a good girl. Here."

Maggie opened her mouth obligingly, swallowed, and shook her head. "We're older now, Sister Clegg."

"Yes," Sister Clegg replied. "You are. And I'm not surprised that my son still enjoys your company. That he seems to enjoy it more and more, even—when you give him the time of day, that is. You're a girl with quite a few charms. Not the least of them, that you're like none of the other girls in town."

At this speech, Maggie looked incredulously at her.

"Well, I'm sad to see how surprised you are that I'd say it. Don't you ever take time out from all your worrying lately to think of things like that? Girlish things, like who you might marry one day, or sparking and such?"

"I—I'm not that sort of girl," Maggie answered. She held her hand out for the spoon.

Sister Clegg handed it to her this time and set the bowl in her lap. Maggie could feel the warmth of it through the quilts.

"What sort of girl?" Sister Clegg asked.

"The sort who should have thoughts of sparking and marriage."

Sister Clegg frowned. "Why?"

Maggie shrugged. She didn't want to talk about her lack of refinement, about what Ma Alden had said so many times recently, about Maggie making a fool of herself going after the Clegg boys. The darker thought hovered in her mind.

She couldn't face it. "I'm not a good girl," she said instead.

As if hearing her thoughts, Sister Clegg took Maggie's chin in her hand. "You would be welcome in my family, Maggie, if you ever had reason to be," she said. "I know I can't choose my daughters-in-law, but you'd be one of my choices if I could. And . . . you've got to get this through your head. *It wasn't your fault.*"

Maggie sat, looking into Sister Clegg's clear blue eyes, and couldn't quite believe it. But why would Sister Clegg say nice things to her? Maggie had nothing to give her. It had always been Sister Clegg's charity that had Maggie sitting in her living room, hemming handkerchiefs and learning to sew.

It reminded Maggie of another moment, when someone had taken her chin in their hand and given her a talking to. The contrast was completely stunning and completely confusing. Maggie felt the moisture well up at the corner of her eyes. She turned her head away again. "You shouldn't have to do this for me," she said.

Sister Clegg let go and sighed. "Maggie, I'm going to tell you a story. No, keep eating while I tell it. I want that bowl empty soon as you can manage it."

Maggie sat back against the headboard of the bed and sipped at the broth.

"Once, a family moved into a little house outside the walled fort of a pioneer town. It wasn't Provo. It wasn't even here in Deseret, I don't think. But it was in a part of the territory far from any large settlement, and so the people there tended to rely on each other a lot for help with harvesting, tending children, and sharing what little food they had during the winters. It was a small town, and the ground they planted on was not really very good, and so they barely scraped by each winter. But they were happy, nonetheless. They had each other's society, and they knew that what anybody had, they all had. And so they got by.

"When this new family first moved in people tried to be neighborly. Someone would go by every couple days or so, even though they lived far out enough to make it a morning's or afternoon's task. Knowing how hard it was to weather a first harvest and planting season out there on the prairie, the friendly townspeople would bring gifts of eggs and flour and other goods from time to time.

"But each time somebody paid them a visit, these people acted like they weren't all that grateful. They seemed tetchy and uncomfortable, especially the father of the family. They would receive the visitors with cool courtesy, but they refused all the gifts brought to them.

"Well, you know how it is in a small town, where people have nothing much to entertain themselves with. People in town talked about the family. First they just considered on how strange, and to themselves, these new people were. But then there were rumors that began, about how the father was likely an escaped convict. A whole elaborate story began to form about the father. In the end, the townspeople became convinced that he must have done something truly terrible to make him so afraid of being discovered, and thus, of the society of neighbors that, to all in the little town, seemed the most natural thing in the world.

"In the course of that year, the new family was very little in town. They never went to town functions or even church meetings. They stayed by themselves, in their little cabin out on their own fields, several miles from the town walls.

"One day, there was a terrible lightning storm. Those kinds of storms come up quietly and cause all kinds of havoc; I know you've never seen one, Maggie. It was like that out in Missouri, though. Well, anyhow, this particular lightning storm had caused a lot of damage to the property of one of the prominent members in the little town. And as he was going about chopping down his dead trees and repairing his roof, which had been struck and burned by lightning, he suddenly thought of this family. He suddenly remembered that there happened to be a tall, magnificent old oak tree that stood a stone's throw from the little cabin, prime target for lightning. He wondered if they had weathered it all right.

"You see, Maggie, this man, who later became the mayor when the town grew large enough to need one, was full of charitable kindness and wisdom. He hadn't given ear to the rumors that had spread throughout the town. He knew how people could be and was wise enough to give ear only to truth. So he decided to visit the family. He rode out, the morning after the storm, on his little pony only to stop by and see what the damage may have been, but he brought nothing with him because he knew it would only be refused.

"When he got to the house, he saw his fears hadn't been off the mark. The tree was in a complete ruin; the trunk cracked in two. The branches that remained were scorched by the fire of the lightning. It was lucky for the family, the man thought, as he went to knock on the door, that the rain put it out and the house didn't catch fire as well."

Sister Clegg sat back now and observed Maggie for a moment.

Maggie shrugged and settled the empty bowl into the hollow of her lap. She nodded at Sister Clegg and clasped her hands, interlocking her fingers, and stared at them. "Good story," she said.

"Isn't finished," Sister Clegg said.

"All right."

"There was no answer at all to his knock. He thought it was strange and leaned against the door to see if he could hear anything. All was silent. Just for politeness's sake, he knocked again and waited before he tried the door. It opened easily.

"The sight he found was terrible. The whole family lay dead, Maggie—dead in the house. The state of them when he found them was awful as well; it was clear they had been dead for some time.

"The man rushed back to town and told everybody what he had found, and immediately a group of volunteers was got to go in the house and carefully take care of the mess and the bodies.

"It was a sad thing. And the saddest part of it all, Maggie, was the fact that they got the most help from their neighbors only after it was too late, when they weren't alive to let their pride get in the way of their needs.

"The people in the little town held a small service and buried them. Being a small town, everybody came. The little graveyard was full, even though nobody in town really knew the family. The people later speculated that it was likely that the family died from an illness, or from bad water, and living so far out of town, they couldn't make it to town to ask for help. And as nobody regularly visited them, there was nobody to know about their plight and intervene before it was too late for them all."

Maggie had finished her soup. She sat, with her fingers interlaced over her stomach.

"Well?" Sister Clegg said, picking up the bowl and spoon.

"Is that a true story?

There must be a hint of the skepticism she felt in her voice, because Sister Clegg's brow furrowed. "Don't know, Maggie. But it could be. Something like that could very well happen. It's something you ought to think seriously about, if you really plan on striking out on your own, and taking care of your sister, to boot."

"I take what people give me!" Maggie cried. "All the time. All winter I have. I've swallowed and gulped down my pride. And now she's back with the Aldens, so it don't matter anyhow."

"But that's just the thing," Sister Clegg interrupted. "There ought to be no pride at all. Be proud, Maggie, to live in a place like we do, where you can take and give and get by, and know you are cared for by a family as big as a town."

Maggie sighed. Her frustration made it almost like a growl. "I don't have anything to give in return, though. I'm fair useless. It's not the same. I—I reckon God's punishing me, Sister Clegg." She glanced at the older woman's face, at the serious expression there, and quickly looked down at her hands again.

"Nonsense. I believe God can feel your sorrow wrench at Him same as anyone else who loves you, Maggie. Tragedy strikes at all of us, and we all blame ourselves for a while before we get through it. And Maggie, don't forget Ephesians. There are seasons. Seasons of receiving, and one day, your season of giving will come. You give us all a gift Maggie, in just being who you are."

Maggie squeezed her fingers together so hard that the

tips turned white. "But what if I end up—what if I have little chance to give back in my life."

"Well, in that case, you give back in kindness, in cheer and neighborliness, and in thanks and letting others have the blessings of doing for you. But I doubt that what you worry about will come to pass, Maggie. You're too pretty and too smart, and far too determined to end up the way you fear you will." She nodded, almost to herself. "Stay with us a week, Maggie. Please let me get you back to health before you go off on your own again. Let me be a mother to you for just a little while."

Maggie shook her head. She felt tired, too tired to take all this in, and it really didn't matter, anyway. The rotten, awful feeling at her core, the knowledge of what she had done, was all she could feel and care about. "Thanks," she croaked out and slid down in the bed and pulled the covers over her head as soon as Sister Clegg left the room.

It was like things had completely upended on Maggie. She had been scared to sleep before, but now her dreams were not what she dreaded. It was life, and the awful realities that faced her there. Her dreams were nothing in comparison.

THE LETTER

MAGGIE STAYED THE ENTIRE WEEK AT THE CLEGGS', JUST AS she had promised. She was so miserable that she was glad that they all mostly left her alone.

The room she stayed in was the only one off the main room on the first floor. After the first two days, she got up and helped Sister Clegg with sewing and mending as she usually would do, but retired to the room early in the evening.

Henry came in every day for lunch. Maggie didn't know exactly what to say to him. She generally avoided looking at him, and he generally avoided her. But every time he came in, she felt her heart beat oddly, and she knew where he was at every moment.

A few times he came over to her and said something joking or teasing, but Maggie just didn't have the heart to respond as she usually did.

"You feel like going fishing?" he asked one morning as he was getting his boots on.

This brought Maggie out of her fog. "What? There's likely at least six inches of ice over the pools!"

"There it is." He grinned at her.

Maggie frowned at him. "What?"

"That look."

"What look?"

"Like you're sure I've completely gone off the deep end. I've missed it. I've been tempted to turn cartwheels in the middle of the floor, these past few days, just to see it again."

Maggie snorted but couldn't come up with a clever response. Her mind was muffled, somehow. It was stuffed with so many tangled thoughts and worries that nothing came through clearly.

"I've been wondering if getting sick gave you some kind of brain fever or something."

Maggie blinked at this. She shook her head and went back to her sewing.

Henry sighed then and went out the door.

Maggie looked up and watched him through the window. She could see him all the way out to the street, up until he turned the corner.

Christmas had come and gone while Maggie was whiling her time away in the Hosters' loft. She was glad. She did not feel like celebrating or socializing. She said hardly a word to any of the Cleggs except, "thank you," but she said those words a lot. She felt compelled to say them.

She thought of Giovanna often. She felt so much, so many things all mixed and inseparable, when she thought of her sister, because immediately she would think of her other sister, and bring back the horrible images from her dream.

Or perhaps they were memories.

Maggie worried so much over Giovanna, thinking

of Jed and Uncle Forth and Ma Alden, that she felt sick almost all the time. Jed would, no doubt, be extra teasing and cruel toward Giovanna now. He had gotten a reaction out of Maggie and out of Patience, which was what he liked. And his pa clearly wouldn't stop him or lay a hand on him. And Maggie knew that Ma Alden wouldn't do much either; she had never intervened on Maggie's behalf.

But Maggie also knew that she could not take care of Giovanna. It would be worse for Giovanna to live with Maggie, who had let her nearly die of cold and had killed their baby sister, than it was for Giovanna to have to endure the torture of Jed's attentions and the neglect of Ma Alden. At least, with the Aldens, Giovanna was fed well enough and kept warm. And at least she had Patience there to make sure of some things.

The inevitable, horrifying conclusion that was stewing in Maggie's mind was that she should go back to the Aldens'. There, she could at least do something to intervene if she had to. And she couldn't stand it, being away from her sister like this. She just couldn't stand it, even though she knew she wasn't a good caretaker for Giovanna, even though she had felt all of the fire of Giovanna's annoyance and wrath over the past weeks and knew that her sister likely despised her more now. Giovanna had to know that Maggie had killed Noémie. Ma Alden wouldn't keep quiet about it anymore, not when she had felt Maggie's accusations. She would defend her own actions, and, to get back in everybody's good graces including Giovanna's, she would not keep herself from laying out everything that had happened.

Maggie felt the shame of it. The burden was almost physical, pressing her shoulders down, slumping her neck

Maggie realized now that she deserved her lot. By herself,

she was a nobody. Somebody who needed care, who needed charity. With the Aldens, at least she had a future, even if that future was washing other people's clothes up in Great Salt Lake City someday.

It was these thoughts that lead Maggie, at the end of her week with the Cleggs', to bundle up in her shawl and walk slowly over to the Aldens'.

She felt her heart race as she knocked at the door.

A moment later it was flung open, by Giovanna.

Maggie and Giovanna stood and looked at each other for a long moment. Giovanna's eyes were large, her face inscrutable. And then her mouth trembled a little, and the corners lowered.

"Are you back, Maggie?"

Maggie nodded. She felt the heat of shame and heartbreak wash over her. Giovanna hated her now, and it was not surprising, considering all Maggie had put her through, and for nothing. *I am a terrible person.*

Just as this crossed her mind, Giovanna surprised Maggie by throwing her arms around her and squeezing her hard. "I was worried," she said. And then, just as quickly, she let go, slid under Maggie's arm and out the door. "Tell Ma Alden I'm over playing with Scotch and Davy."

Maggie opened her mouth to object. It was habit, but she caught herself in time. She shoved her dismay aside. "All right."

Giovanna stood outside on the path, facing her. "Will you tell her, then?"

"I'll tell her."

Giovanna frowned. "Well—all right, then," she said. She turned around and trudged slowly toward the gate, almost as if she was reluctant to go.

Maggie steeled herself to walk into the empty house. She sat in the rocker and waited, feeling jumpy and nervous. She picked up some darning and began on a sock, for the sake of keeping her hands busy, but soon put it on her lap and crossed her hands over it.

When Maggie finally heard footsteps outside, she felt relieved and sick all at once. She looked at the door, waiting for it to swing open.

When it did, she was so relieved to see Patience that she almost cried.

Patience stopped still in the doorway. "Well, hello."

Maggie nodded.

Patience walked into the living room, and Maggie leapt out of the rocking chair, moving toward her usual place on the hearth. The forgotten darning rolled onto the floor.

"No, you can sit there," Patience urged.

"No," Maggie replied. "No, I'll just—" She sat down on the warm bricks, scrambling to pick up the tangled wool and darning needle. "Is Ma out somewhere?"

"Over at the Forths'." Patience sighed and sank into the rocker. She pulled something out of her apron pocket.

"What is that?" Maggie asked.

Patience colored. "I'm just doing a little bit of lace."

Maggie nodded, unwilling to ask more questions in spite of her curiosity. Why did Patience need to knit lace? It wasn't like her to be so vain, and she wasn't mad about getting her trousseau in order as Etta had always been.

"Ma'll be over to make dinner," Patience remarked.

"All right." Maggie felt the nervous flutters start again.

It was almost a welcome respite when, a moment later, the door opened and Ma Alden walked in, loaded down with a large bundle of linens. "Dale's got some mending," she called out, backing into the room. Patience leapt up to help her, and Maggie just sat in the chair, trembling.

Ma Alden set the linens down on the floor. She froze for a moment when she saw Maggie. "It's right cold out," she said, fumbling over her consonants.

"Yes," Maggie replied.

Ma Alden stood there a moment, as if searching her mind for something further to say. She turned, finally, back to Patience. "All right, well. Let's cook up some ham with the potatoes and onions this time. Dale's coming over."

Maggie flinched internally at the mention of Uncle Forth. For something to do, she reached out and grabbed at one of the linens. "Got a thimble?" she rasped.

Patience and Ma Alden turned and looked at her in surprise.

"Sure," Patience said. "Use mine. It's in my workbasket there against the wall. Needle's stuck in it."

Maggie rummaged through Patience's workbasket until she found thimble, needle, and thread. She picked up a linen sheet and realized that it was soiled.

"You need these washed?"

Ma Alden looked over her shoulder at Maggie. "Before they're mended, they likely need a bit of washing."

Maggie stood, walked across the room, and picked up the washtub.

"You'll have to crack the ice on the ditch," Patience said.

"Just use snow," Ma Alden snapped. "And put on something warm, for heaven's sake."

"I'll only be out there a minute," Maggie muttered, but she stood in the doorway as Ma Alden wrapped her large wool shawl around Maggie's shoulders.

"You're only a bit of a thing," Ma Alden mumbled. "Still,

those skirts need to be a bit longer, don't they?"

Maggie stared at Ma Alden, feeling like the world had suddenly tipped on its edge.

Ma Alden avoided her gaze as she tucked in the ends of the shawl. "Be quick, it's no weather to be out in." She turned and shut the door behind her.

Maggie stared at it for a full minute before she walked out into the middle of the field to find clean snow. She bent and scooped it into the washtub with her bare hands. They turned red with cold. Maggie didn't really feel them. She bent and scooped up snow and dumped it, feeling like a piece of machinery with gears and pulleys that moved automatically.

She felt like she was living two separate lives at once. There was her body—going about tasks, and her mind and heart, which were full of something red and boiling, and unbearable.

"Hey," a voice cut through her thoughts.

She looked up, and saw Jed Forth.

"You're back now, eh?"

His tone was belligerent.

Maggie stood and squared her shoulders and gazed at him. She suddenly realized that she wasn't afraid of Jed, for herself at least. He could do nothing to her that would be worse than what she was already feeling.

He moved a step closer, as if he sensed a challenge.

It might be lucky for Maggie that the door opened at that moment, and Ma Alden stuck her head out.

"You got enough wash water yet? Oh, there you are, Jed. Come on in and get warm. Where's your pa?"

Maggie stamped her snow off and set the washtub on the hearth to warm. She sat on the little stool, and took some wool stockings from the mending basket. "Where's

Giovanna?" she asked Patience in a low tone. "She said she was going with the Hosters but it's almost dark."

Patience looked up from her lace. Her eyes slid in the direction of the stove, where Ma Alden was busy. "Schoolhouse, most likely," she said.

"Oh." Maggie stared at the stocking, fingering the large hole in the toe.

"Hook's right there in the yarn."

Pa Alden came in, covered in snow. When he saw Maggie, he grinned and patted her on the head on his way to the fireplace.

Uncle Forth came in just as Ma Alden was serving up dinner. He sat in his usual place at the hearth, opposite Pa Alden.

It's like nothing ever happened. Aside from Giovanna going to school, and Ma Alden's slight strangeness toward Maggie. It was almost like before Cedar, even, with Pa Alden acting cheery and easy once again.

It was unbearable.

"Heard anything from Great Salt Lake City lately?" Uncle Forth began, and Maggie knew they were in for it. He never asked the question because he wanted to know what somebody else had heard.

"No." Pa Alden looked up and a flicker of amusement crossed his face. "I suppose *you* have, though."

"And so I have." Uncle Forth nodded. "Judges've convicted Brigham. Brought him to court, and laid it all out there. Fine show, from what I hear. Ol' Brigham was properly set down."

"That's not what happened." The words spilled out of Maggie's mouth, and she thought for a moment they had come from somebody else.

Everybody stared at her.

"Sorry," Maggie muttered. "Didn't mean to say it out loud."

"Well, missy, why don't you tell us what makes you so sure of yourself."

"Dale, you hush yourself," Ma Alden snapped.

It was a strange moment. Uncle Forth looked at his sister, and Pa Alden looked at Maggie, and then at his wife. And there was something in the exchange of glances. Something that changed the balance, somehow, of the personalities in the room. And then there was a strange, exultant look that crossed Pa Alden's face, so quickly that Maggie couldn't be sure she had really seen it.

"Well," Uncle Forth continued after a moment. "Way I heard it—"

"You can leave it, Dale," Pa Alden cut in. "News leaks down so slowly from the city this time of year, and passes through so many shady channels and highways. I'm betting we'll hear better news come spring, when we can get it ourselves firsthand."

Maggie stood then. She couldn't stand how everyone seemed to be looking at her, but not looking at her. "Reckon I'll go—I'll go over and see if Sister Holden needs me," she said.

"Take the wrap," Ma Alden said, in a voice that brooked no argument.

Maggie wrapped the shawl around her shoulders and headed out the door. She waded through the snow, feeling it wash against the shins of her boots, and stumbled through the drift and onto Seventh. She sped her pace as she walked down the street. The pumping of her heart and the rush of blood felt a little better.

"Hey!" A head poked out of Stewarts.

"Hello, Andrew."

"Pa's got a letter for you."

Maggie felt a trickle of pleasure. It was a startling feeling and drew her to the store like the warmth of the fire. "All right," she said. "Can I come in and read it?"

"Just make sure kick your boots off."

Maggie hurried inside and took the letter from Brother Stewart's outstretched hand. She sat down on the floor, with her back against the barrel in front of the little stove. She tore it open.

"It's a long one," Maggie murmured to herself, and leaned back on the barrel to read it.

"Hey-O."

The voice wasn't as strident and playful as usual, but it was unmistakable. Maggie's lighter mood, brought on by the letter, induced her to turn and grin at Henry.

He looked surprised for a moment, and then a grin spread over his face as well. "Saw you go in from across the street at my pa's shop," he explained unapologetically. "Got a letter then? From Mariah?"

"Yep."

"Can I sit next to you and read it over your shoulder?"

Maggie scooted over to make room for Henry's back against the barrel. He sat next to her, so close that their knees were touching.

Maggie felt, in that moment, like some magic came over her. The world seemed madly bright, and her heart was full of some strange, bubbly feeling. It made her impulsive. Without even thinking about it, she laid her head against Henry's arm and held the letter in between them.

Henry's arm stiffened. He went completely still. Slowly,

gently—as if he were trying not to scare away some wild creature—he shifted his arm so that it lay lightly around her, and her back rested on one side of his chest.

It surprised Maggie, the alien impulses that overwhelmed her in that moment. She wanted to put the letter aside for a moment and turn, and gaze up into Henry's face. She had this strange desire to embrace him. And there was something fluttery and nervous, like those strange, stomach-twisted feelings she'd had, thinking of him all the time, after that day he had given her his coat.

Maggie suddenly remembered it, then. That embrace, in the snow. Embarrassed and worried that he might guess her thoughts, she kept her face trained away from Henry as she laid the letter on her lap. It took her a moment to focus on the words in front of her and not Henry's arm around her.

Maggie frowned as she read the date. It had taken a long time getting to her. What had kept Mariah from sending it right after she wrote it?

Snow, most likely. Maggie squinted, mouthing the words as she read them.

12 Dec. 1858

Dear Maggie.

This will be a long letter because I have much to say in it, some of which will be hard for me to write you. I want to ask your forgiveness right off, before you even start in. Will you forgive me, Maggie, for interfering and impertnince. But I can't help it Maggie, you have learnt by now what a big nose I have for others affares and how I can't help it. And I love you so much and want your happiness so badly and thought I could provide something of value as I live up here and you're stuck down in Provo with no means of making enquiries & co. & co.

All right, that is too much. So Maggie I will just go to and get it over with. I have been asking my ma to make inquires for me. And so far none of them came to any fru-tion but I knew my Stepfather (whose name you well know) would have a great deal more luck and so I resolved next time he came by, which does not happen often these days, to ask him to make some inquires as well. I convinced Ma to ask him. She could see it was all plaguing my heart, and so she finally gave in and consented to mention to Brother Brigham that I wanted to know about your brother Sam Cabret and where he might be.

At this, Maggie stopped reading. She folded the letter on itself and put her hand to her mouth. "Oh, my," she managed.

"I'm sorry, Maggie," Henry said. "Truly, I am. I know how much you've thought about your brother."

Maggie looked at him. "What? Sorry for what?"

Henry was silent for a moment. "I forgot you're a slow reader," he said finally. "You'd better finish the letter. You mind . . . you mind if I stay here with you?"

Maggie gazed at him for a moment. Slowly, she opened the letter again, only dread was the emotion she felt now. What could make Henry look like that? Only something terrible.

She leaned forward and read quickly now, skipping words she couldn't get right away.

When Brother Brigham came down, my Ma had me go over to a neighbor's for the day. When I came back that night, she assured me she had asked him the two questions I have been plaguing her about all these weeks. She said Brother Brigham had taken down the name I told her about and he would go see about it. He told her it was likely a Brother Toronto, who herds sheep on Antelope Island, would know something of your brother as all the Waldensian Saints (I guess there were a few families who traveled from the same part of Italy as your parents and they call themselves Waldensians) kept track of each other in the City and tended to be tight knit, and Brother Toronto felt sort of like a caretaker of them since there aren't too many living in this valley who come over from Italy, and Brother Toronto is a Secilan. At any rate he was certain he would be able to find out good information. I give you these details, Maggie, so you can be sure my information comes from good sources.

I can't tell you what tenderhooks I was on for a while. I was so anxious to hear news that I got a thrill every time anyone mentioned Brother Brigham. Which is often, of course. But I didn't hear anything at all until yesterday. Brother Brigham happened to be going up to the canyon for some business with a party coming through, and he stopped by Sugar House to see my ma on the way.

Ma tells me that Brother Brigham was sorrowful, Maggie. He was clearly sad to have to bring news that your brother died a few months ago. Your brother traveled down to Ephraim to do more herding during the move, so at least you don't have that to plague yourself about. Your brother was never in Provo.

Ma told me that Brother Brigham asked Brother Toronto about Sam Cabert, and he was cut up about it as well. Didn't know he had sisters in Provo. Though it was odd, for Brother Toronto apparently talked of sisters in

Pleasant Green. I didn't think you had any other sisters, Maggie. And Pleasant Green is the point that reaches out toward Antelope Island, and I guess has become sort of a gathering place for the few Italian Saints. So maybe your brother thought of these people as his family and thus called them his sisters.

I guess what happened is, there was an accident and they couldn't get him to the mainland fast enough to see a doctor. And they couldn't signal from the island like they usually do when there is an emergency. They tried, but there was too much fog.

I feel wretched, but I might as well get all the bad news out in one writing, and hope you forgive me this awful letter. You have been wondering about judges and rumors about people coming over. Well, I did not think much on it but asked Ma to ask about that as well. And I guess you were right. Someone has come into town. His name is Cradlebaugh. By most accounts he seems a reasonable man. Brother Brigham told my ma that those he has talked to thinks he will be reasonable and follow in the path of Cummings, upholding the will of the people and bishops. But he (the new judge) has told one or two people (acc. to my stepfather) that he means to go down to Cedar to get a good look into all that happened down there before coming up to Provo and setting up court there.

That is all I know, and I beg you do not worry on it too much, and you forgive me for interference in your affairs and bringing you the worst news as a result. But I figure you would want to know, Maggie. And I figure you are a strong soul. Stronger than anyone I've met. So I figure you will get through it all just fine.

Please write me back soon as you can and reassure me that you don't hate me and that you are all right.

With love,

Mariah.

It took Maggie a moment to digest. She stopped and set the letter down for a moment, after the part where Mariah gave her the information about Samuel's death. And then she picked up the letter and read the rest of it more carefully, in case there was anything else. And then she read it once more from beginning to end.

"You all right?"

Henry's voice startled Maggie. She had almost forgotten he was there.

"Fine." Maggie folded the letter up and put it in her pocket. "I've got to go."

"You sure you're all right? You know, Maggie—that part about the sisters in Pleasant Green—"

"I'm fine," Maggie snapped. She shrugged his hand off her shoulder.

"Maggie, I don't think you are," Henry said. "Maggie, let us help you!"

"I don't need help," Maggie muttered. "There's nothing you can do anyway, Henry."

She walked out the door into the snow. She felt oddly empty. It was good, because she knew she ought to be feeling a lot worse. Maybe if she just kept on going, kept her feet moving, she wouldn't have to feel it. Like hypothermia, if she just kept moving, maybe she would survive.

She made her way up snowy streets, off to the side to let others pass. She felt the soft brush of the snow banks against her skirts.

At the edge of the town blocks, the cold began to seep into her, making her bones throb. She stood there a moment, looking out on the wide, white expanse of the empty fields east of town. She sat, suddenly, in the snow, with her back up against a fence post.

She gazed up at the mountains. Squaw Peak had always looked, to Maggie, like it had been created for the express purpose of jumping. *It's a giant jump-off point, jutting out over the valley so that you could fall thousands of feet without hitting anything. Maybe it even gave you enough time to lose all your senses, before that final, terrible crash into the earth.*

With their blue color and caps of snow, which trailed in lacy white lines down their sides, Maggie could almost imagine they were giant waves, big enough to reach her, there on the edge of the fields. She could almost sense a little bit of motion. They were slowly coming for her. They would take her, and sweep her up, up, up, over their tops, and fold her inside of them, and she wouldn't have to think or feel anymore.

Maggie stood then. She couldn't feel her legs, but she didn't need to feel them. She could still walk, and so she did. It gave her a tiny edge of pleasure to wade through the snow, to break a new path in all the soft whiteness.

At first she thought she would just wade over to the edge of the mountain and begin to walk up it, and get as far as she could, but her feet took her in another direction.

The last of the Chaberts. Giovanna is an Alden now.

Because I can't take care of her.

The thought brought the first edge of pain, and then it overwhelmed her. She stumbled and nearly fell as it descended on her like the giant mountain-waves she had been imagining, crashing over her and covering her in blackness. She kept moving, only because she suddenly had the fierce, aching desire to visit Noémie.

We're the two last Chaberts. The two who can still be together. Who aren't buried on the plain, or in Great Salt Lake City. We can be together, at least. Me and Noémie. It's fitting, as I was the one who killed her. We were the last two pieces that made a family, and so we can at least be together.

The riverbank was a lot higher up if you tried to find it east of town, so Maggie circled up around the north side of the fort; the newer one that touched the northern edge of the town's walls.

This is my real home, Maggie thought as she came through the homestead door. *This is the last place my family was.*

She could remember so much right now. She didn't know why, but Samuel's face came readily to her mind as she lay there next to the hearth. She saw, clearly, the crook in his nose, where he had broken it. It had happened when he was chopping wood over out behind the little brick house in Italy.

Pink brick, Maggie remembered. Pinks and yellows, made of clay from the ground there. The hearth had been made of bricks that dried in particularly fine, bright colors. And the fire made the rose of the brick seem like it glowed, like it was a sunrise in the middle of the tiny main room of the Chabert's little house in Italy.

"Il fait froid aujourd'hui. Pensez-vous que les missionnaires viendront par?"

Maggie's mother stood at the fire, stirring it so that sparks flew out, leaving ashy spots on the hearth. She wiped these away quickly with her palm.

"Ils sont assez difficiles. Particulièrement difficile, compte tenu qu'ils sont Américains."

Maggie's father chuckled and sat back in the wooden chair, leaning so that it balanced on the back legs only, and rested his feet on the warm brick.

"Allons-nous vraiment y aller, Philippe? Maggie, mettre la main sur de la bouillie."

Maggie started at her mother's voice and snatched her hand out of the warm porridge that sat on the table, along with a pitcher of cream.

A white pitcher, with yellow flowers.

The image yanked Maggie out of the warm memory. She shivered on the dusty floor of the little homestead, curled up next to the hearth.

They're all gone. Noémie and me, we're the only real Chaberts left. Noémie's out behind the house. And I'm in here, waiting for Mama and Papa and Samuel.

She shivered. After a while, strange, delicious warmth stole over her. It made her drowsy. She shifted in and out of sleep, with her father's bearded face, her mother's soft, fine expressions to keep her company at times. Eventually the room faded and there they were again.

Mama kneaded bread over in the corner, and Papa sat back in his chair, repairing some metal instrument. Giovanna was a baby playing on the floor, and Samuel was teasing Maggie, poking at her with a stick he'd whittled.

"Ne pas! Mama, le faire taire!" Maggie cried.

"Samuel, ne taquine pas votre sœur. Elder Snow et Elder Stenhouse sera ici bientôt."

Samuel kept poking Maggie, his face twisted with delight. It began to hurt.

Maggie cried. "Stop!" She pushed him away.

He leaned in and shook her, hard.

"Stop!"

Suddenly Samuel's face became Pa Alden, who was shaking Maggie awake.

Maggie gasped as she felt the cold, and her own shivering and aching bones. There was a blaze in fireplace, as if the fire and her dream had somehow magically come alight in the cold hearth of the little homestead. And there was a scratchy, rank horse-blanket wrapped around Maggie's shoulders.

"You're going to be all right," Pa Alden said. "I think I've warmed you up enough. But an hour more, Maggie, and I'd've lost you." He wrapped her in a fierce, tight embrace. "What were you thinking of, girl? You were like to freeze to death up here; only way I knew was your friend Henry came by, worried you'd gone off. And your ma worried herself sick, looked for you in all the usual places—Cleggs, Hosters, Holdens. I just happened to think I should try up here. Your ma's likely still running around like a headless chicken, looking for you."

His breath stirred the hair on top of Maggie's head.

Maggie pictured her mother's face, and then remembered. Ma Alden. Ma Alden was looking for her? Worried about Maggie?

Maggie glanced up and studied Pa Alden's face. It was grim, serious. He wasn't lying, she didn't think.

Well, Pa Alden had never been much good at lying, anyhow.

But it just seemed impossible, that Ma Alden would have that much energy and concern on Maggie's behalf.

"Likely she was worried what people would say." The words slid out of Maggie's mouth, and she was immediately sorry for them, because Pa Alden froze and then slowly moved Maggie away from him, holding her at arm's length.

He looked at her for a few moments. His expression was stern.

Maggie quailed inside, and she couldn't meet his eyes. She had never seen Pa Alden look like that, ever.

"Your ma loves you, Maggie."

Maggie nodded.

"No, don't just agree with me. I need you to hear this. Patience tells me you already know what happened to baby Jane."

"Noémie."

"Your baby sister. Don't matter what you call her nor what your ma calls her, you both loved her, Maggie. You *both* loved her."

Maggie's eyes and nose prickled. She folded her arms across her chest and stared at them.

"It was an accident. You were scared, so much from what happened to your family you barely talked to anybody. Baby was your only comfort. Anyone could see that. You held her whenever your ma put her down. Rocked her, held her, whispered words to her nobody could understand. We all knew she was your comfort. Your mother understood that."

It was too confusing for Maggie. The "your mother" brought up images of the dark-haired woman Maggie remembered from Italy, not Ma Alden. It stirred feelings, too many feelings. She felt hot tears start down her cheeks.

Pa Alden pulled her close again, rocking her. "It was an accident, and it was something that broke all our hearts, Maggie. Not just on account of baby Jane's death, but just the downright sadness of it all, that the thing you loved most—that she—" and at this, his voice broke.

"That I killed her."

"It was a terrible accident," Pa Alden managed, but his chest shook and his voice was hoarse. "Good people accidentally do terrible things sometimes, Maggie, and the Lord takes care of it. He—the little children—they go to him. Your baby sister is happy and warm and fed better than any of us, Maggie. She's happy, and with your ma and pa, where she truly belongs. God takes care of his children, Maggie. This life is just a blink, and then the sadness and pain and guilt and hurt are all over. But we got to live it to get there. And if we live it right, we can be happy in spite of it all. You make my heart happy, Maggie. You're one of my favorite things here. When you came to my family, I felt blessed beyond measure, girl, to have such a smart, pretty, sharp-thinking, funny, handy little daughter. I was blessed with two daughters I never expected. You're my blessing, Maggie, and I aim to hold onto you."

Maggie felt like her whole body was shaking. She couldn't think or pick out any feelings. It was just raw and red, and it spilled out of her in an endless stream of hot saltwater, down her face and neck, soaking the horse blanket and her already damp collar. "I don't know as I can live," she said, finally, "knowing." She looked up at Pa Alden.

He gazed back at her. Maggie was overwhelmed at what she saw there, in his face. "But I love you," she added. She choked on the words a little and immediately felt her face turn red.

"It's mighty good to hear it," Pa Alden said, giving her a squeeze. "Maggie, I think I ought to tell you something. Something about what I've been struggling with lately."

A prick of curiosity somehow made it through Maggie's tumult of emotion. "The Injuns at Cedar?"

Pa Alden shook his head. "Don't try to smooth it over, Maggie. You know, after the way Dale's yammered on. 'Tweren't the Piedes."

Maggie pulled away from Pa Alden and sat, cross-legged

in front of him, studying his face. Was he going to tell her what happened?

Why did she need to know? That was the other question. Why did she want to know?

"I don't name names, because God's judgment is just," Pa Alden said after a few moments of brooding silence. "But I was there, and I could've said something. Told me they was just fixing to harass the Fancher Company, teach 'em a lesson for all the harassing they did coming their way through the settlements. I knew better . . . I know those men. I knew the tribes in the area. I knew the feeling out there. They were stirred up, afraid, raring to fix a finger on a trigger and aim at anything. I lived through Haun's, Maggie." He gazed at her again, his face full of some emotion that she couldn't really interpret.

"Had a brother die in that one. You never knew your uncle John. He was killed at nineteen; never got married. My only brother. I knew what could happen, and I didn't say anything, just rode away and left matters as they were, and more'n a hundred shot down in cold blood not three days later." Tears were finding their way down his cheeks now. He didn't bother to wipe them away.

"You didn't know for sure."

"But still, I didn't say anything when I knew I should."

"You don't generally say much in any case," Maggie pointed out.

"Don't matter. When the Spirit moves, you speak."

"Did the Spirit move you to tell 'em off?"

Pa Alden shrugged and then sighed. "I was there. Three days before. I talked to more than one person. More'n a hundred souls, squarely on my own head."

"You didn't kill those people. The people who killed them had a choice too."

Pa Alden looked at the fire for a long moment, then turned and squinted at her. "You saying you forgive me?"

"Nothing to forgive. You didn't do a blessed thing. Plenty of men could've said something. Maybe if you said something, you could've—you would've—" Maggie shrugged. "Maybe you wouldn't be here now."

Pa Alden nodded. "It's a sight easier to forgive someone else than it is to forgive yourself."

Maggie frowned, brought her knees up to her chin, and glared at them.

"But that don't mean we aren't required to forgive ourselves, same as everybody else. Scripture says we're required to forgive all men. 'All' means you too, and me."

Maggie squinted back at him. "How's that doing for you then?"

Pa Alden sighed, and then chuckled. "It's a process, Maggie. I wonder sometimes if forgiving's like anything else in the gospel—a journey. You can't stand up and say, now I've got perfect forgiveness. Perfect means, you're always trying to do better. I can say I'm doing better at forgiving myself now than I was a while ago, and I hope I'm better still as time goes on. But can anybody say when they've finished forgiving?"

Maggie shuddered involuntarily.

"One thing I did realize, though, Maggie. Me not forgiving myself? Made me so I couldn't care for you. Couldn't care for anybody, not Patience or Etta, or your ma or Giovanna. Couldn't stand up to your uncle, neither, when you needed me to that day when you left."

Maggie nodded.

"You forgive me, though."

Maggie nodded again.

"Well, maybe if you learn from my lesson, you won't have anything real serious happen to those you love, before you right yourself over all this, Maggie. People love you, and they need you, and you can't let them down. They've invested themselves in you, Maggie. You should've seen Henry's face when he came by. And Giovanna—"

"Giovanna hates me."

"No. Giovanna feels safe with you, Maggie, and she does remember your ma and pa before, I guarantee you that. You're that connection for her. Without you, all that's lost. You keep it fresh in her mind, tell her what she is. Where she's come from, and that's something special and important. She needs you."

Maggie nodded.

"If you don't mind, Maggie, I'd like to bless you. A father's blessing."

Maggie frowned. "You haven't before."

"I've failed you in a lot of ways. But I don't mean to anymore."

Maggie shrugged, feeling self-consciousness overtake her. "All right, if it'd make you feel better."

"That's just fine," Pa Alden said.

And there, in front of the fire, Pa Alden lay his hands on Maggie's head and blessed her. Maggie didn't listen to the words so much; she was too startled at the feeling of peace that seemed to steal in and sweep her away, the way the fire-light in the room suddenly seemed to congregate around the both of them. It wasn't really a light she could see; she more, felt it. And she wasn't really sure she felt it at all, she was so tired, and so fuzzy-headed. But the peace was there. It was undeniable. She felt her body shudder, and something left—something intangible, but it left her feeling lighter than air.

When he finished, Pa Alden pulled Maggie to him again and gave her a fierce squeeze. "Fine, then?" he asked.

"I reckon we better get back to—to Ma," Maggie replied, avoiding his gaze.

Walking back through the snow with the smelly blanket around her shoulders, Maggie felt embarrassed and self-conscious about all that had happened inside the cabin, but the feeling of peace didn't leave. It stayed with Maggie and seemed to affect the world around her too. The snow drifted down peacefully. The soft, white snow muffled her steps and covered everything in a blanket of serenity. Along the river, the big, curving tree limbs, branches, and twigs were all traced with perfect white frosting. Everything looked and felt right, and Maggie was right, as well—a part of the picture. A girl walking home with her father.

Maggie glanced up at Pa Alden and felt a kind of warmth rise up in her throat.

They got to the gate just in time to see Ma Alden come barreling out of the house again. "You found her?" she shrieked. "You ungrateful chit of a girl, you've given all of us such a scare. Get inside. You're lucky I don't hide you—right now I feel like I could take the skin completely off of you."

Maggie looked up at Ma Alden. "Sorry," she said.

Ma Alden frowned at her. "Well, get on inside before you freeze your toes clean off."

Pa Alden put a hand on Maggie's shoulder and gave it a squeeze as they went in the door.

Maggie watched Ma Alden out of the corner of her eye as she bustled around, serving her up some stew, putting a blanket around her, scooting the rocker she sat in closer to the fire. *It's almost*, Maggie thought, *like there's a new light on*

Ma Alden that casts different shadows. Right now, instead of the stern, cool, dismissive woman, Maggie saw a worried mother, tending a child she cared about—tending Maggie.

It was odd, but Maggie didn't have any room in her heart in that moment to argue.

BACK TO ALDENS

THINGS WERE DIFFERENT, BUT THEY WEREN'T. IT WAS LIKE the depression in Maggie's spirits, with the burden that she suddenly carried, had not only let loose all the anger and frustration she contained inside her at her foster family but gave her a sort of patience. She sat, weary from all she knew, and with the burden she now had to live with. Her fingers took her mind off it, but she didn't have the energy to jump up and run off, the way she used to.

Ma Alden took Maggie's new inclinations in stride, without questioning her. She had her stay inside with Patience and gave her different tasks. Instead of hurrying through messy chores and then running off to find something to do away from the house with Henry or Giovanna, Maggie sat in the rocking chair next to the fire, mending linens or clothing, or darning. She had even begun a little bit of embroidery, though it was wobbly and her stitches, unpredictable.

Ma Alden startled Maggie once, observing over her shoulder as she fumbled with stitches. "You ought to go over to the Cleggs' sometime," Ma Alden sniffed. "You need some work on those knots."

It came out sounding displeased. Maggie had realized lately that Ma Alden always sounded displeased, even when she was exceptionally pleased about something. She couldn't be happy so that people could see it. *It's like happiness is a private thing for Ma Alden, not to be displayed if she can help it.* If you wanted to know how Ma Alden felt about you, you watched what she did, not how she talked. Why Maggie hadn't been able to understand this before, she didn't know, but it was a strange comfort to see displeasure directed at everything and everyone—Patience, even.

Maggie had a lot of guilt about Henry. Pa Alden's description of his worry ate at her. She didn't see him anywhere. When she did go over to the Cleggs' one morning, she forced herself to ask after him.

The loom's lulling rhythm stopped. "Went up to the city with his Pa and Samuel," was the mild reply. "Said they mean to stay a month or two."

"What for? Ouch." Maggie held a length of linen away from her.

"Those buttonholes can be beastly. Here." Sister Clegg handed Maggie a cloth to staunch the trickle of blood coming from her thumb. "They've been hearing a few troubling rumors and went up to shed some light, bring back some news."

"About the judges?" Maggie blurted out, before she could stop herself.

Sister Clegg gave her a bemused look. "Your friend Mariah ought not've meddled in the thing, but yes. And it's partly on account of that letter of hers they went up, I won't lie. Added to other things David's heard about town."

Maggie gnawed on her thumb. "What do you reckon could happen?" she asked after she had finished another buttonhole.

"Nothing much. President Buchanan himself gave the order for Johnston to keep his troops on the other side of the mountains. There might be a bit of a battle between the courts—if they bring in new judges to oversee the ones we have. But that's just part of living out here in the wilderness. Government and the people who live here, battling it out and trying to find a good balance of who's in charge."

"The prophet's in charge," Maggie said, frowning.

"Well, that's all well and good for now, but it can't last long when people who aren't in the Church move out here. And if we ever want to become a state, we've got some things to figure out."

"Why would we want to become a state?"

Sister Clegg shrugged, but her hands kept moving quickly over the loom. "There's good things about it. And bad. We'll just have to see how it all plays out, won't we? Best advice I have to give, Maggie, is don't worry over things you can't do anything to change."

Maggie felt that this was a completely dissatisfactory end to the conversation, but she knew a dismissal when she heard one. And in spite of Sister Clegg's advice, her mind ran away with her, coming up with all manner of frightening scenarios, up to and including Henry being killed at bayonet point.

"When do you think they'll be back?" Maggie looked over the shirt and sighed. All the buttonholes were gaping. "I'll need some bigger buttons."

Sister Clegg stood, stretched her shoulders, and took the shirt from Maggie's lap. "I'll give it to Henry," she said. She gave Maggie a wicked glance. "I'll tell him you sewed it, and he won't complain."

Maggie felt her face grow red. "Guess I'll head on over back to the Aldens'," she said.

"Take some muffins," Sister Clegg replied, bustling into the kitchen.

Giovanna seemed to enjoy school. She came home pink-cheeked and excited, with a hundred stories about the schoolmaster and the older boys in class. Lizzy Twelves sat by her even though she was two primers ahead. It took Giovanna away from Maggie a good deal of the day and made it so they had hardly any time at all together. They had their old pallet back and slept together still, but there were no more stories, and no more whispering at night after the lights went out. It was like Maggie and Giovanna didn't know exactly what to say to each other. Maggie's heart ached over it, but she didn't feel she deserved any better, after what she had put Giovanna through.

And every time they lay down, she thought of that other, horrible thing. The sheets, crumpled around Giovanna seemed often, to Maggie, like it might hide the still form of a baby. She felt a startled sort of horror every morning when she woke up, and when she moved the sheets so that they lay straight, a keen sense of loss took over.

It was just her and Giovanna. There was no baby anymore.

Every time Maggie started feeling the guilt of it all pressing on her and growing unbearable, she tried to think of Pa Alden and what he said. And the burden he carried and how she loved him. It helped. It didn't hurt less, but Maggie felt like somehow she could bear it, whereas before, she couldn't even face it.

January wore away and became February, and still

Maggie didn't hear from Henry. She had hoped he might write her a letter.

One morning, Shedrick Holden and George Bell passed right by Maggie as she was going to Stewarts to see if the post had come. They were so absorbed in their conversation that they didn't notice Maggie. "Cradlebaugh," Maggie caught the name as they hurried past. Talk in the town was beginning to stir, and the tension beginning to grow. Maggie could feel it, even if she didn't hear much. One or two times she walked into Stewarts or into the Tithing House and overheard worried conversation. Generally, the conversation would hush as soon as she entered the room, and the worried tones would change to a friendly salutation, to nods and grins fixed in place, and impatient tapping of fingers or feet on the floor as she did her business.

I hate being a girl, was Maggie's thought on these occasions.

Uncle Forth, like usual, had no such scruples. He talked as loudly and as indiscriminately as ever, in front of Maggie and anyone else who would listen.

"Heard One-eyed Jack's headed up this way fairly soon," he mentioned casually one day. "After he's done examining things down in Cedar."

Maggie glanced at Pa Alden. He sat, whittling as usual. He didn't seem moved at all by the mention of Cedar.

Well, that's changed, she thought. *Maybe he's made peace about it. Or maybe he's heard it so many times from Uncle Forth that he doesn't get startled by it anymore.*

Uncle Forth also seemed to be directing his attention at Pa Alden. Though he didn't look directly at him, his body was turned in Pa Alden's direction.

"Talk is he'll be bringing a passel of troops into town, round up some of the bishops." He stretched the "s" on *bishops* out, as if he were savoring the word.

Pa Alden didn't respond. He kept his gaze on his hands, whittling away.

"Really, Dale?" Ma Alden said. "When do they say he's coming?"

"Soon. Talk is, he landed in Cedar just two days ago. Asking about the Parrish and the Fancher murders, going door-to-door to talk to the folks."

"You think he means to—to come up here, and—"

"They say he's full of the fire of the Lord's justice," Uncle Forth said. He chortled a little. "I aim to enjoy the show. All these bishops here, setting and judging all the rest of us, sure they're beyond the reach of the law. They'll get a nasty surprise. Ol' Aaron Johnson with his passel of wives and great, white mansion, and no thought in his head to account for the killing of—"

"Ain't true," Maggie muttered to herself, thinking of Mariah's letter. Mariah had said that Cradlebaugh was supposed to be decent.

"What was that?" Uncle Forth said.

Maggie looked up at him and realized that he must have heard her. "Nothing," she said.

"No, say it out. Go ahead and speak your mind. Go ahead and rattle off about all manner of subjects you can't know nothing about." Uncle Forth's face was red, and he walked toward her and bent over her where she sat there in her rocker. "You're just like all them here. Spoon-fed facts by bishops that aren't facts at all, speaking up out of ignorance. What can you know? You speak out even though you're only a gimpy, dirt-faced Italian—"

"That's enough." Ma Alden's voice cracked like a whip across the room, startling both of them.

Uncle Forth looked over at his sister for a moment. He shook his head a little, with an incredulous expression on his face, and turned back to Maggie. "You don't know nothing, you ungrateful chit—"

"I said that's enough." Ma Alden walked to her brother and put an arm on his shoulder. "I won't have words like that spoke at my children in my house, Dale."

Uncle Forth stared at her and moved his mouth, but nothing came out. He shook his head, finally. "Got things to do in town. Come on, Jed," he snapped. His son followed him out, hands stuffed casually in his coat pockets. He glanced at Maggie, began to whistle tunelessly, and slammed the door behind him as they left.

Maggie stared at Ma Alden, but all of Ma Alden's attention was focused on her husband.

"Do you believe it's true?" she said quietly.

Pa Alden looked up and gave her a half-smile. "We can't do much about it if it is."

"We can," Ma Alden said, a note of urgency in her voice. "We can leave, Fred. I don't know what I'd do if I lost you, on top of everything else."

Pa Alden rose and rubbed his eyes with his palm. "Move to California?"

"Dale's got connections. We could set ourselves up just fine, Fred. We could—"

"You realize you'd be leaving Etta behind. Elias's not going to leave his family. And Patience is fair on her way to the same situation. Didn't tell you yet, but the McClelland boy came by a week or so ago."

Ma Alden clasped her hands together. "He asked for her?"

Pa Alden nodded. "After a fashion. Asked if he could court her, which means he's already been courting her a while and getting serious about it. Are you going to weather leaving two daughters behind . . ." He glanced at Maggie. "Maybe four?"

Ma Alden's face crumpled. She sat down on the little stool next to the wall. Maggie thought for a moment she should offer the rocker, but then decided not to say anything. She wasn't a part of this. Ma Alden likely forgot she was there, listening.

"I can't lose you, Fred," Ma Alden said finally. "I just can't—not to a judge, not to Injuns, or to blood-murdering sons-of-guns."

Pa Alden knelt beside her and put a hand on her shoulder, and Maggie quietlygot up and left. She walked down the street to the Cleggs'. As she passed the schoolhouse, she had an odd inclination. She walked up to one of the windows and peered inside.

There was Giovanna, sitting in the second row with Lizzy Twelves. She was squinting with concentration at the book on her lap, and her lips were moving. She looked up. Maggie's gaze followed hers, across the room at the schoolmaster, who nodded and smiled.

Maggie walked back out to the street.

"Henry and Sam and your husband back yet?" she asked as soon as Sister Clegg opened the door.

"Not yet," Sister Clegg said. "I just got a letter too—they aim to stay a few more weeks."

Maggie didn't ask if there were a reason given. She couldn't go that far. Henry wasn't hers. He wasn't hers to ask after yet, not like Patience could ask after Will, and not like Ma Alden could ask of Pa Alden.

"Do you need some help today?" she asked instead. "Bet your henhouse is in need of a good mucking, with Henry gone so long."

"I've had Alfie do it. Come in and help me with basting; with the weather getting warmer, I've got to finish the linen shirts for all the boys and David in the next few weeks."

Maggie felt on tenterhooks for the next weeks. People weren't bothering to lower their tone anymore even in the presence of girls. Every time Maggie went into Stewarts or the Tithing House, and even at the few church meetings she went to with Ma Alden and Giovanna, there was talk of Cradlebaugh. Nobody mentioned Cedar right out, but it was implied. It ran under everything, like rapids under the smooth-rolling surface of the Provo River, which was beginning to thaw enough for fishing again.

Maggie thought of fishing—and Henry—a lot. Her mind was so full of what had happened—the embrace, the feeling of sitting next to him as they read Mariah's letter together, which had turned out so awful. Maggie felt crawling embarrassment at the thought of Henry taking her out of the Hosters' loft, likely smelling worse than all the Hosters combined and ungrateful to boot.

Maggie wouldn't be surprised at all if Henry had written her off completely and found some nice girl in Great Salt Lake City to starting paying attention to. She wouldn't be surprised at all, but she realized, more and more, how gut wrenching it would be if Henry came home and didn't pay attention to her.

After all the worry and thought, the actual event seemed anticlimactic to Maggie. She was sitting in Sister Clegg's living room, basting. Her hands were quick now, and her stitches—though perhaps not as neat and perfect as Sister Clegg's—were acceptably tidy.

The door opened, and in they walked, just like it was any other day. Brother Clegg walked in first, followed by Samuel and Henry, shaking slush off their boots on the steps.

Sister Clegg looked up from her loom. The corners of her mouth twitched, and she gazed at her husband. "Roads decent on the way in?" she asked.

"Fair decent," David Clegg replied. "How'd you all hold up here?"

"Just fine," Sister Clegg said, rising from her seat, and touching the top of Maggie's head on her way across the room. "I've had some good help."

Brother Clegg put his arms around his wife, and they were both silent for a moment. Henry and Samuel finished removing their boots.

Maggie felt like she couldn't look at him. At Henry. She was aware, out of the corner of her eye, of him removing his boots, walking over to the fireplace to lay his damp coat. Her insides felt especially knotted up—knotted so badly she couldn't say a single word, like she might even be sick.

He must think I'm crazy. That was her thought as she concentrated on her fingers, on the needle that flashed in and out of the length of linen.

A pair of hands landed on her shoulders, startling her.

"Whose shirt is that?" Henry asked, stirring the hair on the crown of Maggie's head.

"Your ma said it's yours," Maggie said around the lump in her throat.

"Looks fine."

Maggie nodded. His fingers on her shoulders were both extremely unsettling and wonderful, at the same time. She was afraid to move.

"You've stopped sewing."

Maggie swallowed hard and put her needle through the fabric again. The thread knotted and bunched as she pulled it through. Sister Clegg and Brother Clegg were talking with Samuel by the fireplace, with serious expressions on their faces.

And Henry was there, behind her, with his hands on her shoulders. If she turned and looked up, she would see his face: his blue eyes, the shock of light hair that was likely standing up in damp, irregular tufts all over. Likely he'd be smiling at her—

"Maggie, are you afraid of me?"

Maggie turned then. "No," she said indignantly.

"Why won't you look at me then?"

"I am looking at you," Maggie retorted.

She was looking at Henry. His hair stuck up, just as she'd expected. His eyes were clear, his face pink with cold. Maggie felt like running her hand over the top of his head, smoothing it over.

There was something different though. Henry looked tired. The weariness—on Henry, it was expression she had never seen before.

Henry's eyebrows rose. "You're awful quiet. Bee in your bonnet?"

"Reckon I—reckon it's—" Maggie tried, and failed to come up with one of her usual smart remarks.

A smile spread slowly over his face.

"What?" Maggie snapped.

"Nothin'." Henry reached over and fingered a little curl on Maggie's temple.

Maggie felt her heart race away with her. "Don't know why you keep sticking around here," she finally managed. It was as close as she could get to saying what she really wanted to say.

Henry's eyebrows shot up again. "What do you mean?

I've always stuck around. So've you. We're friends, Maggie."

There was something dissatisfactory about that remark, but Maggie couldn't lay her finger on it. "After bundling me out of the Hosters', I mean," she said finally. "And the way I run off—ran off and left you the other day. It's like you—it's like we—your brother Samuel said."

Henry crouched down then, next to her chair, and looked up at her. There was a curious expression on his face: half frown, half smile, and laughter in his eyes.

"Well, dagnabit, say something," Maggie snapped.

"Reckon you said it."

"Said what?" Sister Clegg asked from across the room.

Maggie flushed. The three adults had stopped talking and were now looking at Maggie and Henry. How much of her blubbering had they just heard? Maggie hadn't thought she could be more embarrassed than she had that day Henry carried her over here, and Sister Clegg washed her and put her to bed. But she had been wrong.

Henry jumped up, his face a little pink. "Want to go fishing?"

"Go fishing *where*? There's still ice on all the pools," Sister Clegg remarked.

"We're due up in Kolob," Samuel said. "Sorry to break up such a sweet reunion."

Maggie had resumed her stitching, keeping her gaze trained on her fingers, but she felt her face flood with heat. She looked at the crooked, uneven line she had made and stifled a sigh.

"Right now?" Henry complained. "Can't a fellow sit down after a long trip and eat a proper dinner? Brother Bell will be fine for another hour or two, without us."

"No, son." David Clegg's voice was grim. "This is

serious. Talk is Cradlebaugh is due in town this week sometime. And he's brought some of Johnston's men along for the trip. He's been taking men out of Springville already, and Bishop Johnson has had to leave town. He's already up in the canyons."

Maggie shoved the linen aside then and leapt up. "Cradlebaugh? But I heard he was coming peaceful, not like to make war on us."

Brother Clegg gave Maggie an apologetic glance. "Wish I didn't have to worry you with talk like this, Maggie. But there's no hiding anything, now. There've been mixed reports in the past. But it's undeniable from what I've heard that he's got a bee in his bonnet about this. He's been holding meetings at night, alone, and gathering his case. He's already used some of Johnston's men, already arrested a few men from down south. Talk is, he's got subpoenas ready, going to be issued for dozens more, most of them the prominent men from settlements from here all the way down to Peteneet. And he went back to Camp Floyd, likely for more soldiers. He's got his eye out to pin the whole Cedar mess, and the murders down south too, on the bishops and high priests and probate judges—all the leadership in the valley."

Maggie's heart thumped against her chest like a bass drum. "Can—may I tell my pa?"

"There's no way of keeping it a secret, so tell whomever you like," Brother Clegg replied. "Like I said, Bishop Johnson's already left his home in Springville. And Elder George A. Smith's encouraging the rest of us to be ready for whatever may happen."

"Whatever may happen," Sister Clegg repeated, frowning.

"See you, Maggie," Henry said, holding the door open for her.

"We'll collect Hy and Moses at the shop in town on our way up," Brother Clegg was saying as Maggie ran out, hastily bundling her wrap around her shoulders as she went.

On the way, she slipped and fell in a puddle of slush on the corner of West Main and Seventh. She arrived at the Aldens' dripping and filthy from the waist down, but she didn't care at that moment. She flung the door open. "Pa Alden's got to get up to the canyons. Cradlebaugh's coming with troops! Brother Clegg said he'd be here by week's end—"

Ma Alden, busy stirring the stew pot over the fire, stopped still and turned. She stared at Maggie for a long moment, without seeming to take in her filthy appearance.

"He could go with the Cleggs," Maggie continued. "They're headed up right now—he could meet them at the store—"

"He won't go," Ma Alden cut in. She sat down in the rocking chair and ran her fingers through her hair. "I've been trying to get him to—to think about leaving. He won't. Only time he's said anything to me, he says the truth will come out and since he's not killed anybody, he thinks he'll be fine."

Maggie walked across the room. "What did he do? Down in Cedar? Did he have anything to do with the shooting?"

Ma Alden shook her head violently and then shrugged. "He's never talked to anyone about it."

"I figured he said something to you."

"Not me either."

"He was talking to me about it t'other day." Maggie bit her lip. "Was trying to comfort me, I think. So, don't be mad he'd say something to me, Ma, please."

Ma Alden shook her head impatiently. "What did he *say*?"

"From what he was saying, I don't think he was down there. Not when it all happened, but he feels like he knew, before, what might—"

"I already knew that," Ma Alden said and rose from her chair. She walked over to the stove and stirred something.

"I'll make him," Maggie heard her mutter. "I'll tell him—I'll tell him he has to go, or I'm going without him. I'll tell him—" Ma Alden snatched the wrap from the floor, where Maggie had left it, and ran out the door.

Maggie sat in the empty rocker. She turned it toward the fireplace and watched the flames dance. She got up and stirred the stew, and then sat again.

It felt like the fire was playing along her nerves. She kept seeing Pa Alden's face, and Henry's and the Cleggs'. She thought of the stories from before. The stories that people in town would tell when the mood became solemn and sad and loved ones were remembered, about the violence that had followed the Mormon settlers from place to place before they made the long trek west. Stories: angry mobs riding through small towns, tearing and stealing and shooting and slicing men open, taking women and children.

They were the same sorts of stories that Maggie had in her mind from her childhood in the village in Italy. Waldensians: that was what Mariah had called the group that had traveled over from Italy to be with the Saints. But Maggie remembered another word for them—the word that the Italian members, all from the same high mountain valley had used for themselves: *Valdois.* The Valdois believed they were saints, too, and clung close to their gospel in the face of persecutions.

She thought of the stories as her mother had told them.

They had seemed like fairy tales to Maggie, the stories told before bedtime of the courage and faith of the Valdois, when the soldiers came to take them hundreds of years before. They were fantastic stories—almost unbelievable—of the ragged villagers rolling giant piles of logs down the slopes, taking out whole lines of soldiers the Catholic-led government had sent up the mountain to route out the Protestant "apostates." *Dieu nous a favorisés*, Mama had said—God favored us.

Maggie thought of Giovanna, and Jed. She thought of Pa Alden and Johnston's soldiers, and Henry, who was likely riding up through the mountain passes right now to be with the Legion.

She thought of the image from her dream: men, mud, and blood. And guns.

Was God on their side? If women and children and men were killed, shot down, and people had justified it somehow to themselves through things that they thought the prophet had said, God must be very angry.

Maybe we're being punished. But, then, why . . . Henry hadn't anything to do with it. Why him?

Pa Alden had, though. At least, he felt like he could have done something about it, prevented some part of it, maybe. But the guilt of all of this had already nearly driven him to a breaking point. Couldn't that be punishment enough? Wasn't God merciful enough to understand the thoughts and intents of somebody's heart, in spite of the horrible things they might do? Or not do, when they wished they would have.

Maggie felt as if all she could do was rock, while the thoughts moved in her mind like a drunken flock of birds—circling and spinning and running into each other, without any sense of direction.

The door banged open, and Giovanna came running in. She stopped short when she saw Maggie alone there.

"Where's Ma and Pa?" she asked, edging into the room.

Maggie looked up at Giovanna, at the sudden anxiety in her expression, and felt, if possible, even more terrible. "I'm sorry, Gigi," she said.

Giovanna frowned, her face a mix of puzzlement and annoyance. "Lizzy Twelves invited me for supper. Do you think Ma would be all right with that?"

"I shouldn't have just—taken you," Maggie continued relentlessly. "I thought I was keeping you safe, and making you happy, when I took you to the Hosters'."

Giovanna set her books down on the hearth. She sat there next to them, leaning her elbows on her knees, and looked at Maggie. "I know," she said simply.

Maggie felt her eyes and nose grow hot. "You're a good girl, Gigi."

"No, I'm not. I was a brat, Maggie. I know you want to make sure I turn out all right, and you were worried about Jed and the way Ma Alden treats us."

Maggie stared at Giovanna. "You sound very grown up," she replied at last.

Giovanna shrugged. "I'm not a baby. I guess I got mad at you because I feel like you treat me like one. I was tired of you bossing me. But I wasn't nice about it, and I'm sorry. I—I know I left and acted bad before that. But I wouldn't want you to go away, Maggie. I've always had you."

Maggie was beginning to feel a little bit of the tightness in her chest ease. "I'm glad Ma Alden's sending you to school."

"I told her I was going." Giovanna's voice was matter-of-fact. "I'm tired of her treating me like a baby too. Well, I mean, I used to think it was nice not to be bossed. But I was getting bored, and none of my friends were around during the day because they were all in school. And I know, Maggie"—some of the ferocious expression came to Giovanna's face, drawing her eyebrows down—"that I need to learn letters. I'm not stupid. I know I can't just play all the time and end up—" She shrugged.

"End up what?"

Giovanna shook her head, turning a little pink. "Well, I won't be like you, at all."

"Like me?" Maggie was truly puzzled now—a mix of hurt and bewildered. "I never got to go to school after Papa and Mama died, though, so it's not the same."

"No," Giovanna said, not quite meeting Maggie's eye. "I mean, I want to. Be like you. You know how to read, and how to write, and how to sew. And before you were doing all that with Ma Clegg, you were fishing and doing all the outside chores and you—" Giovanna shrugged. "You're smart, Maggie. You know things. And you can get on by yourself, and do what you want. That's why Henry likes you."

At this, Maggie felt her face go completely red. "He doesn't."

Giovanna gave Maggie a look of deep disgust.

"Not like that—well, maybe," Maggie amended.

Giovanna rolled her eyes. "I'm going to finish my schoolwork over at the table before I go over to Lizzy's."

That's a good idea. Maggie didn't say it. She kept her face blank of the approving smile that wanted to spread out over it.

"What's going on in town?"

Maggie batted away her first instinct, which was to tell Giovanna not to worry over it. "Johnston's coming with some men. Over the—the Cedar business."

"Pa Alden going into hiding?"

Maggie whirled around and was surprised again by the canny, matter-of-fact expression on her sister's face. "I don't know."

"He better get up into the canyons soon. Bet that's why Ma Alden's gone. She left, to go after him and warn him, didn't she?"

"Likely that's why," Maggie replied faintly.

"Don't worry over it, Megs. Pa Alden can take care of himself too."

Maggie felt like she couldn't swallow her astonishment. Who was this creature, sitting at the table in the room with her? The attitude was not unfamiliar: calm certainty, an edge of bossiness. Dark eyes and formidable eyebrows. Her anxiety and worry over her sister had blinded her. Completely, thoroughly blinded her.

"You know," Maggie ventured, with Pa Alden's advice at the back of her mind. "You—Giovanna, you're an awful lot like Mama. Mama Chabert, I mean."

Giovanna set her book down with a thump. She frowned ferociously at Maggie, but it was playful and self-conscious. Maggie could tell that really, her sister was very pleased at what she had said.

"She used to look at me just like that," Maggie added, hoping she wasn't pushing her luck.

The corner of Giovanna's mouth twitched, and she brought her book up again. But Maggie noticed she didn't turn any pages for several minutes.

A large party of men arrived in town two days later. They rode in from the west. The snow was falling fast and thick, which made it hard to see much of anything. But from where Maggie stood with her family at the corner of J and Seventh, it seemed an anticlimactic thing.

There were plenty of people on the side of the road, watching. It was hard to see much at all, but the shapes of the men as they rode past—bundled up, hunched over, wet and snow-covered—made Maggie feel sorry for them more than anything else.

John Cradlebaugh rode in first. He sat up tall as he passed them and kept his gaze straight ahead. Maggie could see there was something strange about one of his eyes; the focus was off, so that it looked like he was looking in two directions at once.

Two men followed behind him on horseback and following them were a few dozen soldiers and some army wagons. There were men sitting in two of the wagons: a few Indians and a few people dressed in plain clothes, with several soldiers sitting opposite.

Maggie thought she recognized a few of them.

"Witnesses," Uncle Forth said. "And that riding with Cradlebaugh—that's Cap'n Heth, and Marshal Dotson there, see, just behind them." There was satisfaction in his voice.

Maggie felt like kicking Uncle Forth, as she watched Ma Alden's grim face and saw her stiff, hunched shoulders.

Next to her stood Pa Alden. He had an arm around his wife, but some of the tension and reserve, which Maggie had been so glad to see gone these days, had returned to his countenance.

He had refused to go into hiding, even when Ma Alden sat on the hearth next to him and pleaded and cried.

He put his arms around her to comfort her. "I'm not leaving, Ella," he had said. "I haven't done anything wrong myself. And if they need material witnesses—if they ask after me, it ain't moral for me to run away. I do know some things."

"What things?" Ma Alden asked immediately, her face paling.

"I know some of the people who were involved," Pa Alden admitted after a moment. "Or at least, I know those who were talking of it in the beginning."

"But—that means people might have a reason to . . . to want you gone," Ma Alden countered immediately. "That's what I'm worried over, Fred. I'm—I know you're not capable of . . . of murder. I've never doubted you that way. I'm more worried about what other bad men might worry you know. What they might think to do to you."

"Ella," Pa Alden shook his head at her. "Thanks, Ella, for not doubting me. But I can take care of myself."

Ma Alden and me, Maggie had thought as she sat and knit, and watched the scene from the corner of her eye. *We're two peas in a pod.*

She thought it again now, watching the soldiers walk past. She couldn't help but glance anxiously at Pa Alden and wish for all the world that he were up in the canyons with the Legion.

With Henry. Well, at least he's out of harm's way. And all the Cleggs. Half the men in Provo're up in that canyon, leaving their wives and children to cope with all this.

The last of the soldiers passed Maggie. She watched the line turn left and begin walking alongside the city run, by Town Square.

"Where are they headed?" Giovanna piped up.

Pa Alden looked down at her. "Don't know. Cradlebaugh's setting up court somewhere, I imagine."

It turned out to be the Seminary building, which caused some outrage.

"Soldiers all 'round, and wagons blocking every entrance," Sister Harrison complained to Brother Stewart an hour later.

Maggie and Giovanna, Patience, and Etta and Ma Alden were crowded around the stove at Stewarts store, along with what seemed to be half the town. Maggie had seen several men disappear upstairs as well.

Brother Stewart leaned across the counter. "Talk is Cradlebaugh's to issue some bench warrants soon as he gets set up."

"One-eyed Jack," Brother Harrison muttered, eliciting chuckles from several in the room.

"I ain't fixing to go, no matter what he sends after me." Andrew Stewart's face was pink with excitement.

"Now, now." Brother Stewart shook his head. "Law's in his court right now. Much as we don't like the soldiers here in town, a subpoena's a subpoena. And it's not just white men he's holding. He's got some Indians as well. This is a federal court. He's got some laws to work within. We got rights, too—it's not like he can hold us without bail. Long as we obey our part of the law, I reckon he'll hold up on his."

There were snorts and amens at this.

"But we're not part of the states," Andrew argued. "Why should we follow the law when it don't apply to us?"

Brother Stewart turned on his son, giving him a look such as would have made Maggie shut her mouth tight. "We are Americans," he said. "I ain't renounced my citizenship yet."

"Let's go," Ma Alden said suddenly. She had followed the crowd to Stewarts, mostly because her brother had seemed keen to go. Uncle Forth leaned against the wall, his arms folded. He watched, almost as if he were enjoying a show. Jed stood next to him, whittling on something and whistling in the maddening, tuneless way he'd taken on as of late.

It grated on Maggie's nerves. "Yes, let's," she said and tugged on Giovanna's hand.

"Where's Fred?" Ma Alden asked as soon as they entered the door.

Patience and Will were sitting together on the hearth. They both jumped a little.

"Don't know, Ma," Patience said when she had recovered.

Ma Alden groaned and threw herself into the rocker. "He should've gone up to Kolob with your boy," she said, when Maggie sat in the little stool and picked up her sewing.

It was too much.

"He's not my boy," Maggie snapped.

Ma Alden's eyebrows rose. "No? Sure seems like it to me." She settled back in the rocker, apparently feeling better now that she had passed some of her ill temper on to Maggie.

"Well, seeing as how I'm not fit to keep company with boys like him, and will likely end up a washerwoman, I don't see how it matters." Maggie stood and flung her sewing into the scraps pile. "I'm going to take a walk."

"Where?" Patience asked. "I think you shouldn't be going about town, Maggie. Who knows what all those men might be capable of." She shuddered.

"I can take care of myself." Maggie threw her wrap back on.

"I'll come with you, Maggie," Giovanna said, jumping up.

"No, you won't." Three voices spoke it at once. Giovanna looked from Ma Alden, to Patience, to Maggie. She frowned ferociously, folded her arms, and plopped down on the hearth next to Patience.

Maggie only had to step outside to know that she was being foolish in the extreme. She immediately shivered, as her skirts were still wet from being outside all morning. And just as she got to the road, three men on horses rode past.

Soldiers.

One of them turned and looked at her as they rode past, and if Maggie wasn't mistaking it, she thought he might have winked.

She shivered inside, wishing herself invisible.

A figure strode up toward the gate. Maggie felt a thrill of fear. She turned quickly and started back toward the house.

"Hey, Maggie-girl," Pa Alden's voice floated through the snow. "Tell your ma I'll be in by dinnertime. I'm going to stop by the Seminary building."

Maggie whirled around, half relieved, half horrified. "You're going to—why are you going there?"

"I'm going to offer myself as a witness," Pa Alden's quick reply came, and he strode by the gate, increasing his pace.

"Don't!" Maggie called after him. "You don't know what—we don't know what they're going to do! Pa!"

But there was no reply from Pa Alden. He continued along the street until the corner and turned west.

Maggie's heart felt like a lead weight in her chest. She trudged back to the door and waited in front of it for several minutes before opening it.

Her news brought exactly the reaction she knew it would. Patience gasped and became tearful. Ma Alden shrieked and ran about the room for a moment, and then she threw on her own wrap and went out the door like a runaway carriage, bumping the rifle off the wall where it was mounted next to the door. The door slammed so hard as she left, the windows rattled.

Maggie bent and picked up the rifle, setting it back in its nails.

Giovanna stood and crowded in next to Patience on the hearth.

"Suppose I'll go after him," Will said heavily and rose.

"No," Patience snapped.

It surprised Maggie, and Will, and Giovanna.

"Don't be stupid, Will."

Will stood there next to the hearth. He scratched his head and then sat again. After a few moments, he stood. "I've got to do something," he said in almost a pleading tone. "I—I s'pose I'll go over to the Walls'. Ask Nancy where the Legion's got to. If I'm not mistaken, they're likely mobilizing right now. I've not drilled with them before, but . . ." He shrugged.

Patience didn't say anything as he left, but she looked at the door after it closed for several minutes.

Maggie had to wonder how many other scenes like this were happening all over town. Men leaving, women sitting on their hearths without anything to do but worry and ache and live inside their heads.

"I'll get dinner started." Maggie walked to the stove.

Patience, Maggie, and Giovanna kept dinner as long as they could, and then ate it together, alternately staring out the window in the kitchen and watching both doors. Darkness came, leaving the three of them sitting around a candlelit table. Maggie couldn't finish her stew. It was an hour past the time they would usually retire that the door finally opened. Ma Alden walked in, obviously tired and bedraggled.

And alone.

"Where's Pa?" Patience's voice cracked.

"Cradlebaugh's holding all the witnesses." Ma Alden flung her wrap in the direction of the door. It landed in a heap on the floor. She sat in a chair at the table and stared at the half-empty bowl of stew in front of her.

"That's mine," Maggie said. "I'll get you some."

"Holding him?" Patience asked. "How? You mean—he's been arrested?"

Ma Alden shrugged. "Cradlebaugh issued the bench warrants and some of the men he asked for came forward, including your Pa, fool that he is. His name wasn't even on the list. But he must've convinced the judge he knew something because he was 'retained' along with all the others who came forward voluntarily."

"But," Patience started, then stopped when she saw her mother's expression.

"I don't reckon I'm going to talk much on it," Ma Alden said. "I'm not hungry. Let's all go to bed. I'll see what Dale can do about it in the morning."

Maggie woke late. It was the sound of wheels on the street that woke her. It took her a few moments to remember, but when she did, she leapt out of her bed.

And found an empty house.

"Dagnabit," she whispered to herself as she threw on clothing. She didn't bother to lace her boots tight, and she grabbed the first wrap she could find. It was Giovanna's and a little too small to cover all of her arms, but she ran outside anyway.

J Street was churned up; the middle was near to a foot deep in mud and slush. There were a few men on horses, but Maggie saw that they weren't soldiers. In fact, one of them looked like—

"Brother Bell!" Maggie called out and ran to the fence.

Brother Bell moved toward Maggie's side of the road. "Yes, ma'am." He nodded at her. "Fine day, isn't it? Wish the roads were better, with all the traffic in town. Likely the snow'll melt off before tonight."

"Yes. What's going on in the Seminary building? What're they doing with witnesses? Will they let 'em go when they've talked? You seen Ma Alden or Patience or Giovanna? How long do you think—"

"Whoa," Brother Bell said, and tugged on the reigns so his horse halted in front of Maggie. "Now, what're you saying, Miss Alden?"

Maggie didn't bother to correct him about her name. "What's going on? Pa Alden's been taken—by that judge, and Ma Alden's in a state about it, but I woke up and everyone was gone—"

"I'm not sure what'll happen," Brother Bell said. "That's what we're all coming up to see. People from as far out as Peteneet—Cradlebaugh's summoned a jury and sent out subpoenas. Bishop Johnson's hightailed it with some other folks up in the canyon, and it's likely he'll stay there after Cradlebaugh's arresting all those he subpoenaed yesterday. I've got to hurry, ma'am, I'm sorry. I'm due in court to record the proceedings. I know you're worried after your pa, though. Why don't you ride with me and I'll drop you off before I cross through the patrol, or whatever it is Cradlebaugh's calling it that's got our streets all choked up around the Seminary building."

Normally Maggie would have been too shy to accept, but a second later she found herself taking Brother Bell's hand and sliding up in the saddle behind him. "Thanks," she murmured.

As Brother Bell had said, the streets surrounding the

Seminary building were full, chock-full. People crowded around, as close as they could without provoking the soldiers that stood guard. The wagons were now lined up in every open space, like a blockade.

Brother Bell handed Maggie down. "George Bell," he said.

One of the men nodded and moved, allowing him to pass through.

Maggie recognized him from before—he'd been one of the two men riding up front with Cradlebaugh, as they rode into town yesterday. *Dotson.*

She turned and walked across the street, joining the crowd there.

"Your pa been released yet?"

Maggie turned and saw Liz Ellen Hoster. "What you doin' here?"

"Brother Higbee's been called in to jury," Liz Ellen replied.

"Where's your brothers?"

"Over at the Higbees'. I told them to stay there."

"Why're *you*—" Maggie stopped, as Liz Ellen gave her a particularly gruesome grimace. They stood next to each other on the side of the road, jostled by the crowd when people moved through it. Several walked up to the line of soldiers, but the Marshal shook his head at each of them.

"Why're we not allowed past?" Maggie whispered.

"Dunno. Is that not how it's supposed to be?" Liz Ellen shrugged.

"Dunno," Maggie repeated. "Well then, Ma Alden must be around here somewhere, and Patience." She began to edge her way through the crowd, looking for signs of any of the Aldens. She made her way along the block south of the

Seminary building, and then turned the corner and started up the western edge. Everyone was restless, watching the soldiers, talking to each other quietly. The tension was palpable. "Heard he's fixing to bring in Mayor Bullock."

"They say he wants Bullock."

"Bishop Johnson's gone up in the canyon. Elder Smith and Bullock'd do well to follow 'em, after what happened yesterday."

"They'd better not take in Bullock—they're not ready for what would happen," Maggie heard this when she had made her way about halfway up the block. The voice was familiar. She turned every way, standing on her tiptoes to try to see out over the crowd, or at least over a shoulder or two, and finally spotted him—Uncle Forth.

She saw the rest of them when she had edged through enough bodies—Patience, with Will next to her. Giovanna stood between them, clutching Patience's hand. Etta Mae and Ma Alden were close to Uncle Forth. "With this little group of soldiers—no, they'd need at least a few hundred troops," he continued, folding his arms and looking up over the crowd. "Marshal looks nervous. He should too."

"You think they'll bring over more soldiers?" Etta asked, her face pale and taut.

"Where's Elias?" Maggie asked, moving closer to them.

"Pasturing the sheep with Jed," Etta said.

"Up by the river?"

Etta made a shushing noise.

"They'll not go after him," Uncle Forth snorted. "Don't you worry, they're after bigger game than that."

"My poor fool of a husband," Ma Alden said, shaking her head. "Heaven knows when Cradlebaugh'll free him now."

"You should be glad he's in there, Ella, and not out here."

Uncle Forth lowered his voice and glanced over his shoulder. "He'd be dead in a ditch within the week if it was known, generally, he's willing to talk about what he's seen."

Fury boiled up inside Maggie. She watched Ma Alden's drawn, tired face and longed to say something that would put Uncle Forth in his place, but she had no words, no knowledge, and no idea of what her uncle's reaction might be, and whether Ma Alden had the energy or inclination to step in and defend Maggie right now.

She settled in beside Patience and Giovanna to watch. The crowd around them continued to press and move against itself, and the murmurs became more audible and more agitated as the day wore on.

"Let's go back for dinner," Patience said.

It had to be long after noon, Maggie thought. And she hadn't realized it until Patience said it, but her stomach was hollow with hunger.

"Reckon I'll go up to the pastures and see what the boys are doing," Uncle Forth said, shoving his hands in his pockets. "Don't look like there'll be much action here for a long while yet."

"I'll stay here," Ma Alden replied.

"I'll bring back some food for you," Patience said. She took Maggie's hand with her free one, and the three of them slid through the crowd in the direction of their home.

CRADLEBAUGH

It didn't take Cradlebaugh very long to do exactly what the people in town seemed most worried about. On the eighteenth, he issued a bench warrant for Isaac Bullock and had him in custody before nightfall.

The next day, it seemed to Maggie that the town had doubled in size. People, animals, and wagons and carts lined the streets. It reminded Maggie of last spring, when everyone had come down from the city to get away from Johnston's men.

Well, now they've come up to see *Johnston's men*, was Maggie's thought. The irony made her feel a little better—a bit of humor in a very dark situation.

The Alden house was somber these days. Maggie felt Pa Alden's absence keenly and worried over him every moment of every day. She felt like there must be a bruise on the inside of her rib cage, where her heart had beaten itself against it these last few days.

She also thought of Henry. She tried to shove these

thoughts aside, but they kept siding into her mind, making her feel guilty for spending even a moment of her attention and grief away from Pa Alden.

Henry's up in the canyon with his pa and brothers, Maggie kept reminding herself. Not that it's any of your business, she would add mentally, but couldn't help but feel a bit of rosiness, a little piece of happiness, at the thought of their last, hurried encounter: Henry's eyes, the way he looked, the way that smile spread over his face.

She shivered, though, thinking of what might happen. What was she, really, to him? And was she even capable of being whatever it was he wanted from her?

Ma Alden was often absent these days. Jed and Uncle Forth were staying in their homestead by the river "to keep track of the sheep," as they said it.

Well, it wasn't all that far-fetched. Maggie realized this when people began pouring into town from south, west, and north. Though she doubted anybody would steal the Aldens' and Forths' animals, it was a very confusing time. You never knew who might be riding next to your fields, scattering your animals.

If the mood at the Aldens' was somber, the mood in town could be called dangerous. A roil of emotions and people, lining the streets around the Seminary building, packing into Stewarts and the Tithing House, congregating under the bowery for hurried discussions and far-fetched plans to break out all of the witnesses that Cradlebaugh had arrested, "Without bail and without rights," as Brother Bell put it. The arrest of Mayor Bullock had been the thing to put it over the top of the dam of wanting to be law-abiding, not wanting to stir up the pot, for the people of Utah Valley.

"Aaron Johnson had some visitors last night," Stewart

drawled, leaning over his counter as usual. He said it loudly, talking over the buzz of conversation.

Heads turned, people jostling to get closer to the counter.

"They get him?" Brother Bell asked. He leaned on the counter as well.

"Wives and children all right?" Eliza Bell asked, almost at the same time, sliding her head under her husband's arm.

Brother Bell pulled her tight to his side.

"No, he's not gone back to Springville. Up in the canyon still. From what I heard, the family made out all right. Came to the door in their night dresses, and scolded the soldiers into submission, threatening them with pillows and blankets and such, with kids running like mad all over the place."

"Enough to scare any man into submission," Brother Holden quipped, coming down the stairs.

This set off a nervous chuckle through those crowded around the counter.

"We need to send a letter to Cummings," Stewart said.

"Aye," an unidentified voice called out, and then the noise broke, people chattering away, trying to yell over each other and pushing to get closer to the counter.

Maggie, who was standing by the door, began to feel a bit frightened at the press of bodies and frantic movement. She managed to push past two men who entered as she left.

She took a deep breath of fresh cool air and waited for her knees to stop shaking before she started back to the Aldens'.

She kept her feet on her boots as she walked, in case any soldiers might happen by and try to wink at her.

The crowd ranged all along Seventh this morning. Maggie turned right to go up a block, hoping that Eighth would be less crowded, giving her an easier path.

She had just crossed K, when a bunch of men, marching

in odd procession, began to pass her. Maggie moved to the side of the road and watched the neat lines of men go by, spattering slush up their plain wool pants and boiled-wool coats. They had rifles over their shoulders.

They marched in the direction of the Seminary building.

"Hey, Mag."

Maggie thought she heard it as one line of men passed her. She started and scanned the line frantically—it had sounded like Henry.

But Henry was up in the mountains.

Henry's supposed to be up in the mountains, with his brothers and pa, Maggie argued to herself, *drilling*—

Her heart sank.

That was likely Bishop Wall leading them. Leading them toward the Seminary building—to do what? *What could they do*, Maggie argued to herself, *when Johnston's got more than a thousand more men waiting on the other side of the mountain if he asked for them?*

Maggie quickened her pace, changing her route to follow the troops.

Giovanna was in the schoolhouse, just across the street from the Seminary building. If shots were fired—

She began to run, spattering herself with the gray, soup-like sludge that covered the street. She slid a few times and almost ran into people as she entered the edge of the press that overwhelmed the block of H Street, Eighth, Seventh Street, and G Street.

"Excuse me," she mumbled, to herself, really. Nobody was listening to her; they were all watching Bishop Wall's ranks advance on the Seminary building. Johnston's troops, previously lolling about, laughing, leaning or sitting on the wagons, began to scramble into order. They stood at all the openings, tall, stiff, with grim faces turned toward Eighth.

Marshal Doston came forward and called out an order. The soldiers slid their rifles onto their shoulders.

It was too much like Maggie's dream. She felt her heart throb inside of her. Fear made her clumsy; she slid and fell into a melting drift.

"Here," someone said and grabbed her elbow, helping her to her feet again. Maggie looked up and saw an unfamiliar face. She pulled out of his grip.

"Thank you," she muttered.

She was soaking wet, and her thighs were starting to go numb where her skirts stuck to them. The wind hit her, and she shrieked and began to run again, through the unbroken snow on the west side of the block just north of the Seminary building, toward the little log schoolhouse.

She banged on the door with her fist.

Nobody answered.

Maggie banged as hard as she could. "Giovanna!" she called out.

Immediately the door opened. Maggie tripped and almost fell into the room.

"Get over here," Brother Jones hissed and tugged Maggie by her elbow over to where the rest of the children were huddled around the stove, sitting cross-legged on the floor. "We're holing up here, till the danger's passed—"

"No," Maggie sputtered, thinking of soldiers pouring into the room, splintering the wooden door with their heavy boots and bayonets. "Giovanna—"

Giovanna stood up. "Thank you, Brother Jones." She hurried outside with Maggie.

"The Legion's come in," Maggie said.

"You're all wet. Let's get home, Maggie. What're you

doing?" Giovanna stared as Maggie waded back into the drifts.

"I've already broken a path through it. There's no way we'll get anywhere soon in the crowd here. Come on." Maggie tugged at Giovanna.

"Where're Ma and Patience?" Giovanna asked. "Stop it." She snatched her arm away from Maggie.

"We—they're in, out there, somewhere," Maggie gestured helplessly at the crowd that lined Eighth Street, now so thick with people that all wheeled traffic was effectively blocked off. "Wait!"

She ran after Giovanna, who had begun to run in the direction of the crowd.

"Ma! Patience!" Giovanna cried.

"Hush!" Maggie hissed at her sister, clamping a hand over her mouth.

"Let me go!" Giovanna squirmed out of Maggie's grip again. She ran toward H and made a left.

Maggie couldn't keep up with her. Her legs were so cold, she couldn't feel anything below the knee, and her thighs burned.

She stumbled and slowed to a walk.

The best she could do was to find Patience and Ma Alden and try to get them to convince Giovanna to go back home.

The Legion was stationed on all four streets. They stood in the middle of the road, in front of the crowds, facing the soldiers. When Maggie got down to Seventh, she saw Marshal Dotson and another, taller man, standing in the road, arguing with Bishop Wall.

"Clear your men out." The taller man's voice carried, sharp and clear in spite of the snow and crowd, which had fallen into complete silence.

"Can't do that, Heth," Bishop Wall said, scratching his chin. "You've got our mayor in there a prisoner, and we aren't going to sit by and watch you drag him out of here and around the mountains without so much as a by-your-leave from Governor Cummings."

"Governor Cummings's got no say in this," Marshal Doston spoke up now. There was the bite of frustration in his voice. "Johnston's and Cradlebaugh's authority comes straight from Buchanan. Don't need a by-your-leave from the governor."

"Seems to me there was a piece of paper delivered lately from President Buchanan that said you had to leave us alone," Bishop Wall argued. "Seems to me Cradlebaugh's overstepping a thing or two, bringing all these hired thugs into our town, taking our civic leaders hostage so they have to sit and listen to him spew out vile and poisonous slander all the day long."

"Stand down," Captain Heth barked. "If anyone attempts to break my line, I'll order my men to fire on the crowd."

"Well, that would sure be a sad situation," Bishop Wall nodded. "As I've got three times the men you do, Heth. I reckon I know how it'd end."

Just then, as if to confirm Bishop Wall's words, a stone flew out from the crowd. It missed the Marshal by only a few inches, and instead hit a soldier that stood behind him, right in the head. The soldier stumbled in the snow, holding his head with both hands, and the crowd erupted. The people bunched behind the Legion started shouting and picking up whatever they could find—mostly snow.

"Ready," Captain Heth called out, his voice carrying through the noise.

"Stand at attention." Bishop Wall turned to the men standing behind him.

Marshal Dotson moved hastily behind the line of soldiers.

"Aim," Captain Heth called, and both groups of men obeyed, the Legion without even waiting for Bishop Wall's order.

Maggie put her hands over her mouth. "No," she whispered. "No, no, no."

There was a long, tense moment, as each man waited for the other to call out the next order.

"Stand down," Captain Heth said finally, and his men lowered their weapons.

"At ease," Bishop Wall said to the Legion. "And no more stones, do you hear me?" He addressed the crowd now, his face stern. "Everyone drop them, now." He turned back to Captain Heth. "Release Mayor Bullock."

Captain Heth was frustrated, Maggie could tell. He stood silently for a moment, glaring at Bishop Wall, and then turned abruptly and walked toward the Seminary building.

The crowd was quiet again, waiting. When they saw Isaac Bullock walking out of the Seminary building, the cheer went up, startling Maggie so she felt her heart nearly stopped. He walked out to the crowd, grinning, as people began to pat him on the back and congratulate him.

Maggie hurried through then, and standing on her tiptoes, strained to see if she could spot Giovanna or the Aldens.

"Don't start celebrating yet," an angry voice called out.

Maggie was still struggling through the crowd, but as everyone turned back in the direction of the Seminary building, she found herself pushed into the street. She nearly fell headlong again but managed to save her balance by grabbing the sleeve of one of the Legion that stood close to her.

It was Cradlebaugh who had spoken. There he stood, next to Captain Heth and Marshal Dotson. "Glad you're in such a celebrating mood," he growled. "Makes me feel generous." He glanced at the crowd that lined Seventh. "Here, then—I'll let all the prisoners go. How do you feel about that? Since I don't seem to have the favor of local law enforcement," he gestured angrily toward Bishop Wall, "I figure you can take care of things yourselves."

A line of men began making its way out toward the crowd. Maggie spotted several Indians and some men she didn't recognize.

"But, sir," Marshal Dotson stammered. "They're wanted for other matters—"

"Well, since these people feel the law ought to be in their hands." Cradlebaugh shrugged.

"You'll be letting all your witnesses go too then?" Bishop Wall spoke up.

"They're still testifying."

"But you've dismissed the jury."

"I aim," Cradlebaugh raised his voice, "to get a real and true account of what's happened in these parts and bring it before the Congress of the United States. And don't think," he added, squinting and pointing at Bishop Wall, "that this is over."

"We've sent an appeal to Cummings."

Cradlebaugh snorted and shook his head. "On your own heads be it." He turned on his heel and headed back in the direction of the courthouse.

Maggie felt horrid inside. She watched Bishop Wall as Cradlebaugh trudged through the snow back into the Seminary building.

"Maggie," someone called out to her.

She jumped, and whirled around, nearly losing her balance again.

"Easy, there." It was Henry.

Was it really? Maggie could hardly believe her eyes, but there he sat on top of an Indian pony, wearing the long gray coat that the other members of the Legion all wore. "Let me give you a ride," he said, stopping his animal just in front of her.

"No thanks," Maggie said when she had rediscovered her voice. "I've got to find—"

"Giovanna's fine. I just talked with your Ma Alden and Patience. They're over along on the other side of the block."

"Are they going to release Pa?"

Henry shrugged and then shook his head. "Don't figure Cradlebaugh's going to let any witnesses go until he feels satisfied with what he's got from 'em. Hop on, Mag. I'll take you home."

"I . . ." Maggie stopped herself. She could walk, but why would she? She was wet, her legs were almost completely numb, and she felt miserable. She could get up out of the snow and have a quick ride home. "Thanks," she finally said, taking Henry's hand and allowing him to place her on the saddle in front of him.

"You're soaked through," he exclaimed when she settled into place.

"Sorry."

"It's okay. Go warm up in front of your fire. I've gotta ride back up into Hepsedam before nightfall."

"Hepsedam?"

"Where we're staying in the canyon; that's the name we've given it. Don't tell anybody, of course."

Maggie nodded.

"Maggie—you, you don't reckon you might want to come along with me? Up into the canyon?"

Maggie felt warmth flood her system, making her eyes water and her face tingle. "Don't reckon it'd be proper, Henry," she managed at last.

"You've never cared about propriety before."

She took a breath to steady herself. "Well, Henry, I figure you want to see me." She nodded at the saddle horn. She couldn't bring herself to turn and look at him. "Like, sparking. Tell me if I'm wrong." This last part came out in a rush.

It took several agonizing moments for Henry to answer. "Well, I figure I do," he said. "If you're of a like mind, of course."

Maggie felt suddenly light as a bird, like she might burn up, like she might burst apart at the seams. "Well," she said, covering her smile with her free hand, "if we're going to be seeing each other, we ought to do it proper. I'm thinking of your ma and your pa and all those who might look sideways at us if we continue as we been."

"Been how?" Henry's arm found its way around Maggie's waist. She touched it, lightly, with her fingers. "And Ma'd never judge you that way, Maggie."

Maggie frowned and passed over his latter statement, unwilling to argue at that moment. "I mean like going off fishing alone and all that."

"We need to take a chaperone fishing." Henry chuckled.

"Well, no. Well, maybe." Maggie shook her head. "I dunno, Henry. I'm not all that good at this yet."

"Me neither. Reckon I'll have to ask Samuel a lot of truly embarrassing questions."

Maggie nodded. Then silence stretched out between them. Maggie's throat felt constricted. She wanted to say a million things, wanted a million things to happen, but she had no idea how to get herself, or them, started. And she was frightened, for some reason. Her stomach had never been so knotted on itself.

"Maggie, do you fancy me?" Henry finally broke the silence. "Don't—I don't want you to be doing this as a favor to me, or because you miss spending time with me and you figure it's the only way now we're older."

"Do I fancy you?" Maggie nodded, again at the saddle horn. "Well, I s'pose I do."

"You suppose? Be sure about it, Maggie. My heart can't take much more of a beating from you than it has already."

"Henry . . ." Maggie felt a lump form in her throat. She cleared it. "I reckon you don't have to worry over that, I like you plenty. And I—I'm sorry for how crazy I've been acting lately."

"Just lately?"

Maggie had no heart to chuckle at this quip. "Whatever I done to make you sad, I'm sorry for it, Henry."

The pony stopped in front of the Aldens' home. Maggie's heart was beating so fast, she was afraid it might break out of her rib cage. She forced herself to turn and look at him. "I reckon," she said, hoarsely. "I reckon I want the same thing you want, Henry. If I'm understanding you."

Henry's smile spread out over his face, just like it had that evening at the Cleggs'. His eyes glowed, and the sun shone on his hair, which was damp and tousled.

Maggie put her hand up to smooth it. She felt the smile start across her own face as well. She wanted to do more—to embrace him, squeeze him so tightly that he hollered, but she didn't. It was like the moment was a fragile piece of magic, like anything might disrupt it. Maggie could hardly believe it as she felt the damp strands of his hair wind around her fingers.

"Consarn it," Henry murmured. He put a hand on her shoulder, as if to draw her closer to him.

"I haven't been able to get in to see him yet," Ma Alden's voice pierced the quiet.

Maggie made a face at Henry. "Help me down," she said. "Quick now."

He frowned but obeyed, and Maggie was down from the pony in a flash.

"They won't let anyone past," Ma Alden continued, coming around the corner with Patience in tow. "As if a poor, bedraggled woman could—Maggie-girl, there you are."

"Be careful up there," Maggie mumbled at Henry.

"See you in a little while," Henry replied. Traces of the jubilant smile were still on his face—tugging at the corners of his mouth.

It made Maggie squirm, but she managed a small smile of her own. "Soon as this all gets taken care of," she said. "Tell your ma I said hello."

"Tell her yourself. Likely you'll see her before I do. I don't have time to stop on the way up."

Ma Alden and Patience walked over to where Maggie was standing. Maggie watched the snow and slush as it was flung back from the hooves of the pony as Henry urged it into a trot. He sat, tall and stiff, as if he knew she were watching him and wanted to appear at his best advantage.

"Nothing's likely to be taken care of anytime soon," Ma Alden said as they went inside.

Maggie nodded, keeping her face turned away so nobody could see her face change color.

So Ma Alden had heard a little of it, at least.

She made her way quickly over to her usual spot, on the

stool by the wall, and took up her mending. She didn't want to talk or look at anyone right at that moment, for some reason. And she felt like her face must show everything—she felt like it was permanently red.

Patience sat in the rocker, next to her. She picked up her knitting and stared at it for a moment, then set it down again, and stared off into the distance.

"You get a chance to talk to Will before he went up with the others?" Ma Alden asked from the kitchen.

"No," Patience replied. She sighed and grabbed her knitting needles. Their rhythm of clicks sounded loud, to Maggie, in the silence of the room.

"Where's Giovanna?" Maggie asked suddenly.

"Went off with Etta and Elias. They're feeding her supper."

Maggie nodded and bit her lip, concentrating on keeping her darning stitches tight and even.

It was useful, Maggie decided as she sat there, even if it was tedious—stitches occupy the mind and hands awfully well.

"I think I have a headache," Patience said. "Can I go lie up in your room, Ma?"

"Sure," Ma Alden said. "Just come down in time to help me get supper on. Maggie, have you done the milking yet?"

Maggie stood, obediently setting aside the darning.

"Get some dry clothes on first. Those skirts are too short, anyhow. I think I may have one of Etta's old work dresses. I'll go look. Henry paying you company then?"

It came so suddenly and without precedent, that Maggie didn't have any time to be flustered. "Well—yes," she said, "I think so."

Ma Alden nodded, frowning. "Not much of a surprise,

but glad there's an understanding—it was worrying me for a while there, the way you two always went off, old as you are. You talked to his ma about it?"

Maggie felt the color flood her face again at this. "No."

"Well, she likely knows already anyhow. Wasn't hard to see he fancied you."

A sudden surge of anger replaced Maggie's embarrassment. "You . . ." She couldn't even get the words out, she was so flustered.

"Here, I think this'll do," Ma Alden said, tugging something from the crate of odds and ends that she had pulled out from under Patience's bed. She held out a faded blue dress, of calico. It had three buttons in the bodice, shaped like little flowers. "It'll be too long for you. I think if you work quickly though you could do a makeshift hem right now and we'll do it proper later. I don't want you wearing that outside." She stepped back, looking Maggie up and down. "Really, that one ought to go to Gigi. It's too short for you."

Maggie stared at Ma Alden. The anger hadn't receded, but she knew it wouldn't do any good to express it. "You—I thought you disapproved of me going 'round with Henry."

Ma Alden raised her eyebrows. "What gave you that idea?"

"You said I—you said his ma wouldn't appreciate it, that I shouldn't keep company with him because I wasn't fit company for him."

"No," Ma Alden frowned. "I never would've said that."

"You said his ma'd likely want him to—to see someone of good family, not foreign."

"Well," Ma Alden said, "I've always tried to give you a bite of reality, Maggie. I don't feel it's moral to give you and Gigi expectations and be disappointed . . . I've always felt like

I ought to teach you hard work so you can shift for yourselves if need be. But if Henry's paying court . . ." Ma Alden shrugged. "Who am I to argue with that. I'm happy for you. He'll have a trade in his pa's shop, and he'll have land, and likely you'll be a first wife or maybe an only wife if you can keep convincing him the way you've done."

"I'm not convincing him," Maggie snapped.

"Well, fine," Ma Alden replied, tossing the dress to Maggie. "You don't got to have your nose in the air about it. I'm saying you done a good job on him."

Maggie felt the anger boil and then dissipate. There was no use, really. No use at all. "Thanks," she managed.

"Be quick about it, that poor cow's waiting for you. And you don't want to be out too long after dark. Who knows what might come in off the street these days." Ma Alden shuddered.

A while later, Maggie rested her cheek against the cow's warm neck for a few minutes. She thought of Pa Alden, freezing in a tent or wagon—where were they keeping the witnesses? Her heart felt like a band was squeezing it as she thought of Henry, up in the canyon with his brothers. She thought of the soldiers, sitting on horses, spitting in the streets, and winking at people.

A surge of raw fury rose up inside of her.

Who were they, those men, to come into Maggie's town, hold Maggie's pa prisoner, and send good men like Henry, Hyrum, and Bishop Johnson up into the mountains. Pa Alden and the other witnesses had come forward voluntarily—who was Cradlebaugh to hold them like prisoners?

Will he ever let Pa Alden go? Maggie wondered. Bullock had gotten off, but the town and Legion wouldn't take such a stand for the sake of one farmer.

Maggie felt her anger turn on the town and its people, the sanctimonious faces in the crowd—how many of them had some involvement in what had happened in Cedar? How many of them were holding back, trying to save their own hides, while Pa Alden, Henry, and Mayor Bullock paid the price for their cowardice?

And what if it was true, what Uncle Forth said? What if there were one or two people who were willing to do something horrible, if they got a chance, to keep things quiet? Whoever it was, they had killed women and children. They wouldn't stop at killing Father Alden, not if they thought he might be a threat to them. Maybe Pa Alden really was better off where he was.

Maggie sighed and plunked herself onto the stool. She grabbed hold of the cow's two back teats and saw her left hoof twitch, then raise slightly off the ground.

"Sorry, Bess," she said, letting go and patting the cow's leg. "Don't upset my pail—I'll be gentler. Just got a lot on my mind."

HEPSEDAM

"DON'T PUT THAT ON," MA ALDEN SNAPPED AT MAGGIE.

Maggie wrinkled her brow at Ma Alden. "You said I could have—"

"We're shearing today."

Maggie raised her eyebrows. "Today? Do you think that's—"

"Got to be done," Ma Alden said. "Can't afford to lose this year's yield. And with your Pa still . . ." She broke off, looking down at her hands. She gave the washboard a last, furious scrub with the square of flannel she was using to clean it. "We need everybody up in the fields today," she said finally.

"Giovanna too?"

"She's already over at the schoolhouse."

Maggie frowned at her own hands and saw that her darning had tangled around two of her fingers.

"All right, fine," Ma Alden said. "Go and get her too, then. I don't fancy leaving her in town either, with all that's . . ."

Ma Alden couldn't even say his name. She couldn't talk about it. Maggie wondered if it was because she didn't want to break down in front of Maggie or if she was trying to keep her thoughts completely away from the subject; go on with life—pretend nothing was happening.

"All right." Maggie rose from her chair. She put the wrap on, laced up her boots, and stepped outside.

It was miserable. The sun hadn't come quite up over the mountains yet, and so the churned-up, muddy landscape was shadowed and treacherous. Maggie walked carefully along Eighth. The soldiers stood there, lined up as usual. The crowds had just started to gather for the day's exhibition. Maggie watched as the jurors, apparently just arriving at the Seminary building, filed past one of the soldiers and toward the front door.

Maggie gazed up at the building for a moment. It was three stories, made of brick, wider and taller than any other building in town. It had stood for as long as Maggie and the Aldens had been there. Maggie knew that it was built to be a home to Elder George A. Smith, who was the presiding Church authority in the area, but he had surrendered it to the town, saying it was too fine to be a residence; it ought to be purposed for social gatherings and Church meetings.

And now it's being used against us. Maggie turned her back on the scene, walked up the shoveled path to the schoolhouse door, and knocked timidly.

"Good morning," Brother Jones said when he opened the door.

"I'm here for Giovanna," Maggie said. "We got to get up in the fields for shearing."

Brother Jones sighed. "I ought to just cancel school." He moved aside so that she could get past him.

Maggie looked over the half dozen students scattered over the mostly bare benches. “Looks like it.”

“I certainly wouldn’t mind. I don’t fancy sitting here in this room, right across the street from that,” he shrugged. “But Bullock is being stubborn. He says I must keep the term going.”

Maggie shrugged. “I’m sorry. C’mon, Giovanna.”

Giovanna frowned. “I don’t want to go up to the fields today,” she said.

“Nor do I. But the sheep’ve got to be sheared.”

Giovanna slapped her book shut and gathered up her pencil. She didn’t look at Maggie as she marched out the door.

Just as they got free of the drifts that lined Eighth, Maggie saw the Seminary doors open. She stopped on the street, grabbing Giovanna’s shoulder.

“Pa Alden,” she said.

It was true. He was there, walking out of the doors, along with three other men. He looked, if possible, gaunter than the last time Maggie had seen him. As the four men approached the line of troops, several more people exited the building, and Marshal Dotson. “Jury’s been dismissed, and these witnesses. Let ’em pass,” the Marshal barked. “We’re moving out—get everything in order.”

Jubilation broke out in the crowds surrounding the tabernacle. “Get the Legion and the band!” someone called out. “Give ’em a proper send-off.”

Giovanna ran toward Pa Alden when he walked into the street, past the soldiers. He seemed taken aback by the sight of her, hurling at him like a human cannon, but a weak smile broke out over his face and he grabbed her up, and pulling her to his chest.

Maggie finally moved her feet. She walked to him and put her arms around his waist. "Ma Alden will be tickled. Let's go right home," Maggie managed in spite of the thickness in her throat.

But when they opened the door and Pa Alden walked in, Ma Alden did not seem happy. She stood, put her hands to her mouth, and grew very pale. She put her arms around Pa Alden. "You've got to leave town," she said hoarsely.

Pa Alden pulled back and looked at her. "I'll be fine, Ella."

"No," Ma Alden shook her head. "No, I'm not going to stand by this time. You said it'd be fine, and you got yourself jailed. You said it'd be fine and Maggie run off and nearly froze herself. This time, Fred, I'm *putting my foot down.* You get your hide up into those mountains, and when all the soldiers leave, we're leaving, too."

"Ella," Pa Alden shook his head. "I've got to stay. Cradlebaugh didn't let go all the witnesses. He plans to take the rest over to Camp Floyd—"

"Well, that's a right shame," Ma Alden cut in. "And I'm sorry for their families. But I have you back now when I thought I'd never see you again, and I don't aim to let go of you. Or to let you waltz back into danger, no matter how noble your intentions. These men—" She shook her head, sitting and putting her hand to her chest. "Dale likes to go on and on, and half of what he says is just his own mouth running away from him, but Fred, there've got to be people worried about who you'll talk to next. And if you go back and get tetchy with the court again, likely they'll take you with them back 'round the mountain. And who knows what'll become of you then? Nobody from here will—"

Maggie was unable to look away politely; it was too

surreal, seeing Ma Alden give way to her feelings. To see her shoulders shaking, her head buried in her hands.

"Ma Alden's right," Maggie said. Her face burned—she knew it was presumption, speaking up like this, but she couldn't hold back. "They've killed already, Pa. Whomever it is. And they know you know who they are. They know you're willing to talk, now, too—now you've already volunteered yourself a witness. When all this blows over, if it ever does." She shrugged, thinking of her conversation with Sister Holden. "Somebody's bound to think of a way to get rid of you. People can come up with all sorts of justifications . . . all sorts of reasons, ways to twist the prophet's and other peoples' words so they can stay righteous and still do what they want."

Ma Alden pulled her hands away and looked up. "She's right. I never heard you speak so many words of sense together, Maggie. But she's right, Fred. Mayhap you'll listen to her." There was a tinge of bitterness in these last words.

"Where's Patience?" Maggie asked, more to break the awkward silence than because she really wanted to know.

"Off with Will. Oh, that's the other thing!" Ma Alden exclaimed, standing. "Now you're free, Fred, Patience and Will're straining at the bit. She's been telling me near every night now they want to rush the marriage. Wanted you there, that's the only thing that's keeping Patience in check. But there'll be no keeping them now you're free. Likely want to get in and do it tonight."

"Tonight?" Maggie exclaimed. "Are—but ma, you won't be able to do anything fancy, or have fiddlers—"

Ma Alden shook her head. "Hang the fiddlers. I'm of Patience's mind right now. Hurry up with the marriage, then we can all leave," She gave Maggie an odd look. "We can all leave for California," she said finally.

It was a shock, though Maggie had seen the possibility already, of course.

She had never taken it seriously, the idea of a move. Uncle Forth ran on about so many things, and Ma Alden ran along with him, but they were all talk. That's all it had been—talk.

Ma Alden seemed serious about it, though. Over the next few days she nagged Pa Alden until he had the wagon box repaired and pulled out the canvas of the old cover. She washed it, and had Maggie go back over the seams. The thick, tough thread blistered Maggie's fingertips as she thrust it through the layers of canvas, hour after hour during the day.

It was just Maggie now, sitting in the room with Ma Alden. True to what Ma Alden had said, Patience and Will got married the next morning, after all the troops left Provo. That had been an evening to remember. When the soldiers finally got all of their supplies packed and began their march out of town, the Legion and the band was ready for them, along with perhaps the biggest crowd that had ever lined the streets of Provo during the entire Cradlebaugh incident. The Legion saluted them as they left, but the band was more irreverent, playing the tune of "doo-dah" triumphantly, the brass loud and comic and the drums catching a rollicking beat, stirring the crowds to a frenzy. People turned cart-wheels in the streets, little boys and girls thumbed their noses at the soldiers, women clapped and do-si-doed along with the men. They all followed the soldiers to the end of town, watching until the procession faded from sight.

It at once embarrassed Maggie and made her proud. It also made her angry, the thought of the few people who were now going to get away with murder, but she was jubilant, thinking that she would be able to walk down the street without fearing she might run into a soldier. She felt suddenly light and free again, more at ease than she could ever remember feeling. The whole town acted like they were drunk on something.

Patience and Will are completely mad with it, too Maggie thought, watching them exchange their vows in Bishop Wall's front room a week later. Even he was beaming—the bishop—unable to hide his grin or produce the solemnity that the occasion usually required.

Patience giggled—something Maggie had never heard her do—and said "Sure," when it came to her line. Bishop Wall had to correct her, make sure she said yes properly. And Will's eyes gleamed, and he pulled Patience to him and gave her such a kissing that Maggie had to turn away, feeling the color warm her face. The image of Henry slid into her mind; the thought of what it might be like, kissing him like that.

She shoved it fiercely away now and waited by the door until it was time to leave. Patience and Will were exchanging pleasantries with the bishop.

"Seen it coming a long while," he declared, wiping his forehead with a handkerchief.

"Me too," Will said, sliding his thumbs into his suspenders.

"Don't be silly." Patience giggled again, swatting at him.

"So I hear from your uncle, you'll be off to California." This, Bishop Wall directed at Pa Alden, who stood grinning with his hands in his pockets.

The grin immediately slid off Pa Alden's face. "Ella's been discussing the possibility," he said.

Bishop Wall nodded, suddenly serious. "Well, I'd

consider it, Fred." He nodded again. "I'd sure consider it . . . considering." He shut his mouth as if biting off the rest of his words and nodded again, looking at the floor.

Patience and Will looked at each other, smiles gone. Patience flicked an anxious glance over her shoulder at Ma Alden and gave Will another, more significant look.

They're not going, Maggie suddenly realized. *If Ma and Pa leave town, Patience and Will are staying here.* The look had said it all—anxiety. And the guilt in Patience's face, the way she looked at Ma Alden without really looking at her.

Maggie stopped in the street, watching the others go on ahead of her. She gazed at Etta and Elias, who were furthest behind in the party—at the way Etta's slight waddle betrayed her current condition.

Etta won't leave either. Maggie felt her stomach become something like stone. *Not now. And Elias won't leave his family—his ma and pa and uncles and aunts and brothers and sisters only a half-day's ride away, in Peteneet.*

The guilt choked Maggie.

When Ma Alden had made her ultimatum on the day the soldiers had left town, just a week or so ago, Maggie's immediate thought had been that she was staying in Provo whether the Aldens left or not. Her worries, quickly shoved to the back of her mind, had been about Giovanna and persuading her to stay and having to say good-bye to Pa Alden, if it all really came down to it. She hadn't thought it through at all, because thinking about it had been too much insanity with everything else.

But what if Ma and Pa Alden did leave?

They'd be leaving alone, leaving all their family behind.

Maggie's heart felt like it had twisted on itself. She ached inside, thinking of Pa leaving all of them. She shivered then, and felt her heart beat faster, thinking of Giovanna going with them, without Maggie.

The Aldens were all due in the fields to finish shearing. The Forths were already up there, waiting for them.

Maggie stood in front of the little oval-shaped mirror that hung on the wall. It was Patience's—likely she'd be taking it with her to whatever house she and Will eventually set up for themselves.

She stared at her reflection and the neat, dark coils that hung on either side of her face, at the way her hair gleamed, smooth against her head, coiled neatly at the back. Ma Alden had helped her that morning.

She hadn't even said anything in preface, just grimly attacked Maggie's hair with the brush, while Maggie did her best not to wince or cry out. And when she had finished, Maggie didn't recognize herself.

Ma Alden had gazed at Maggie in the mirror for a long moment, nodded sternly, and turned to some other task, leaving Maggie to stand at the mirror, feeling like she had entered into some other world.

And standing here again, looking at her reflection that seemed more like her mama's—more like a memory than her own face—Maggie felt like something was ending. Or beginning. In any case, either was frightening.

Maggie turned from the mirror and hurried to unbutton her white dress—the one Sister Clegg had given her—and helped Giovanna to undo her buttons as well.

They piled into the wagon—now with canvas stretched over it, there was a welcome respite from the gentle trickle of flakes that came down from above.

"Hope it doesn't get any worse," Uncle Forth remarked. He drove, sitting on the front bench between Ma and Pa Alden.

"I see a patch of blue sky coming in from the south," Pa Alden stated.

"Let's hurry up there and see if we can get it all done today then."

They were using the old homestead as a makeshift shearing station. Maggie leapt from the wagon into the soft, pristine snow, feeling it cover her ankles in quietness.

The fields were soft, the air muffled by the snow that came down slowly. She walked over to the old homestead, watching as the Forth boys herded another half dozen sheep onto the wood floor inside, which was damp with melted snow. She saw through the narrow doorway that they had a fire going in the fireplace.

One mercy about the snow is that they've been out of the dirt for going on two weeks. The wool won't need much washing.

She moved as if to go inside with Ma and Pa Alden and Giovanna but couldn't bring herself to do it. Something stopped her there at the door, and she stared on the Aldens, Forths, and Giovanna as if they were a tableau, lit by the flickering of the fire and the dim light that came through the high windows of the homestead. They immediately fell into a rhythm. Pa Alden and Uncle Forth would each grab a sheep and hold it, Jed would shave them quickly with the shears, letting the wool off in smooth, perfectly cut lengths that Ma Alden and Giovanna quickly gathered and began to pick through.

Maggie turned away and walked around behind the cabin.

The wood marker was nearly covered by snow. Maggie dusted the ground with the end of her shawl, kicking and clearing it away with her boots as well. She sat then, next to it, ignoring the damp seeping through her skirt, and thought of Samuel.

Why hadn't he been able to stay alive? Couldn't he have managed it, at least? He had gone off without any counts against him—no illness or injury, like their parents. And he had been twelve, strong and tall for his age. He hadn't been a helpless infant like Noémie, for Maggie to—

Maggie closed her eyes and said something like a prayer under her breath, steering herself away from the thoughts and memories that seemed so ready to rear up and take her over again.

She had to be there for Giovanna.

But did she really? What if she was left here, truly the only remaining Chabert, left to carry all these memories?

One person doesn't make a family. While she thought it, the image if her mother, so like the one that she had seen in the looking glass that morning, came to her mind and with it, the familiar sensation that something had tight hold of her heart.

Maggie shook her head impatiently. She stood and brushed her skirt off.

"Is that where the baby is?"

Maggie composed her face and turned to her sister. "Yes," she said.

Giovanna walked over to stand next to Maggie, looking down at the patch of ground that she had cleared. "I don't think it was your fault, Maggie. You didn't mean to do it. I think baby Noémie probably forgives you."

Maggie shook her head. "I'll find out one day I guess."

"That won't be for a long time, though. You should probably not worry over it too much until then."

Maggie stifled a chuckle. She wished it were that

simple—she could stop worrying over it. Put off the worry and just wait and see what happened one day, when she met baby Noémie in heaven, and they could clear the matter up between them.

She looked over at Giovanna and was startled to see a tear running down her cheek. "Oh," she groaned. "Don't, Giovanna. Please don't."

"It was likely my fault, anyway, Maggie. You sleep still at night. I'm the one who tosses and turns and tangles the linens up."

"But if I hadn't been disobedient, she wouldn't've been in our bed in the first place."

"So we're both to blame."

"No." Maggie put her hands on Giovanna's shoulders, shaking her a little. "You're not to blame. Stop crying."

"You cried. A lot. I'm allowed to too, aren't I?" Giovanna glared up at Maggie.

"Girls," Ma Alden said, coming from behind the house. She stopped short when she saw them, and the cleared patch of ground. "I—they—we need you inside." She whirled around and hurried back around the house.

The day was long and dim. The blue sky never arrived, but the snow never poured down, either. It just threatened above them, in skeins of cloud the same grayish-white color as the wool that they gathered and carded. After dinner they switched tasks, and Maggie's arms trembled as she crouched, holding the delicate neck of a lamb in her arms while Jed carefully swiped the sheers along its spine.

Suddenly, there was a terrible noise. It was strange, low in resonance, louder than Maggie had ever heard in her life. It shook the little homestead and made Maggie's ears ring.

All in the room stopped what they were doing. The

sheep spooked, wrestling away from those that held them, clattering, and skidding on the wet floor in all directions.

"Cannon fire," Uncle Forth said finally.

Maggie made an incredulous noise and then quailed under her uncle's glare.

"No, Maggie, I reckon he's right," Pa Alden said slowly. "Let's get these last ones shorn, everyone."

All in the room turned toward Pa Alden. He still knelt there, with a firm grip on the ewe that Ma Alden had been shearing. "Come on, it'll be dark before we're finished and we'll have to come up again tomorrow." He gestured impatiently with his head in the direction of Maggie's lamb, which was trotting the circumference of the room, bleating, trailing half its coat on the floor behind it.

Maggie grabbed the little animal and knelt with it again. Jed knelt beside her and finished with a few efficient swipes of the shear. "Dumb little son of a gun," he said, grabbing the lamb's muzzle and shaking the little animal's head roughly. "Likely wool's half gone to a waste."

"Stop it." Seeing Jed's face, Maggie was immediately sorry that the words had escaped her.

"You're full of lip today." He grabbed the half unraveled bun at the back of her head and gave it a tug.

Pa Alden released the animal he was holding and stood. "Leave her alone."

Jed gave Maggie's hair another giant yank before he let it go—so hard, it made Maggie's eyes water. *Glad the others are here*, was her thought. *Or I wouldn'ta got off so easy.*

It was so quick, what happened next, that Maggie didn't have time to process it. The whole room gaped at Pa Alden, and at Jed, who was now headlong on the cabin floor.

"Don't you move," Pa Alden said easily, setting a boot

over Jed's throat when he tried to sit up.

Jed's face was red, furious, his eyes darting around the room. His hands grabbed for Pa Alden's foot. Pa Alden must have applied a little bit of pressure, because Jed gasped suddenly and went still.

Uncle Forth made a furious noise and set down the shears he had been sharpening.

Maggie caught the look that Pa Alden threw over his shoulder and felt like she had gone colder by a few degrees. "Stay where you are, Dale. Your son needs to learn a long overdue lesson."

Uncle Forth stared at him for a long moment. He turned and sat quietly back down on the hearth.

Pa Alden looked down at Jed. The silence in the room buzzed. Maggie felt like the ringing in her ears had multiplied tenfold. "Next time you touch one of my girls, you'll get the hiding of your life." His voice was quiet, but everyone in the room heard every word.

Jed was shaking a little as he stood. He looked down at his shoes, avoiding eye contact. He threw the shears onto the floor and stalked outside, slamming the door behind him.

At that moment, there was another cannon sound, even louder this time. Maggie's breath was taken away, as if someone had knocked her in the chest. The shears rattled on the floor.

"Fred," Ma Alden's voice was plaintive. "Fred, let's go."

"There's three more sheep to shear."

"I don't care about the blasted sheep!"

Giovanna squeaked, surprised that Ma Alden would use such a word.

Maggie took up the shears that Jed had thrown and managed to cut the rest of the wool off the lamb's little rump. It wasn't as clean as it could have been, but she knew Pa Alden wasn't going to leave until the sheep were done.

"Go where, Ella?" Pa Alden's voice was pleasant and languorous again. He grabbed one of the two remaining ewes.

"Go—well, somewhere."

"California." Uncle Forth stood, rubbing his shoulders. His fury had receded, but his tone held a kind of grimness.

"You all packed and ready to go?" Pa Alden asked mildly.

Maggie knelt and began shearing the ewe he held. *He won't leave until they're all done*, she thought. "Hepsedam. Or Kolob," she said quietly.

"This is no time for jokes, Maggie." Ma Alden's voice shook.

"No," Maggie said. "Not like in the scriptures. There's a place in the south canyons. It's where the Legion sometimes drills and where some of the—the people have gone to hide. They call it Kolob. And Hepsedam's the name of the camp up here in the mountains. Henry's up there right now with the Cleggs, and Bishop Johnson, and some others."

Ma Alden grabbed the other ewe, startling it so that it bleated. "Get those other shears over here, Dale," she snapped.

They cleaned up, put the sheep back to pasture, and loaded all the wool into the wagon. Maggie and Giovanna sat on top of the load. Giovanna moved close to Maggie, who put an arm around her. "We going to California, Maggie?"

Maggie was startled by the question. She thought for a moment but still couldn't come up with any kind of response. She gave Giovanna's shoulders a little squeeze. "Don't know. Reckon we might have to decide."

"I want to stay here."

"What if Ma and Pa leave?"

"I'll stay with Etta. Or Patience. Or—or I could stay with you. At the Hosters'."

Maggie shook her head. "That's not a good idea."

"Why not, Maggie? We can—"

"Well, we don't know if it's going to happen anyhow, so let's not get our feathers in a ruffle over it," Maggie snapped.

The wagon jostled over the fields. It was a nicer ride with the wool to cushion them.

"Hey!" a voice called out.

"Ignore them," Ma Alden hissed. "Let's just keep on."

Pa Alden slowed the mules. "Hello there, Brother Hall."

"Don't go by canyon way," the man called, trotting his pony up to them. "I'm telling all the travelers. Bench's teeming with soldiers."

"Was that cannon fire then?" Uncle Forth asked. "Where did they fire? Did they fire on the town?"

"No. It came off the benches. Just shooting a couple practice rounds, I expect. Or that's what I'm sure they'll say on it. Don't doubt they thought of the fact we'd all hear, for ten miles around—"

"How many troops?"

"News from up in Evansville says eight hundred crossed from the valley up onto the benches. Camped there last night, headed along the benches down south. This afternoon some came down into the east fields and bayoneted a boy."

"Bayoneted?" Ma Alden gasped. "What—?"

"Talk is it was a scuffle over some sheep. Guess they were shearing, and the soldiers were causing trouble, scattering them. Likely wanted to take one up into the canyon with them, I'd think. The boy put up a fight."

"But was he—"

"Thanks," Pa Alden cut her off. He saluted Brother Hall and started up the mules again.

Uncle Forth, who had risen in his seat to hear better, cursed and clutched at the bench's wooden back.

Ma Alden craned her neck, looking over her shoulder at Maggie. "Where's this Hepsedam place, then?" she said abruptly.

Maggie blinked. "Don't know where it is myself. Henry and the Cleggs go up there."

Ma Alden nodded and turned back around. "You two can go by Cleggs' after we've got all the wool out of the wagon. No, Fred, you're going up there tonight. Until this all settles down." Her voice cracked.

Pa Alden didn't argue. He heaved a sigh and clucked to the animals, bringing them into a trot.

The wool made a giant pile in the little side room where Patience usually slept, now Etta was gone. Would Patience and Will be sleeping here tonight? Maggie hadn't thought to ask.

They'd be sleeping in a bed of wool if they did and wake up smelling like sheep.

This thought, funny though it was, did little to cheer Maggie as she pulled on two wraps, a scarf, and a muffler. The air had gone dead and cold on the way back, making Maggie's teeth chatter and her fingertips numb.

It was no time to be venturing up in the canyon.

Pa Alden and Maggie set off, walking quickly down seventh. Their breath steamed out in puffs of vapor. They didn't talk.

A few minutes later, Maggie knocked on the door.

Hannah Clegg opened it.

"Where is everyone?" Maggie asked, glancing around at the empty room.

"Sheep shearing," Hannah said. "I've only got Orson and my little boy here. All the other boys're out at the herd."

Maggie's stomach felt suddenly hollow. "Did Henry—did all of them come down from the canyon to help with shearing then?"

Hannah nodded.

"Are—did you hear if they're all right?"

"All right?" Hannah frowned. "Likely they're back up in the canyon by now."

"There was a tale told to us on the way home of a boy who was bayoneted by a soldier whilst he was watching over sheep," Pa Alden said, putting an arm on Maggie's shoulder. "A dozen families have herds in the fields east of town, Maggie. Don't worry over it too much."

Hannah stood and stretched, glancing at Pa Alden. "You hungry, either of you? Betsy left some baking and there's stew left from dinner."

"No," Maggie said, just as Pa Alden nodded.

They sat at the table. Maggie forced down a few bites of biscuit and stew, and then watched Pa Alden eat. It seemed, to Maggie, that he moved even more slowly and deliberately than usual, as if he were pushing back against everybody hurrying him.

Including Maggie now. She sat and tried not to chew her nails as she watched him take the last few bites.

"We aim to go up to Hepsedam," Maggie said, taking his bowl and putting it in the tub where other dirty dishes lay, soaking. "Do you think you know of anyone still in town who knows the way up?"

"You're going to go up there?" Hannah's brow wrinkled. "No place for a young lady—up in those canyons. Sleeping in canvas tents, with all those men around."

Maggie glanced at Pa Alden and kept her mouth shut.

"Well, Stewart's in the store, I think. I saw the light on when I looked out just now. He could give you directions, maybe. Though it'd be foolish to go now. Sun's going to go down within an hour, I'd think."

"Thanks." Maggie tugged at Pa Alden.

He rose and carefully put his coat on, one arm at a time, and checked his gloves to see that they were snug inside the sleeves.

"I'm coming up with you," Maggie snapped when they got out on the streets. "Don't bother about arguin'."

"Henry's likely fine, Maggie."

"I'm tired of people talking to me about Henry."

"All right, then."

Pa Alden whistled a cheerful tune as they approached Stewarts. There was a light on upstairs, Maggie saw. She gave the door a good pounding, waited a few moments, and then pounded again.

"Likely abed for the night," Pa Alden remarked.

Maggie gritted her teeth and pounded again, this time with both fists, using all her body weight.

"All right, all right," a voice called. "I'm coming down." The voice grew louder. "Don't go breaking my door in."

Brother Stewart stuck his head out. He had on a stocking cap.

It would have made Maggie giggle if she had been in that sort of mood. "We need directions up to Hepsedam."

"Now?" Stewart shook his head. "Don't leave now. You'll get lost if you've never been, catch your death wandering all over the mountainside—"

"I was fixing to go up tonight, Pa," a voice called from behind them.

Maggie looked over her shoulder and saw Andrew, who carried an armload of firewood.

"Not by yourself, son."

"No. I'm going up with the Turner boys; they've been in town today to settle some business and aim to be up at camp tonight."

Brother Stewart sighed, rubbing his eyes with the back of his hand. "Fine. You two have a ride?"

"We'll go by home and take the horses," Maggie replied quickly, before Pa Alden could get a word in.

"That'll be just fine. You take the mare, son. She's been up that way so many times she'll likely find it better than you all stumbling around in the dark. Good night." And unexpectedly, he shut the door in their faces.

Andrew grinned at Maggie, dropping the firewood on the front step. "He'll remember to get it in a few minutes," he protested at Pa Alden's look. "He's in a state over his supplies. Guess with all the traffic on the road, and the weather, he wasn't able to get some things in he was counting on. And business is down, with everybody gone up out of town."

The ride up into the canyon was as cold and miserable and jostling as any Maggie had ever had. *And that's saying a fair piece. Considering some of the times on the trip across the prairies.*

She pulled her wrap tighter around her shoulders with one hand, keeping her other arm tight around Andrew's waist. She had been embarrassed at first, but it was only sensible, Maggie knew. Pa Alden, by far heavier than either of them, should be the one to ride alone.

The two Turner boys were already saddled and ready to go when Andrew, Maggie, and Pa Alden got to their place.

They rode in front, right now, stopping now and then to look for signs Maggie wouldn't be able to pick out if her life depended on it.

"I'm g-g-going to make Henry teach me," she whispered, giving her numb lips something to do.

"What was that?" Andrew called back over his shoulder.

"Don't pay me any mind. How much further?"

"A good ways. We've got to go slow in these conditions."

"How can any of you see?"

"There aren't that many good ways up in these canyons. Turner boys know it well. They've been up and down this every day in the worst conditions. I been up a fair number of times myself. We're going the right way. Don't worry. I'll get you safe to your fella."

Maggie heard the impertinence of his tone, but she didn't care anymore. "If he's n-not bayoneted."

There was no answer, and no more talking for the rest of the ride. Andrew was obviously in a state of deep concentration, keeping his eyes on the snow and both hands on the reigns. Maggie shivered. She breathed into her shawl, hoping the warm breath would collect in the fold of fabric that covered her chin and mouth. She said disjointed prayers in her head. *Father, please help us get there . . . Help us see him . . . Help us not come up against any troops . . . Help us stay alive and not freeze or lose any toes . . . Help us have a good time, please, Heavenly Father . . .*

Maggie shook her head. Have a good time? What was she saying? "H-how much farther?" she slurred.

"We're nearly there," Andrew replied after a long minute's pause.

He was right. It was only a few minutes more before the Turner boys turned into the forest. Snow was falling off the branches above in wet, chilling clumps; Maggie leaned forward to avoid getting any on her head.

Maggie saw canvas tents and then an opening in the trees. The sky above was clear of clouds. The stars were brighter and clearer than Maggie had ever seen them. Somehow they made her colder—all those millions, in their brilliance, scattered across the sky.

"Anybody have tent room?" Pa Alden asked when they dismounted.

"Where are the Cleggs?" Maggie said at the same time.

"I'll answer both your questions. Cleggs likely have tent room. Follow me."

They dismounted, corralling their animals with the many others at the edge of camp, and wound their way around canvas tents, makeshift lean-to's, even a little cabin or two. The tents glowed against the darkness with the lantern and candlelight of those inside them. Maggie could see the shadows moving and hear the murmur of voices.

"Settling down for the night," Andrew said unnecessarily. "There's Cleggs over there." He pointed at a few tents grouped around a smoldering little fire. There were two long, cut logs by the fire.

Henry sat on one. He was gesturing enthusiastically, talking to somebody who had their back to Maggie.

She didn't really think. She ran, calling his name.

He stood and squinted into the darkness, and she came barreling at him like an undone caboose.

"Maggie," he said, when he got his breath back. "What in tarnation you doing up here?"

Maggie couldn't get enough breath to answer. She hung on him, burying her face in his neck.

He patted her back. She kept her head down, and after a

few moments, the mortification descended on her. She clung to him tighter with the idea that, if she didn't look up, she wouldn't see his face, wouldn't see anyone who was looking at her. She had the feeling the whole camp must be there—looking at her, at them, and thinking bad thoughts. How could she have come up here? What had she planned on? Was she going to sleep in a canvas tent with a bunch of men? What would Sister Clegg think when she came back down the canyon tomorrow morning?

"Maggie, you're fair squeezing the life out of me," Henry said, trying to detach her fingers from the back of his neck.

"Sorry," she said. She released him and stared at her feet.

"You must be cold."

"There was a boy bayoneted in the east fields today."

"You came up all the way to camp to tell me that?"

Maggie managed to look at him, finally. "Thought it might be you. Hannah said you all were shearing the sheep today—" She felt the notorious trembling of the corners of her mouth.

Henry's face crumpled too. He pulled her to him and wrapped his arms around her so tightly she almost couldn't breathe. "Well, it wasn't. We didn't go down to shear today like we planned. Heard word from Bishop Evans that Dotson was coming with more troops—oh, crikey, Megs. Will you stop? I'm fine. You're here, I'm here, and I'm fine. Like to put a piece of cool, hard metal into Dotson's head, though."

"Your ma'd likely wash your mouth out, she heard words like that coming out of it." Maggie pulled one of the ends of her shawl up to her face and wiped it. She blew her nose and coughed a good deal. "Sorry."

"Sorry, nothing. Let's get you warmed up. Ma's up here too. Did you know that?"

Maggie felt a dart of emotion—equal parts fear and relief. "No."

"Where were you going to sleep?" Henry chuckled, but his voice held a note of bewilderment. "You are one for running around like a headless chicken. Well, with you here, I s'pose we can give you and Ma a tent to yourselves—"

"Pa Alden and Andrew Stewart came up with me."

"All right, that makes a little more sense. Glad to know you weren't haring off in the dark on your own. We men'll squeeze then. It'll be fine, we've got two other tents and plenty of men here are dozening up—hullo, Fred."

Maggie whirled around to see Pa Alden and Andrew. They were chatting with someone else—Maggie couldn't tell who, because of the dark.

Pa Alden looked over at them. "You found him, then." He nodded at Maggie. "Fit as a fiddle, without any bayonet holes through him. Glad to see it."

Maggie felt the heat in her face. She wiped her nose again, this time with her sleeve.

"Stop that. Ma's likely got a handkerchief or two," Henry said, tugging at her arm. "Let's get you warm."

Maggie and Pa Alden followed Henry over to one of the tents. "Ma," he called, tugging at the flap. "I've got Maggie and her pa here."

Maggie felt her face grow warm again, and her heart speed up. What would Sister Clegg think of her?

Sister Clegg had a shawl wrapped tight around her when she came out. Maggie could see she had on a nightdress—*who brings a nightdress with them to camp in a snowy canyon?*—and her boots weren't laced.

"Hello." She squinted at Maggie. "Wait a moment—I'll have David clear out and bunk with the boys."

"Ma, Maggie come up because she thought I'd been bayoneted."

"Well, I'm glad you weren't, though there are days . . ." Sister Clegg retreated back through the tent flaps.

"Where are we sleeping then?" Pa Alden asked.

"We'll figure it out," Henry shrugged. "Why'd you come up here, anyhow? Just keep Maggie company?" Suddenly his face changed. Astonishment spread out over his features. "Hey—they let you go! You . . . they let the others go, that's right." Henry was nodding. "So, you going to hole up here for a while? That's likely smart."

"Ella seems to think so."

"Ma Alden wants to go to California," Maggie blurted out.

David Clegg poked his head out of the tent. "Hello, Fred. Got to get my bootlaces done up again, and then it's all yours, Maggie. Sorry to keep you in the cold."

Maggie shook her head.

"You—you figure she means business?" Henry asked her, in a quieter tone.

Maggie couldn't see his face. "If she does, I reckon I aim to stay with—well, either Etta or Patience or the Hosters. And I'm sure that Ma Alden'll get done what she wants to get done. You know the states she gets into. Uncle Forth's been talking her ear off about Sutter and gold and California all these last months. I know Ma Alden. She's made up her mind. I don't know." Maggie shook her head again. "I don't know if I should stay with Liz Ellen. I've already imposed on her enough. And Patience and Etta're both, well, newly married. Maybe I should just . . ." She shrugged. "I don't know what I aim to do, Henry."

"You all for shipping out to California, then?" Henry

addressed Pa Alden, now, who was standing silently behind Maggie, his hands tucked into his pockets.

"Reckon it'll be what happens. Let's get some shut-eye." Pa Alden turned on his heel and walked away.

"He doesn't seem too happy about it," Henry observed, watching the dark shape of Pa Alden's silhouette move toward one of the other tents.

"He's not."

"Giovanna going with them?"

At this question, Maggie felt like her heart was being squeezed again, hard. She almost couldn't breathe. She shook her head, giving herself a moment to regain her voice. "Who knows what'll happen. I don't have much hold over Giovanna anymore. None of our family's—of the Chaberts, there's nobody. Nobody left of us, aside from me, Henry. She's an Alden now."

"She loves you, Maggie. She needs you."

"That's not the only thing there is, Henry. I can love her but I can't take care of her. Maybe if I was a year or two older, or . . ." She shook her head again, her face burning.

Brother Clegg emerged from the tent then.

"Don't worry over it," Henry said, patting Maggie's head. "It'll work out the way it's supposed to."

Maggie shook her head. "It's too bad Samuel died. Only a few months ago, too. He'd have . . . maybe then, I . . ."

Henry's expression grew thoughtful.

"Come in, Maggie," Sister Clegg called.

"It wasn't really properly done, though," Henry remarked, as if to himself. "Though I give Mariah all the marks in the world for trying. Name was wrong, and it was a third-hand thing. Maybe we should—?"

"Come in and shut the flap." Sister Clegg's voice was terser, now. "Henry, go to bed."

Maggie scrambled into the tent, making a mess of her bootlaces as she fumbled with them.

"Let me do that. Your fingers are nearly frozen together." Sister Clegg gave Maggie a small smile and bent to help her unlace her shoes.

"Sorry."

"For what?" Sister Clegg raised her eyebrows.

"You're always having to undress me, like I was a baby, or something."

Sister Clegg made a dismissive gesture with her hand. "Don't worry over it, Maggie."

"I was stupid, coming up here like this, wasn't I?"

"We all do unwise things when we're worried about people we love."

Maggie squirmed and looked at her hands. "Sorry," she repeated.

Sister Clegg made a frustrated noise. "Stop being sorry. You're human, Maggie. That's nothing to be sorry about. And I don't feel put upon, taking care of you and teaching you. I want you to feel like I think of you as a daughter. I don't know any other ways to help you understand that."

Maggie slid her feet out of her boots, biting her lip to keep from apologizing a third time. "Thanks."

"Well, you're always welcome. Now settle down so we can get some sleep."

Maggie curled up on the swath of bedding that was laid out on the rocky ground. Sister Clegg put a quilt over her, and then lay down next to her, pulling another over herself.

Maggie lay there and listened to the sounds of camp: low

voices muttering, the flapping of tent canvas in the wind, the sounds of fires being banked, the whuffling and snorting of horses nearby.

Safe, Maggie realized blearily, as she approached that dreamlike state of almost-sleep. *I feel safe.*

With Sister Clegg breathing deeply next to her, high up in these mountains, surrounded by tents full of men that she knew—good men, who would likely rather be with their families that night.

Maggie's last coherent thought was something to do with the eight hundred troops, camped out on the bench, just below them, and still she felt safer than she could ever remember feeling. Safer than she had felt in a long time, at least.

HELLOS AND GOOD-BYES

THE NEXT MORNING, MAGGIE WOKE SUDDENLY. SHE blinked a few times at the canvas that stretched over her. It was bright, and the air had a white sort of quality. *Snow*, Maggie thought. *And I'm up late.*

She sat up and saw that Sister Clegg was already up for the day. She hurried out of the bedding and straightened her skirt as best she could. Her hair was a mess. There was no help for it, without a comb and some time and some water. Maggie pulled her shawl on over her hair, and, wrapping it tightly around her chest, she pulled open the tent flap and stumbled out into a drift up to her knees.

It was still snowing. Great white flakes came down thick and fast, piling on Maggie's arms and head. She saw people, movement, but the sound was all muffled due to the snow.

"Pa! Henry?" she called into the dead air. She wandered around for a few minutes.

"Here," a voice came finally, and Maggie felt a warm mitten on her elbow. She turned and stared into Sister Clegg's friendly gray eyes.

"Where—?"

"Your Pa's been put on patrol duty with David. Henry and Moses have gone to town."

"I'll go down too. If you're going?" Maggie asked.

"I'll be back down to Provo when there's a favorable report about the situation. Today, troops are crawling all over the bench."

"Then how'd Henry and Moses get through?"

"They're not going down to Provo. They're up to the city to take care of some business. They aim to keep to the heights and forge a way over where the troops're at."

"Must be a pretty important business takes them up to the city." Maggie frowned and folded her shawl more tightly around herself. "In this weather . . . Considering everything."

"Henry seemed to think so. Moses was willing to put his end of it off another week."

"Well . . . what do we do in the meantime?"

"We'll look around and see what we can do."

All day long, Maggie and Sister Clegg busied themselves about small tasks. They took over cooking duties and served men in shifts as they got back from patrolling. Maggie had all the news she could have ever wanted about the movements of Johnston's troops along the bench, sitting and listening to the various groups of Legion members as she served them.

"Legions are mobilizing all the way from Evansville, up at Battle Creek, on down to Peteneet," Brother Turner declared over his gruel and salt pork. "Every settlement's in open revolt. I don't think even eight hundred soldiers, strung out along the benches, will be able to keep things under much control. When they had their hundred all congregated in the center of Provo," he said, shrugging. "'Twas a different story, then. Good luck to those troops if they run afoul of any o' the natives too, you ask me. They're causing an awful lot of ruckus. No doubt we'll be left to deal with the aftermath."

Maggie tried to shut the picture of Henry and Moses out of her mind. Hard as she tried, she couldn't help worrying over them, alone, on horseback, winding through the canyons and finding away across the mountainsides above the line of troops. What if *they* met with some of the "natives"?

If Maggie hadn't been so absorbed in her own worries, she would have seen them mirrored on Sister Clegg's face. The older woman served up the men and went about seeing to sicknesses and the small injuries that had occurred in camp with far less cheerful conversation and a grimmer countenance than usual.

Bishop Aaron Johnson was one of the last company. His tall, broad figure was unmistakable even with all the added layers of clothing. His face was broad as well, his eyes set further apart than most men. He had thick, arched eyebrows and a full head of hair, and his voice was a resonant tenor—you could hear him from quite a ways away. He came to dinner in deep conversation with another man whom Maggie didn't recognize at all.

"See, thing is," Bishop Johnson said and sat on one of the cut logs by the Cleggs' little fire. He slapped a spot next to him. The other man obediently sat, and accepted a bowl from Sister Clegg. "From what I've heard about the testimony you gave, you've not been entirely truthful in this whole affair." Bishop Johnson ran his fingertips through his beard and pursed his lips. "That's the bone I've got to pick with you. Not the fact you went to Cradlebaugh, but that you've stretched some truth, I think. And I can't reckon—I can't quite figure, why that might be. That you would have a call to be untruthful. If you really did it for your conscience's sake, then why didn't you follow your conscience clean through to the finish and tell nothing but the absolute truth?"

"Eat it before it cools down. Won't take much time at all," Sister Clegg broke in.

Bishop Johnson bent over his porridge and spooned some into his mouth, keeping his eyes on the other man, who sat with the air of someone who'd been hit over the head with something. He looked at his hands, flexed his fingers, and studied his nails.

"It was a lot," he said finally. His voice was much deeper than Bishop Johnson's, and softer too. Maggie had to strain to hear it.

"How do you mean?" Bishop Johnson set to now, shoveling bites in as he waited for the man to elaborate.

"He said all sorts of things to get us to talk. Leading questions, like. It weren't easy to—" He shrugged. "And you have to admit, Aaron, that business with the girl could seem mighty fishy from the outset."

"Leave her out of it," Bishop Johnson said mildly, but there was something in his tone the brooked no argument. "You—nor anybody else, really knows about that affair. You all think you know everything, but it's between me and Parrish, God rest his soul. And God knows mine too, and he knows yours, Tom."

Tom, whoever he was, didn't seem to Maggie to know what to respond. He set to and shoveled down bites of porridge. "Tastes just fine," he assured Sister Clegg in his gravely tones.

Sister Clegg gave a curt nod and moved to stir the pot and fry up some more salt pork. "Come on, Maggie," she said. "Let's leave these men to their meal."

"That man testify at court?" Maggie asked a few moments later.

"Likely," Sister Clegg replied. "Sounds as if that's the case."

"Ma Alden's worried Pa is in danger." The words came out finally, like a cork out of a bottle. "They're talking about California, she and Uncle Forth—Pa Alden's wore down, I think. I figure they'll do it. I think they'll leave, soon as the soldiers leave town and clear the way. And Giovanna'll—"

Sister Clegg placed a hand on Maggie's shoulder. "Don't worry over what you can't fix," she said quietly. "Maybe something will change. Maybe there will be a blessing that will make all your worries a nonety, Maggie. Pray, and try to keep your worries down to a low simmer. I don't need any more pots boiled over today."

Maggie studied Sister Clegg's face, suddenly noticing the unusual lines of worry and strain. She nodded and didn't say another word about it.

The good news came in the late afternoon. "They're moved on for now," Bishop Wall declared. He stood up on a tree stump and cupped his hands around his mouth. "Listen up," he called.

Men who were busy about taking down their canvas tents, rolling up their bedding or loading up their ponies, turned in his direction.

"We can go on back to town. Cumming's sent notification for Johnston's men to retreat, as all the settlements are in a state of open revolt." He turned to Brother Bell. "Those were the words he used?"

At Brother Bell's nod, he sighed. "Well, troops've been ordered to make their way back on the other side of the mountain, and I think it's understood we can resist arrest at this point. We've got Johnston and Cradlebaugh on the one hand, but Cummings is our governor, and that letter from Buchanan's the last word on the issue, I think. Dotson and Heth have been put in their place. Be ready to move again at a word. But get on back to your families."

There was a scattering of cheers. Most men simply nodded and turned back to their work.

"They all look tired," Maggie said.

"I think we're all tired. My soul's tired," Sister Clegg agreed. "C'mon. Help me break camp. We'll bring you on down to the Aldens'. You can rest easy that your pa's likely safe for a while now. Eye of the hurricane, I'm thinking, but it's something."

Maggie kept quiet, packing up the bedding and rolling it, taking the canvas down and folding it, loading up two ponies and helping to saddle and cinch, though those were tasks that she had never had much hand in before.

As they rode down from the canyon with the Legion, Maggie wished Henry was there. She thought of him, and of Moses, riding to Great Salt Lake City. Had they made it to Point of the Mountain yet?

Likely they had, Maggie decided. Or would by that evening. And then they'd likely be scot-free, in the governor's hands, at that.

She wondered, for the hundredth time, what sort of business would be so pressing as to take Henry and Moses up there at this most inconvenient and dangerous time. Half a dozen times, she turned to ask Sister Clegg and then shut her mouth.

She was simmering; Sister Clegg was simmering. They were riding next to each other, each thick in their own thoughts.

"You fixing to go to California with the Aldens?" Sister Clegg asked suddenly.

Maggie shivered. "I—I've been thinking I'll stay. With the Hosters. Or with Patience or Etta, maybe. But maybe I ought to go with Ma and Pa? Giovanna's said she wants to stay with Patience, but—" Maggie shrugged. "She's only a little girl, and she'd go with Ma and Pa if they told her to, of course. In the end, that's what would happen, supposing Ma Alden were to insist on it."

"And then you would go too, if Giovanna did."

"Now Samuel's gone, and it's only me and Giovanna left in our family—the Chaberts—I mean, I don't know what'd tie us here. I mean, I don't want to leave the Church, or the people 'round here, but . . ." She shook her head. "Maybe our obligations are to the Aldens."

"Your family is your family, Maggie," Sister Clegg declared. She slapped her pony's neck with the reigns and sped up a little, so she was even with Maggie. "You're a Chabert. And an Alden. You're Mother Chabert's girl, and your Ma Alden's girl, and mine and Henry's girl, too. Make sure you consider on that. Family's not something you lose. You only gain more as you go on in life and get more people who care about you."

Maggie nodded. Her throat felt thick, but she willed herself to keep from boiling over.

That Sunday, the Aldens all went to church. They went to the schoolhouse, which was packed so full that people could hardly breathe, squeezed in as they were. Giovanna plopped herself on the bench between Patience and Will, who exchanged amused glances over her head. Maggie sat next to Pa Alden, with Ma on the other side. Etta and Elias were across the room.

Maggie was glad for the break. Ma Alden had been

packing, cleaning, and setting Maggie to tasks that kept her on her knees from dawn until dusk.

"We can't leave soon, Ella," Pa Alden reminded her every now and then. "There won't be anything to feed the animals. Ground's still frozen."

"Won't be all the way across," Ma Alden argued. "And there might not be another chance to get out of here, Fred. This isn't over. Your friends in Cedar know it ain't over too."

Your friends in Cedar. That's what Ma Alden and Uncle Forth had taken to calling whomever it was that Pa Alden had to fear might do something rash to keep him from testifying again.

Maggie shook her head and shifted her weight. She was being squeezed so that she couldn't even flex her elbows without digging them into somebody's side. "Can you scoot just a little?" Maggie heard Giovanna ask, in a fretful, complaining sort of tone.

"Can't," Patience replied. "You want to sit on my lap?"

"Sure," Giovanna replied after considering for a moment.

"Hush up," Ma Alden hissed, leaning across Maggie.

Maggie strained to see over her bent back. Brother George A. Smith would address them today. He was making the rounds—spoke in the Seminary building that morning and was going to the bowery after he spoke here in the schoolhouse.

The door opened again, drawing annoyed glances from all who were in the room, except Maggie.

She stared and felt her legs tremble. She stood, without thinking.

Two young men had walked into the room. One of them was Henry, with a wet overcoat and the misshapen felt hat drooping on his head. And the other . . .

He had Maggie's nose. And her mother's eyes. And her father's crooked chin and thin lips, and an untidy thatch of hair stood up on the top of his head in dark curls.

"Samuel," Maggie choked the name out, and then she was picking her way through between the benches, heedless of the disapproving hisses and Elder Smith, standing there at the front of the room, watching Maggie instead of talking.

Giovanna got up too, taking hold of Maggie's skirt.

"We'd best go back outside," Henry observed. He leaned away from the door enough so that Maggie could duck under him.

Samuel and Maggie stared at each other for several minutes. Giovanna, suddenly shy, folded her arms tightly to her chest and stood, half-hidden by Maggie.

Samuel stretched out a hand, and Maggie took it, surprised to feel the real flesh of him.

"*Ça va*, Magdalena," Samuel offered, finally. "*Comment la vie a été pour toi?*"

Maggie felt like she had entered one of her dreams. The only time she had heard French, these last few years, had been in her dreams.

"*Bon*," she replied, feeling helpless and unable to say anything. What did you say when there was too much to say, and not enough to say? And when the whole situation was just so surprising.

"I can't quite believe it." Maggie put her hands up to her cheeks, feeling the warmth against her cold palms.

"I believe it," Samuel said, grinning crookedly.

That crooked smile. Father. Maggie shook her head. She was dreaming, wasn't she?

She turned to Henry. "Well, how did you find him? Why did you *think* to find him, after Mariah said—*where* did you find him?" Maggie didn't know where to look. Her gaze went from Henry to Samuel, and back to Henry.

"I just did a little asking over in Pleasant Green," Henry shrugged and put his hands in his pockets. "Had the right name to hand, while, after all, Mariah didn't. Brother Brigham had your brother confused with another of Brother Toronto's—but, well, why don't you let him tell you?"

Maggie turned back to Samuel, opened her lips, and then closed them, shaking her head. She kept shaking her head, feeling mortifying tears well up inside her, threatening to spill out of her.

Samuel still had hold of her hand. He pulled her up against him roughly and gave her a few pats on the back. "You look well, Maggie."

His English was much furrier than Maggie's—full of the sounds of Italy, of Mother and Father as they were learning it from the missionaries.

Maggie felt caught between two worlds. She didn't know where she was standing. She was suspended between her own present—which five minutes ago had seemed so entirely real—and her past, which came rushing back to her, overwhelming her with memory and color, feeling, and the personalities and family that she had once considered comfortable, real.

"I—*Bon*," Maggie shook her head. "*La vie c'est bon, et Giovanna . . .*" Maggie pushed Giovanna forward. She stood there, chewing a nail and looking at Samuel.

"Are you my brother?" she asked.

Maggie snapped out of her odd reverie and made hasty explanations to her sister, who gave him an awkward embrace. Samuel chuckled and lifted Giovanna up on his shoulders and carried her that way, over to the Aldens', where Maggie served some food.

"This is where you've lived for all these four years?" Samuel asked, between polite bites of biscuit. Maggie noticed he scooped his beans with the biscuit and ate them together, and remembered suddenly that her father had done the same.

"Yes," she said. "Me and Giovanna."

"And Noémie?"

Maggie felt like something heavy had landed in the pit of her stomach.

"Noémie died," Giovanna answered for her. "She's buried by the Forths' old homestead if you want to see the grave."

Samuel nodded. They were all silent for a moment. "Mama was sure she wouldn't live very long," Samuel said finally. "She had hope the people could save her, but she was far gone by this time. By the time your family was able to nurse her. She was too skinny."

"The Aldens," Henry supplied. He wasn't looking at Samuel, he was gazing at Maggie, watching her with a face full of the pain that Maggie felt but could not readily express.

"She got fat," Maggie said.

Samuel set his biscuit down and gazed at her.

"She got better. Ma Alden nursed her. Noémie was well and happy. I—I rolled over on her one night." Maggie looked down at her plate, tracing the smooth surface with a fingertip. "Ma Alden was always telling us not to take her in the bed. I—I reckon I didn't listen or didn't understand or just didn't want to—obey, maybe. And she died. I'm so sorry, Samuel."

"I'm sad to hear of it," Samuel said a few moments later.

"I—I know. It was my—"

"I'm sad she died," he interrupted, looking up at her, finally. "But happy she was comfortable for some time before she died."

Maggie stared at him. Had he completely misunderstood what she said? Ought she to repeat it in French, maybe? "*Il a été à cause de moi elle est morte.*"

"I hear you, Maggie," Samuel shook his head. "It wasn't your fault."

Maggie laughed, a strange, frustrated sound that sounded more like a sob. "How come people keep saying that? It was my fault. I did it."

"No," Giovanna snapped. She turned red and avoided Samuel's quick gaze.

"I remember," Samuel said slowly. "Mama's body couldn't give her enough heat, and Pa had died, so on the trail, in the tent, I tucked her between the two of you"—he pointed at Maggie and Giovanna in turn—"so that she wouldn't freeze at night. I told you to keep her always close and keep her warm."

Maggie frowned at him.

Her thoughts were churning, and her insides all knotted. She stared at this dark-haired stranger with similar features and wondered what part he had in her world. He was taking up her burdens, sharing them. Maggie couldn't remember the last time that someone had shared the burden of memories with her. She felt lighter, maybe. But also confused. "It wasn't *your* fault," she said.

"You were obeying me, obeying your mama and papa," Samuel shook his head. "You did what you knew. You took her into your bed to keep her safe. I wish I—I'm only glad, Maggie, that you got good people to care for you. I have worried so much. I have thought of you three girls, wondering. When we rode down to Evansville, I looked for you."

"I looked for you in Provo." Maggie forced herself to smile, and then it became real as she saw the crooked grin he returned to her.

"Well, that's some good talk and good food," Henry declared, putting his boots up on the table, completely shattering the moment. "And I reckon I'm ready to sleep for a whole week, uninterrupted."

Maggie looked at Henry. "Thank you."

He nodded at her, the corners of his eyes wrinkled like he was trying to hold back a smile.

"I've given notice to Brother Toronto," Samuel said. "When your friend came to talk to me, he said you and Gia were going to have to leave with your . . ."

"The Aldens," Maggie supplied.

"He said you were leaving for California."

"I wasn't sure what I was going to do. But your being here changes things. Maybe?"

"I was going to stay here with Patience," Giovanna snapped. It was the first words she had said in Samuel's presence. She seemed to regret them immediately after. She went red as a turkey-comb and, resting her chin and mouth against her fists, she stared up at Samuel with a skeptical expression in her large, dark eyes.

"I hope my being here changes things," Samuel said, addressing Maggie's unspoken question. "Would you mind living with me instead, Gia?"

Giovanna studied him for another moment. "I guess we can try it out. I'm-going-over-to-Lizzy's." She flung this last part in Maggie's direction, talking so quickly that Maggie could barely understand it. She jumped up from the table, running out the door before Maggie could respond at all.

"She's so much like Mama," Samuel said, watching her retreating figure through the kitchen window.

Henry had his hat in his hands and was twisting it.

No wonder it's such a sodden mess all the time. Maggie turned and began to walk toward the back door that lead into Stewarts.

"Hold up there, Mag. Don't go in just yet."

The pleading note in Henry's voice caught Maggie's attention. She turned slowly on her heel and frowned at him. "I've got to get this letter out. Mariah likely thinks I'm upset at her. I want to make sure she knows—"

"I know, but it can wait another minute or two."

"Andrew's going to leave any minute. What else *can't* wait a minute or two?"

"Ah, Maggie." Henry sighed and looked at her with such a dramatically tired, gloomy expression.

Maggie wasn't sure whether to laugh, or be concerned. "What bee's gotten in your bonnet, Henry? Hurry it up. I really want to get this in today's post."

"Maggie." Henry shook his head. "Maggie, Maggie, Maggie. I really like you. I really do."

Maggie felt her face go pink. "Uh-huh," she said, glancing around to see if anybody was listening.

"Quite a bit, in point of fact. You've got a lot of great things going for you. The way you look, and talk sassy, and smell, and—"

"Smell?" Maggie frowned at him.

"Well, now, never mind about that. What I'm getting to is . . ." He twisted his hat a little further, and Maggie thought she heard it rip.

"Well, spit it out,"

"Well, it's hard to, *you* know . . ."

"No, I don't know," Maggie snapped. "What, do I stink? I've been working in the fields, getting the ground ready for the front garden, Samuel thinks he can get some seed wheat from Turners—"

"Shut your yap a moment, girl, and listen!"

Maggie raised her eyebrows, startled, and frowned. "Well, this better be good."

"Well, darn tooting, I sure hope it is," Henry said. "I, uh . . . I was figuring you might owe me a kiss or two."

"A kiss?" Maggie couldn't help but shriek. "A kiss?" She repeated it in a whisper, looking around again, mortified that somebody might have heard.

Henry folded his arms over his chest. "I'm sorry, but I sure think you owe me one. After I rode up past all those soldiers on that bench. I've been thinking on it and thinking on it, and I wanted to do it smoother, you know, more gentlemen-like, but Maggie . . ." Henry shook his head, tossing his hat on the ground. "You really aren't the type of girl a fellow can creep up on. So I finally decided just to say it right out. Hope you aren't mad at me."

Maggie felt her face go, if possible, a shade redder. "No," she said.

"No, you won't kiss me, or no, you're not mad."

"Not mad," Maggie mumbled. She moved a step toward Henry.

He looked at her, carefully examining her face. "You mean you don't mind a pucker or two, maybe?"

"Well, long as we're back here," Maggie stuttered, unable to meet his eye.

She felt his arms around her, warm and wiry and strong.

"You've got to look up at me, Maggie, for this to work."

Maggie looked up and saw Henry's face close to hers, felt his lips touch hers carefully, softly.

It was too much. She slid her arms around his neck and

pulled him up against her and kissed him. There was no thought to it, only feeling, only the dozens of daydreams she'd had over the past months about this very moment, wishing for it as much as she was afraid of it.

When she pulled away and saw the startled look on his face, she couldn't hold back a nervous laugh. It sounded silly and high-pitched and made Maggie cringe immediately. *Heaven help me*, she thought. *I'm turning into Julia Harrison.*

"Well, I reckon I've been good and kissed," Henry said conversationally, taking her hand as they walked through the door.

"Well, you go on about it as loud as you are and see if it happens again anytime soon."

"I think I might just owe *you*, now. Got any other long-lost relatives I could ride up after?"

"Hush, Henry." Maggie nodded at Brother Stewart and handed her letter to Andrew.

"Any aunts, maybe, you didn't know crossed over? I hate to be in debt to people."

"Quit while you've gotten ahead. That's my advice," Maggie called over her shoulder as she left through the front door.

"Don't aim to," Henry called after her.

A bubble of happiness welled up inside Maggie as she walked along Seventh. It was a feeling that surprised her—peaceful, whole. Untinged by guilt or worry for the future.

EPILOGUE

Maggie walked into the Aldens' old home—her home now. The Aldens had given it to Samuel, in return for the Indian pony he had ridden into town. *Well,* Maggie thought as she tidied up after breakfast, *really it was a gift.* A gift from a mother and a father to their two daughters, Maggie and Giovanna.

Ma Alden had cried. It had been such a strange sight that Maggie hadn't even thought to be uncomfortable, watching it happen, to see her foster mother sniffle and pull out a handkerchief to hide her face.

She had given a fierce hug to both Maggie and Giovanna. She hadn't said any words at all. She just turned abruptly and climbed into the wagon.

Pa Alden had spent a little more time over his good-byes. He held Maggie in his arms and stroked her head. He lifted Giovanna up off her feet, even though these days she wasn't too keen on that sort of thing.

"Take care of each other." The husky note in his voice

brought Maggie's tears to the surface as well. "I'll do my best," she had said.

The two girls followed the wagon to the edge of town and watched until it disappeared behind a rise in the landscape.

"I'm sad, Maggie," Giovanna had said.

"Me too," Maggie had replied. It was a curious feeling—an achiness she hadn't expected. She knew she would be sad about not seeing Pa Alden again, but she hadn't guessed how sad. And there was some sorrow, some sadness about Ma Alden too. A lot of it had to do with lost opportunities, and Maggie knew, in that moment, that some of the fault had been hers.

"Well, let's get on back," Etta had declared, feeling her back with a grimace. "I don't want to stand around in this state."

Etta and Elias decided to abandon their ruined little cabin and take over the Forths' home. Patience and Will had their own little brick home on the edge of town. And of course, Maggie and Giovanna and Samuel had taken the Aldens'.

And now, they were gone. Off to California. Life was suddenly so different. But not so different, either. *It sure is an odd feeling.*

Maggie scrubbed at the dishes. Carefully, she wiped the yellow-patterned white china and set it on the draining board. She sat in the rocker by the hearth and picked up the thick, worn Bible, the Chabert family Bible that she had thought about and mourned over so often lately.

The Bible that, miraculously, Samuel pulled out of his knapsack the first night they spent together as a family.

"You have it!" Maggie had shrieked.

Samuel had looked at her, bewildered. "Well, it's supposed to pass to the oldest."

"No, I know, I just hadn't thought—I didn't . . ." Maggie could almost have laughed or cried. Or both the same time. "Will you read us some?"

And Samuel sat down right then and read the first chapter of Genesis. The French vowels, the succulent consonants—they ran like a river through Maggie's mind, making the room seem a little warmer.

Miracles are funny things. Maggie ran her finger over its worn cover now. She opened it—looking, as she had hundreds of times since Samuel's arrival in Provo— at the flyleaf.

Magdalena Bounous Chabert. Right there, written in that familiar flowing, elegant hand.

And above it, in slightly different writing: Michele Cardon Bounous.

Then Phillipe Adolphe Cardon.

And at the top, above all the others: Samuel Cardon Chabert.

My great-great-grandfather.

They were right here in front of her now. Four generations, names and dates etched right on the page, by different hands—the hands of her family.

Family. *Famille.*

She now had a family.

But she couldn't think of the Aldens and relegate them to the status of not-family, really. They'd been her family for too long. Pa Alden was certainly family. The ache of mourning in her chest told her that.

Patience. Etta. Ma Alden too, and even Uncle Forth and Jed.

The thought came into her head: *a person doesn't choose her family, they just are.* Maggie nodded to herself. It sounded wise, possibly true.

For that matter—well, she also had to think of Sister Clegg. Nobody who washed you, the way a mother washes her babe, could be anything other than family.

Henry.

Maggie's lips curled up at the corners, thinking of him.

Well, and the Hosters too. They had to be family. She'd lived in their loft for weeks.

She watched Sister Holden's upright figure come by the fence, the sun painting her hair in a fiery halo of orange.

Yes. Who can know when a piece of family might walk by?

DISCUSSION QUESTIONS

1 Why do you think Maggie reacted so strongly to finding her mother's name on the mattress? Was she right to react that way?

2 Why do you think Ma Alden acts as she does towards Maggie? Do you think she cares for Maggie?

3 Who is Maggie's truest friend, or friends, in all of this? How does she reciprocate? What does she have to learn about friendship?

4 The Mountain Meadows Massacre is a very controversial event in the history of the LDS pioneers. How do you think it affects LDS people today? What factors do you think contributed to the events as they played out in the massacre? How can we prevent such things from ever happening in the future?

5 The early LDS settlements were governed by religious leaders. This lead to conflicts when the US government tried to exercise authority in the state of Deseret. How do you think this relates to political issues today? What did the pioneers eventually gain by giving some authority to the government, and what did they lose?

6 Why do you think Maggie had such a hard time remembering her first family? Why do you think she forgot about Noémie? Do you think that it is possible to completely forget events from your past?

7 Why do you think Pa Alden turned himself over to Cradlebaugh? How does it relate to him standing up to Uncle Forth?

8 Do you think it's a good thing that Pa and Ma Alden left for California? What would you do in their place?

9 What sort of process do you think Maggie, Giovanna, and Samuel might go through as they adjust to being a family again?

ABOUT THE AUTHOR

SARAH DUNSTER IS THE MOTHER OF SIX YOUNG CHILDREN. Her childhood journals are littered with poems, stories, and drawings of maps, characters, and places she imagined for her stories. She wrote her first novel at age nine—a rambling combination of *Little Women* and *Anne of Green Gables*, scribbled on binder paper—and tortured her friends by making them listen to the whole thing. Sarah is an award-winning poet; her pieces have been published in *Segullah Magazine* and *Dialogue: a Journal of Mormon Thought.* In addition to writing, she loves reading, singing, skiing, and educating her children at home. Sarah lived for ten years in Provo and grew to love the places, people, and history of Utah Valley.